MW01614307

EXILED
AND THE
TRIAL OF KINGS

EXILED
AND THE
TRIAL OF KINGS

VOLUME I

Zachary Harvey

TATE PUBLISHING
AND ENTERPRISES, LLC

Exiled and the Trial of Kings
Copyright © 2015 by Zachary Harvey. All rights reserved.

No part of this publication may be reproduced, stored in a retrieval system or transmitted in any way by any means, electronic, mechanical, photocopy, recording or otherwise without the prior permission of the author except as provided by USA copyright law.

The opinions expressed by the author are not necessarily those of Tate Publishing, LLC.

This novel is a work of fiction. Names, descriptions, entities, and incidents included in the story are products of the author's imagination. Any resemblance to actual persons, events, and entities is entirely coincidental.

Published by Tate Publishing & Enterprises, LLC
127 E. Trade Center Terrace | Mustang, Oklahoma 73064 USA
1.888.361.9473 | www.tatepublishing.com

Tate Publishing is committed to excellence in the publishing industry. The company reflects the philosophy established by the founders, based on Psalm 68:11,
"The Lord gave the word and great was the company of those who published it."

Book design copyright © 2015 by Tate Publishing, LLC. All rights reserved.
Cover design by Eileen Cueno
Interior design by Jomel Pepito

Published in the United States of America
ISBN: 978-1-63268-827-9
Fiction / Christian / Dark Fantasy
15.01.07

To Michael C. Andrews
In loving memory and infinitely more rejoicing of the life that
was is and is to come. To my brother who now rests, I thank thee
and bid a momentary farewell until eternity takes hold where no
more tears are shed and only love reigns through Christ Jesus.

Let brotherly love continue.
Hebrews 13:1 (KJV)

Acknowledgments

I, the author, would like to take a moment to acknowledge those who helped me along the journey to completing this prolonged task. Although I am the sole writer on this project, it would not have been possible without the love, friendship, and support of all the amazing people who have blessed my life, including the dozens not on this list, you know who you are. I apologize that these acknowledgements are short, but know I cherish each of you dearly.

First and foremost, I would like to thank my immediate family of my father, mother, and two brothers who have taught me so many things and laid the foundation of Christ in my life.

I would like to thank Robert and Priscilla and my friends, Kevin and Tommy, for years of support.

Thank you, Todd, Mandy, Carly, Emmy, and Luke for sharing life with me.

Pastor John, I tip my hat to you.

I give my regards to Scott for both baptizing and giving me my first Bible, which I still own.

Shannon, you were my favorite teacher who inspired me to undertake this venture.

Abraham and Eloisa, truly blessed are you, and your son confirms that.

My oldest friend, Scott, brother in arms till the end.

Tate University, thank you for undertaking the difficult task of publishing this project. You've done a most magnificent job.

To the one who matters the most, Christ Jesus, the one who is I AM. To you, I say thank you for everything, and I pray many come to know you through this and that you are glorified by it according to your will. Truly are you Lord of lords and King of kings. Every day you teach me so much, and every day you open my heart just that much more by example of the cross. I love you, Father.

Contents

Preface

Exiled and the Trial of Kings is the first of a planned four-story series. I am the only writer on this series and have been with it since its inception in the year 2007. I began writing this series during/after God carrying me through the trials of suicide from my youth into adulthood. Through that pain words cannot describe, He made me into someone I could have never imagined. He blessed me with an understanding that could not have been obtained any other way. Only after those long years in hell could I have come to further understand that there are so many out there who desperately need to hear that they are loved, but not just loved by others but by Jesus who blesses man with the capacity to share love. It was in that *Exiled* would come to be created/ written/published and hopefully so much more.

Only in recent years has it been my hope to become a full-time author, but it has always been a dream to live by what is true even though it took me years to figure out what that was. Although a long arduous process from *Exiled*'s initial thought to first story completion, the experience has forever changed my outlook on every facet of life. I have no college degree nor do I have family within the literary community, but by the grace of God, I've been brought to this point. The works of *Exiled* mean the world to me, for it is what the Lord gave me to cope with the world around me as God restored me from the depths, so was this series built from the foundation, for Christ Jesus is the cornerstone for those who have faith in his name.

Today, we live in an age when morality and authenticity seem to be on a sharp slope of a most dangerous conclusion that has been foretold yet not without hope. I believe you, the reader, deserve a better class of a quality-made original story, and it is my sincere hope that I was able to give you that. Granted, we have not met, I want you to know that it was you, the reader, who encouraged me every step of the way, for without you, this project would have not meant nearly as much. Before you start reading this story, I would advise one to hold up one's hands and ask yourself, "What am I reaching for?" Once established, retain that thought on a constant, comparing it in every way to the adventure presented before you, and in that, you will come to your own solid conclusion that belongs to you and no one else, for free will is a gift we were all given.

Introduction

In a nutshell, this story is a dark fantasy set within a medieval backdrop, but the presentation is spiritual in nature adhering to sound Christian doctrine from a nondenominational point of view. *Exiled* is a series that takes place within a world called Vulgata. This is a world cursed by sin to such a level that the very nature of the world is twisted and manipulated by it in both its creatures and settings. Within this world, most people are taken by either madness, theology, or piety, and more often than not it flows within the same river of pandemonium. This is a story that is the beginning of a spiritual epic that will consist of a plethora of stories intertwining into one singular finale by the end of the fourth novel.

This being the introduction to the series, I would like to make one quick analysis to help you out. Although this is the first of the series, it is by far the smallest of all the novels with the second being about double the word count if not more. Every *Exiled* novel in this series is completely connected to a full degree, but each one will be focusing on a slightly different writing style as to shift the focus of the atmosphere presented and to not grow dull. A major factor here is that as each novel is read, it is set up to reveal different meanings as the other three are released at the designated hours. There are certain pieces to have double meanings with the truest not revealed until book number 4, which will shift meanings in books 1, 2, and 3 and vice versa.

Exiled and The Trial of Kings initializes the concept of the holy knights and who they are alongside the core meaning of the Sword of Abraham and its relevance to the story alongside the basic idea of the Exiles themselves. The actual story beginning after the prologue initiation covers the accounts of two main characters. The first is a pastor by the name of Joseph Voltel, a man filled with the utmost empathy, always relying on the word of God to guide him and his family's life. Second is Zacharias, a young man upset with the stained world surrounding him; he holds a great anger toward the idea of God. Eventually, their paths intertwine, and we begin to see just who each of them really is as ideology clashes betwixt the newfound friendship.

I would have to say I've written this series for a long time, and there are pieces within this first one that I believe shine the brightest, making it my personal favorite. The focus of this story becomes Joseph's and Zacharias's journey to what they believe to be the restoration of the holy knights at the rise of the Exiles, but the more one stands by truth, the more the war rages. A great multitude of characters for the series are introduced if only subtly and they will have major parts later on. What makes this first novel so unique is that this is the only one that deals with so few characters so in that the writing style is able to explore much further the psychology of these people, which is probably why I like this one the best. This is a story that delves deep into both setting and character as to really set the foundation of this the series of *Exiled* in the world of Vulgata.

I also wanted to note that for the map and the timeline created for this series that additions will be added for each novel. On the timeline, only very major events are displayed at this time. As for the map, not every city within each nation is listed, only very important ones pertaining to major story elements for this and the other three stories. Some nations contain so many cities in fact that to add them all would make the map look far to cluttered so mostly only capitals are presented. Lastly for the map, it should be noted that it is to advance with each story, so coming in the next story, every nation will be given its national symbol along with new additions, with the final map not shown until book 4.

Disclaimer

As to clarify any potential discrepancy, it should be noted that project *Exiled* is a series clothed in metaphorical light. This is a heavily allegorical piece that also contains a fair amount of hyperbole and personification to further the direction of themes established. It is not the goal of these works, or I, as the author, to misuse scripture in any way shape or form. I hold true that the Bible is the infallible word of God given us by our loving Father as to guide us to the path to heaven by the Holy Spirit after entering eternal companionship with Christ Jesus through the cleansing of baptism (acceptance of him as your lord and savior) and repentance of sin in his name.

I also confirm that we, as men, are wicked at heart and cannot earn salvation through our own so-called merit. Salvation is only granted through Jesus Christ who was, is, and always will be the final sacrifice bridging the gap from initial sin made at the tree of life by Adam and Eve. With that being said, I would like to note that in Paul's teachings in the New Testament, we, as believers, are called to spread the gospel and to talk to people how they are. We are never to stray from the truth of scripture, but we are to adjust our methods as his ministry did when talking to the Jews and to the many forms of Gentiles. *Exiled* is a work that embraces that ideal to the core, choosing to explore the nightmares of hell and the dreams of heaven as to better let the audience decide what they are going to choose to believe in for we were all gifted with free will.

At the end of the day, this series stands by the Holy Bible from a nondenominational standpoint, trusting in every word written for the pens that wrote the Bible were guided by the Holy Spirit. Backed by constant prayer, this book and series holds its intent in broad daylight in hopes that someone will be saved because of this and that the brothers and sisters of the faith will strengthen their resolve for the difficult journey ahead. It is this series's goal to further enlighten the flock of the countless false prophets, teachers, and leaders that are openly prevalent in today's culture. This series makes arguments on all ends of ideological perception but does tip heavily toward that of a Christian perspective, for a purely objective piece would not be plausible in the realm of fictional storytelling, choosing a main theme.

I, as the author, would like to personally add that this series is not about casting judgment or vengeance, for they do not belong to man; instead, it is my fundamental goal to stand by the order to discern spirits as to safeguard the flock and one's own salvation. Undoubtedly, I (as all men) have fallen short of God's glory and would like to openly admit that there are most likely an embarrassing amount of mistakes within this story and the ones to come. These mistakes are purely my own and I accept full responsibility. As for the victories and what is done properly, they do not belong to me, but they belong to the Lord Almighty for triumph and glory belong to God alone.

In this novel, you will see quite a few scriptures used, all of which are from the King James Version. With that being said, I wanted to note that I'm not declaring the notion that all other Bibles are wrong or false, but I am stating I believe the KJV to be the closest translation from the *Latin Vulgate*. I believe when it comes to Bible translation, one really has to look at the lineage of whether or not it traces back to *Antiochian* or *Alexandrian* origins for the *Antiochian* line is the proper. I believe that biblical canon is the word of God and apocrypha is a most dangerous deception sent from the devil, for canon does not contain error whereas apocrypha is loaded with contradictions, errors, and even worse is that it contains practices we as believers were directly commanded not to partake in such as what *Simon Magus* partook in. The word of God which is holy because He is holy also means as God is perfect so is His word, so in that the Bible cannot contain a single mistake or contradiction from anything written, which immediately rules out apocrypha as being canonical.

Now, the first Bible I was ever gifted was the NIV, which I do still have to this day, and I am acknowledging that a main reason for translations such as that exist because of the change in the English language for the KJV is one of if not the greatest English works ever completed, so for the majority to understand that kind of college level reading wouldn't work out so well. As a fellow brother in the Lord, I would advise you to stay with the KJV as your primary learning source by aid of the Holy Ghost, but I would not advise one to forsake other translations, for I have seen many respond very well to them because they could understand, so in the end, I'd say discern Bible translations the same way we are called to discern spirits.

THE SEVEN AGES OF
OF VU

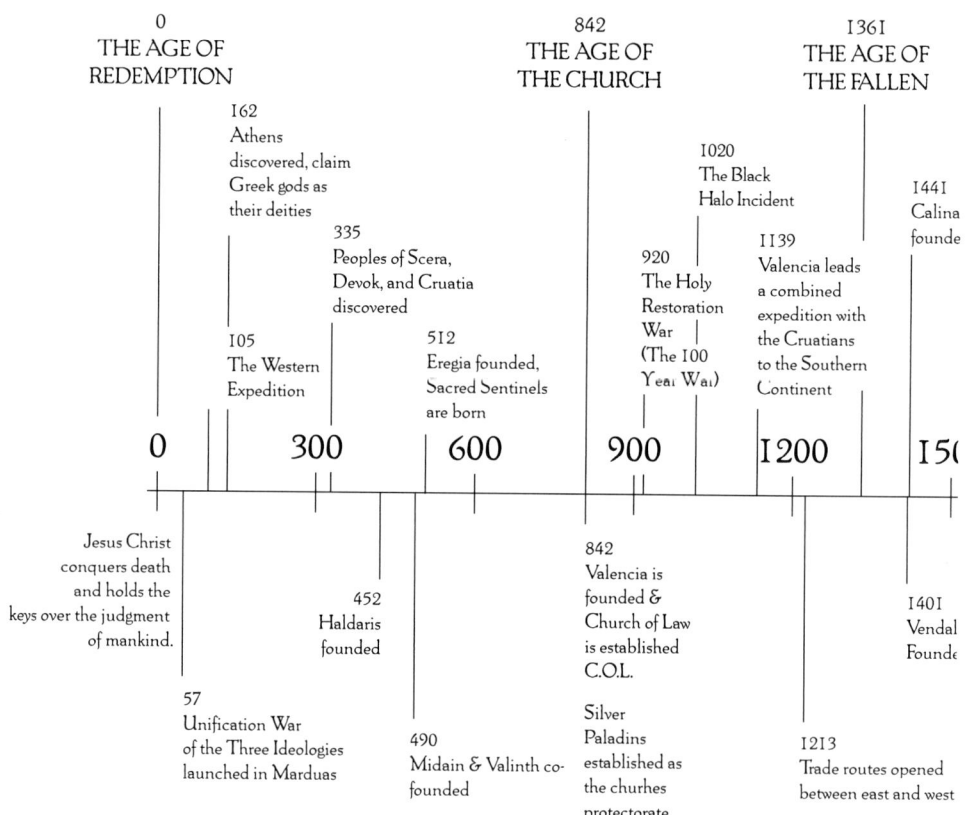

0
THE AGE OF
REDEMPTION

842
THE AGE OF
THE CHURCH

1361
THE AGE OF
THE FALLEN

162
Athens
discovered, claim
Greek gods as
their deities

1020
The Black
Halo Incident

1441
Calina
founde

335
Peoples of Scera,
Devok, and Cruatia
discovered

920
The Holy
Restoration
War
(The 100
Year War)

1139
Valencia leads
a combined
expedition with
the Cruatians
to the Southern
Continent

105
The Western
Expedition

512
Eregia founded,
Sacred Sentinels
are born

0   300   600   900   1200   150

Jesus Christ
conquers death
and holds the
keys over the judgment
of mankind.

452
Haldaris
founded

842
Valencia is
founded &
Church of Law
is established
C.O.L.

1401
Vendal
Founde

57
Unification War
of the Three Ideologies
launched in Marduas

490
Midain & Valinth co-
founded

Silver
Paladins
established as
the churhes
protectorate

1213
Trade routes opened
between east and west

'THE NEW TESTAMENT
ILGATA

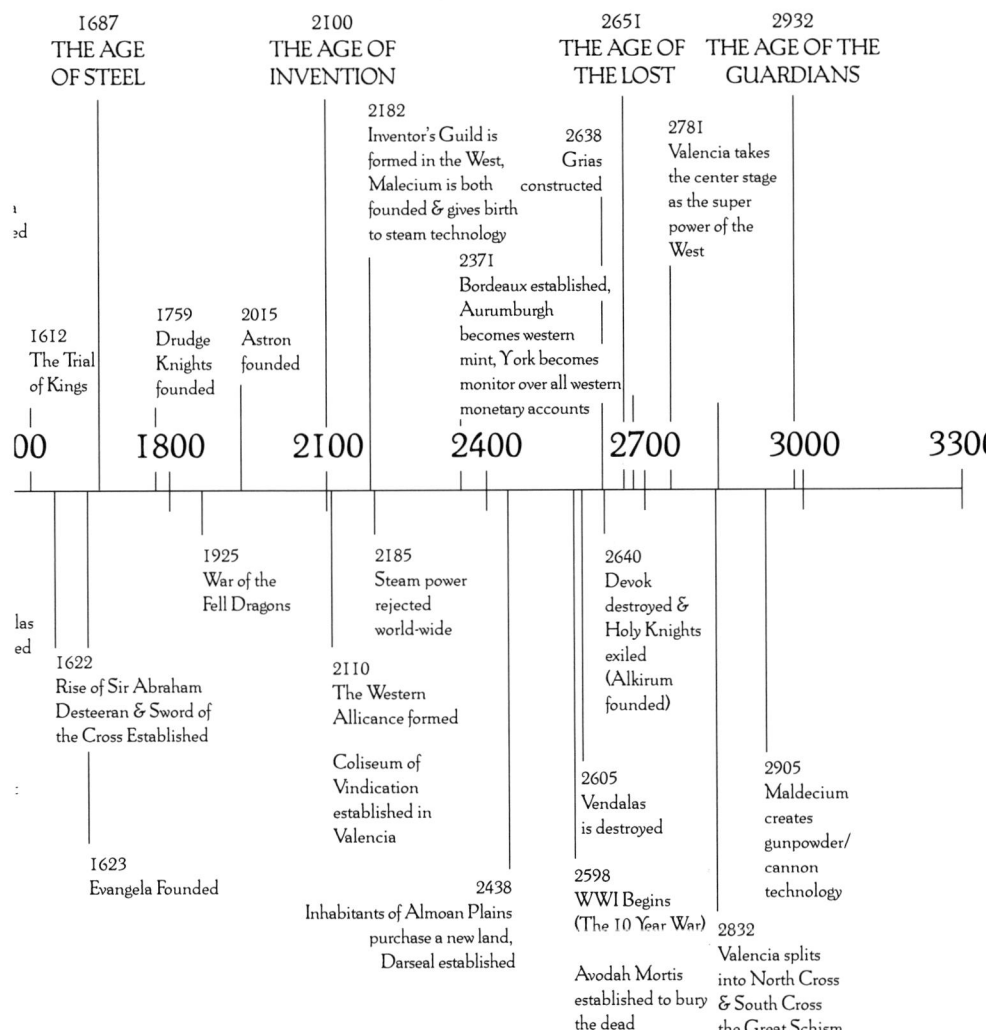

1687	2100	2651	2932
THE AGE OF STEEL	THE AGE OF INVENTION	THE AGE OF THE LOST	THE AGE OF THE GUARDIANS

2182
Inventor's Guild is formed in the West, Malecium is both founded & gives birth to steam technology

2638
Grias constructed

2781
Valencia takes the center stage as the super power of the West

2371
Bordeaux established, Aurumburgh becomes western mint, York becomes monitor over all western monetary accounts

1759
Drudge Knights founded

2015
Astron founded

1612
The Trial of Kings

1800   2100   2400   2700   3000   3300

1925
War of the Fell Dragons

2185
Steam power rejected world-wide

2640
Devok destroyed & Holy Knights exiled (Alkirum founded)

2110
The Western Alliance formed

Coliseum of Vindication established in Valencia

2605
Vendalas is destroyed

2905
Maldecium creates gunpowder/cannon technology

1622
Rise of Sir Abraham Desteeran & Sword of the Cross Established

1623
Evangela Founded

2438
Inhabitants of Almoan Plains purchase a new land, Darseal established

2598
WWI Begins (The 10 Year War)

Avodah Mortis established to bury the dead

2832
Valencia splits into North Cross & South Cross the Great Schism

ATA
34
SEA OF
THE VULGATE
North Cross
Philippi
Jerome's
Channel
Chaos
Mountains
OK
Noxious Mist
Schism's
Wall
Royal
Navy
Alexandria
GOLEME
(SAMARIA)
Caves of Falethroar
Void of Cain
House of the Fallen Wing
SEPTUAGINT SEA
VALENCIA
Keystone River
The King's Dam
Drudge Knights
Citadel
Halls of
Sovereignty
Romulus
South Cross
Constantinople
The Forlorn
Gorge
Tigris River
MARDUAS
Talrock's Spire
Dolgorum
Cliffs
ng's Higway
Wardens
Keep
Grias
Slave
Networks
Concrite
(Jerusalem)
Hive of Glut
SEA OF TARENE
ltar of the First Sword
ISRAEL
Industrial
Desert
Zeradins
Oasis
Bone Trenches
éol
AVODAH
MORTIS
Bethlehem
Pyramid of Mecca
Desert of
the Exiled
Continent's Peak
Hebron
AMERITH
The Great
Aqueduct
Falling Stars
Inlet
Labyrinth of Daedalus
EAUX
Unknown
Subterranean
Tunnel
Lorns
Dunes
VOLSTROM
(JUDEA)
SARDONIC SEA
nge
eyards
Taurus
Mountains
Thessalonica
Corinth
Babylon
Aurumburgh
Crete
ATHENS
The Mechanical City
New Albatross
RAYITH
Astron
The Crystal
Mountains
Ephesus
Haunted Coasts
CRYPHA
The Church
of Sodom and the
City of Gomorrah
CLYPTIC OCEAN

N
W   E
S

Prologue

The Holy Knights

Long past the madness of both a century-long Restoration War and failed expedition to the unknown southern continent, the Age of the Church had come to an end after 519 years. Man had turned from the goal of maintaining the purity of the church and had fallen into the trap of dogmatic expression in which their leaders believed they could contain God within human tongue and false tradition. With this came a celestial sign from the heavens, and man was unsure whether this sign was of God or the fallen one, Lucifer. The sun and the moon rose irregularly, void of correlation for months. The great church that had ushered in the era of personal custom was based in the west in the nation of Valencia whose capital was Alexandria. This church was known as the Church of Law (COL) and the seeds had now been sown for a split that would later divide the mightiest nation of the west. Its church divided on the issue of whether to follow the Law of Moses by sacramentalism or salvation through faith in Christ Jesus. To the east sat the entirety of Marduas, which was all the gathered nations of the east, including Jerusalem. Throughout the Age of the Church, the nations of the world played to the isolationist type of role in order to better contain the purity of the church and protect themselves from outside influence, so they thought. . To no avail, the fall plunged to the world below, for unhumbled man had improperly placed his faith, unknowingly using the word of God as a weapon for the evil one whose deceptions are limitless. The veil of protection was lifted from Valencia and its sphere of influence lost in the west. Valencia was attacked in those days by grotesque and terrible creatures from the land, ocean, and sky. Their crops would not yield bountiful harvests as they once did while sickness and plague beset upon the once proud and noble empire of church, custom, and crown.

To the east, a far worse sign had appeared, for a seeming judgment had fallen upon the entire region. Far south of Jerusalem, the black pyramid of Mecca divorced of capstone sat proudly deceiving men. Thousands of acolytes dressed in the night's embrace marched into the structure, dragging with them numerous amounts of tortured slaves. Inside of the tombs of the black pyramid, the screams echoed, for in the deepest of its chambers lay a great sacrificial pit, and at the bottom, an even darker cube-like building standing forty-three feet high. It rested upon the grave of the greatest of the fallen dragons; this one was born of guile. One by one, the slaves were butchered by dull axe and sword as to further the pain pleasing the lords to come. The thousands of acolytes dumped each limb ecstatically into this crater to the depths chanting together in foreign tongue; as for the sand, it began to turn black itself from the gore. The earth let out a considerable cry, sounding an indescribable boom, shaking the hardened hearts of the disciples of a most unholy cause. The smell alone from all the bodies would have warded off any who cling to the path of life, but these men were drawn to it; they were in love with this—the fragrance of death. It excited their carnal appetites, making it impossible for them to concentrate on anything holy for even a second. Atop the four faces of the chamber, they could see star streak across accompanied by a petrifying meteor in the shape of the blasphemous dragon. He was seen consuming countless souls of the earth outside the realm of time. From the dragon's mouth, a lone meteorite was spit out into the cube that lay within the pit, and together, the acolytes worshipped in the purest of delusional fanaticism. A godless anchor married to 666 chains fell from the midpoint of the ceiling littered in unlawful tongue, each demanding the desecration of the church as it lowered into the trench of bodies. It turned hotter the deeper it went until it began to rise with the block of deception. When it was fully raised, the door projected a lavender glow whilst absorbing sound and warmth. It did not open but instead vanished, and from it, the unspeakable sight of an arch-demon bound by these many chains was revealed. His black heart derived from his father knows only hate, and from that, he draws a berserk-filled rage, setting him free. Only a single shout is given by this abomination as he tears his heart from his chest by those massive claws befitting for the reaper's scythe. Standing before the acolytes in a white yet stained coat of skin, this monster stared breathing heavily with dark yellow eyes and wounds drenching the altar. Before the now unnerved acolytes could act, he slammed his fists to the ground, demanding further sacrifice, and like cages of blade, the sand rose up around the followers, tearing apart their flesh until the truest form of their sinful nature was exposed in both muscle fiber and skeletal frame. The suffering reached such a level, an undoubtedly disturbing grin overtook the demon's face as the anchor above began to swirl counterclockwise laden with sacrificial limbs received from the pit. The blood stained the walls, creating pure shadow. From this shadow, another rose, sucking up the sand around him, taking in the words from the disciples who had lived and now died in sin. This arch-demon's eyes were a glowing crimson and the shadow flowed much like mist around his body; above him, an even darker cloud hovered, constantly raining blood from the floor upwards. He held a great book with a Luciferian seal upon it, and as he opened it, he was so pleased to the scene painted around him that his ear-shattering laughter dislocated his own jaw, giving him further pleasure. The two arch-demons appeared outside before the entrance of the pyramid before the last disciple who bowed before them. This man of a false intoxicated spirit had led everyone into this trap purposefully as to gain his own glory. Atop the pyramid where no capstone sat, blood flowed down each of the four sides like sludge; on each of these sides, a massive face arose boiling from the intense heat. Each of the four faces moved in unison before speaking in words sounding of crashing wave. A final demon mounted on a pale horse appeared as the capstone wearing a crown made from lamented branch with heads attached, each bearing their eternal judgment. His armor is a ceremonial red and black, but the cape is a black hole forged in the fires of hell directly from Satan's pride. Raising his sword to the sky, the meteorite spat out by the dragon could be seen floating above him, both increasing and decreasing in size simultaneously. He rode down to the other two arch-demons, and the three made the final acolyte the alpha prophet of their cause. The man standing before their dark infernal presence purchased his want of boundless pride before the three and the four faces upon the pyramid held a devious smirk. The beast in white skin called himself The Spirit, the one wrapped in darkness The Word, and the one on pale horse The Crown. He was the eldest. These were the three sons of Satan and their prophet became a prelude of many to come and preach their name all along the east as risen lords to a one omnipotent god of infinite form that should be worshiped by all who seek his secret worldly knowledge. In each of the four faces' mouths upon the pyramid, demonic children appeared and were eaten alive. Their moans of absolute pain overtake the newly appointed prophet, showing him the end of the world. The blood now pours as a river through a broken dam unto the damned, sealing a covenant of evil around Mecca. So began the Age of the Fallen in the year 1361. For over two centuries, the three brothers lay with thousands and thousands of women, who essentially sold their souls to be with false gods and yield their unholy tainted offspring. When these women conceived, they conceived what is called a Nephilim— half-man, half-demon—but it also should be noted that they were giants ranging from eight to thirty-six feet tall on average. These Nephilim, being a hybrid (abomination) of both man and demon, were unable to reproduce.

> There were giants in the earth in those days; and also after that, when the sons of God came in unto the daughters of men, and they bare children to them, the same became mighty men which were of old, men of renown.
>
> Genesis 6:4 (KJV)

The Nephilim, now numbering some two thousand in the east, answered to the three brothers who were their fathers unto their god. There were only two thousand after all these years because the lion's share of these vile offspring was consumed by the three sons to curve their gluttonous appetites that could not be filled. Both men and Nephilim worshiped the three brothers as they slipped into all the forms of government in the east. They undermined all worldly laws to enslave man by the use of their foul worldly knowledge. The only problem left was those of Hebrew tradition (Amerith) who refused to follow the known-to-be demons who were in allegiance with Beelzebub alongside untold amounts of other darkened generals. The Nephilim were ordered to slaughter all who refused to follow, both Jew and Gentile, and so for centuries, hundreds of thousands, if not millions, were slaughtered in the name of these false gods. Humanity attempted to resist, but mortal weapons held little to no effect. The west chose to hide these things were happening until one day, a man escaped the east that was sealed in what some would call a biblical season of death. His words spread internationally of the demons' eventual plan to campaign across the west when all had been harvested from the east. The Valencian populace, now informed of this terrible evil enslaving the east, understood the severity of the implications made and was forced to confront the issue. This was taken all the way up to the king of Valencia by the church, and orders were given to launch a holy crusade into Marduas to cleanse the world of evil; the year was 1608. The king gathers man, horse, and sword and a force of 150,000 strong is summoned before the Church of Law and prepared for the eastern campaign, led by the churches elite force of 15,000 silver paladins. The silver paladins were sharply split over the authenticity of the crusade, and most said that it was not the will of God at this time, so two-thirds did not participate. 155,000 of the Valencian crusade march east, and the western world witnesses the launch of this holy war, wondering as to the root of this sudden militaristic movement. Thoughts of the Restoration War reverberated throughout the high courts of the land and the shadow of worry returned just as before, just as an anxious heart weighs man a down. The crusade marched through the Dolgorum Cliffs into the Forlorn Gorge where they were met by 2,000 Nephilim and the three sons of Satan. Numbering only 2,000, the force seemed trivial before 155,000 of the king's finest, but these lumbering giants who had the faces, strength, and demonic black armor/weapons from hell were a force not to be trifled with. The brother known as The Crown dismounted his pale horse and dug his hands into the earth, calling upon Lucifer's name. His cape blotted out the sun, and the three brothers united inside, portraying the face of their father overlooking the battlefield. The Valencian crusade was immobilized for their faith could not protect them from the pure spiritual attack and the Nephilim crushed them with ease. Each man's heart was locked in heinous nightmare as all 155,000 were slaughtered while the demons carried their bodies and mostly limbs to construct a massive mazelike wall around the entrance unto the east. These men all died because they partook in this crusade, but not of noble intent, but of a want to establish their own majesty of national patriotism to make this event the crowning achievement of Valencia before the earth Vulgata. Many wicked and foul things occurred at the construction of this wall. The Nephilim partook time and again in demonic orgies with animal and dead body alike. They rejoiced at the triumph of this structure and would even maim each other to bring gratification to the three sons of Satan who would restore them by use of The Word's sorcery from his incorporeal book. At the entrance, there was a lone sentinel named Cerberus, a three-headed demonic watchman standing tall in ungodly armor made from the skulls of horse and men before what was deemed the gates of hell, he was the gatekeeper. A single man was set free to bear witness to the church of the dread that was seen in the battle. This man was released because he was the only man within the crusade who held a true faith to the Lord God, and it was that faith that saved his soul, for even in the midst of total annihilation, God does not forsake those who solely trust in His holy truth found in Jesus Christ.

The west bears witness to the twisted wall of human bodies and the demon standing at its gate, and the world of Vulgata now knows of the truth: that man is not alone. In Valencia, the church and its king watch as their once powerful military sits decimated, propped up on a stage of mockery, and none know of what the next answer is. It was in this day the original concept was drawn for a united world military, but disagreements due to national sovereignty quickly halted the project. The king later decides to declare The Trial of Kings to all the nations of the west in which any who can defeat the three brothers and the Nephilim will be made a king and the empire of Valencia his prize. For four years, warriors came from all over the west to attempt to earn the prize of kingship, but all who traveled east were drawn into Cerberus's trap into the maze of death. Whenever an army would ride to the wall, the Nephilim would return and ward them off, so the use of force of arms was widely ruled out, now unanimously by world leaders. Valencia was under martial law at the time because its denizens believed that the end of the world loomed on the horizon, so needless to say, pandemonium had found its home. Out of desperation, each nation vowed kingship over their lands, praying a warrior would rise up, but no cries were louder than that in the east where people were absolute slaves to this evil.

In the year 1612, four years after the king's decree of the Trial of Kings, there was a young man by the name of Abraham Desteeran who lived among the peoples of Scera. In those days, Scera or Nation of the Forest was held in high renown by most of the world, untouched by ever-advancing science or anyone who wasn't pure in Sceran blood. Abraham was a seventeen-year-old hunter of common birth and thought who was a man that fully believed in Jesus Christ with all his heart and had prayed diligently for four years for a hero to rise up to save those suffering in the east.

That night, deep in prayer, Abraham felt an unnatural pain; he was one with the sorrow of those suffering in the east because their cries had reached the Lord God. Abraham wept for these people to the highest level a man could, begging God with all his soul for Jesus to release them from their bondage of death. He had prayed for seven hours, and when he opened his eyes, standing before him was an angel of God, shining in a brilliance of light he could not understand. The angel then spoke unto his heart, "Your faith and prayers have reached the Lord Almighty, be joyous in all things for you are favored in the eyes of God, the Father!" The angel instructed Abraham that he was to construct a sacred sword hilt to certain specifications that would be given by the Holy Spirit.

That morning, Abraham awoke to a holy piece of lumber from the tree of life with a ceremonial blade to carve it with. The pure white piece of lumber was so incredibly tough that it took him all of three years to carve it into its perfect specifications. This hilt was made of only this lumber, but he was also to carve in special notches along its inner handle to hold some sort of cloth, which was not to be assembled in his day. Abraham was ridiculed to the point of being deemed insane by the denizens of the forest, but there were many who did believe God had chosen him as the instrument to deliver the east from evil.

Close to three years after Abraham had started construction of the sword hilt, the walls of Jerusalem had finally fallen to the evil one. This had been the only truly safe place in the east and had stood its ground for hundreds of years against the three sons of Lucifer. Jerusalem had now become a den of sin, drinking from the nefarious cup of the eternal harlot that had shared her crimes with all the nations of Vulgata. It was now the mother of all demonic spirits that hovered above the city in a never-ending storm of hatred that attacked the souls of all those spiritually unprotected who either entered the city or gazed upon it. The three brothers met at Golgotha (Cavalry) where Jesus Christ was crucified over 1,600 years prior. They reveal their plan to the numerous false prophets that their goal was the destruction of God's people and more so to turn as many as they could from the faith for they saw no victory in the first death.

Abraham, now twenty, had finished the sword hilt and believed the task to be over. Although, he wasn't actually sure what was to come of this sword hilt or why God had chosen him for the task. That night, as he prays, he offers the hilt to the Lord, and the same angel of the Lord returns and commands his second task as the carving blade returns to the angelic wings. Abraham is commanded that he is now to take seven years and take a feather of the holy white dragon Atyrael and forge it into a block of holy metal from heaven. The angel leaves, and Abraham is not happy with the angel's decree from the Lord because the three years were remarkably difficult for him to endure. Now he is supposed to take another seven-year period on this, and he can't yet understand as to why. Abraham awakens to the four-foot long white feather and the block of holy metal with a ceremonial hammer beside it. For the first few weeks, he refuses to start on it until one night, in a nightmare, he can see the people of the east suffering like he is there. He awakes that night with his spirit one with justice grasping the glorious mallet that holds to the appearance of divine retribution. Now he begins its construction, and for seven painstaking years, he forges the blade. These seven years are not hard for Abraham because the Holy Spirit reveals to him to take it one day at a time, to not dwell on the past or worry of the future, but instead focus on the Lord's gift that is the present. The sword is forged by fire, water, and spirit, and every day, Abraham gets closer and closer to his righteous destiny given by the grace of the Lord. That night, after ten years of spiritual labor, the blade is combined with the hilt, and the angel of the Lord appears to Abraham. The angel blesses him and deems that the Sword of Abraham is now complete and takes the sword and knights him: "Sir Abraham Destecran, firstborn of the Gentile Holy Knights, arise!" Abraham is so full of the Holy Spirit, he is momentarily blinded because of the magnificence of God, and as the light dissipates, a heavenly full suit of complete white armor with golden lining is presented with the sword encased inside. A scarlet cape rests around the armor, further drawing Abraham's soul. The helmet that rests on the sword's hilt is crowned with a metallic dove and wings to the sides at a slight curve pointing to heaven. The shield is grand and formidable, holding much like the armor in appearance with seven golden lamp stands. One by one, they light, for they are the seven Spirits of God that are the Spirit of the Lord, wisdom, understanding, counsel, might, knowledge, and fear of the Lord. Upon the chest plate, a golden cross forged in the image of a sword gloriously shines, three points indicating the hilt and the bottom the point. This same image is present on the broad pauldrons and a fourth rests on the cape; these are the spiritual guardians of the four winds.

Here, the angel reveals to him that he is the knight to defeat the three brothers and that this ten-year process of building the Sword of Abraham was for God to forge him into the man he needed to become to glorify Him properly. Abraham gave thanks to the point that the angel smiled, having to remind him to equip the full armor of God. As he began to equip the armor, the angel spoke this scripture:

> Finally, my brethren, be strong in the Lord, and in the power of his might. Put on the whole armour of God, that ye may be able to stand against the wiles of the devil. For we wrestle not against flesh and blood, but against principalities, against powers, against the rulers of the darkness of this world, against spiritual wickedness in high places. Wherefore take unto you the whole armour of God, that ye may be able to withstand in the evil day, and having done all, to stand. Stand therefore, having your loins girt about with truth, and having on the breastplate of righteousness; And your feet shod with the preparation of the gospel of peace; Above all, taking the shield of faith, wherewith ye shall be able to quench all the fiery darts of the wicked. And take the helmet of salvation, and the sword of the Spir'-it, which is the word of God: Praying always with all prayer and supplication in the Spir'-it, and watching thereunto with all perseverance and supplication for all saints;
>
> Ephesians 6:10–18 (KJV)

Upon equipping the armor, which covers his entire body, Abraham is surprised at its incredibly light weight and perfect fit from its superbly heavy plated appearance. He also notices that on his belt of truth, to the rear that a Bible, is encased in a protective armor attachment that is also concealed by the cape.

The year is now 1622, and Sir Abraham Desteeran, the first holy knight, marches into the city of Alexandria of the nation of Valencia on a Sunday morning. The brazen and incandescent armor draws the crowds, and all who look can feel the glory of the

Lord around him. Sir Abraham walks up a hundred feet of stairs to the Church of Law; his cape drags but does not collect dirt. It instead polishes the stairs to perfection. Atop the climb, silver paladins produce reverence by means of bowing, but Abraham demands they bow only to the Lord not to him. The holy knight opens the massive doors to the current mass that was taking the offering. The king who was about to place his tithe is interrupted by this, and thousands who are in attendance rise along with the clergy. Each step taken by the holy knight separates the hearts of the true believers and the false. A church member assigned to the organ gives way to the command of the Holy Spirit, and a celestial-sounding tune never heard by man overtakes the structure of worship. Every believer can feel the presence of Christ Jesus, and they begin to weep at this miracle. Abraham makes his offering by pulling the sword from the golden sheath cast in light before the king at the great altar holding a profound Crucifix accompanied by decorations striving for perfection. The Sword of Abraham is the size of a claymore, but is of the weight of a dove's feather to Abraham; the blade itself speaks of the piercing word of God in the sharpness of complete appearance. The sword is baptized in the waters of sanctification along with Abraham, who reaffirms his faith still wearing the armor; the king then sends Abraham out to fight Cerberus, also giving him his blessing. Another divide is seen as a multitude of clergy argue that no work is to be done on the Sabbath, but Abraham states this scripture,

> The Lord then answered him, and said, Thou hypocrite, doth not each one of you on the sabbath loose his ox or his ass from the stall, and lead him away to watering?
>
> Luke 13:15 (KJV)

Thousands of citizens go to see if this man can do what no other can: conquer a demon.

Abraham gallops to the Dolgorum Cliffs on a white horse given him by the king and then gallantly steps forth on the plains to the gate of bodies known as hell's gate. Cerberus peeks one of his heads around the corner, then stammers out, but he does not walk like things from the earthly dimension; he walks and moves like how a clock ticks each agonizing second. Seeing Abraham, his three heads laugh as he approaches and points his two-handed axe made of sharpened bone fastened together by a strange hair-like wire. Each of its three countenances are different, but all holding black rings around their eyes; staring from the left, the first head is pale. The next is halfway rotted away, and the final is skeletal in nature, but the bone is all black; they are the three stages of death and decay. The demon was remarkably obese, hued in charred skin, and as Abraham came within steps, the first face smiled, the second went into shock, speaking backwards, and the third let out ferocious and repeated screams of profanity. In a calm yet chaotic-sounding low-pitched tone, Cerberus's heads state in unison, spitting on itself, "Finally, God hath sent one of His precious sons of light. Oh, how we shall enjoy the defilement of your frail human body." Abraham stares down the demon with just eyes, gifted from God of a coming judgment as the demon's armor begins to urinate and defecate on itself from the mouths of the horse and men attached to his armor. Cerberus would frequently attach new parts to this armor from would-be heroes attempting to pass this hell's gate. In one hand, Cerberus grabs a skull off the pile of bodies and crunches down on it with his left head, and the right begins to consume his own feces, letting the majority run down his body. The middle head only stares and begins to weep, speaking in the voice of a child taken by tear, "I cannot wait. I wish to rape him now. Let us initiate!" Both hands grab the middle head violently and crush the eyes. The harder they push, the louder the unsettling high-pitched squeals become; the two heads turn to the center. "No, fear, pleasure, then feast! That's how it's always been and always will be!" After that, he turns around and stomps into the maze of bodies. The center face turns completely around, breaking its own neck, and watches him during this exit, also bleeding profusely down the cheek and back. Sir Abraham Desteeran kneels and prays to Jesus Christ and asks for strength. He then stands and draws his sword, entering in behind the demon, ready for the day of battle. He steps forth into the maze and the bodies begin to cry out in pain, but what is more frightening are the sounds of hell overtaking them by unimaginable devilish screams, screeches, and laughter. Abraham traverses the maze that descends into the very grasp of Satan himself; it is absent of light. Spiritually, Abraham can barely handle each step, but it was the ten years of preparation that forged his spirit to this point to be able to withstand this. An unusual silence sets in, and as he travels further along, it gets cold in both a physical and spiritual sense. Detestable and sickening sights appear before him of demons in hell torturing those who did not make it to heaven for man's merit is naught in terms of salvation. Falling to the ground, he weeps for those lost to the flames of perdition and then begins to shiver at the grasp of not adrenaline but divine providence, for he is ripe with the Holy Spirit. "Cerberus," Abraham screams in such a mighty voice that the call for justice shakes the ground. A potent light is projected from the wings of the dove on his helmet. In the darkness, he can hear a grotesque grunting sound until he can see the giant naked body of Cerberus from the back. Gradually, each head turns around, but his body continually rapes the corpse of a dead man. Two of the heads engaged by this sexual action become further excited by Abraham's presence, but one of them states, "Soon, this is to be you. Are you not afraid?" The holy knight is indeed not afraid and is thrown into a rage, but not a rage like a normal human being. This is a Godly anger; this is the feeling given when the truest violations of God's holy word are witnessed. Charging him, Abraham powerfully swings his sword and the demon vanishes; the sword crushes the remains of the molested body and delves mightily into the ground. Noticing black liquid resembling what could be surmised as demonic seed (unfruitful) on the man's corpse, Abraham reclaims his blade then slams down the hilt of the sword into the ground, commanding Cerberus to appear with all the force of his diaphragm. The sword lets out a shockwave in the ground that brings the labyrinth crashing to its knees in a foretold bow. Cerberus is buried under the bodies, and his three heads sit poking out taken by profanity. Abraham, seeing this, sprints over to commence the fight crushing bones with each saintly footprint. From the demon's mouth, his words weave spells of fire that spread across the ruins, buying him precious moments of survival. The axe underneath his body sprawls open and the wire-like fiber streams through the mountain of bone, paralyzing Abraham's feet in place. Cerberus is able to free himself and, in turn, launches his assault, barreling through corpses as to crush the holy knight. Unable to break free from the fiber, Abraham is overtaken by the fire, but his cape protects him from becoming burned alive by producing a waterfall encircling his body. Cerberus, unaffected by the flame, grabs Abraham through the water in his violent clutches, tossing him to the ground. The wire that had bound his feet attempts to pull him into the bodies, but Abraham cries out, "I AM!" Immediately, it uncurls from him, returning to the earth, and Abraham, grabbing the sword, holds to a devastating slash, hacking off the lower half of Cerberus's stomach. The demon is cast aside from this divine blow and is left kneeling, attempting to pick up the intestines rapidly spilling forth unto a pile of its own. Standing before the monster, Abraham strikes him without mercy as he proclaims the word and majesty of God. Cerberus screams, yelps, and weeps for how much more do the demonic fear God than man? Cerberus, who was mostly hacked to pieces, looks at the holy knight as he threw up on himself and its other mouths began to consume the chunky excrement, hoping to regenerate. The first holy knight raised the sword to the sky and red-hot magma flowed from the tip of its blade onto the demon's skulls, burning it alive in the fires of judgment.

After the defeat of Cerberus, he cut off its last head, giving the victory to the Lord. Returning to Valencia, he presented it to the king, showing that the demons could only be destroyed by having complete faith in Jesus Christ. He then asked for every able-bodied man who was a genuine believer that could join him on the true crusade that will vanquish this foe from the earth. Abraham had received this command on his ride back to Valencia. 2,500 silver paladins join Abraham as do 2,500 commoners. All had one thing in common: they all had faith in Jesus and understood that his call had come for the righteous men to march in the face of injustice. Standing outside the Church of Law, all 5,000 stood by Abraham as the citizens gathered gave praise to the Lord Almighty. That Sunday, the king offered him all the arms he would need, but as the 5,000 prayed and opened their eyes, an angel of the Lord came upon them. All of the men were knighted at once and became the first 5,000 holy knights, each given the armor and various weapons from heaven. These men were spiritually hungry and so the Lord fed the 5,000 that day. Here it was established before the church that they would be known as the SOC (Sword of the Cross).

Meanwhile in Marduas, the three brothers prepare for war against the one who killed Cerberus. Infinitely outraged, the Nephilim are thrown into a furious rampage and murder tens of thousands of their own followers by their demonic malice. All 2,000 Nephilim coat themselves in the blood of their sacrifices, and the stench is almost unbearable especially for the sands of the earth. They line Jerusalem with thousands of crosses that they crucify anyone and any living thing they can find to in order to give themselves peace that they cannot nor will ever attain.

Now known as general to his men, General Abraham Desteeran launches the proper holy crusade east on the seventh day after a week of prayer, accompanied by his army of 5,000 holy knights. All of Valencia watches as they ride off the island, and people are united in prayer for the last chance the west has before the inevitable tide of darkness makes western landfall. The holy knights trample over fallen hell's gate, and as they ride over it, the ground swallows up the bones of the damned maze, for the truth of life does not hide or conceal the way it presents that path in all its holiness in broad daylight. They arrive at the Forlorn Gorge where the first but false crusade was slaughtered, and standing in the distance, they can see a lone Nephilim general with the mountain at his back. The general's horde of a thousand strong rises from the sands, crashing weapon and fist into the ground with hatred for those who have been sent in His name. He then gathers his men into a massive phalanx against the horsed knights. The Nephilim clad as colossal black knights stand higher than most structures found in Vulgata, attesting to their delusional pride that reaches for the sky. They begin to curse God's name openly in front of the knights and verbally glorify malevolence, self-worth, and sexual immorality. The holy knights are uneasy and half of these men have never seen battle, but Abraham standing in front of his men rallies them. He rebukes the evil by counsel of the Holy Spirit and leads his men in prayer, asking for God's perfect guidance; every knight clings to the Bible upon his belt of truth then raising it to the sky. Great celestial lances double, if not more, the size of a worldly lance appear in the grasp of every holy knight, and it is revealed in their hearts that it shall be the sons of light to initiate battle against the sons of darkness. Every horse is now coated in heavenly armor, just like the knights. Abraham then declares, "It is not the righteous that fear evil, but evil that fears the heart of the righteous man for he walks in the divine will of God!" He pulls his legendary blade and points it to the Nephilim's forward army as all the knights raise lances unto Zion. All 5,000 holy knights become full of the Spirit and ride with all their might as the thunderous hooves of even the horses command the hatred of that which is evil. A profound and constant gust of wind hits to the back of the charge and pushes them to unprecedented speeds. Behind the charge, the sun comes into view, blinding the Nephilim, five thousand capes flow led by five thousand spears pointing to the enemy of the flock. The knights crash through their ranks piercing bone, armor, and carapace of the enemy, the sound is deafening to all. Madness emerges as both man and demon are meshed in the battle for justice that has raged since the dawn of thought. Horsed knights slash with the sharpest of blades and axes, dislocate and break bones with war hammers cast in punishment, withstand attacks by armor of such a loving embrace that the soul cannot be harmed, but most of all it is the reflection of their faith gleaming off their shields that the demons cannot overcome. The knights held close in spirit begin to climb the giants and their love for one another as brother gives them the valor to continually fight. The Nephilim covered in holy knights from their legs to their backs try to throw them off, but the holy knights' will is stronger as they cut down the monsters and they crash to the ground. Vertically, horizontally, and diagonally, the demons bring down their blades and hammers unable to immediately kill the holy knights for their protection is pure. Like branches of tree, the body parts of the Nephilim impact the soil and the bloodbath of them leaves an oily pond reeking of sulfur. Abraham is saved by his two greatest knights, Isaac and Jacob, whom together, lop off the legs of the nefarious general. Abraham banishes him to hell before he plunges the mighty sword into his heart, then cleaving to the side, covering it in putrid demonic flesh. The general's body slides off into the pond, and blood sprays down Abraham's armor as the knights look upon their noble leader. Slowly, he opens his visor that drips constantly and kneels, stabbing the sword into the dirt, giving the triumph to the Lord; the holy knights follow in suit. When the sword is removed, a burning bush is seen that catches the lake into an inferno, it incinerates the wolves further ensuring the victory.

The battle is won, but Abraham's heart weighs heavily for the 500 lost brothers who gave their lives for the cause of justice. Where each of these men fell in combat a patch of majestic garden rests like a sacred tombstone untouched by sin, the bodies were gone. They then begin the ride to Jerusalem; this is a four-day ride. As they arrive, thousands upon thousands of crosses line the road into Jerusalem with bodies and parts of bodies crucified and attached to them. Starlit clouds swirl over the once holy city with a never-ending lightning and rainstorm that bellows dreadful cries across the lands. A group of slaves runs up to Abraham, begging for them to save their people who are held in bondage by the demonic hordes. Abraham is taken with compassion and tells them to pray as the glory of God descends upon the unclean spirits. In the city, the other thousand Nephilim await, fortified with great bows, ready to fire upon the knights, and somewhere hiding inside the unholy brigade sits the three brothers who are initiates of this suffering. Screams can be heard all around the city from those trapped inside calling for the Lord at the sight of the horsed saints; the one brother known as The Spirit emerges with a young slave woman in claw. Held high, the arch-demon pulls her legs from her body, generating a sound of pain no one should ever have to hear. The sound is muffled after moments of pain by him crushing her throat to the point; her head rolls down the monster's forearm into his mouth which he then executes a leisure chomp. "Lucifer," Abraham shrieks across the battlefield followed by the loudest crash of thunder man has heard since the Old Testament when sin entered the world. Abraham readies his men once more and yells out this scripture:

> Truly my soul waiteth upon God: from him cometh my salvation. He only is my rock and my salvation; he is my defence; I shall not be greatly moved. How long will ye imagine mischief against a man? ye shall be slain all of you: as a bowing wall shall ye be, and as a tottering fence.
>
> Psalm 62:1–3 (KJV)

Like the lances had appeared when needed, their shields doubled and tripled in size and the armor upon the horse began to rise up further shielding them. The holy knights rode into the city with their shields of faith held high as flaming arrows the size of men rip apart the very ground their horses ride, creating many a crater to trip upon. Tens of thousands of slaves began to escape the city as holy steel clashed with demonic flesh. High above the city, the storm raged as a dim light could be seen attempting to penetrate. One of the holy knights looked up and screamed for the men not to give up hope for the angels were fighting with them, and the men pressed onward as their faith reached peak heights. Nephilim crashed through the buildings, cornering the knights along the streets, but their brothers leapt from the highest structures bringing bladed retribution from the heavens. In the midst of the city at war, Abraham came face-to-face with the brother known as The Spirit. He was the greatest deceiver and attempted to trick Abraham by offering him power in the demonic realms. It had no effect on Abraham, so he then engaged The Spirit in combat as Isaac and Jacob entered melee with the royal bodyguards. Isaac and Jacob quickly dispatched their opponents, but Abraham's foe was far superior, being the strongest warrior of the three. The first son of Satan swipes his jagged claws that extend out in a three-foot-long curvature and knocks down Isaac and Jacob violently. Abraham is caught by one of the fingers through the visor gashing his forehead to cheek grievously. High above the city of Jerusalem, in the swirling storm of diabolical initiative, the titanic anchor that had brought the false Spirit into the world from the pyramid began to plummet. It hung like a perverted dining hall chandelier and from the mouths along its metallic surface flowed out the 666 chains. At the order of the first son of Satan, these chains began to whip down in all intensity, killing demon, knight, and slave en masse. Thousands of holy knights rushed into home, market, and whatever could provide defense against this unbeatable adversary that tore apart the city. Free of frightened restraint, Abraham, Isaac, and Jacob courageously held their ground against the false Spirit in this the battle for Jerusalem. Debris crashed through the city; with each crack of the torturing whips, they took delight in pain and long-suffering. They needed it for they were it. The chains began to converge on Abraham's position, but behold, another great miracle would occur for the holy knights did not enter this war alone. The neighs of thousands of horse were heard in a single stampede as they took the median of the city. Each horse began to grab the chains by their muscular jaws, and together, they ripped the anchor from the sky; that day, the Artorias breed was born. Abraham brought down the false Spirit by careful instruction from the Holy Spirit that guided every attack of the blade. His steel catches between the claws and came in unto the palm. The monster in turn grasps Abraham with that same hand, but like a lever, Desteeran rotates his weapon forward with all his strength, cutting from shoulder to dismemberment. Isaac crushes the kneecaps with his war hammer forcing the arch-demon to bow; whereas Jacob kicks his back and plants his spear from skull to ground winning the fight.

Having lost one of the brothers and most of the Nephilim, they ran into the remnants of Herod's great palace. Numbering 2,000 at this point, the holy knights enter into the palace and the remaining Nephilim bar the gates and windows with their hulking bodies from the outside for it was a trap. Standing outside is the second brother, The Word, who begins to use the word of Satan to summon forth tens of thousands of lesser demons. These monsters held numerous deformities and had blades and other weapons spliced into their naked burnt flesh. This was a far worse foe than the Nephilim, still none of this compared to the true horrors of hell. These tens of thousands of lesser demons began to crawl up the sides of the palace and flood through the windows like water and pour forth into the main room. These demons are different; they are not controlled by thought but only chaos; their level of aggression is so high that they tear flesh from themselves charging the saints. It is like a nightmarish flood as they slip and fall everywhere in the sopping floor covered in their vomit and blood. The holy knights gather by the main stairwell and make that their defensive line to make them converge from one direction as to give them a chance. Try as they might, they cannot defeat the now 50,000 flooding inside, so Abraham knows at this point what he must do for the survival of his men and better yet the glory of the Lord. Abraham clambers up the stairwell, exhausted, and tells his men to hold the line as he enters the rear gatehouse. Waiting for him there is his white steed covered in a majestic thorn-like armor that was not there before. Abraham cuts the chains of the rear drawbridge, which comes crashing down on thousands of lesser demons. He rides out into the endless regiments of hell spawn, and none of them can touch him as they can see an enormous pair of angelic wings clad in golden armor protecting his body. The wings themselves guard Abraham's spirit as each golden feather that is the armor forms into heavenly swords. Like charging angels in flight, the army of celestial swords smashes through the forces of The Word with ease. Abraham continually rides for The Word, which the monsters go berserk, all converging on him, falling over one another, desperately trying to rip him from horse. Approaching The Word, the wings around Desteeran open and create a holy explosion as they dart in every direction creating such widespread death to the army that they back initially. The Word and Abraham engage in combat, encircled by now over a hundred thousand lesser demons that are unable to approach. The Word is encased in a long black cloak that he uses as a weapon for the fabric shifts and flows as bloodied water, stabbing and clawing at the knight. In his left hand, he reads from the book of the dead adorned with a Luciferian seal and a dark green liquid spews from his mouth. In this battle, Abraham cannot get close to the arch-demon for the poison of his speech keeps him at bay it confuses his mind, but in the distance, atop Herod's ancient palace, he can see Isaac and Jacob standing at the peak of the palace holding a wooden cross. Above The Word, the depraved nimbus rains not blood but a jade poison that powers him up the more the duel is engaged. Light breaks through the storm, and The Word begins to shield himself within darkness as Abraham tries to destroy him, and at the same time, the lesser demons climb the palace walls to get to Isaac and Jacob. Abraham remembers the Bible in his belt, and in presenting this, he is able to advance now unhindered by twisted tongue, the fortress of his mind is reclaimed by the fruits of the Spirit. The holy sword obliterates the false Word, and Isaac and Jacob are rescued at the final moment for as the summoner of the vast army dies so does his force as they are cast back to the abyss along with the ancient tome of evil.

The few remaining Nephilim begin to retreat as the last 500 holy knights hunted the stragglers down. Tired, injured, and almost broken from the loss of so many, the holy knights continually push forward as champions of the faith. Abraham never gave up on his men and yet again uplifted them, for Jesus never gave up on him nor his flock. The remaining Nephilim are cornered in the city, but as the holy knights approach, the storm dies down, holding the region in a deafening silence. The sky is blanketed by a crimson veil blood can be seen staining the revealing moon's surface, pouring from a golden chalice of transgression. The last brother, The Crown, hovers above the city on a pale horse with sprouted wings stripped of feather. His countenance strikes fear into the Nephilim, who try and run away, but they are sucked into the storm above. The winds tear apart the city as The Crown reaches the earth; all of the holy knights are paralyzed in place out of fear for their souls cannot handle the level of attack this arch-demon has brought to them. Unlike the majority of material, the knights are not taken into the vortex nor are their horses, but sadly, tens of thousands of others hiding among the city are seen taken to this the void of Cain. Alone,

Abraham charges to the heart of Jerusalem where he meets The Crown sword to sword. A great earthquake overtook the region, and all of Jerusalem fell into the earth along with the holy knights. Opening his eyes, Abraham sees a land cast out from the sun, an endless plain of grave. Desperately, he looks around, calling for his men, but no answer is heard, except the voices now assaulting his mind. The legendary sword is gone, but his armor remains, giving at least minimal comfort if that. Suddenly in the distance, a vast tidal wave comprised of oil and fire as high as it is wide rushes forth, consuming all in sight. Trapped inside are bodies from men and women cast to this infernal plane since the dawn of man. Immediately, he is overtaken, but it does not kill him; instead, he opens his eyes once more and is at the bottom of a blazing chasm. Countless people can be seen being led by endless corruptions and demonic entities. Everyone is naked and no one can speak except in pain or fear. No water, no breath of pure air on this dismal putrid hole of sulfuric damnation. Abraham was capable of doing nothing but could only witness the destruction of those who were not children of God. People were burnt alive repeatedly; limbs were joyfully torn from their bodies. Demons would rape man and woman alike, tearing flesh, so they would have to exist without even skin. Nothing but false hope was given only to further the pain, and all the time, people would cry out to God for his existence had now been revealed to them, but they chose not to believe in Him in life when sign after sign was freely given. Calling upon the name of Jesus Christ, a lone light shone through the chasm and a sword thousands of feet high plunges to the depths in front of Abraham. Crashing like a meteor from space, it sent every person and demon to their knees, and the vast angelic wings around this the word of God revealed Christ Jesus inside. Abraham is filled with sorrow for the sins he has committed and repents reaching for the Lord and for a single moment he can feel the Lord's embrace hold him closely. He is then rescued, and as he opens his teary eyes, he realizes he is back in Vulgata. Both Abraham and The Crown reappear in Jerusalem and the city is left intact for it was a spiritual attack, but through Jesus, the knight had overcome. "Do you not like my kingdom? Do you not know that soon I am to be king of this world for I am the spirit of the antichrist?" The Crown explains. Abraham rises with the very purity of the Holy Ghost coursing through his very being; he then turns to The Crown and says, "If you are the spirit of the antichrist, then surely, you know this passage." Abraham sheathed his sword and tossed the shield to the ground and began to say this scripture for the Lord was now directly speaking through him.

> I am the good shepherd, and know my sheep, and am known of mine. As the Father knoweth me, even so know I the Father: and I lay down my life for the sheep. And other sheep I have, which are not of this fold: them also I must bring, and they shall hear my voice; and there shall be one fold, and one shepherd. Therefore doth my Father love me, because I lay down my life, that I might take it again. No man taketh it from me, but I lay it down of myself. I have power to lay it down, and I have power to take it again. This commandment have I received of my Father.
>
> John 10:14–18 (KJV)

The first holy knight, now stripped of armor, walks up to The Crown, who is terrified of Abraham, for sitting on his head is a crown of glory in the image of a shining halo. Abraham kneels, and a grand shadow of the blessed dragon Atyrael appears in front of them; a single dove then rests on Abraham's shoulder. The false Crown imprisoned in everlasting fear of the Lord states that only a king can defeat another king. Abraham stands, pressing his crown against the arch-demon's chest and looks directly at him. "A kingdom divided shall not stand. Checkmate," he says and the false Crown is forced to bow with such intensity that he is taken by fire. Abraham draws the legendary sword and splits

The Crown's body from top to bottom in half. Worms, maggots, and snakes soaked in his unholy ichor dissolved onto his body as it went back into the ground. All the while, his blood-curdling screams of a pain mortal man cannot comprehend echoed across all of Jerusalem as Atyrael's righteous and mighty jaws ripped him asunder within the shadow, further proving that the foul cannot hide from what is holy and true. Far to the south in the pyramid of Mecca, the four faces on the sides appeared once more, roaring in hatred for their days were short so their boldness was amplified. In the shadow of the pyramid, another dragon watches intently, wanting to sift Abraham but is denied. The four faces disappear as does the dragon but for only a short moment; a ghostlike sight of a transparent capstone hovers above the pyramid, and on this capstone is a single eye of that dragon known as the ancient serpent the devil. The skies over Jerusalem began to break apart and both the sun and clear sky had once again returned. This day, great evil was defeated out of the east and the slaves both Jew and Gentile from all the land came and honored Sir Abraham Desteeran and the holy knights. The 4,000 fallen holy knights gardens could be seen across the city and in Herod's Palace with their bodies gone also. A great feast was held in their name, and on that day, people of all walks of life came to faith in Jesus Christ, for even though the spiritual battle was over, the war was not, and the holy knights preached unto the masses that day still. Abraham and the holy knights gave all the glory of this legendary victory to the Lord God.

Later that night, Abraham met with the last of the holy knights and wept dearly over the loss of their brothers and then gave a fervent eulogy in their name. He said that they have now gone on to be with the Father in heaven and their names would never be forgotten in the Book of Life for their valiant sacrifice. Together, they said good-bye to the freed people of Jerusalem and headed back to Valencia to proclaim the good news to all people that good had prevailed by faith. Before the holy knights left the east, Abraham appointed elders among the slaves who were already believers in Christ who had been in hiding for some time. These men were now free to openly preach the good news of the kingdom of God for all to hear. After passing back into the west, Abraham turned back one last time, remembering the faith and bravery of the 4,500 men he had not yet known who gave all so that freedom could be given to all. Isaac and Jacob picked up Abraham's spirits by reminding him of all the people and children that were saved because of their sacrifice and better yet all who would come to know Him that sent them. Abraham watched as the holy knights raised their swords one final time to their fallen brothers and said in unison, "I am the way, the truth, and the life!" Many days later, when they reached Valencia, the king, the church, and the citizens greeted them with a great parade and offered him the crown to the Valencian Empire. Abraham turned it down for he showed that the Lord had given him a crown and his kingdom was to be far to the west. They said their good-byes and not a single eye was left dry as the God-fearing holy knights rode away on the center bridge of the seven bridges of Valencia, passing the city of Romulus. These heroes in the face of infinite temporal glory remained humble and turned down an entire empire; much work was left to do in the world.

Far to the western edge of the continent, the 500 holy knights rode until they came upon the point where the continent dropped off into the ocean. The angel of the Lord appeared to the holy knights and guided them across a bridge made of light (Faith's Bridge) to a small continent of their own. After they crossed, it turned into a two-mile long bridge in a bright flash of lightning. Here on the first steps of what was called Evangela, they were instructed to build a white bell tower (Covenant's Bell Tower). From the deeds accomplished by Abraham, righteousness was counted towards him by the Lord for he had obeyed the commands of the Holy Spirit, also understanding that these victories were God's. On this day, the Lord made a covenant with

Abraham to serve Him and to remain humble in obedience to the Holy Spirit and to never forsake the name of Christ Jesus from this land. This new nation, Evangela, was to live righteous and upright lives, never forgetting the Lord who blessed them with the land, and for that, this nation was untouched by the corrupted nature of the world. Also, this was to be a nation of and for all people, regardless of race or ailment or status. Abraham was to be the king of this nation, for the true Trial of Kings was proven in his quest, which was nothing more than a reflection of the spiritual truths shown in Christ. The bell tower was the seal of this covenant, and whenever it rang, it was His call for the holy knights to disperse in the world to protect the innocent, stand against injustice, love the lost, and above all else, to glorify the one true God who gave His only begotten son Jesus Christ so that all the world may have the chance at salvation. Here, Abraham gave his last words to his men before they began to build Evangela: "Let us never forget what the Lord has done for us, and today, let us set the precedent that the Holy Bible will be the roots of this great nation as long as we stand and with it the truth of the Christ whose name is Jesus and that only through faith and repentance in Him may salvation be gained!"

They went on to build the capital city of Antioch and the first structure built was the Church of Salvation (COS) in 1623. This was a nondenominational church whose first 500 were of many a denominational background. In Antioch's main square stood a tablet presenting the Ten Commandments for all to see and remember as their core principles.

For the next thousand years, the holy knights honored the covenant and rode out to all nations, crossing Faith's Bridge every time the bell tower beautifully chimed. They fought wars against mighty beasts born of sin; they defended the western lands and spread the gospel for all to hear. Loved and revered, the holy knights never gave up on people or their nation of Evangela that later became the third largest superpower in WWI. They changed the world, and just as quickly, they were gone a thousand years later, which tossed things back into a state of turmoil. Although gone, one mystery did remain for at the birth of Evangela, another task was given: the holy knights were to wait for the sacred day of the Exiles. Generation after generation, they indeed did wait, passing on the knowledge to their sons, but the Exiles never came, and so was the account of Sir Abraham Desteeran and the holy knights.

ACT I
DESCENT

1

Fated Black Rose

The year is 2984. It has been 376 years since the end of WWI, and relations are kindled once more between east and west. Three major superpowers hold the keys for the dawn of a new age in the world of Vulgata: (1) Valencia, the nation of the church; (2) Evangela, the free nation of all peoples; (3) Marduas, the unified empire of the east. Valencia and Evangela hail to the west and have long been allies since even before the Great War. Marduas sits reunited for the second time in human history as nations can only speculate to the interests of the new crown. Marduas had been subject to religious warfare since speech was introduced and no belief or army was ever able to unite it, except for WWI, which was made out of a common hatred for the western religious ideology. Only four years earlier, a lone man had reawakened the sleeping giant and united the entire east. Known as King of the Slaves, Victor Carthright, who was once a slave himself, now soars even above the status of the Valencian Church of Law. This upcoming year would prove to be very special for Carthright has received royal invitation to attend the Week of Commemoration in Valencia; this is the first time since WWI that the easterners have been granted audience to western banquet. It is unknown the size of force Marduas controls, but it is known throughout every western nation that if they were to attack, it is a war they could not win, that is not without the holy knights who once led them through WWI. King Victor Carthright also controls the most powerful knighthood in the land known as the Drudge Knights that are said to number in the tens of thousands. Sharply divided over how to react over the issue along with the current political atmosphere neither Valencia nor Evangela can decide whether to join or take a stand as public sentiment becomes an ever-rising factor. Although Valencia has always been the nation of the church, they are at the brink of civil war over the issue of salvation through Jesus Christ through faith in Him or to stand by the Laws of Moses. These days the divide goes far deeper than ever for the incorporation of apocrypha unto canon is said to cause a second Reformation. The Church of Law is the cause of this split, and it remains the battleground for both Northcross and Southcross, the two dueling factions of Valencia. In that, Valencia focuses a large quantity of its military on her homeland security if civil war was to ever break out. It is said that their nation could never defeat Marduas, but at the same time, Marduas could never defeat them. This is due to the Valencian Empire sitting on its own island and the only possible assault is by one of the seven bridges overlooked by the famous bridge city of Romulus. Valencia holds the only known naval force in the world and use cannon-based technology; it is radically advanced in a world subject to sword. These cannons resemble that of revolutionary war types, except far larger and frighteningly more devastating. Valencia along with Maldecium is one of only two nations that are known to currently have gunpowder-based weaponry. Lastly, Valencia has the greatest military in the west of close to if not more than half a million soldiers currently enlisted to the crown. The church in this day retains a 15,000 silver paladin elite force of her own, but they move by order of the church not the crown. Evangela struggles with its own perplexing burden of holding its own state in check by power of the judges. Evangela, who was founded upon faith in the Lord, had exiled and murdered the last of the holy knights 344 years ago in the year 2640. The first free nation for all peoples in the world had as a whole turned its back on what they were founded on and instead decided to follow the always changing philosophies of moral relativity. Its government was no different, for Evangela was ruled by a noble-based parliament, which was locked in a bitter struggle for power between two political parties conceived before the exile of the holy knights. Evangela's government was quickly becoming known as the most corrupt in all the land, for it had destroyed the once legendary nation of the holy knights by the rule of sinister partisanship, their agents are the lobbyist and the bureaucracy. Evangela holds the second largest military to the west of well over 300,000 men at arms. To this day, the members of the Church of Salvation in Antioch still hold on to hope in the falling empire of Evangela and pray that one day the patriots of their country will return. The time of Sir Abraham Desteeran and his holy knights have long been forgotten by the rest of the world, and darkness yet again seems to be returning to a land that does not care.

East of Evangela rests Calina, otherwise known as nation of the arts. A piece of artistry itself where the Starras Mountains stand tall and the lakes reflect the clarity of the sky. Subject to many a rainstorm, the endless flowering fields only enhances the beauty of this nation built upon a plethora of small village. Calina crowns their love of fine culture from musicians, artists, and playwrights to the simple but vast gardens planted all around the home front. The culmination of these pursuits serve not only as their capital trade but to advance outlook upon humanity for it was here that the first playwrights were born of the stage. The original playhouse sits in Malastay capital city of Calina, but as for our story, we shall be visiting a much smaller and most peaceful village known as Salem.

High above a lonely yet majestic mountaintop sits this city, overlooking the breathtaking grasslands where an ongoing serenade to nature is given by a constant gale. Individual fingers of the mountain encompass the city much like trees surrounding a lake; some even say it is the loving protection given by the hand of God. Home to roughly two hundred citizens, this is a small village where everyone knows everyone. They live and band together here as many of the societies do in the world of Vulgata for most creatures are vile beasts littered across the earth. That year, the harvests were better than they'd been in decades, so good fortune seemed to favor them. The denizens of Salem were a jovial and simple people who enjoyed their lives together and everyone had a love of the professions of both humanistic and natural expression. Most of the jobs here were of painter and musician, but a true playwright had not come along since the days of Fanero Malchior who had gone on to change the world once he left Salem. Among this village, there was a single red cottage that remained perched on a hill quietly monitoring the city, which in its own right was quite large for a mountain town. This was the home of Joseph Voltel who had been gone for well over a year, but this day, he was to return to his wife Penelope and his six-year-old daughter Mariana. Although Joseph was settled here as a pastor, he would still occasionally travel off into the world to deliver the word as a missionary. Penelope, his wife, was one of the only female writers in all of Calina for it was frowned on in those days, but Joseph always encouraged his wife to pursue whatever the Lord had called her to do. She was a writer of children's stories, which also was a very new concept to the times. This was a true believing couple who let the Lord lead their marriage, and everyone was able to learn from their longstanding examples.

One brisk morning, young Mariana awoke to the fresh smell of baking cookies from the downstairs kitchen. The adorable six-year-old girl with curly brunette hair and a bright red bow sitting atop her head sprang out of bed. "I wonder if Mommy is downstairs or writing upstairs," she said aloud to herself. "I know I'll sneak a few cookies for myself and Mr. Sebastian." Mr. Sebastian was Mariana's imaginary best friend who was a patched-together small teddy bear she kept in a knitted rucksack Joseph had made for her before he left. The six-year-old bundled herself up for the cooler weather and threw on a blue coat. She crept down the stairs as quietly as possible and asked her bear to watch her back for her mother. Now peeking around the corner into the kitchen, she could see dozens of the freshly baked prizes. Her eyes gazed and mouth watered as she looked around for her mother yet again, but she was nowhere in sight. Her little finger pressed against her lips as she glanced around wondering if she should do this or not; the decision wasn't difficult to say the least. "All right, Mr. Sebastian, I'm going to go for it. Make sure not to say a word," she quietly whispered to the teddy bear who had two different-sized black buttons for eyes. Carefully, she stepped into the kitchen on her toes closer and closer to her preferred entrée, which was oatmeal. "Yes," she had accidentally yelled out with excitement. She then ran under the kitchen table and sat still without saying another word listening for any footsteps or angered voice. Minutes went by, no trace of her mother, so she stood back up, grabbing an entire plate, and stuffed it in with the bear. Immediately, she ran out the door and ran down the hill from the red cottage almost falling down the hill. "Mariana," a lovely parental voice called out. Mariana looked back and it was her mother. Her beautiful mother Penelope stood at the doorway smiling, brushing her lovely dark and flowing hair out of her eyes. "Don't forget to be back by the afternoon, okay, dear!"

"Yes, Mommy, I love you," she said giggling as she ran off into the village.

Penelope held an all too familiar grin, knowing Mariana's plan, then went back inside and sat down at her desk, which was littered with papers being assembled for her just finished masterpiece. A story titled "Faith of a Child" that was about a child who was born and then abandoned to the forest raised by an angel of the Lord. Later, when the child came of age, he would fight a terrible evil that threatened the sacred forest. "Oh, Joseph, you're finally coming home," she said as she kissed a painting of him on the mantle by her oak desk. Penelope held the portrait close and began to pray for his safe return home with her year's work laid out before her.

Mariana makes her way into the silent inner village of Salem as the sun is soon to rise. She passes by the town's old and only bakery with its own windmill and stone base behind it. By every building, an array of flowers are cultivated to perfection of all types from daisies to chrysanthemums. Mariana arrives at an almost forgotten graveyard at the edge of the city by a pond where the wind blows just enough for her bow to fall off. "My bow," she exclaims then scolds Mr. Sebastian for not holding on to it for her. The little red bow catches an old iron gate, then flies in the wind all the way to a gravestone that reads: Simon Peter Voltel 2966–2982. Below that sits another inscription that also reads: "The Hearing Rock on which Salem rests." Mariana picks up her red bow and takes off the rucksack in which she then removes the dozen cookies from the kitchen back home. "Simon, I brought these here for you today just in case you get hungry," she said under her breath. A single tear rolled down Mariana's left cheek as she caringly placed each cookie around the tombstone, five in front and seven behind. "Mr. Sebastian says he misses you and so do I. I love you, big brother," as she kisses the tombstone with her bear.

The sun begins to rise in the east, Mariana's eyes are drawn to it as does Penelope's back home for they are both focused on Joseph's return for he is the light of their family. The townsfolk begin to awaken, for the daily life of an artist begins at dawn. Music slowly begins to pick up as painters and writers take to the streets with canvas and quill in hand. Young Mariana, who is rumored to be the spirit of curiosity and imagination, begins to interact with many of the townsfolk. During this, a conversation is heard between some of the locals passing by about the dozens of missing ladders, which Mariana begins to wonder thoroughly about. Mr. Royalton's hammer can be heard forging a sword as the village's only string quartet rivals the pounding steel from the main square. Mariana watches every strike against the steel and loves the sparks, also asking for a sword. Mr. Royalton chuckles and says that perhaps she can when she is older; he then drops the red hot metal into a barrel of ice-cold water and steam rises along with the hiss of cooling steel. Looking at this finely crafted blade he was preparing for Joseph, he saw the little girl take off in the corner of his eye.

Back home, her mother Penelope meets with a few of the townsfolk as they prepare a feast for the return of Joseph. All kinds of splendid foods and goods are brought to dozens of tables all set up just below the little red cottage on the hill. "Well, I wanted to thank each and every one of you for helping me prepare this today. It really means the world, and I know it will to Joseph," Penelope said blushing and touching hair above her eye while her lips curled slightly. They laughed because they could all see that even after all her years of marriage, the mention of her husband's name still tightly held the reins of her heart. One of the townsfolk asked her how excited she was for her husband to finally be returning from his last trip abroad. Penelope gave a sort of half smile, then began to chop up a variety of vegetables. In a tender way, she explained, "He is the light in my life, the proof that Jesus answers prayers. Joseph brings out the best in me, regardless of the mood I'm in. We've been married a long time, and to this day, he still romances me and cherishes the words I have to say even when they're not very interesting. Joseph would lay down his life for me and Mariana in a heartbeat, but more so, he is the man Christ tells him to be, not the world. I pray for his safety and return every day and for his travels to finally be coming to an end is a magnificent blessing." Penelope then cut her hand slightly on the blade, which surprised her as she wrapped the bleeding finger in a cloth. She then peered, and while surveying the village, she stated, "But I want my husband to be happy and pursue what the Lord has asked him to do. So if this wasn't his last trip, although I'd be displeased at first, I'd come to realize that God's wants are so much more important than ours. When you can rest in that, all things seem to fit into place." After she had finished saying this, her cut abruptly stopped bleeding and she began to wonder what Mariana was off doing.

Meanwhile, in the eastern section of Salem, Mariana had made her way to an old stone made bridge that spanned over a small stream. Traversing it, a grouping of hills could be seen as she then began to sprint across to reach the summit. Halfway up the tallest of these hills, she tripped and fell down face first and then began to roll down the entirety of it. Quite tough for a young one, she laughed as she rolled to its base and asked her bear if he was all right. When she finally got to the top, she surveyed a plateau where an old broken-down playhouse sat, reminding Salem of meritorious days long past. A single stoop outreaches in the shape of a ram leaving room for only one to roost. Years ago sat a manmade suspension bridge connecting all the way to the top, but due to years of non-repair, it had collapsed. Many a lovely play once was written here, but none with the same grandeur as Fanero Malchior's "The Inlet's Dream." It is said that sometimes a lone violin can be heard late at night, playing from within the playhouse. Mariana had come here many times over the past few months for she wanted to explore the forgotten playhouse, but it was impossible to gain entry, but today would prove to be fruitful. Off to the side of the plateau sat a thicket where she entered and found a ladder propped to the side of the cliff. Behind the plateau, out of the sight from the front view of the playhouse, a series of ladders reached all the way to the top; they were placed all over the back of the small cliff reaching to the playhouse. "My wish has come true," Mariana shouted while jumping in the air, swinging her bear in every direction. Standing before the first of a surplus of wooden ladders, she yelled out to her bear, "Better hold on because here we go!" She began her ascent, racing the eternal clock of the sun. The ladders shook and rattled, and the bear bounced about in her rucksack as her little red bow swayed with each new height attained. Now reaching the top, the playhouse's main entrance was blocked by massive debris and there was no way inside. Around back sat one final ladder going up to the roof of the old broken-down arts building. Now towards the top of the structure, many feet above the city of Salem and hundreds of feet above the mountain's base, she could see across the lands. The windy grasslands were seen to the northeast were as usual the blades of grass swayed in unison for miles to the prevailing winds. "All right, Mr. Sebastian, don't let me fall off the roof," she said as she began to walk to the roof's center where a massive hole sat and beams creaked by each step. At the edge, there was yet another ladder leading all the way to a stage where actors and writers alike once worked tirelessly together for the love of story.

Mariana took out Mr. Sebastian from her rucksack and told him to check first if it was safe and then tossed him all the way to the bottom, hitting the center stage. A single circle of light was fixed upon the lifeless bear from the rooftop for he was the star of the show. Mariana climbed down to him into a decent-sized yet glorious but aged gothic style playhouse. An ominous presence lingered within the room as there was little to no light. The walls were lined with bronze statues of fallen angels and demonic creatures all staring at the main stage. Above the center stage stood a group of holy angels who were mounted on horseback riding out to vanquish evil and above them stood a figure cloaked in a represented golden light pulling a double-edged sword from His mouth. "I don't like these statues very much, they frighten me," she explained while shielding her eyes from the demonic statues beyond the stage. Mariana crossed behind the main curtain and hundreds of costumes, masks, and stage props were sprawled about on the wooden floor. Filled now with excitement and awe, she began to play with all of it as she sat Sebastian on a chair to watch her try on the costumes. She then found another small bear and dozens of ranging outfits, so she dressed up Mr. Sebastian as a groom and the other bear as a bride naming her Mrs. Elysia. She dressed herself up as a pirate, claiming all the loot, first inspired from an imaginative treasure box now raised to life and opened by realities key. Mariana then waltzed out onto the front stage in the light where she had descended. As she married the bears, the holy angels of light and the demonic cast in shadow served as the witnesses. Then with her vast imagination, she pulled out the pirate sword prop she had found and pretended to kill a monster that was trying to kill the newlyweds and ruin the wedding feast. She put the two into the old rucksack and proceeded to look around until she found a small formation of red roses behind the stage props. The peculiar thing here was that amidst of all these was a single black rose. As she plucked that one, she said to the newlyweds, "I'm sure Daddy will love this as a gift," for Joseph, her father, was to most likely to return within the hour. She gently placed the rose in her rucksack between the bears and began to leave the playhouse the same way she had entered. As she stood on the roof, she looked down into the playhouse one last time and a gust of wind blew the red ribbon down onto the stage and she then left, knowing she had many more bows at home. As she left the view of the ceiling, a figure cloaked in the darkness walked on to the stage. Only the figure's hand could be seen reaching out into the light grabbing the ribbon as the figure then lifted it up and crushed it in his grip. The demonic statue's eyes seemed to be fixed upon the figure as the sun began to set.

Mariana returned home, still wearing the pirate hat, and sitting in the kitchen was her mother Penelope reading her Bible; she was in Romans. She lay it down, hugged her daughter, and gave her a kiss on the cheek. "How was your day, dear?" She pulled out the new bear she had found. "This is Elysia and she is married to Sebastian now!" The bears were still dressed in wedding clothes and her mother asked where she had gotten all of this, including the pirate hat. Mariana knew she would get into a lot of trouble if her mother knew where she had gone so she switched the subject. "Mommy, look what I've found," and she pulled out the black rose and handed it to her. "This is my present for Daddy when he gets home." Penelope examined the black rose for she had never seen anything like it, but before she could attempt to get all the information out of Mariana, she heard someone yell Joseph's name. Penelope and Mariana dashed outside where the entire village was gathered around the only route into Salem. Riding up the steep hill on a white horse was Joseph Voltel; the village cheers him back home as he gets off his horse and runs to Penelope and Mariana who in turn do the same. Joseph, who was a gray-haired man of fifty-two, beheld the happiness of a child at the sight of his family. The family embraced each other as the town applauded their beloved friends return. Joseph takes his wife to his right and his daughter to his left hand as they walk together to the feast prepared for him.

Later that night, after the time of the party, which in fact went wonderfully for the Voltel family especially, Joseph prepares to put little Mariana to bed. He walks in with candle in hand, with the other, carrying his daughter, who had fallen asleep in his lap at the party that night. Laying Mariana in her bed, her eyes partially open. "Daddy, I love you," she says as she falls asleep virtually instantaneously. Joseph smiles, then places the bears on both sides of her, giving a long anticipated kiss on the forehead. *I hadn't noticed the two married bears at the party tonight, hmm, perhaps a wedding feast*, Joseph thinks to himself. He then begins to pray over his child and standing in the doorway is Penelope with her arms crossed lovingly gazing upon Joseph. No words are said as he stands up and meets his wife in the kitchen where they sit down over a pot of tea she warms over a fire. "That was a lovely party you put on for me tonight, dear," Joseph said, caressing her hand. "Oh well, you know, anything for the man I love," she replied as her eyes fluttered back towards him alongside a beautiful smile, but this was a smile only a wife can give to her husband. This was a smile where to this day she still felt slightly embarrassed by it, because the simple truth was no matter how long thou art married, new things will always be revealed. Still, something didn't seem right, and although she knew in her heart it was linked to the trip he had been on, she asked regardless, "How was the mission's trip?" He grasped his cup of tea slightly tighter than most would but did not drink it yet; he then looked down for a moment, contemplating his answer. Penelope had never seen her husband this uneasy before so it worried her all the same. "Dear, what is it?" Joseph then raised his tea and scratched his brow with the glass while replying, "All that could have been done was accomplished, but still no trace to his whereabouts." Penelope walked over and hugged her husband, kissing him on the cheek, and acknowledged the statement. "God will answer all prayers, you taught me that. It's going to be all right, honey."

"I know and you're right. I guess that I just really felt this time was going to be different, but the Lord will reveal in His time so patience is key," he replied. The two held each other close, resting their hearts into one another, each wondering how the other had been but knowing now at this moment each had longed for the other. "Joseph, you look older, you look tired," Penelope stated, stroking his face. He blinked only once, looking past his wife before asking, "Have I failed, have I misled everyone and deceived myself?" Penelope flicked him in the head, gaining his full attention. "Nothing is going to happen that isn't in God's will, so in that, we can trust. You have always trusted in the Lord and done what He asks of you. Sometimes, the worse things seem the better. The closer you get to the Father's will, the more the world that hates Him is going to try and bring you down. You did teach me this after all." Her words touched his heart before they were fully spoken, and without saying anything back, he gave his wife a long lasting kiss, which in itself said I love you. Joseph then stood. "What a mighty celebration this day is and praise be you're here to share it with me." He then reached out his arm and asked her for this dance and they began to slow dance in the kitchen. "Oh, I almost forgot I have something for you, Penelope," he exclaimed a bit too loud as he laughed because he could have woken up Mariana. Reaching into a bag, he presented a breathtaking music box that was cast in ivory. As he turned around, Penelope was gone, but she returned to the kitchen quickly with her novel, "Faith of a Child." The two presented their gifts to each other and lovingly accepted them, but Joseph sarcastically stated, "Well, I think you've outdone me by just a bit. I did not know this was a contest."

"Oh, shut up. You had plenty of work to do," Penelope answered back as she playfully smacked his shoulder. Before they began to dance again, Penelope had remembered one thing that Mariana forgot to give her father. She went into her room and grabbed it from her rucksack and gave him the mysterious black rose. Joseph examined it for a moment for he had never before seen such a thing.

"Penelope, do you know what this is?" he asked.

"I have no idea, but there is a strange sort of beauty, don't you think?"

"This rose is a bad omen. It represents evil's love of eternal death."

Penelope felt bad that she had not known that right away, but before she could speak, Joseph pulled out a vial of holy water and let a single drop course down its soulless ink-like stem. The jet-black rose shriveled up, closing like a dying spider as steam slightly rose from what appeared to be a burning ember inside the bulb. "It's all right because we are spiritually protected, but we as a family and a village should keep our wits about us to the best of our ability for prelude is married to action." They then decided to turn in for the night after Penelope tossed the shriveled black rose outside that was taken by a rogue gust. "I'll have to ask her where she got it tomorrow," Joseph whispered to himself before they turned in.

Late into the next morning, Joseph, who had slept in, woke up to an excited Mariana throwing the bears at him to wake him up. "Mommy has breakfast ready. Wake up, Daddy," as she was now hitting him with a pillow.

"I'll be right down, sweetheart," he replied as he knocked her away with his own pillow partnered with an assault of a hug initiated by the father. The family sat down, giving thanks to the Lord for breakfast, and ate joyfully together. For most of the day, they lounged around the house, talking to one another, catching up on unshared adventures. Sometime in the evening, a group of the village's hunters armed with long and composite bows arrived. One of them spoke, "Joseph, we're glad that you've returned. We've spotted a large grouping of deer amongst the grasslands." They knew that Joseph loved to hunt, and at this moment, Joseph couldn't resist game or an easy meal for his family this close to home. He looked to his wife and she looked back at him and gave the nod so that he could join his brothers on the hunt. "I'll go on one condition: I've been promising this young lady for some time I'd teach her how to hunt," Joseph said, picking up his daughter.

The hunter replied, "Ya, that's fine. Perhaps she'll bring us good luck and a child is never too young to learn the fine art of hunting." Joseph got himself ready as Penelope dressed Mariana quickly. They then left with the hunters out into the windy grasslands.

The hunters, numbering eight, broke up into groups of two as they spread out across the grasslands hoping to yet again spot the multitude of deer. Joseph and Mariana took an eastern path over a large stream that ran across flowing directly from Salem. "Mariana, I have to ask you a question, and I need you to be truthful with your father," Joseph said as he had his composite bow in his left hand and quiver on back.

"What is it, Daddy?" she answered, bobbing her attention with eyes lovingly wide.

"Well, I was curious as to where you found the black rose." Mariana had noticed it was gone that morning from her rucksack and had been looking for it the entire day. Slowly, she explained where she had gotten it at the old playhouse where the ample amount of ladders twisted all the way up the plateau. Joseph got down on his knees and put his hands on his daughter's shoulders, smiling and hugging her. The sound of running water could be heard as Mariana's eyes began to wander hoping that she wasn't going to get into trouble. "Oh, I see," he said making a ridiculous face to make her laugh. "It's probably best this stays a secret between us, okay. I don't want your mother to worry." Mariana smiled and tilted her head as she gave her father a kiss on the cheek then forced him to make a pinky promise on the important matter. Just then, they heard a branch break, and not far off, the group of deer was sitting by a beaver's dam, drinking from the stream. Joseph put his finger to his lips signaling for Mariana to be quiet as he reached for an arrow out of his quiver. His heart began to race as he crept forward, not yet drawing for the shot. Mariana put her tiny fingers over her mouth to remain mute, standing as a young statue. Joseph drew his bow and had a magnificent buck dead in his sights as he then steadied his aim. Everything stopped, and far off in the distance, a loud yelling could be heard from one of the hunters. The buck ran off with the rest of the pack and Joseph listened diligently in the direction of the sound where he could now make out that someone was yelling for help. "Mariana, stay right here. Someone's in trouble," he shouted to her. She shook for a split second because it scared her but then began to run off with her father deep into a small wooded area regardless of his command. The calls for help were getting louder, and as Joseph was then sprinting in to help the other hunter, he became separated from Mariana who was now lost within a labyrinth of brush. "Daddy," she screamed back again and again, but no response was given. The trees were barren and stripped of their bark, yet the sunlight was unable to pierce through. Alone in the woods, Mariana began to frantically search for her father, but fate, it seemed, had other plans.

The grip of silence captured the region, and while running, innocent Mariana tripped over a log and landed face first into the mud. She pulled herself out, covered in tears, mud, and terror as something could be heard rustling about in a brush-covered thicket up ahead. The noise wasn't normal; it sounded as claws running up and down a tree. Crying too hard to breath, Mariana called out, "D-d-daddy, is that you?" Instantly, the scratching noise ceased; trembling, she pulled out Mr. Sebastian and proceeded to step to the brush. Lying in front of the brush was the crumpled black rose Joseph had poured holy water on, for the night winds had carried it to this very spot. She bent down to pick it up, recalling that her father had asked her about it and implied it not being a good thing. As her hand touched the black rose, a shadow stood wrapped around a tree watching her every move. Its hand reached out to her and Mariana was one with the shadow. She went to look up and the presence disappeared from the tree and everything turned to shadow but herself. Holding Mr. Sebastian close, Mariana nervously spoke, "Sebastian, do you think Daddy is going to save us?" As she stood up, the eyes of a grotesque corrupted beast of the earth emerged from the brush and was almost face-to-face with her own. Its face looked as if it were the flesh form of a moss-covered demonic dragon with twisted antlers on the top of its skull and its ears. The monster's eyes were a deep yellow with an emerald tint but it had no eyelids, so it was locked in a permanent gaze as if damned to do so for the entirety of its life. Mariana was frozen in horror, and the beast's mouth opened up with jagged obsidian-like teeth that sat in two rows. A poisonous gas also came forth from its lungs and out its mouth as it began to breathe heavily, savoring the meal to come. Mariana jumped back, and the beast stood out of the bushes at over eight feet tall. The hoof type legs of the beast were crooked in a way that didn't make sense and its lanky arms with humanistic hands fused with claw like nails dragged lifelessly along the leaves on the ground. The creature's back was covered in long black quills, which were the noise Mariana had heard scratching against the trees. Its body was littered with a prickly type of grass-looking substance that was of an extreme jade coloration. The child began to run away, and the creature strafed sideways with its eyes never leaving her. Running with all the might her little legs could muster, Mariana arrived to an old stone bridge atop the stream. Halfway across the bridge, she could see the beast running down the stream on all fours as it then climbed up the side of the bridge. It peered over the side, frightening her, which caused Mariana to fall backwards. Clenching her bear tightly to her heart, now petrified, she closed her eyes tightly, calling out for her father. The beast slowly began walking towards her, letting out a disturbing and distorted goat-like noise. It swayed eerily, but the magnetized eyes that never blinked seemingly drew it to her, it was fueled by the fear it was exalted by it.

The beast stopped only steps before Mariana, for a figure held in a travel-worn cloak over old leather armor stood in front of Mariana as she kicked her legs, moving back along the bridge to get away. The man drew a massive two-handed claymore with some kind of specialty crest on the cerulean sheath strapped to his back. The mysterious figure lowered the blade to his left shoulder and readied his attack. At the same time, the lumbering beast that was standing over eight feet tall got down on all fours, twisting its head so violently that the beast's eyes began to hemorrhage. They both charged the other and the man's claymore locked with the monster's twisted antlers as it then attempted to pull the sword from his grasp. Unable to gain the blade from the monster's powerful grip, he pulled a dagger from his overcoat and jammed it into the monster's back, causing it to squeal in the goat-like sound not of true nature, but the pitch transitions constantly from low to high. The man pulled the dagger towards him violently past the shoulder, causing the corrupted animal to rise quickly, but as it did, he continually pulled the blade over its shoulder and down its chest. The skin was pulled off, leaving its shoulder, back, and chest bones exposed. Green blood gushed in untold amounts from its deep gash as its eyes began to lose coloration. Crying out in pain, it let out a ferocious last attack with its final breath of toxic existence and stabbed the hero with its claws through the chest. Afterwards, it fell to the ground and shook violently and the same shadow Mariana had seen stood within the cloaked figure's shadow with a demonic grin, but it also moved around as he did not. Picking up his sword, he pointed it at the shadow as Mariana sprinted over to the man. The other hunter's calls could be heard along with Joseph's for his daughter. Mariana hugged the man's leg, still crying, covered in mud as the monster's sour stench lingered. She looked up at the man whose entire face was hidden, but his eyes which were hazel spoke of a disillusioned pain. "Thank you, mister," she said, staring at him with all the love a child could show, but the man remained without word or acknowledgement as his own blood dripped out of his chest onto the bridge. She attempted to say more, but the man nudged her off him and as fast as he came to save her, he was then gone. At the other end of the bridge, the man turned around one final time and the two synchronized eyes as the man sheathed his blade and held his palm close to his bleeding heart. She could sense a deep spiritual hurt in this man who walked away, and behind him, the black rose fell on the bridge where his blood had stained. Mariana stood alone on the bridge unsure why the man had left as the creature's corpse rots and its bones boil in a pool of its own venomous poison. "Come back," Mariana cried out repeatedly, stomping her feet until she had no voice left.

"Mariana, Mariana," Joseph screams as he runs to her with the other hunters. "It's the Murkan you had spotted," he said to one of the other hunters who were calling for help earlier. Joseph grabbed his daughter and held her close; she was covered in mud and had traces of blood from both that man and the creature. "What happened? Are you okay? Are you hurt?" Joseph clearly spoke to her as she sat there in silence. The other hunters examined the broken body of the Murkan whose shoulder was split by steel and fine steel at that. "This must have been a warrior to stand toe to toe with a Murkan by the use of a sword," one of the hunters spoke aloud. The hunter walked over to Mariana and asked if this was the case. Mariana looked up and said as she was holding on to her father, "It was like one of Mommy's stories, an angel saved me. But, but his face was covered up. The black rose, see it's over there." Right there, Joseph, who was a man of keen perception, thought and also believed in signs from the Lord knew that this must have been linked to where she found the first black rose in the broken playhouse. Joseph returns home with the hunters and his daughter, knowing Penelope will not be happy with him. They enter through the door and Penelope drops the plate she was carrying onto the ground in shock of her daughter's appearance. "Joseph, what has happened to our baby?" she said, covering her mouth as she ran up and grabbed her. The hunters attempted to explain what had happened, but she smacked Joseph across the face and then immediately hugged him, apologizing. "Penelope, there's something I have to do and I can't explain at this time, but I'll be back before the night is out," Joseph stated with a dire sense. Penelope knew that it was important and she trusted her husband's judgment. Leaving, he instructed some of them to stay at his home and the others to guard the mountain pass into Salem.

Joseph made his way to the plateau on the east side of the city where the old playhouse rests alone. It was now dusk and he had found the hidden ladder that Mariana had explained to him. He climbed all the way to the top and down into the playhouse, and every ladder had newly spilled blood cascading down its steps and rails. Once reaching the dark stage, a flash of lightning lit the room of all the statues of divinity. A storm made its home outside and a relentless rain begins to crash onto the stage with a succession of lightning, revealing more of the playhouse. He begins to climb the main stairwell and is led by a trail of blood. "Who are you?" Joseph says to himself. As he continues to climb the stairs, a feeling of the utmost sadness overtakes his soul. He gets on his knees and rebukes the feeling by the name of Jesus Christ and then rises back up and presses on. At the top of the stairs, there is a large collection of blood upon the stone floor. "He must have rested here," Joseph considers extremely concerned. The trail then leads to a door at the end of the forlorn hallway. Joseph opens the door nervously, yet when he enters, it is a room of song where the walls are lined with parchment of sheet music. "Perhaps more than just a lone vagabond," he says to himself as he examines a violin resting on a mantle above a fireplace. Rain is heard smashing in great force on the ceiling of the playhouse as thunder and lightning strike together. The blood leads to one final door and Joseph knocks. No answer is given. He knocks again. "I'm going to enter now, do not worry, I am a friend." Joseph opens the door very slowly; it is the stoop in the shape of a ram which is absent of ceiling, rain floods sight. A man sits in the corner drenched in ruby stain, looking to the sky, but although the Murkan had injured his chest, the true wounds were from his arms. In his right hand, a bloody dagger sits for this man had cut his wrists so deeply that he was soon to die. To his left hand, he was grasping an alabaster box close to his heart. His broken eyes barely gave Joseph notice. "Oh dear God," Joseph said quietly as his heart skipped a beat and he rushed over. The man had tried to commit suicide and lay there without spirit or hope. Joseph was choked up over this and began to bandage his profusely bleeding wrists with a piece of his cloak he tore off. "You're going to be all right, it's going to be okay," Joseph exclaimed, trying to get the man to regain consciousness. The man looked up and spoke in a despondent voice, "Death besieges." Joseph grasped his shoulders and explained in all empathy, "You are not alone and Jesus isn't going to give up on you here." It was impossible to tell whether the stranger's or Joseph's cheeks had more tears or rain soaking them, but at that moment, as fate met choice, the broken individual passed out. Joseph finished bandaging him and pulled out a small rope from his pack he had brought with him to hunt. He tied the man's body around and then strapped him to his back so that he could carry him more easily down the ladders. Doused from the rain, Joseph entered his home exhausted and then fell to the floor bringing the corpse plummeting with him. "Help him," he said, gasping for air as the hunters and his wife came running to them. That night, after they did all they could for the man, they were forced to wait and see if he would survive. "Whether this man lives or dies is up to God," Joseph explained to his wife and the hunters. That night, Joseph and Penelope sat praying over the man who had saved their daughter's life. Later that night, he sent Penelope to bed as he stayed with the man praying until the sun had risen for Joseph's compassionate heart had taken great mercy upon him. But where was it he had learned such a thing in a world so utterly broken and alone? It is often said in Vulgata that when a child is born we are to rejoice fully and when they cease, we mourn bitterly without end. The truth is, rejoice is a sacred seed made to grow once well rooted on the rock, but whereas average plants sprout up and later wilt unto death this crop is very special for this gift is made to grow forever. Love and laughter in the Lord is something that begets itself for it is itself, in that praise we can see not to be trapped in the sorrow of loss or worry but be thankful for the days we did have and the many more that will come to pass together, eternally.

2

Forgotten Lamb

For three days, the man slept in a tranquil bedroom of the Voltel household, and for those days, they were unsure of whether he'd live or die. That Sunday morning, he rose on the third day as light broke its way through the window and illuminated the room. The man glanced around, seeing a few pictures on the walls and his belongings all set aside, including his sword within the scabbard. Containing little to no memory of what had happened after the battle, the man stands out of bed in his drawers wondering how he had arrived at this location. His skin is painted in countless scars, but none worse than the one upon his back, the one pressed deeply as a sizable scorched handprint. He glances down at his arms that are bandaged, and as he tightens his fists, he remembers through a jolt of pain that he had tried to kill himself. His chest hurt from the wound given him by the corrupted forest creature known as a Murkan, but that was not the real source of his pain. At the foot of the bed, his clothes were resting on an old stool, they were washed and folded. This included both his travel-worn cloak and his leather armor, but underneath were shirt and pants not his own. Atop this pile was an alabaster box at which he gazes upon for several seconds but does not open, it is his.

Dressing himself, he gradually realized that he was enormously hungry for he had been out for days, but more so, he wondered who the man was who had saved him. Emotions of self-worth pierce his persona, twisting into an ever-worsening cyclone of mental destruction. Overwhelmed by this nameless emotion, he sat in the corner of the room and began to have trouble breathing as spiritual torment deep inside was crushing the very fiber of his being. His hand folds over his eyes and forehead while his other slopes down the cap of his knee. No words nor sound, only the silent pain and frustration of being utterly alone, isolated from the thought of humanity. The tear ducts fill but do not flow. Who is that man underneath the skin, acutely reaching for freedom by means of a salvation verily present yet unattainable? Suddenly, a knock was heard at the door, but he does not stand, he does not speak, he prays to not be discovered in his weakness.

The knob turns and the door opens, but no one is there. Light from outside stretches across the wooden flooring, and for only a moment, he looks before clenching the fist upon his kneecap tightly. Footsteps begin to walk up the stairs, and in walks Penelope. His fingery veil shrouding his countenance opens faintly and his hazel eyes are revealed. Penelope stares and smiles a way only a mother can. "May I sit beside you?" she asks. He nods a yes out of politeness. Now sitting beside him, Penelope twirls her thumbs and bobs her head. Her eyes glance up to the ceiling, searching for the words to say, but the expression of joy ready to burst grows exponentially. "So how are you feeling?" she asks excitedly. Removing his hand, his eyes roll awkwardly toward her; he is unsure how to respond. The man is young, dark haired, and handsome but bears the expression of a lost child. Most notably were the eyes; these were the eyes of one who hath endured many a trial or perhaps one prolonged. "Where do you come from? Are you a warrior? Are you hungry?" she presses further. His mouth opens, but words do not instantly rise, but instead, it transfers into a subtle laugh. "I-I could eat," he says.

"Oh, good, no, not good, this is great. I have much prepared," Penelope yells, followed by teeth fully present. He held out his hand to her and introduced himself. "Hi, my name is Zacharias," he said with a sound of doubt in his voice. Penelope threw her arms around him, hugging tightly; she had truly caught him off guard. "I'm so glad that you are okay my name is Penelope!" Zacharias blushed a deep crimson color and seemed more embarrassed than appreciative. "Do people not hug where you are from?" Penelope jokingly asked. His eyes looked everywhere but in her direction as if he was attempting to mentally escape the situation. Now staring at the floor, he replied, "I, I don't really know anyone" he is ashamed of this. Penelope could see the sadness in his eyes and feel the pain of his spirit, but instead of dwelling on that, she felt compelled to positively raise his emotions, motivation is her specialty. "Well, we're just gonna have to change that," she exclaimed with her hands on her hips and a single eyebrow rose for she was now standing. "Now come down for breakfast, you haven't eaten in days, young man." Penelope then walked downstairs as he slowly followed. Smelling all sorts of breakfast food, he secretly smirked but quickly relinquished that returning to nervousness and then sorrow. "*If I lose this momentary peace I'm going to die, I cannot bear another day, please help me someone help me!*" Walking around the home of the Voltel family, there were so many simple things that were beautiful to him, ranging from drawings to the general atmosphere of a home that cared which drew long past days of precious nostalgia. Now entering the kitchen area, he sat down at a table filled with a plethora of hotcakes, bacon, eggs, sausage, etc. Penelope gifted him two large plates with three large glasses of milk, forcing him to promise to consume everything as to regain his strength. Attempting to work his way through the mountain of food, Penelope began to ask him question after question. "So where do you come from?" she asked yet again. His eyes squinted in curious demeanor with a piece of bacon hanging out of his mouth. "Vendalas was once my home."

"You came from Vendalas? I didn't know people still lived there." He took a drink of milk, then wiping away the moustache left from it, he explained, "Vendalas may be nation of the ruins, but it serves as home to those of us with nothing left." She could see that it was a touchy subject for him, so she darted over to her next question. "Well, how about other things, family, friends, the arts? What brings you to Calina and better yet to Salem?" Putting his hands down on the table, he crossed them together and looked right at Penelope who was constantly smiling for she was happy to have him in her home and better yet to make him feel welcome. "Can we be honest here and skip the formalities?" Zacharias politely asked in a calm voice.

"Ya, sure," Penelope said, slightly bewildered.

"I thank you for your hospitality, but we both know I came here to die," he explained, absent of personality.

Penelope began to laugh and quickly apologized, "I'm sorry, probably the worst time ever to laugh, but you seem to be pretty alive to me right now."

"I guess you're right," he included with smirk and a minor eye twitch. "That was a fantastic meal by the way. Your family is lucky to have a mother like yourself."

Penelope then looked at him with a serious face. "I can tell about people and you're a good man, Zacharias." Ignoring the compliment, he asked where he may find the man who saved his life. "Believe it or not, that was my husband, dear." His heart skipped a beat, for he had not yet put together this was his home. Then dropping his fork, he felt bad that he had not known or said thank you to her as of yet. Before he could, Penelope answered, "Oh, and there's no need for thanks. You're family now, okay." His belly now stuffed, he asked if families attempted to kill each other by overfeeding them. Penelope tossed a fork at him jokingly and told him to go out and find Joseph at the church on the other end of town. Zacharias walked back upstairs, grabbing his sheath, attaching it to his back, contemplating on the term "family." Now returning down the stairs, he checked the sharpness of the blade and examined it from his engagement with the Murkan since it had struck its powerful antler. In the kitchen where Penelope was cleaning up, he sheathed the massive blade and checked his side dagger. "You know, that's a magnificent blade. Does it have a name?" Penelope asked intently.

Zac held the hilt to Penelope, stating, "Titulus is his name."

"Wow, this is heavy. Do you always go out ready for war?" Penelope said, attempting not to drop the sword. Reclaiming Titulus, he clicked his dagger into his overcoat as he proceeded to the door. Before stepping outside, he states, "Life is war."

He travels down the hill from the little red cottage and proceeds onwards into the main area of Salem. It was now the beginning of winter, but the snow had not yet blanketed the lands. A gust of northern wind catches him, reminding him of the coming winter's season which was superbly short in Calina yet ridiculously long to the southwest and everlasting in Valinth. Thinking to himself, he wondered what the man who saved his life would be like and what was he going to say. Also flashing through was the image of the young girl from the bridge. He truly had hoped she was all right and had forgotten to ask Penelope about the girl. The wind refused to allow him to keep a continuing thought by blowing away each theory; he tried to decide on for the speech with this man. It was as nature itself was trying to keep him from planning this meeting. Entering the town, it was remarkably quiet and all of the shops seemed closed; this was due to it being Sunday, the day of rest, which Salem honored. In the center of the town sat a marvelous plaque with the Ten Commandments inscribed. "I'll never understand why people follow such archaic traditions. The world has enough trouble surviving without extra burden from man-made laws," he said to himself, shaking his head. As he was about to leave the main square, all the citizens came out and began to give him a standing ovation. "The hero of Salem," one man yelled, another patted him on the back, and another lady gave him a handful of daisies. He was bright red for he didn't know any of these people nor was he a fan of the spotlight. They then offered for him to have dinner with the town that night in his honor to show how the Lord had used him. "Uhmm, thank you, but no thank you," he exclaimed, pulling away. "I really must be going. I have to meet with Joseph." The people all smiled and watched him stroll down the streets towards the edge of town. A few blocks down, he came across a lonely yet majestic art gallery dressed in the humble decor of Calina's rich history; the colors are silver, yellow, and blue. Wondering what kind of paintings they sold, he was lured inside by his curiosity. An elderly couple sat behind the counter knowing who he was but didn't mention anything about his heroics. Zacharias nodded a hello to the senior citizens as he glanced up and down at marvelous portraits of kings, knights, and castles. To the back of the shop, there were paintings of angels ascending to heaven and others of various depraved creatures that existed within the world of Vulgata. One picture in particular caught his eye so he reached out to it with eyes of vengeance. The old man stepped beside him. "That's the beast you defeated, was it not?" he asked. The picture was of a Murkan rising out of a swamp as if possessed. Before Zacharias could speak to him, two tiny arms grabbed his leg squeezing tightly. He looked down and it was the little girl whom he had saved. He was scrambling in his mind for she had thrown him off his axis of comfortability. She had done the unthinkable she had shown love to someone who did not know love. The old couple laughed as Zacharias poked the child's head, asking for his leg back. The adorable brunette girl of six now with a blue ribbon looked up. Her eyes were glowing with all the love a child could offer as she stated, "I'm Mariana." Zacharias who had little to no interaction with children in his life answered back in a joking manner, "What a coincidence. That is my name too." The old shopkeepers were completely oblivious to understanding the satirical nature he was using to make fun of introductions, but as they say, sarcasm is not for everyone. Mariana laughed because children normally understand the intentions of adults more so than adults do. "You're lying, that's a girl's name. I'm really glad you killed the monster that was after me," Mariana said while examining the portrait with him. For several minutes, they remained by the painting as Mariana's noggin rested into the side of his leg. He then proceeded to leave and the child began to follow him as if she was a lost puppy. Every time he glanced back, she would hide in an alley or behind a signpost. Finally, Zacharias stopped and sat down at a bench, and as he did this, she came and sat beside him. Mariana reached over and pinched his nose, and as soon as his eyes looked over, she acted like it wasn't her. "You know, I'm really glad I saved you," he stated with a false seriousness. Mariana continually smiled as she was mesmerized with him, which became very calming for his deeply troubled spirit. "Am I close to the church?" he asked Mariana. "You want to go to my daddy's church, follow me." Yet another alarm went off, he had now realized that the woman Penelope was Joseph's wife and this girl Mariana his daughter. Lost in thought on the bench, he wasn't really getting up to move, so Mariana grabbed his right hand and began to pull him in the direction. "Okay, I'm going," Zacharias answered as he was led by a child. Much like in the small wooded area where he had fought the Murkan, there was another small stone-made bridge crossing a stream that flowed from a hidden spring atop the peak. It rose high above, and from it, the stream ran throughout the far side of Salem. On its other side sat an old church with a waterwheel constantly rotating. Mariana started to drag him across the bridge and he stopped for a moment because he wanted to take a gander at the view. "C'mon," Mariana screamed in his ear.

"Maybe I want to take a look around first," he stated while flicking her hair. Although they had only just met, they acted as if they were brother and sister to one another; he felt peace being with this child. When she finally forced him across the bridge, Mariana went into the church, but Zac went down beside the stream where he found a pile of tiny rocks and began skipping them across the water. Thinking to himself, he wondered as to what he was going to say to Joseph but better yet as to why he was still alive. "Well, I owe him this much, I suppose," he said as he threw one last rock into the water. The rock bounced seven times and landed on top of one very large rock where it somehow remained dry, but he didn't see this for he had already turned his back and headed to the church's main doors

Now standing before the tall oak doors of the church, he noticed two things. First, a lovely bell sitting atop made of cast metal and then a hand carved cross on each door. The unique thing was that door handles were two horses jetting out in opposite directions with their front legs raised up as they stood on their hind legs. He pulls open the door to a decorated yet compact lobby area where a rack for overcoats sat. A miniature aqueduct draws life from the waterwheel outside into a lone fountain. There are no statues by the fountain; instead, flowers are placed in front of it, various in type. Moving on, he enters into the main chapel area that is built to house no more than two hundred. It was completely empty, so he decided to take a look around. At the altar sits a small oak table with words: "This do in remembrance of me" (Luke 22:19, KJV) carved into the front of it. Behind that sits a large wooden cross on the wall extending to just about the ceiling twelve feet high. He walks, brushing his index finger upon the table, wondering what those words meant, and puts his entire hand on the bottom of the cross. Staring to the top and then the center of it, he is reminded of his grandfather who had passed on many years ago. *"If I kill myself, I go to hell, if I live, I'm already in hell, what do you want from me?"* he thinks to himself. A tap on the table behind him is heard. "Hello, my friend," Joseph spoke in a friendly and enthusiastic voice that held untold wisdom. This startled him for he thought he was alone. "Is this your church?"

Joseph smiled and replied, "It is not my church, but I am a servant who is blessed to preach the good news here."

"Well, whose church is it then?" Zac asks unknowingly.

"It is the Lord's house for all who wish to enter," Joseph replies. Rotating from the pastor to the cross, he scratched his chin and then ran his fists across his nose. After this, he went and sat down in one of the pews as Joseph came and sat in front of him on the altar stairs. "So why do you do it?" Zacharias asks calm yet secretly baffled.

"Do what? Live the life of a believer?"

"Yes, I am curious as to what would lead you to that conviction." Joseph pulled out his Holy Bible out of the side of his coat and set it on the step. Placing his palm on the cover, he looked to the young man and asked, "What led you to saving my daughter?" Taking a minute to himself, he thought and realized what it was that he was doing and answered, "It's not God if that's what you're thinking. I did what I did because it was the right thing to do!" He realized he was now standing up and apologized for raising his voice.

"It's okay. I was just curious is all," Joseph said raising sprawled fingers and smile to ease the situation. Joseph then stood up and helped him out of the pew. Now both standing, Joseph continually stared grasping his hand like you would a sword. In all seriousness, the pastor's eyes said the words he was soon to say, "Zacharias, you are my brother for you saved my only daughter from the hands of death." Feeling a strange sense of honor from this God-fearing man, his trust moved closer to his word if only slightly. "And you saved me from the blade of my own hands, that is a debt I could never pay," Zac replied. The warrior then let go of the almost alliance-like grip because he felt he wasn't good enough to have that kind of fellowship with a man as good as Joseph. "I'm sorry, Joseph, but there are things about me that you could not comprehend. I really must move on for your own safety." Joseph walked down and put his right arm on the back of Zacharias's shoulder and asked if he would honor his family and stay with them for the short winter. "My wife and I could really use the help, and my family has seemingly already fallen in love with you," he stated while chuckling loudly. Drawing his sword, he held it out in front of him, facing up, glancing upon the cold barren steel. A single tear ran down his face as he explained, "This sword has always been there for me. Sometimes, I wonder if men can be born of this uncaring metal denied of heart? A home is for those who have a reason to exist, a purpose, but me, a man with a stolen past and a damned future, the only rest I will find is in death for he is my shadow and I his slave." Now proceeding down the aisle of pews, Joseph begins a counter statement of his own, "Are we not all slaves to death, my friend? Do we not all have a debt we could never pay? No man can overcome it alone or by his own means." Looking back again, Zacharias gave one last account, "You are not wrong in your interpretation of death, Joseph, but the death I speak of is far more real than most men could ever come to imagine. I'd love nothing more than to live with you or your family, but I am a cursed man who could only bring woe unto your household. Your family is beautiful and has given me a reason to live if only for a short while, good-bye, my friend." Together, they nod a farewell as the vagrant begins his final exit, his return to exile. Reaching the end of the chapel, Mariana came out from behind one of the pews with tears in her eyes. "Don't go. I want you to stay and be my big brother," Mariana sobbingly confessed. His heart stained with potential regret made it hard for him to keep walking toward the tall oak doors, but it was for that reason he had to leave. "Mariana, come here. Do not hinder the man from making his own decisions. He is an adult and you are to respect your elders," Joseph said to her. Mariana ran back over to her father and cried into his leg even after the man had left. After leaving the church, he began to run as fast as he could to get away from the town. When he arrived at the only road that led out of Salem, he turned his sights out over the vast lands of Calina and proceeded down the long narrow hill of the mountainside. Towards the base of the hill, he had an argument with himself in his mind. "You know you could have stayed and perhaps found some measure of happiness. No, no, there's absolutely no way I could stay and bring harm to them because of my plight. Those are good people and they do not deserve that. It's not your fault death plagues your soul to administer his eternal will upon the earth. I made the choice to follow him and I deserve to reap what I have sown. That man saved my life and that does make him the only one to have done so." Zacharias was so conflicted over the issue he drew his sword, screamed loudly, and cleaved a rock in two. "Leave me, false voices! This mind is still mine!" Gasping for air, he fell to his knees, desperately searching for a reason to keep moving on, a reason to avoid fellowship. Then after traveling for a while, he returned to the bridge where he had defeated the Murkan and noticed a teddy bear. *That was the same bear as the little girl's*, he thought. Picking it up and holding it close, he knew he had to go back to return it but not just for her but for himself.

That night, Joseph and Penelope sat within their kitchen with Mariana over a candlelit dinner. A windstorm picked up that night for they were common in Salem and battered about the roof of the cottage. Mariana always loved it as she sat on her father's lap and they listened to Penelope read them her story, "Faith of a Child." There was a knock at the door, but they didn't realize at first from the windstorm, so the knocking got louder. Joseph went to answer the door; lo and behold, it was Zacharias. "Sorry to bother you all, but I think this is Mariana's," he stated, holding out the bear. Mariana ran up and grabbed it for it was the female counterpart to her favorite bear, Mr. Sebastian. "You found Mrs. Elysia," Mariana yelled as she hopped around delighted.

"Surely you didn't come all this way just to bring back a teddy bear," Joseph asked, raising his entire self. Zacharias who had been only purely serious or sarcastic in nature as of before changed slightly this time with a peaceful smile they had not seen. It was the smile of a man who one would guess had a level of weight taken off his shoulders a normal man could not come to understand. "I was wondering if the offer still stands?" Now Joseph loved to play games with people because that is how he enjoyed getting close to them and making them feel a sense of kindness and kinship. Responding to the question of the offer, he peered to his wife and winked, then turned back to the vagabond, "What offer are you talking about?" It was amazing to Penelope and Joseph just how vulnerable this man was and saw that their joke had backfired as he sunk into a noticeable depression. His hands moved timidly and eyes scrambled, but most noticeably, his lips moved for a second, but the words did not come out. Solemnly, he answers, "I-I'm sorry," as he backed up to the door shadowed by darkness. Penelope bounced out of her seat and scolded Joseph, darting to Zacharias, stating, "Oh, honey, he's just kidding. He has nothing better to do with his time. We'd love to have you live with us."

"Oh, thank you, it-it means the world," Zacharias said from the bottom of his heart while Penelope hugged him. Still proceeding out the door, Joseph asked where he was going. "Well, I was going to go to the stable outside. That is where I can stay, right? Which I am truly thankful for." Penelope looked at Joseph and him at her and they both laughed together. "You know for someone as well-spoken as yourself, it shocks me you're oblivious to certain things," Penelope stated. Joseph waved for him to follow. "Come, we have a spare bedroom in the attic." So the family took him up to the attic, which actually was a remarkably cultured room where he would be staying. There were numerous relics in this attic collected from all over the world. Old maps, charts, and a surplus of rare books about the history of all sorts of things from the Restoration War to the joining of the western alliance to more current events such as the unilateral monetary system for the entirety of the western nations, this was generated out of Bordeaux nation of finance. "Joseph, what are all these things? It is remarkable that you have so much."

"Ah, an eye for history, I see. I like to learn as much as I can about the glorious world around us. It helps with my passion if you will." He loved the old world map of Vulgata and had never witnessed one so detailed before; it was encased in glass hanging on the wall drawn from fine ink. "You know that was made by my grandfather and given to me by my father the day I became a man," Joseph stated as he gladly approached.

"Were you close with your father?" Zac asked politely.

"Yes, I loved him very much, but he has moved on to heaven now." Although only a common map to most, to a wanderer, a marvelously designed map such as this serves as a sort of bible all in its own. It would be then that the concept was born into Joseph's mind that his new friend had been searching for something for a very long time, if not most of his life. Zacharias then apologized for his father's death. "Thank you, my friend, but on another note, I'm grateful that you are going to stay with us throughout the winter, no matter how short the snowfall."

"Just make me one promise, Joseph, if anything seems unusual, ask me to leave, please," Zacharias said while sitting on the bed.

"I mean no insult here, Zac, but you are a strange one. I haven't seen a character like you before, but that's a good thing. It means you're genuine, not letting the world corrupt you. To be yourself is to search for truth. Working as a pastor and quite often these days as a traveling missionary, I see the worst sides of humanity and the travesties caused in the world by nature, science, and religion. My point being more often than not you don't get to really talk to people because they put up a front or a fake persona, they stick to societal norms that change abruptly. Sorry I'm getting a little off subject. I just want you to know that I'm excited to have you as a new friend and you honor us by staying here, that's all." Joseph then tapped his hand on the banister twice before going downstairs and just as the door shut at the bottom of the stairs so did it open again. Mariana came running up the stairs carrying both her bears, which bounced off each stair. Zacharias watched as he was lying down and gave a coughing laugh. "What are you up to, little one?" he asked. Mariana explained that she wanted to sleep in that bed tonight, but just then Penelope also came up to fetch her daughter. "Is she bothering you?" Penelope asked.

"No, it's fine. I think I'm going to turn in now though." Penelope took Mariana, double checking if he needed anything before leaving him to the quiet night's long assessment.

Many hours into the night after all had fallen asleep, the winds grew far more violent, and the old cottage creaked with the night. Zacharias awoke soaked in sweat with tears of dread in his eyes as he could feel the terror of a demonic figure forming amongst the shadows of the already pitch-black attic. Frozen in fear, he could not move, think, or act, but his eyes remained solely on the figure within the darkness that paled in comparison to whatever it may be. The figure did not move nor did it speak, but its eyes spoke as they pierced first his mind, then body, and finally his soul. An immense pain of helplessness overtook his heart as the word "Manistof" repeated over and over in his mind. He fell out of the bed, choking from lack of air as his heart rate pushed through the roof; he felt as though he was going to die, but unlike before, he did not want to die now. "No, I don't want to die. I can't die here. I can't put this family through that, after all they've done for me, they gave me a reason to live," he said this to himself as he struggled to stand up. After he had finally regained his composure, he discerned the figure clearly and spoke back to him, but at a low volume for everyone else was slumbering, "You will not harm these people," as he grabbed his blade underneath the bed. The dark figure spoke inside his soul, laughing in a deep lawless tone. "You really think a piece of steel made from this cesspool of sin, shit, and self-arrogance you call a world can hurt me? Do you even think anymore or have I so infiltrated your personal barriers that you are losing control? You seem to forget you are my slave and that means everything you have belongs to me first and last. I will take the souls of everyone you love just like

I did your worthless grandfather and everyone else you've loved. There's nothing you can do to stop me, but I will say as long as you keep this hope that is indeed folly, it does bring me pleasure to destroy it. Perhaps you shouldn't waste the Voltels' time and just end your own meaningless life and do them the favor of freeing their souls from my master and I." Zacharias inspected his already deep wounds beneath his bandaged arms, knowing he had come close, but Joseph had intervened. The dark spirit replied, "Go ahead, the process has already begun and the lines of your resolution already drawn within your tainted skin. Just know, my master has the ability to torture, desecrate, and destroy every spirit he gets his hands on, and the longer you take to finish our contract, the longer both they and you will suffer." The door at the base of the stairs then creaks open and Zacharias's heart skips a beat for at the moment he believed the spirit had gone on to the Voltel family. Mariana's eyes could be seen peeking as she came sneaking up and saw him standing with his blade facing the wall. "What are you doing up here this late, Mariana?"

"I had a nightmare that you were in trouble so I came up to make sure you were okay," she replied. Zacharias lay back down in the bed and Mariana walked over with her two teddy bears. She put one bear in front of her and the other in front of him. Zacharias, who was still slightly shaking out of fear from the dark spirit, felt a sudden peace emerge as the child fell asleep on his shoulder. "Thank you for saving me, big brother," Mariana whispered as her precious head nestled into his shoulder more. Something about the child had pushed away the spirit and he understood this; that night, he was granted the most peaceful sleep he had experienced in well over a decade.

The next morning, he awoke to both teddy bears sitting on top of him and had realized that Mariana was gone. Springing out of bed, he rushed downstairs, and as he reached the bottom, he crashed into the kitchen. Joseph, Penelope, and Mariana stared at Zacharias as if he were crazy. "That hungry, huh?" Penelope said as she fixed him a plate, and everyone began to laugh, himself included. Now sitting at the table with them, he began to eat and forgot that this family prayed before they ate. Staring now at Penelope, he let a piece of bread fall out of his mouth, which made her shake her head. Joseph began to chuckle as Zacharias and Penelope went back and forth. "Do you know how to chew your food, young man," she yelled.

"Huh, what do you mean?" as he let the rest fall out of his mouth onto his shirt. Mariana loved it and laughed alongside her father as Penelope bewildered by why this was funny turned her confusion against Mariana and Joseph. Finally, when all was calm and they were about to pray, Zac turned to Joseph and laughed before saying, "I'm sorry, you're going to pray, aren't you?"

"Yes, would you like to join?" he replied.

"I, uhm, don't know how to pray, is it okay if I watch?" Joseph and Penelope nodded in approval. He then watched as Joseph, Mariana, and Penelope joined hands and gave thanks for the meal. Joseph closed his eyes, lowered his head, and began, "Dear, heavenly Father, thank you for the food in front of us that you have so gracefully provided. We offer thanks for the many blessings you have given in our lives and also for bringing Zacharias to our home and family. Please, Lord, forgive us our sins committed and watch over this family in Jesus's name. Amen." Zacharias, who didn't understand the concept of prayer, respectfully asked Joseph why they pray. "To thank Jesus for all we have in our lives," Mariana responded. Joseph raised a fist of triumph.

"Well, that's it. She hit the nail dead on."

"I see. I don't know anything about that man."

Joseph then answered, "I could tell you about the blameless lamb if you'd like to hear. You would honor this home by doing so."

"Perhaps I'll hear of this lamb or what not another time," Zacharias spoke while secretly rolling his eyes as he began to eat. The rest of the Voltel family smiled and began to eat alongside him.

3

Bond of the Family

For many weeks, Zacharias lived among the Voltel family, helping them with everything he was able. He assisted Penelope with common house chores and cooking to the even simpler things like putting Mariana to bed, which she grew very fond of. Joseph was assisted by Zacharias in cleaning up the church by the stream. Along this span of time, they grew closer as friends, especially after the first snow had come to pass. Among these things Zacharias lent his hand to chopping lumber, he admired that the most. After a while, he began to chop trees and lumber at night once the day's work had already been completed. Both the townsfolk and the Voltels took notice to this for he began to do this for the entire city of Salem. Time and again, the denizens of Salem attempted to befriend him, but they were always met by a despondent and distant reaction of mannerly disinterest. Promptly, they began to realize he was an introverted individual who chose to face life alone for the most part. The strange part being was that although he would not form these bonds of friendship, he was still helping all of them through the winter by storing firewood for them. Most made the assumption that this service was how he showed he cared for others, so they did not take his waywardness offensively. During those many weeks leading into the thick of winter, Joseph politely asked Zacharias abundantly to attend his sermons on church Sundays. He rejected the invite each request and instead pressed to further advance his work ethic without restraint.

Waking up early one Sunday morning to Mariana pulling his arm, he was awake but pretended to remain asleep. "Wake up, you're going to miss church again," she yelled to him. The all too common morning yell came for her to come downstairs and leave their guest alone was heard from Penelope. The wanderer turned homebody descended the staircase dressed in sleeping attire to Penelope who was clothed and ready for morning service. Joseph was already at the church whereas Penelope was now preparing Mariana. They began to stroll towards the door when Zacharias asked, "No invitation this week?" Penelope brought out a unique facial expression of excitement that spoke of a genuine delight, which was soon followed by an extension of her palm. "Well, come on, we're gonna be late," she added.

"I was actually just kidding. I really had no intention of going," he replied. Penelope's eyes sank and then locked onto him as hawk's prey. "You're lucky I'm a loving woman or I'd strike you sometimes," she jokingly said. As they left, he sat down alone and wondered to himself what a church sermon was actually like. *I don't understand how they are such nice people and yet they follow fabled traditions like God*, he thought angrily. Zacharias crossed his arms on the table as he sat in the chair behind him followed by resting his chin unto himself. Looking down on the table, his eyes became disillusioned to reality and he had entered a realm where thought and space join as a one singular being pulling one from time. "I don't understand why so many people I've met in my life believe in religion. Vowing your life to false oaths and man-made traditions to so-called celestial beings you can't even see. How can gods even exist? It makes no sense to me. This world made of suffering, hate, and greed, what kind of god would allow this? People like Joseph are just primarily good people who choose to be good. They just need that extra crutch because they can't understand that they made the choice to do the right thing." Then a voice not sounding of his own interjected words into his thoughts: "What is the right thing?" He jumps back into actuality, searching around, wondering if the same shadow had returned, but not this time; this was of his own platform of thought alone for it was a deceptive thought from his own heart. "What do you want with me, Manistof?" Zacharias angrily shouted further, understanding that his individuality was becoming further compromised, the fortress of self was beginning to falter. The voice was now as an innocent-sounding child asking him, "What is the right thing?"

"Whatever it may be, it's not you!" The dark spirit began to ask him why he didn't want to be his friend anymore in a sincere-sounding lost voice. He then returned to the attic to prepare for the day, attempting to disregard the voice without pause. It then asked the question that it knew would set him into a rage. In a distorted version of Mariana's voice, it spoke, mixed with false tears, "But, but I wanna be your little sister, why won't you just love me?"

"Don't you ever speak of her again, you son of a bitch," he screamed out loud with all the force of his diaphragm. The dark spirit then laughed in a low-toned demonic pitch pleasured by his anger. "It seems to me I've found your weakness, and soon, she and this family will die because of you, just like all the rest." Zacharias fell to his hands and knees, gripping his skull and crying all the while the spirit began to speak backward. "Go away, leave me be, Manistof!" Reaching for his sword, he began to hold it tightly till his grip hurt. "How many times must I tell you worldly metals nor force for that matter can hurt me, for I, we and us are your masters," the spirit began to exclaim. The spirit then gave a command, "You are broken and lost, and today, you will take your own life!" Zacharias's eyes jetted up for he was still on his knees as the remaining tears on his face dropped to the floor that had accumulated into a miniscule puddle of sanity soon to dry. "Why must you do this to me?" he cried out in the utmost pain both physically and spiritually. The shadow then appeared on the wall once more for it had not shown itself since many weeks prior. "Because you are mine and I purchased you at a great cost to me, you paid with initial sin and the wage is death." The shadow then began to creep across the floor by his fingertips, inching closer to Zacharias. His sword turned black as it wrapped and folded itself around the edges then guiding the blade against his throat. "Here, I will help you ease the pain," the demonic spirit explained, now sounding friendly. Zacharias's entire being shook with fear as he then spoke, "I-I can't p-p-p-put Joseph and his family through that. They've done too much for me. They're my friends, no, they are my family and they said they loved me." Instantaneously, the spirit left the sword known as Titulus attaching itself to a small table and began to scream at him, "Damn you and damn them. You either take your life now, or I'll fucking take the entire family with me to hell! They don't love you, and they never will. You are nothing but a bastard child, a forgotten nightmare, a plagued burden upon the already damned world! Do you know what happens in my hell, boy? I rape the souls of whom I choose when I choose. I consume the flesh of men on my command, I curse what is righteous, down here I am a god and all worship me!" Zacharias stood up, ready for war, rebuking the monster's words while smashing the table the shadow sat upon with his sword. "I may not always know what the right thing is, but I know when something is evil and you are it! Everything that is wrong with the world rests in you, and one day, justice shall find you, demon! I may not know how to defeat you, but I will find a way, you coward without honor, perhaps if you had any honor at all, you'd reveal your physical self and face me! Your words of trickery and deceit will die with you when I find a way to destroy you with my grandfather's sword, Titulus!" At the end of this statement, the spirit left, and he then stood in the attic by the destroyed table alone breathing heavily. "I need some air," he said to himself as he went outside to grab one of Joseph's horses in which he let him use to gather lumber. Zacharias mounted the white horse and slowly came down the mountain path, but unknown to him, he was being tailed by another.

Meanwhile in the church, Joseph was preparing to give this week's sermon on the family unit. Joseph stepped up to the altar and first led the congregation in prayer which was everyone from the city of Salem. "Well, how is everyone doing today?" Joseph asked. Receiving only nods and smiles, he could feel the warmth of the room around him. "First of all, I'd like to thank everyone for coming out on this ever so chilly morning to hear the warmth of the Lord's word. Today, we're going to be covering just what the term *family* means." Joseph then opened his Holy Bible and read:

> And the rib, which the LORD God had taken from man, made he a woman, and brought her unto the man. And Ad'-am said, This is now bone of my bones, and flesh of my flesh: she shall be called Woman, because she was taken out of Man. Therefore shall a man leave his father and his mother, and shall cleave unto his wife: and they shall be one flesh.
>
> Genesis 2: 22–24 (KJV)

Joseph peered up at the congregation and spoke of how the Lord had established marriage by two becoming one and how it was a sacred act to be honored forever between man and wife. "So I ask you if two have become one what does that truly mean?"

Mr. Royalton, the old blacksmith, spoke, "I believe it means that man cannot break apart what God has brought together."

"Magnificent response," Joseph stated. "Now if a husband and wife have become one and that is the family brought together by the Lord God, we can conclude he calls for solidarity in Him. Now if we turn our Bibles to Proverbs, it says:

A wise son maketh a glad father: but a foolish man despiseth his mother.

Proverbs 15:20 (KJV)

"We can now see that in a family we are supposed to bring joy to our parents by obeying and not dishonoring them. So if the family is one solid unit established by the Lord made to honor Him things begin to make a clearer picture, do they not?" The congregation nodded in approval, and Penelope lovingly tilted a blissful grin to him. Joseph slightly smiled to himself as he glanced. He then continued the message as he was now walking around the aisles with Bible in hand. Joseph opened his Bible to Mark:

There came then his brethren and his mother, and, standing without, sent unto him, calling him. And the multitude sat about him, and they said unto him, Behold, thy mother and thy brethren without seek for thee. And he answered them, saying, Who is my mother, or my brethren? And he looked round about on them which sat about him, and said, Behold my mother and my brethren! For whosoever shall do the will of God, the same is my brother, and my sister, and mother.

Mark 3:31–35 (KJV)

Now closing his Bible, Joseph had Penelope come and stand with him by the altar. "As you all know, Penelope and I have had a young man living with us for the past few weeks in our home. For those of you who do not know his name, it is Zacharias, although he has not revealed his past as of yet. There is something absolutely special about this young man who I may add saved my daughter's life, and we are so blessed to have him here in Salem. Jesus once explained there was no greater love than to lay down one's life for their friends. Well, that man was willing to put his life down for my family, so in that, he is a part of our family and I ask that we all pray for him together. He has been through more than any of us know, and now having overcome another obstacle, he is greatly susceptible to spiritual attack." Joseph's eyes watered for he truly loved his friend and Penelope put her arms around her husband. Penelope then began to speak, "Zacharias has such a big heart. I believe that Satan is trying to destroy him. Let us pray for him as a family and call upon the holy angels to protect him and, most of all, for the Lord to show him mercy and to open his heart to the love and truth of Jesus Christ." The congregation then gathered and joined hands as they all prayed for a man seen but not yet found. Both Joseph and Penelope had realized Mariana sneaking out earlier in the sermon, but they both knew that she was going to be with her newly beloved older brother.

Far off to the northern grasslands, he trained with his sword around the same dark wooded area he had saved Mariana from the Murkan. The trees were now wholly stripped of leaf and bark. Standing with his sword, he clenched the hilt mightily as he reached the middle of the same bridge he defeated the foul opponent. Holding his blade to the sky, he called the name of Manistof to reveal himself, but no reply was given. "Where are you?" Zacharias began to bring his claymore unto the wooden frame of the bridge with all his strength repeatedly. "Show yourself now," he screamed as he swung the sword wildly and without caution. Further and further, his anger escalated into rage as he began to lose grip on control that ended up throwing him into a berserk state. The sword stuck so far into the rail of the bridge that he could not pull it out. "Dammit, dammit, give me the sword, you bastard," he stated furiously toward the bridge as if it was a living entity. Finally, he pulled the blade free, and on the next swing containing all of his might left, the sword broke and the hilt flew out of his hands and stabbed into a sheet of ice coating the stream. "Grandfather," he said to himself, choked up without hope. "I am sorry, I cannot handle this anymore," as what was left of his tear ducts emptied. Then two small hands wrapped around his back and began to cry with him. It was Mariana who held as tight around him as a six-year-old could. "Big brother, don't cry," she said, doing the same. He picked up the child and gaped at her face. Slowly, he began to smile, thanking her. Holding her close, his heart opened up to a level he had not felt since he was a child himself. "I will never let anyone harm you, Mariana."

"Please don't leave me, big brother, promise you won't leave like Simon Peter," Mariana stated, greatly saddened. Feeling a true and deep connection with the child, he realized at that point she had a brother who had died some time earlier. Together, they would then make a pact that neither would ever leave the other behind. Mariana pulled back and gave him a small peck on the cheek as he then put her down and retrieved the sword from the ice. After he had picked up the sword, Mariana had asked if they could go riding on Grear, her father's white horse. "Oh, I did not know the horse's actual name, thank you for informing me," he stated. He then lifted her up and set her on the horse so she could hold on while they were riding. Now Grear was a marvelous white horse given to Joseph as a gift only two years ago from another friend in his ministry who had traveled north to the mythical forest realm of Scera. Zacharias asked over his shoulder with a rejuvenated smile "Are you ready?" She wrapped her arms around him, indicating that she was. Pulling the reigns hard, the horse reared up on his hind legs, neighing to the bridge crossed then folding to a sprint toward the never-ending grasslands where unattainable dreams seem not so distant after all. Faster and faster, Grear catapulted across the plains pushing to his maximum velocity. The horse itself seemed to love the opportunity to gallop with all his strength. Eventually, they came up to a minor yet wide gap across the Pishon River. For miles, no bridge was seen, but Mariana wanted to cross for she had never set foot on the other side; this was an adventure that could not be passed up. The water was known to be remarkably deep, and in the current temperatures, to fall in could procure a disastrous outcome. Then again, to reach the other side was something else entirely; it was a chance, no, it was proof that to start a new life was plausible for all who could endure the journey to cross and that was worth everything. Zacharias was weary to attempt this, but Mariana placed her trust in him entirely and urged him to do this. Questioning on whether to do this or not, he ran across a single memory of his grandfather explaining the concept of faith, and if one was to believe in that intimate most sacred feeling within their heart, God would grant it if it was in concordance with His will. "All right, let's go across together," he said to her intently. She then prepared herself as Zac got off Grear and checked the saddle, reins, and Grear himself. "Looks like we're good to go, but let me make sure Grear wants to attempt this." He then stood in front of the horse and asked, and as he did, the horse dug its commanding hooves forcefully into the dirt as if preparing to charge past the gates of hell to get to heaven. Now mounting the horse once more, Grear began to start at a slow determined pace without order, but once Zacharias gave his signal by his feet, the horse began to run, and soon, the run advanced to a gallop. Thundering across the plain, they could see a flock of sheep in the distance that were watching from the other side of the river, they were being led by a single shepherd. Right before the jump, both began to yell as the horse Grear launched across in all belief. For that moment as they hurdled across the river's surface, Zac felt like he was once again alive. Landing on the other side, they jumped off the horse taken by joy, love, and laughter for they had just barely made the jump. Lying on the other side of the Pishon, they watched the clouds in the sky without care or worry in the world. The shepherd who had seen this in the distance gave a loud whistle and applause; he was then seen carrying one of the younger injured lambs around his shoulders. "This is what heaven must be like," Mariana said aloud as she patted Grear on his head, which was lowered. Zacharias did not reply but instead watched the sky, wondering if heaven really could ever exist in a land cursed without hope. For the rest of the day, they rode around until nightfall, trying to find a way back home because the incline was too great for them to attempt a jump back.

Back at the Voltel household, Joseph and Penelope sat on the old swing located at the hilltop in their backyard that overlooked the expanse of the Starras Mountains. They were watching the sun set as Zacharias appeared on the horizon with Mariana asleep on his shoulder. Joseph winked at his wife. "You see I told you they were fine, dear."

Penelope glared back at him. "Oh, it's not me that was worried. I think you're just confirming that to yourself, I know he will always look out for our family!" When they reached the home and got off the horse, Zac carried passed-out Mariana to her parents. Joseph went to say something, but Zacharias handed him his child while putting his pointer finger to his lips, signaling to let the child sleep. Joseph obeyed and handed him over to Penelope to put her to bed. After the horse was put up in the stable, Zacharias explained to Joseph, "You know you have a fine horse, there my friend."

"Yes, Grear was an amazing present for my fiftieth birthday. He was presented to me by an old friend by the name of Aurelius Garlen."

"Who is Garlen?" he asked.

"Oh, just another friend in the ministry, he's currently residing in the forests of Scera. You'll meet him someday. I'll see to that. But don't take his stoicism as offense it's just his nature." Now inside, the three adults sat down to have some tea after dark. Penelope poured them each a cup. "So where did you two run off to today?" Zac took a drink. "Well, I, uh, went out to train with my sword and it broke," as he had just remembered. Penelope rotated to Joseph and Joseph to Zacharias. "Sounds like you were training pretty hard to me," Joseph stated. "You know you've been working yourself pretty hard, why don't you take a break for a few days?" he continually added.

Zacharias lifted up his head. "Evil never rests, can we?"

Joseph spoke curiously, "I didn't know that you believed in evil."

"Everyone knows of evil, but few acknowledge the idea of good existing outside of the human heart. I personally believe that both good and evil affect the world, my only difference in thought from yours is that good only comes from what we as people make it," Zac answered. He then also added that he believed Joseph and Penelope were good people; he just didn't believe in whatever god they followed. Joseph sighed slightly and then returned to his normal composure that was always seemingly positive. "Zacharias, you're free to believe in what you want, but I want you to know that Jesus loves you and I believe he has led you to this home for a reason. You are a part of this family now and I want you to know that. The only thing I have left to say on that is Jesus is the head of our family, so perhaps, he is here more than you perceive." The young conflicted man stepped over to the window studying the moon, longing for assurance "Sometimes, I don't know what to believe in, Joseph, there's more to me than even I know."

Joseph then spoke in a way Zacharias had not yet heard, "I know that dark spirits follow you, and it's because they want to destroy you for who you will become in the eyes of the Lord." He turned to Joseph as lightning for he was completely correct in his assumption of dark spirits tracking him. "How could you possibly have guessed that?" Zacharias asked.

"Like I said, Jesus is head of this family and reveals all things in one's household especially spiritual matters." Joseph and Penelope hugged him also asking if they could pray over him. Zac could feel the presence of the same spirit that had been following him. "The one who has been following me is here now, Joseph, please forgive me, I think it is time I go." Penelope held an intent eye but could see nothing. Joseph grabbed his Holy Bible and rested his hand gently upon the condemned man's head. Penelope latched her arms around his back in a firm grip, and Zac was now trapped powerless to the force that could be felt in the room. "You have no power here, demon, and this man is a part of our family now, he is one of God's children," Joseph sternly spoke. Penelope quietly prayed calling upon the name of Jesus Christ to protect him. Zacharias began to lose vision and motor function as things began to fade away in his mind. "In the name of Jesus Christ, the son of God, I command you through the power of the Holy Spirit to leave this man, demon. You have no power over this man and no power in my home, for we worship the one true living God, the Lord Almighty. By the sword of the Spirit that is the word of God, I rebuke thee and command thou return to the fires of hell." Zac then passed out and Penelope held him from smashing onto the floor. As Joseph picked him up, he felt the spirit leave the home, and as the feeling deep in his heart went away, a single black rose was left sitting in front of them. Joseph picked it up, knowing the truest meaning of this black rose, but when Penelope asked him, he only discarded it into the fire where he explained it belonged.

Zacharias slept for two entire days after that incident. He remembered what had happened the other night and went downstairs as Joseph and Penelope sat by the fire. "Hey, he's alive, you see I told you he was tougher than you thought, Penelope," Joseph said to her.

"I did not say that," as she knocked him across the head. Comedy aside, Zacharias moved the conversation forward and thanked them for sending away the dark spirit. "Exactly how did you do that anyways?"

Together, Penelope and Joseph answer, "We didn't. Jesus did." Although not conscious or fully aware when they called out the demon in Jesus's name, he still did not believe them. Neither Penelope nor Joseph pressed further. "So do you feel better?" Joseph asked. At first, he curled his lips inward, then made a surreal look. "I'll be honest, I do and I feel badly. I do not understand it," he replied in sincerity. Penelope answered back, "Patience follows his own clock."

"That does make sense, and speaking of time, I have a schedule to keep. I must be returning to work," he exclaimed, grabbing his overcoat and proceeding outside. Joseph walked outside behind him, but instead handed him an old rucksack that was his. As he gave him the gift, he asked him a favor, "Will you travel five miles east of here to a grouping of old pines? There is a plant there I need you to harvest. I know it's a long trek, but it would really help." Joseph also gave him an old botany book with a picture of the plant he needed.

Later that day, he arrived to the designated location. Searching high and low for the entirety of the day, he could not find the plant Joseph had asked him to find. "Where is this thing? Perhaps it does not grow here anymore?" Knowing only a few hours of light remained, the decision was made to return home. A jolt of sorrow then latched itself, knowing he had failed the task. When he had reached Salem, it was dark, and no one was home at the red cottage on the lonely hill. The town was almost completely silent, but he could hear lively chants from a large group of the locals. When he reached the other end of the city, he could see a large grouping of fires with all the city of Salem gathered round. The people were merry and exuberant, dancing around the fires alongside a mighty feast. Out dashed Joseph with open arms. "Joseph, I couldn't find the plant you had asked for."

"Of course you didn't, the item I sent you out for doesn't exist in those parts," Joseph said, patting him on the back.

Zacharias tilted like a confused dog. "Wait, what do you mean it doesn't exist?"

"I had you go out there so we could set up this celebration for you." As Joseph was stating this, many of the old hunters gathered around Zacharias and dragged him over to the fires. All of them held beautifully handcrafted beer steins all enhanced with unique designs of their own. The most notable was the one they presented him as a gift; it had the four base elemental symbols of fire, wind, water, and earth surrounding a fifth in the center that was holy. As they presented it to him, one of the hunters explained this beer stein's name was "The Guardian". Holding it, he thanked them to a wide degree for he had not received a gift since he was a boy. "Well, drink up," one of the hunters stated as he filled it with Calina's finest ale. Raising their beer steins to the air around him, they deemed him the newest family member of Salem, then clashed their drinks together. Penelope watched happily along with many of the villagers as he attempted to finish his brew with the seasoned hunters who drank theirs roughly three times as fast as he. After he had finished, he had to catch his breath for a minute because he was never known to have partook in an alcoholic beverage before this point. After that, Joseph, standing behind his friend, presented him with his sword that had been reforged. "Every warrior needs a weapon," Joseph yelled out.

Ecstatic over this, the young man's eyes opened wide. "How were you able to fix this?"

"It wasn't me but Mr. Royalton, the master blacksmith, if you wish to call him that." Mr. Royalton sat along the other side of the fire and tipped his hat to them.

Zacharias drank no more that night for he was feeling the effects of the drink quite well. His soul was eased and his smile flowed with the festivities, and for the first time, people saw him in lightened spirit. "I've never seen you laugh so much," Joseph yelled from across the party. Throughout the night, everyone sang, danced, and mingled, everyone loved their now opened-up newfound friend.

Toward the end of the night, Joseph led Zacharias away from the party as it was dying down to the old graveyard to Simon Peter's gravesite. "This is the brother Mariana spoke of to me, isn't it, Joseph?" Turning from the gravestone to the party, Joseph answered, "Yes, he has gone up to heaven now, probably sitting beside my father as we speak." Remembering his feeling from crossing the Pishon days earlier, thoughts of heaven resonated with jubilation, but Zac did not fully understand. "I wanted to bring you to this spot because I have one more gift for you." Joseph reached into his pocket and pulled out a medallion with the Voltel family crest engraved upon it; it was a dove ascending. A circular metallic crest that shown a marvelous white splendor with gold fringe along the edges and a single hole at the top to put a string or chain around to wear as a necklace. "It is made out of Hagios Adamantine Metallon (Holy Unbreakable Metal), and as the bonds of this family can never be broken, so shall this signify you joining us forever. I wanted to give this to you here in front of Simon Peter's resting place because he would have loved you all the same and I'm sure he was there the day you saved Mariana." He hugged Joseph as brother and thanked him for everything he'd done for him thus far. "Joseph, I am not worthy of such a kindness," Zac spoke, gazing at the sacred crest. Returning home, he caught Joseph off guard. "You know, I never fully thanked you for originally saving my life. I wanted to kill myself for two reasons: one was that no more harm would come to anyone because of me. More so I wanted to because I've been alone since I was six years old and I finally couldn't handle it anymore. I've seen things I could never begin to explain nor do I think most would believe if I told them. My point being is that you've shown me that good people come from all walks of life even the church in which I thought to be evil. Joseph, I have been cursed by the touch of death and all I get close to die because of me, knowing that can you still accept me as family?" Still walking toward the house, Joseph did not answer right away but instead waited until they came close to the house. At the door, he turned and, in his own way, exonerated him from that burden within his heart, but it wasn't really Joseph who had done it. "None of us can avoid the first death, so curse or not means nothing in the vastness of life. Did you ever consider perhaps that curse was bound to you to keep you from getting close to anyone? You're the kindest man I've ever met in my life. Don't blame yourself for others' deaths when you're already doing the best you can to save them. To worry beyond the threshold of what we can control will only destroy oneself, both emotionally and spiritually. Don't dwell on the past or worry of the future, instead focus upon the present. Fault in all men is that we believe we can change things but what gives me peace is knowing Christ in all ways is perfect so that I don't have to be." Joseph patted his friend once more on the shoulder and then went inside. Armed with this new concept of knowledge, Zac pondered over it for a few minutes before returning to the attic. Sitting on the bed, reflecting further all that had happened this day, snow blanketed the region outside the window. Alone, he said to himself, "Could this family finally have defeated Manistof and shown me the way? Has dream overcome nightmare?" Falling asleep, he battled in his being if he was free of this curse or if something else loomed on the horizon for the ones he had come to love. Either way, he'd learned a magnificent truth about the bonds of family on this day and was thankful to a level most will never reach.

4

Guardian of Salem

Part 1: Counsel

The bell atop the church rings prominently along with screams and yells echoing across the streets of Salem. Zacharias hastily got dressed and grabbed his sword, running outside meeting Joseph. "What's going on?" he asks the pastor. Joseph told him to follow for he would explain on the way. In all urgency, they ran outside and dashed toward the cities square where they could see a gathering of the majority of townsfolk. "They're sounding for battle," Joseph stated as they ran up to the crowds that were encircling something. A young girl of sixteen lay dying, also being treated by the locals. The right arm had been torn off below the elbow and large patches of skin were missing all over her body. Pieces of bone and sinew could be seen where her arm used to be, which most could not bear to see. Blood froze overtop of the ice as it gushed out of her grievous wounds. They tried to get her into a cabin, but she refused to until she spoke to the spiritual leader. Joseph now presented in front of her knelt down embracing her. "What is your name, child?" he asked, feeling the utmost level of compassionate mercy. She looked up to him with a single eye for the other had been ripped out, and below that, claw marks ran down her fair cheek and skin. "C-Cecilia." Choking on her own blood, she grasped her stomach, which was missing a large chunk seemingly taken out by a massive razor sharp set of teeth. "Th-they've d-d-d-destroyed Malastay," she said as she coughed, spewing her blood all over Joseph. Now reaching for him, he held the dying young girl ever closer and gave one last statement, preparing her for her journey to the other side. The crowd grew in silent tears as she attempted to speak her final words: "D-d-don't lea-leave o-o-our people to die by the m-m-monsters-s-s-s. P-p-please t-t-take the pa-pain away y-y-you are the g-g-g-good s-s-shepherd-d-d." Her hand brushed against Joseph's face as his hand pressed her forehead for he was praying over her fervently to send her home. When Joseph had finished his silent prayer, her tears froze, leaving a red trail drawn as her life faded away in a single breath. Snow began to fall once more, but no one was paying attention to that. Joseph rose with her in his arms as Penelope jumped into the crowd and grasped her heart immediately drawing sorrow. No words could be said by anyone as he walked to the edge of the city where they buried her in their cemetery that morning. Joseph was the only one to give words and would explain that things even as terrible as this were in God's plan. While stating this, he fell to the ground and wept over the girl he had not known. Penelope held her husband as did many, but Zacharias's heart at that moment saw only vengeance for whatever had done this.

An hour later, after Joseph had prayed for guidance, he met with the entire village and the decision was made to launch an expeditionary force to Malastay, the capital city of their nation Calina. "My fellow brothers and sisters of Salem, I wish that we could have saved her, but that is not up to us, the Lord has far more important plans. I'm asking for every able-bodied man to join me on our journey to finding out what is happening in

Malastay. As you all know, Calina is the smallest nation in the west, and with that being said, we have no formal or unified military. In times of need, we defend our own just as Zacharias defended my daughter. I will think no less of any of you if you wish not to come, I am sure we shall meet some kind of wicked force of nature there." Many of the men stood up and the wives of the ones who didn't urged their husbands to join the expedition. In all, thirty-one joined, and that morning, they said good-bye to their families before they set out. In the kitchen of the Voltel household, Joseph and Zacharias stood prepared for conflict as Penelope finished packing their provisions for the short and potentially dangerous trip. "Joseph, I didn't even know you owned a sword," Zacharias said to him.

"I may be a pastor, but that doesn't mean I won't defend my family or the flock in times of need," he replied with a wink and a pat on his shoulder. Joseph readies his bow and packs the arrows into the quiver tightly. The middle-aged pastor then draws his own one-handed sword that is finely crafted, holding the image of the sun on the hilt. "Where did you get that from Joseph?"

"Oh, this was a gift made by Mr. Royalton for me. Truly marvelous!"

Mariana said good-bye to them both and asked her father why they were leaving. Kissing his daughter on the cheek, he explained, "I go to defend others just like you." He then went outside and began to prepare his horse Grear as Penelope then approached Zac.

"You be careful out there, young man," she said as her eyes started tearing up.

"One of the few things I can do well is handle myself in a battle," he said as he grasped the hilt of his reforged blade.

"That's what I'm afraid of, just stay by Joseph's side and protect him for me, okay."

"Trust me if a decision was to ever be made, it will be him who returns, not I." He then joined Joseph outside, who had a brown mare with him; she was the second horse in his stable. "You ready Joseph?"

"Not quite. I have one more surprise for you. I had intended to give you this under better circumstances, but this seems about right." Joseph mounted the brown mare and patted her neck. "Her name is Jesibelle, she was my old horse before Grear, and I think she misses me. Well, seeing as you two have already been acquainted, hop on. Grear's all yours now."

Shaking his head in disbelief, he mounted the white stallion. "Joseph, I can't accept something like this, it's too big."

"It's already done, the deed's signed over to you, just make sure to put your signature down on it when we return." Together, they rode to the main square where they met the other thirty-one men ready for the short journey. Not a one of them was under the age of forty and less than a fifth of them held bows with small swords for they were hunters. The rest were writers, painters, and musicians who had grabbed swords passed down from their family lineage. Zacharias knew most of these men probably didn't know how to use these weapons effectively, judging from the dullness of the blades. Mr. Royalton came prepared for battle, but Joseph asked him to stay as to watch over Salem, although he listened, he was unhappy by this; needless to say, he was indeed a solid warrior in his day. Joseph prayed for protection over the group, and together, they rode out traveling southeast but more so south than east. The village gathered on the hillside to see them ride out to defend Malastay.

Heading down the mountain pass, the snow fell without mercy and a journey that should have taken just over a half day would now take three times as long. That night after pushing forward for the day, Joseph, who was leading, called for them to search out shelter for the night. A hidden cavern was found that contained a waterfall inside that had not yet frozen. Here they huddled around a fire for the night as they took turns every half hour keeping guard over the entrance. The men were afraid of what they were going to find in Malastay, for the girl was so gravely injured, they knew no man could've done that to a human being at least any in these parts. Zacharias stepped over to Joseph who was standing alone by the waterfall that carried in the moon's sapphire glow. Joseph's hair appears far more gray than usual and his wrinkles seem multiplied "How are you feeling?" he asked him. Joseph was smoking tobacco out of his pipe, which Zacharias had never seen him do. Then pushing the matter further, he implied, "It's about that girl, isn't it?"

"Yes, what happened to her is a sad truth that is becoming all too common in the past few years." Joseph sat down, urging his friend to sit with him. They observed the water crash dozens of feet below into the cavern, not speaking for over a half hour. The water splashing below impacts heavily, easing the ability to discern the situation to come. "You know I've been a pastor for over a few decades now, I've traveled the lands of the west and even a slight bit of the east long ago. For decades, I've witnessed physical ailments, emotional sickness, spiritual depths of the lost, and the aftermath of warring regions. But only in recent years, have I seen the corrupted creatures of the earth seeming war with man once again." Zacharias looked at him closer and exclaimed, "What do you believe it could be, because over the course of my days, Titulus has claimed victory over many a dreadful terror that has searched me out." Joseph reflected in his mind for a moment as he took a long inhale from his pipe. After he exhaled a vast cloud of smoke, he asked, "Do you know of the Continental Restoration War that began in the year AD 920?"

"I wasn't sure of the year, but yes, I knew of Valencia's attempt to rid the world of the corrupted beasts. Do they not claim it as The Holy Restoration War?" Zacharias asked in return.

"Yes, they do deem it as holy, but that is a separate issue entirely. Back on to my point, it was thought for countless centuries that the majority of these monsters were destroyed, but only in recent years have they began to attack societies in coordinated attack patterns as they once did. Rumors have been circulating as of late that even the great ballista city of Hagan has been under constant siege from fiends long since vanquished. They have always been around, but they've been on the increase internationally and I believe it to be a spiritual sign or harbinger if you will." Watching the moon, Zacharias wondered what spiritual signs really meant. Instead, he answered in a way Joseph did not expect. "It's too bad the holy knights aren't around anymore. I'm sure they could protect everyone."

"Since when did you know anything about the holy knights and what makes you bring them up?" Joseph asked surprised.

"I'm a warrior, Joseph, of course, I know of the greatest military order that ever fought."

Joseph smirked, passing his pipe "Well then, you do know they also were believers in Jesus Christ if you've read the basics."

Inhaling the tobacco too strongly, he coughed. The smoke hits the water and the remnants spiral out of the cavern. "I read about it before but did not fully understand." Zacharias then passed Joseph back his pipe and held out his beer stein under the waterfall to get a drink of water. "Joseph, what is spirituality anyways?" Joseph's heart grasped joy; he had been waiting for such questions to arise from him. "Well, spirituality, hmmm, that can be tricky to explain at first, but let me do my best. You've caught me off guard." As he scratched his head, Zacharias took a drink of water from "The Guardian", patiently awaiting the answer. That moment, a light shone in his thoughts and Joseph grabbed Zacharias's mug. "Do you see these symbols etched upon your mug?" He nodded yes. "Well, take a look here the symbols of earth, water, wind, fire, surround that of holy. Now bear with me for a minute, imagine that each one of those are actual living entities within the world."

"So you're saying spirituality is the living form of the elements," he asked perplexed.

"Kind of, but really focus on this that the elements are alive because they were made to be alive. They are universal proof that our world is ordered in perfection, that a master gardener cultivated this." Full of wonder and a bit of excitement, Zacharias stood up. "I've never thought of that before!"

"Now let me progress just a little further why would things be ordered, would that not point to someone who ordered it?"

"Joseph, I don't think that you're wrong in thinking that God could have ordered all this, but I personally disagree that this monotheistic God you believe in exists."

"Why is that?"

"Well, the way I see it if the God you believe in exists, then the world would have to hold a fundamental purpose for each and every one of us. Fact of the matter is look around us: people die all over from starvation, war, sickness, and the corrupted nature of the earth. If God exists, how could he allow all that? How is there purpose in the very nature of elements you speak of when it is nature that is enemy of man in Vulgata? I'm sorry, Joseph, you know I respect you, but the God you speak of I hold no love toward, but instead malcontent if he does indeed exist. Purpose is what you make it plain and simple." He then drew his sword and held it out to the waterfall; water cascades unto the hilt like tears of a world that did indeed care. Joseph listened to every word he said carefully and took a moment before he gave his rebuttal. "Did you ever consider the fact that it is not God who hurts the world so, but it is sin that comes from the fallen one? Spirituality, at the end of the day, is the represented truth of both heaven and hell. It is the love of God and the hatred of Satan that battle for your soul as long as you walk this earth. You're right in saying you can choose your path and purpose. God gave you that free will to choose." Zacharias both understood what he was saying to a certain extent, but at the same point was confused. "But if you have free will and you believe in Him, are you really making any choices or just obeying a planned process?" Zac asked.

Joseph began to laugh in a good way. "I always enjoy talking with you, you're a great debater, perhaps that may be your purpose." Zacharias laughed alongside his friend and he put his arm around his shoulder. Joseph then continued, "In all seriousness though, all I can tell you is that we have free will, but God just knows what you're going to choose to do already. Before I further confuse you with that, let me elaborate. God who is all knowing knows what you're going to do, but at the same token, He lets you choose what you want to do at the end of the day. With that being said, for those of us who follow Him, how much greater is it for us to know our Father already knows what's going to happen, so we can always trust and rest in what He commands."

"You make good points, Joseph, but if you're trying to convert me, consider that a lost cause." It was then the two went to get some rest for they knew they would need it for the next long day ahead.

The next day, the expedition set out at first light with all haste for the snowfall had ceased. With that being said, they were not without obstacle for night had brought roughly four inches of snow, which kept their horses from the ability to gallop. This was not because the horse could not handle it, but more so because there were many narrow hills around now hidden. By the afternoon, some two miles from the city of Malastay, they could see the outskirts from the snow-covered hilltops. "What is that?" one of the hunters yelled to the group. Focusing, they could all see a thick blanket of snow swirling around the city of Malastay, even though there was no sign of wind around them. The snow reached high above the city, blocking all sight and perhaps even entry. Everyone was afraid to proceed, but Joseph, now reaching the base of the hilltops, had found the main route into the city. "What are you all waiting for? A little snow never killed anyone," he jokingly stated.

"But a tornado of blizzardous shard most likely will," Zacharias spoke to himself.

Another member of the group frightfully exclaimed, "How are we to overcome something like that? Surely, it is the work of sorcery!" The group became extremely uneasy at the mention of sorcery and talk of disbanding and returning home rose immediately. Zacharias dismounted Grear and walked up to the man and yanked him off his horse. The young warrior was indignant by the statement as he held the man by his collar, stating, "That young girl made it to Salem gravely injured and without horse, Are you really considering turning your back now! She died to give us that message, now you owe it to her having come this far already!" Apologizing, the men regained their composure as Joseph gave a silent nod. Buildings were abandoned along the road as they checked each one in groups of five or more calling out to any survivors. "Nothing, not a damn thing," Zacharias said to Joseph as they checked a deserted pub that had been built recently. "Each room empty, each house empty, no livestock, no people, has this become home to ghosts?" Zacharias spoke within his own thoughts.

"Come here quickly" Joseph sputtered. Rushing into one of the upstairs rooms, a letter sat with the marking of a blood-stained hand. The letter read:

Warning: Flee all who dare enter the necromancer's trap for he is cunning and will bring the seven plagues of sin upon your household. Once was Malastay bright and wondrous in the eyes of worldly artistry, now a ruin of testimony to the coming judgment of false merit upon Vulgata. Even now, his eyes are upon you, and soon, his servants are sure to follow. This I say unto you in the year of the Lord 2984.

Signed, Alias

PS: Beware the PLAGGES, agents of a false sevenfold spirit. Their time is short and they have become bold incarnate for the day of their king draws near.

Pride
Lust
Anger
Greed
Gluttony
Envy
Sloth

After reading this, they looked at one another and neither said a word of it momentarily. At the same time, they interrupted each other with their speech, both trying to blurt something out. Joseph then let Zacharias go first as he was about to blow up. "What the hell is that? PLAGGES? Are you kidding me? What is that supposed to even mean?" he ranted.

"Calm down, the only way were going to be able to confront this is through patient judgment. If we lose our wit, we may be lured into an array of traps." "*This must be the work of the House of Magus*" Joseph knows, but to whom can he share such information with? Gathering the men, Joseph read it aloud to them as they were now only a few dozen feet from the swirling veil of snow. "Well, men, what are you gonna do?" Joseph asked, valuing their input. None of them answered, Joseph advanced to the veil, stretching some two hundred feet to the sky. Massive winds could be heard from the other side. Zacharias asked Joseph "Are you sure you want to go through with this?"

Joseph, examining the snowy veil, drew his own sword. "I didn't take you for one to get scared of anything."

Zacharias gave him a dumbfounded glare. "I'll show you who's scared," as he charged forward on foot with all his might. He pierced through the veil by sword first and fell upon the other side for the force of the swirling snow launched him inside. As he attempted to glance forward, the entire city of Malastay was subject to a never-ending blizzard of snow that would continually fall to the ground and be picked right back up by the storm. This made it almost impossible to see anything. Seconds later, Joseph flew in, falling on his butt. "First fall on your ass hurts, doesn't it?" Zacharias mocked Joseph. "You know I'll take the horse back if you want me to," Joseph yelled sarcastically. He helped him up as the rest of the men began to funnel in like cannon balls.

"What is this, Joseph?" Zacharias screamed out for it was hard to hear from the immense howling winds that just began picking up again. "No idea, let us spread apart into three groups of eleven and search for any survivors! We'll regroup in the central building before dusk!" Joseph led one team and Zacharias another, but before they parted, the two locked hands and bid farewell.

PART 2: CONFIRMATION

Malastay, which was composed of mostly wooden structure that ran in parallel, maintained one massive four-way intersection where they had arrived. The city that paid homage to art in its entrepreneurship of the lifestyle held one peculiar aspect that the men could not help but take notice. A great rectangular stone pillar stood erected high above the city in this intersection. In each of its four sides, a single image was proudly fashioned. To the south, a face like a man seemingly enveloped in thought; to the east, the glorious face of the ardent eagle screeching for resolve. On the western side, a lion's roaring face called out for justice, and finally to the north, the most humble ox glancing ahead at the day's toil and labor. Atop this pillar, hundreds of white feathers could barely be seen protruding some twenty feet down. Thirty-three men had entered the snowstorm inside the veil and three numerically equal groups would now part ways. Zacharias's group took to the inner city whereas Joseph's took to the southern route. The final group was to wait between the two groups to reinforce the other in case of emergency. Just like the road into the city, nothing but empty houses were found, not a body or any traces of struggle. It was as if the earth had just swallowed up man and culture as a thief in the night. Zacharias had reached the town hall, which was a gigantic four-story building constructed of limestone. In front of this building sat two rounded guard towers that were also made from the same stone. Together, they entered, pushing open massive wooden doors that stood over ten feet high, holding the symbol of a closed hand upon each. The doors slammed against the walls, sending a powerful echo down the narrow hallways in all direction. To the front of the room sat a large olivewood desk some fifteen feet in length. The winds that entered the building blew parchment to the ceiling, grasping the attention of those alive. Ink ran across the desk spattering left and right, dripping down the front, but amid this, an image began to appear. It was hard to see from the paper floating in their vision until they fell to the ground as rocks defying gravity. Jet-black is the face of ink on the desk, the eyes and mouth are sowed shut. "What is this? Let's go," one of the men demanded. Zacharias steps forward, but it then disappears. "An apparition, perhaps even the culprit?" he asks himself. Behind the desk, two rows of circular stairs wind up the sides to the second floor. Around the two rows of stairs sat a statue of Calina's founder, Fierno Von Pestaeus III, whom lovingly holds a paintbrush to his lips and a violin to his heart. "Hello," Zacharias yelled out, standing by the statue. He could see nothing, but like the door, he could hear his voice echo throughout the forlorn halls. One of the villagers replied that maybe they shouldn't venture to far into the building. At that time, Zac noticed that the paint brush on the statue was red like blood, which he then noticed was actually coming out of the lips. "Evil's art," he said to himself. Drawing his sword, he proceeded into the next room, but all the other villagers who were with him cowardly waited in the lobby area huddled by the desk.

During this, Joseph who had reached the southern edge of the city had reached a series of wells. Each well is frozen at the rim in red blood, reminding him of the final tear of Cecilia. Toward the edge of the swirling veil of snow sat the gallows where a single coat was left swaying among this false winter's breath. "What is that?" Joseph yelled out as he tried to fire an arrow toward the gallows. For a second, an apparition appeared by as some sort of monster watching them, but the arrow was carried off in the wind. "Looks like our arrows are useless in this, draw steel!" At that point, they all equipped swords as Joseph checked the coat, also thinking of his folly in using the bow in these conditions. A note sat inside the coat just like the note in the pub.

It read: We're going to take you just like we took your son Simon Peter Voltel in Hope's Lake.

"What the hell is this?" Joseph said to himself as a burst of pure anger shot through his being. Joseph was not a man to become angry, but this was hard for him for he had lost his eldest son only two years prior and had yet to fully accept this finality as not being his mistake. Crumpling the note, he shouts loudly, then slashes the coat in half. "Joseph, there's a noise coming from this well," one of his men told him. Running over, he could hear the screams of a male teenager who was calling out for his father. "Simon," Joseph yelled down the well for it was the only well without frozen blood lining, blocking entry. "Father, it's me. Help, I've fallen and hurt my leg, help me!" The other men with Joseph knew Simon had died two years ago and advised him not to go. "I must, that is my son," he then began to climb down the long cold iron bars to the base many feet below.

The third group remained in a watchtower as sentinels over the city. Winds began to pick up more and more as night grew ever closer. This group did make a discovery that somehow, the veil of snow was working as a wind tunnel or a vacuum, but the question remained: what was it trying to keep in or extract?

Zacharias, now deep within the archives of the town hall, depended on the light coming from the windows to illuminate his path. Bookshelves lined the walls where a surreal yet ornamented bronze chandelier hung unlit. Something did catch his eye: a colossal book sat in the room that was some three feet long. Unbeknownst to him, it was known as Codex Gigas (The Devil's Bible) and its pages were turned to a portrait of Lucifer on the right-hand side along a portrait of heaven on the left. "I'm really wishing right about now I wasn't alone in here," he said to himself, pacing carefully toward the book. His eyes do not relinquish the curiosity of the Devil's image for he knows it well; he has seen it for many years rotting in the slavery of nightmare. *You, the one who haunts my life, awake or asleep always within my shadow what is your name, are you the master of Manistof?* He took his sword and tapped the image of Lucifer's head with the tip and one of the bookstands fell over behind him. Zacharias froze, dropping his sword, and the chandelier was somehow now lit. Finally, a clue was given as he noticed blood by the bookshelf toward the end of the narrow room where he saw a bloody handprint on the floor as if it were dragged in that direction. "This trail leads up the stairs." He took a minute to catch his breath for he was frightened. "You guys still there!" The others did yell back so that at least gave him some comfort he wasn't alone. Titulus led as he cautiously crept up the stairs. "Bravery really isn't worth it," he told himself. The reddened path led all the way to the top or the fourth floor to the governor's office, which held massive doors just like the entrance, these doors have hands upon them also, but these ones are open. Putting his own against the door, he felt a dreadful feeling like when the dark spirit visited him at the Voltel household. "I have to do this, there could be more survivors or even children like Mariana counting on me." Images of Mariana flashed vibrantly as he kicked the door in.

While this was happening, the group located in the main watchtower began to flee from it for the winds were becoming too strong and the tower began to shake violently. Once they reached the bottom, the tower fell over onto a music parlor crushing its roof.

The men surrounding the well where Joseph had climbed down saw the watchtower crash and ran over to it. Joseph was now left alone in the well as he crawled forward on his hands and knees to the voice of his son calling out his name. Cramped and claustrophobic is the alley ahead, making him unable to turn around. "My son, I'm on my way," Joseph cried out. In his left hand, he lights a torch, placing his hope in this lone light as he ventures across the dungeon below the earth. "Father," the voice of his son cried out repeatedly. Frantically, Joseph began to crawl with all his ability to do so. "Don't worry, son, I'm coming!"

"Father, I'm scared, the monsters, they've killed everyone!" Joseph's heart underwent a massive spiritual attack that petrified him with fear. "Jesus, give me strength," he began to say in a whisper. His knee hit a sharp rock that cut him fairly well, and it was that instant where Joseph realized that was a sign from the Lord and he stopped dead in his tracks. In his head, he began to reason with himself, "That can't be my son. He died two years ago. I buried him with these hands. I've fallen into a trap because I did not listen to God's divine reason. The devil is down here and I his prey." Joseph began to breath in a frigid soulless air that he knew all too well for this was of evil. Unable to turn his body around, he began to back up very slowly, praying desperately that the beast was not behind him. He began to shake uncontrollably as he heard loud footsteps stomping in water only feet in front of him. Joseph still spoke in his mind as he stopped in silence. "Oh, please, Father, don't let me die here. I'm so afraid the evil one has trapped me. Please protect me and give me the courage to glorify you." Joseph put out his flame as he continually backed up drawing his sword and pointing it in front of him for defense. Not too far from the exit, he began to hear the footsteps getting louder slopping around in mud. Suddenly, Joseph, dropped his sword and the footsteps came to a halt. Carefully, he picks up the sword in the darkness, slightly crawling backward. The faint sound of sliding begins to advance from the back end of the tunnel. Loud sniffing could be heard for it had picked up the scent of Joseph's blood. Quickly, Joseph began to withdraw to the exit, yelling up, "Help, there's something down here!" No reply is given for they had gone over to the fallen watchtower. After Joseph had yelled, he could now hear the terrible sliding noise coming at him from both directions, and among all of this, a petrifying scream of demonic nature overtook the tunnels and pierced his soul.

Zacharias had now entered the governor's office, which was also pitch-black, for the windows were covered with tarps reeking of a foul odor. He opened one slightly so that light barely filled the gargantuan office. A single chair is seen by the back wall of the room behind a desk, which had the governor's name etched within the front. Looking around, he noticed nothing of interest except the ceiling of the room went up some twenty more feet along the cold dark limestone. The desk is checked; nothing is found. "Still no clue, yet the blood points to this room," he said to himself, now sitting in the governor's chair. "This place is dead time to rendezvous with Joseph and see if he's found anything." Now standing up and tramping to the door, Titulus is returned to his scabbard. Just about to exit, a faint dripping sound falls to the desk. Still, he could see nothing except that blood was dripping on the desk in ever-increasing amounts. One more time, Zacharias peered upward, knowing slaughter is soon to bestow. "Hello," he spoke with about half his wit. A distinct and harrowing crunch of bone chimes of the feast, blood pours over him. Wiping his face slowly with his hand, he realized he was covered in gore, but he holds his composure, calling on the force of Titulus. "No retreat, not this close to revelation," he says, creeping over to another window readying to tear it down. In his mind, he mentally prepared himself, so he thinks, "No turning back now.

Truth is truth whether you're frightened or not." Pulling down, the entire tarp light filled the room, but could barely reach the top of the ceiling. Hundreds and hundreds of bodies are dead, secreted to the walls by a jade-looking slime. "Oh my God!" A body ripped in half that was missing a large amount of surface tissue speaks. "Run," the man said with a dead stare in his eyes, no eyelids and skeletal frame exposed on his face. "I-i-it's g-g-g-g-g-going to be alri-alright, I'm going to get you down from there," Zacharias yelled in shock as his emotions ran rampant out of sorrow for his fellow human being. The man cried out in pain, vomiting on himself, then dying as his eyes faded to the spiritual realm. Almost hysterically shaking, another noise was heard and dark yellow eyes were seen toward the top of the ceiling locked on him. Zacharias backed up to the side of the room trying to get to the door. All of a sudden, the hundreds of bodies fell in an avalanche all over the room. Knocked to the ground, he was trapped underneath the sea of bodies and his sword was stabbed into lifeless corpse. Struggling to break free, he watched dozens of Murkans crawling down the walls. Desperately, he pulled himself from the bodies and was able to grasp his sword as he slowly backed to the door. The moss-covered beast's obsidian teeth reflected in the light as some held limbs in their mouths. These Murkans were different than the one encountered months earlier for these were far more muscular and had antlers that circulated down their necks with grass like hair sprouting in patches. All of them were slouched over with their lanky arms dragging on the ground and those yellow eyes born without covering were fixed on his every movement. Their bodies moved toward him as their heads sway from side to side pulled by the strings of fate, some walk diagonally, others attempt to slither through the bodies. One step at a time, Zacharias withdrew to the opened door with his eyes and sword fixed to them. Carefully, he edged backward, toe to heel, all the way to the main room of the town hall where the men were waiting for him. "Did you find anything?" one of the men asked. Another shrieked in terror as he noticed that Zacharias's face was covered in murder's delight. "Get behind me now," Zac screamed at the other men. Immediately, they could see dozens of the Murkan crawling down the ceiling and stairwell while others could be seen dragging their arms from doorways along the narrow corridors. The men began to scream in fright running for the door, but Zacharias holds a vigilant eye on the enemy, never breaking rank.

During that, Joseph remained trapped in the well, desperately trying to escape. "Come on," he shouts, scrambling backward on all fours thrusting his sword in front of him repeatedly. Finally, he reached the iron bars where the light came shining in, and as he reached for it, the face of a Murkan emerged from the darkness and latched on to him. It went to bite him, but Joseph used his forearm to smash into the creature's throat holding it at bay as it began biting and slashing at him ferociously. The Murkan grabbed him with its massive claws on his face and forced him to the ground as its spines brushed up against the tunnel walls. The yellow eyes became brighter and larger, the more it injured Joseph, almost to the point of falling out. It then hissed in wicked delight, pushing against him so powerfully that it almost broke his other arm. A green slime dripped from the plague-ridden tongue that divides into three unto Joseph's cranium who in turn cries out for the Lord. His strength heightens and he grabs his side dagger with his right hand as the creature claws at his sides leaving deep gashes. Screaming in a battle cry, Joseph put the blade into the beast's throat and pulled it violently to the side. Multiple jerks are made by Joseph for the carapace is tough until the esophagus is slashed wide. A terrible distorted squeal was let out of the Murkan as a foul thick liquid poured onto Joseph's mouth, almost suffocating him. Falling backward, the beast's yellow eyes lost their color as its body shook and cried out in pain and agony swallowing the pieces of its own throat. Joseph puked all over the ground fighting for air. Others could be heard thundering through the tunnels as Joseph regained his composure, he then got up and escaped into the light. Covered in the green blood of the creature, Joseph sprinted to the center of the city where loud yells and screams could be heard from the other men. "I'm coming," he yelled out to them as the storm became worse and the wind blew harder, denying the comfort of most communication. Now rejoined with all thirty-one of the men, Joseph yelled, "Zacharias, where is Zacharias?" but no one knew. Murkans came out of the framework from each building and the land itself numbering over a hundred. They surrounded all the thirty-one of the men, including Joseph, who were grouped together retreating to a saloon with its own stone stairway. Well, over a hundred of the beasts followed them in a hungry and organized horde that began climbing over each other to get to them. Joseph went to push open the saloon's doors that were solid without windows, but it was barred from the other side. Desperately, the men kicked at the door screaming as the Murkans converged on the position. "We're dead, we're all going to die," they yelled.

"No silent defeat, not for these demons, prepare for battle," Joseph violently shouted as he stood in front of his people sword and dagger second to the spirit of the pastor. Several buildings down, Zacharias was trapped in a weapon's forge where three of the Murkans forced their way in through the windows. Letting out a violent scream, Titulus beheaded the first Murkan with a precise blow. The body of the creature ran around, grasping the place its head used to be as its head yelped on the ground not yet dying. This distracted Zacharias who then smashed it with a powerful stomp from his boot, but as he did this, another of the two Murkans crashed through the ceiling behind him. It swipes at him and he parries by blade while it then attempts to bite him. The beast's obsidian teeth chip on the sword while he then charges forward knocking it to the ground, but as it falls, it grabs his body, pulling him to the floor with it. "Eat this," he yells as he pushes the horizontal blade down on its mouth pinning it to the ground. The top half of the skull is cleaved off gradually, but it continues to fight him. Now grabbing his dagger, he stabs the beast in the kidneys over a dozen times as it smacks him painfully until it dies. "No time, gotta get to Joseph now!" Jumping to his feet, sprinting for the staircase, the last one dives through the window. Laying atop the massive anvil, it grabs him by the side and digs its claws deep into his side. He cries out in pain, chopping its arm off that then remains attached; the beast then knocks his sword out of his hand with the other claw. Noticing a forging mallet in a smith box he grabs it without delay and begins caving the beast's chest in with mighty blows as it sits atop the anvil. The Murkan sits with an almost flattened chest as Zacharias grabs his sword and gains entry to the roof of the building to get a better view. In the distance, he sees the mob of the monsters surrounding Joseph and the others at the saloon staircase. "Not like this, no, I won't allow this to happen to my family!" His adrenaline is pure as he runs across the roofs of each building to get to them.

Joseph stands in front of his men, their backs are against the door and swords pointed out in front. Eerily, the horde crept forward to them one step at a time, taking the occasional swipe feasting on the very fear of man. The Murkans all of a sudden looked up to the roof and began to rattle their long spines like a snake when frightened. Across the city of Malastay, atop the great stone pillar, a magnificent trumpet sounded and the feathers from the pillar shed from the tower and blew toward the men. A voice shouted from the rooftop, "Unto death we march!" Zacharias jumped from the two-story building into the pack of monsters smashing many with his mighty claymore. Joseph screamed for everyone to charge. All of the men stormed forward with Joseph as steel split the corrupted flesh of the monsters. Disoriented, many of the beasts scattered and regrouped elsewhere. Joseph desperately fights through to get to his friend. Murkans swipe, bite, and claw at Zacharias, but he swung his sword around and moved as if the spirit of justice was with him. When Joseph had reached him, the band of the beast had completely fallen back to the gallows.

"Zacharias, you saved our lives. Thank God you're all right," Joseph said, shaking his shoulders. Entered into a persona of combative assertiveness, Zacharias ordered the men further, they listened without question. "The gallows, look, it's the pack leader," he said to Joseph, wiping the mixed blood of man and nature from his eyes with a handful of snow. A Murkan colored as the snow stood over ten feet tall. Six spikes sprawl from the shoulders encircling the crown. "We have to kill the pack leader to defeat the pack, Joseph!"

"You're right. We'll distract if you think you can get to him. You have the fastest legs of any of us!" Joseph gave the orders to his men who grouped up with a newfound valor given them by the bravery shown by the youngest. Before they could, the beasts made another charge at them as the men held their ground. Standing before one of the men, the antlers on a Murkan's neck rose in a twisted fashion. The impossibly sharp antlers jam into the sides of his head and the monster raises him in the air feasting on his face also tearing its claws down his arms so deeply that the gore turned black The holler of the suffering throws the rest into a frenzied state. The counterassault made by the men was fierce, commanding the pain of their lost friend. Relentlessly, Joseph and the others hacked down the beasts chopping limb, flesh, and antler, buying the hero his chance to reach the leader. Zacharias ran to the side of the battle where two Murkans attempted to bar his path, but Joseph cut one in half and warded off the other, bashing the hilt of his blade into its stomach that somehow caused it to defecate all over itself. It falls to the ground in pain; Joseph runs his blade down the spine, opening the battle for the leader. "Go now," he commanded Zacharias who had questioned whether to help Joseph or get the leader for more Murkans were approaching. Zacharias could see other men torn asunder, which only escalated the need to win this in haste. Charging the leader, he gave a mighty war call that overtook the battlefield. Swinging with all his power at its core, the beast jumped back and then counterattacked by swinging its long arm. Zacharias ducked as the beast then turned around and the thousands of spines on its back stood up. One of the hunters launches him out of the way and all the spines shot like bolts of a crossbow into his body. He fell to the ground, causing the countless spines to burrow ever deeper. The pack leader came charging at Zacharias, who swung valiantly, chopping off some of the antler-like spikes. Standing over ten feet tall, the monster bent over and grabbed his sword, much like how a man grapples another in combat. Bleeding profusely on it, he is unable to fully regain his weapon. An ear-piercing squeal came forth from the white Murkan, making it difficult for concentration. Desperately trying to figure out what to do, Zac backs up, refusing to relinquish the sword as the leader bites at him ferociously. His leg brushed up against the well Joseph had climbed out of revealing the plan of action. He then fell backward into the hole grasping his sword, which pulled all the pack leader's fingers off, returning the sword to his control. His shoulder bashed into the stone wall as his legs braced the other side, so he didn't fall down the hole. Barely was he able to get out of the well before it jumped in after him getting stuck in return. Opportunity presented victory and Titulus claimed it by gracefully slashing the Murkan in half in diagonal fashion. Half fell in the snow and the rest to the depths in a pile of slop.

Joseph, who was battling with the others, heard the beast's final mighty roar as the winter storm stopped and tons of snow came crashing to the ground. All the Murkans' yellow eyes became colorless and they were all blinded; they were then easy prey for the sword. Joseph went and helped his friend and the two breathing heavily dressed in sin-stained snow pressed foreheads together looking to the ground. "You saved us all, kid, or better yet, Guardian of Salem." Hurt and exhausted, Zacharias in a half-dazed expression regained his senses. "Let's go home." The pastor grasps his Holy Bible hidden within his coat. They stand before the man decimated by the spines, his skin was now clearly poisoned from the hundreds if not thousands of them. Turning to Joseph with a melancholy stare, Zacharias fought a lone tear of guilt. "I didn't even know his name."

"His name was Davidoff, he was the greatest hunter in our village." Zacharias stood up and put his stained blade back in its blue scabbard as he saw more of the men that had died very painful deaths. "Thirty-three men leave, twenty-two return. Such is the nature of war, but let us not forget what they died for," Joseph said to Zacharias as they gathered the dead.

They stood off to the side on a barren hill, overlooking the city that was now free of the curse. "What did they die for, Joseph? Nothing changes, there will always be more fighting, more killing, and worst of all, more graves to dig. Where is God in all of this?" "The right path is always harder, but it is one the good men must take, I know it's not much, but they believed in you because you saved their lives."

"It's my fault these men are dead, Joseph, I entered the snowy veil first and they followed my pathetic show of bravado, the folly is mine and mine alone." Joseph lays a powerful punch across Zac's face and picked him up, slamming him into the stone wall behind him. "Don't you take that blame! You saved these men's lives! You're too good of a man to carry that kind of blame, I won't let you! Every single one of those men gave their lives for the cause of justice and you led them to victory!" Joseph then put him back down and Zacharias stood there with the wide eyes of an owl that had just received a fresh feather of wisdom plucked from his own hide. He smiled. "You have a good hit for an old man, perhaps all pastors aren't cowards like I once thought." They both began to chuckle. "I'm sorry I struck you, I just want you to stop doubting in yourself so much and start believing."

"It's okay. I needed that, I'm just glad you didn't hit me in the side," which was currently bleeding from the Murkan that clenched his hip. "I didn't take all warriors for wimps over a simple scratch," Joseph jokingly replied. Although slightly unorthodox, the two continually laughed over this in the situation of this tragedy. It was through this gift of fellowship that eased their suffering helping them to cope. This happened away from the men, of course, for some of them had just lost very close friends and brothers. Zacharias stood among the men, readying to speak, but before he could, they cheered his name. "Hail, Guardian of Salem," raising their swords together, chanting loudly in complete admiration. Trudging through the snow, a young woman came out racing to the group. Crying, this young woman of Zacharias's age hugged him. "Thank you, thank you, kind lord," she said to him.

"Lord? I'm not a lord, I'm just a commoner like you," he said, holding her in his arms. "Are there any more of you?" he questioned her. She whistled loudly, and more than a hundred women and children began to emerge from the opened well. Joseph crossed his arms with a discerning gaze "Hey, Guardian of Salem, does the name Melchizedek mean anything to you?" He had no clue what Joseph was talking about.

5

Dirge of Gigas

That night, everyone was forced to stay in the town hall with the 153 women and children who had come out of hiding they were all widows and orphans. The women treated the wounds of the twenty-two left alive from Salem, praising them all the night for saving them from the cursed city. After the battle that day, there wasn't much light left so to make the journey then would have been dangerous. The woman who had hugged Zacharias earlier introduced herself her name was Kelly Aristos. She was a petite brunette with an amber set of eyes and an amazingly strong spirit, for she had led these people to safety.

Joseph sat down beside her, for they were in one of the upstairs offices. "Can you tell us what happened?" Zacharias was also in this room with the two. Kelly stood up and began to explain in a soft yet assertive voice that had not let go the pain and fear her and her people had endured. "We had been staying in the playhouse located beneath this building that connects to all the sewer lines in the city. Only days ago, the mysterious veil of snow encircled the majority of Malastay, and that's when the nightmare began. The Murkans appeared with the tall white one rising from the gallows." Joseph tapped the table and asked, "I see, so it all began with the Murkans first appearance?"

"Well, yes and no, strange occurrences have been happening in Malastay for some months now ever since the governor found the big book."

"Big book," Joseph asked as he tilted diagonally slightly leaning forward. "Yes, the governor has this great big book he was infatuated with for months. They say that he was trying to use this big book to call upon spirits of fortune, and that's when our home became yoked with mayhem. He claimed to the rest of the city that he had found a way to restore Malastay to its former glory." Zacharias was about to open his mouth on the subject but did not want to interrupt; instead, he sat also in a chair, holding the hilt of his sword with the blade touching the floor as he spun it around. His nails dance around the hilt, a feeling known from childhood throbs, but he cannot pinpoint the origin. Is this a memory or just a diluted semblance of what is now archaic to his so called maturity, better yet does he himself have a clue? *Malastay tied to chaos and now death all sown from the seeds of erroneous belief. Is this to be my fate in the end also?* Zac ponders frightened but does not show it; his secret must remain, for he loves his newfound family too much. Joseph rolled his eyes down for a second then up. "Do you know the name of this tome, Kelly?"

"No, but it should be located somewhere in this building, perhaps the governor's office."

"No," Zacharias quickly interjected snapping back into it. Kelly and Joseph looked at him slightly confused. "The governor's office is dead, I checked the room for any survivors an hour ago, but there are none. All I can say respectfully is that the Murkans made that a feeding ground."

"I understand," Kelly replied, sadly sinking into her chair.

"I think I know where the book is you were talking about, Kelly. Is it over three feet long and weighs well over a hundred pounds most likely?"

"Yes, this book is gigantic just like that," she stated.

"It's in the library sprawled out on the table. I wouldn't advise trying to move it. There's a picture of some kind of demon or something on the page it was left on, I've seen it before," Zacharias tried to explain. Joseph raised his Bible and the two turned to him. "The book is called Codex Gigas, meaning Giant Book, some also call it the Devil's Bible because of that picture you described. I would like to examine it if that would be all right with you two," Joseph asked.

"Do you want me to go with you, Joseph?" Zacharias questioned.

"No, thank you, this time I really need to review this alone just for a short bit." Joseph then exited the room.

"I saw you fight the pack leader, you were very brave for someone so young," Kelly exclaimed, batting her eyelashes. Zacharias, unaffected, spoke absent of emotion, "I did what I had to do, Joseph is my family and a family dies without question for one another." Kelly gave a loving smile and kissed him on the cheek. "You have a good heart." Zacharias had never been close to a woman, but had always longed to have a wife to love and to honor and secretly to find his identity in. Turning red, he searched around for an escape route, but she grabbed his arm and sat down by him. Now in this time and age, a man of bravery and moral standard who knew how to treat a woman properly was in short supply. Kelly was also a good young woman who was an emotional wreck from the loss of her people and everyone she knew. In the world of Vulgata where loss of loved ones is far too common, people often find love early in life to dull the pain. It is for this reason orphans and widows only seem to perpetuate all the more. "Do you have a woman in your life?"

"No, it's just me. I'm still trying to figure out who I am," he explained as his eyes targeted everything in the room except Kelly.

"You're a shy one. I like that in a man. It shows thou art humble." Kelly kissed his neck and whispered in his ear, "If you'll stay with me, you can have my body right now." Zacharias stood up, flustered at first. "Oh, I, uh, thank you for the offer, but I really must be going."

"Do you not like the way I look?" she asked saddened.

"No, no, it's not that. It's just I'm not ready," he said with all the embarrassment social interaction with a female could offer. Immediately, she regained her composure and smiled. "I see you're a virgin." He said no words and looked away shamefaced. Kelly hopped over and took his forearm. "I'm sorry, dear, listen you're a noble man. Save that for when you fall in love with the woman you will marry." His eyes spoke in a thank you of their own and he escorted her to the main room to check on the others.

The survivors sat in the main room huddled together for the night. Joseph in turn reviewed Codex Gigas. *I never thought in my lifetime I'd see this, what a fantastic find*, he thought to himself. Inspecting the picture of the Devil on the right-page and the picture of heaven on the left, he recalled a past memory with his son Simon Peter. Joseph ran his fingers across the picture of heaven, but would not touch the image of Satan. Before he further investigated it, he noticed something sticking out of the back of the beautifully handcrafted tome. "What is this?" A grouping of parchment not of it lay tucked away to the index. Joseph studied the notes for the next two hours, making a most profound discovery, but he would decide to wait to a later date to reveal it to anyone else. Joseph then returned to the main room. Everyone was now asleep including Zacharias, but Kelly sat at the top of the stairwell overlooking the statue. Joseph strolled up the stairs and sat beside. "What are you still doing awake?" he questioned her.

"I can't sleep, a piece of me believes those monsters aren't dead."

"It's all right, Kelly. I have my men keeping watch outside in shifts and at each end of the corridor," Joseph reassured.

"So is Zacharias your cousin or something?" Joseph shone with delight. "He is my family, but not of blood relation." She looked at him with the utmost curiosity for ideas like that had been forgotten in their world for many generations. "Why the strange stare, young one" he asked as he noticed the statue.

"Are you one of the men of God I've heard about in fable?"

"You do me much honor, child, but all I can say is I'm a man who loves Jesus Christ and he asks me to spread the truth loving those in need. Do you believe in him?"

"I do," she said, presenting all the emotions of her heart. Then sorrow returned to her. "I have a confession to make."

"What is it?"

"I made a mistake and did something I'm not proud of earlier. It's just so hard anymore. Everyone around me is dying and the evidence of Jesus seems to be slipping away in my life." Kelly then cried into Joseph's arm. "Zacharias is a good man as you are, and I tried to offer him my body so he wouldn't leave me." She wept in his shoulder as Joseph put his arm around the young girl and spoke tenderly, "Listen, child, Jesus loves you and we all make mistakes, he understands what you're going through."

"I know, but my people are all murdered and everything is falling apart. I don't deserve to be saved by the Lord." Once she had settled, Joseph wiped away her last tear. "You're still alive, so clearly God has not abandoned you. You're right. No one deserves the Lord's mercy or grace, but that's what is so amazing about Him. Out of all the sins we commit and the rebellion mankind chose, Jesus freely offers salvation in his name, never forsaking those born of the Spirit." Joseph then explained, "But you have got to sleep, these people are going to need you for the journey ahead tomorrow, okay? Never forget that in all things, rest in the grace of what Jesus did for all of us." She nodded in understanding and thanked him for all he'd done. Joseph then pulled out one of the documents that were hidden within the index of Codex Gigas and reviewed them further. In the notes, Joseph had found out that the governor was calling upon dark spirits to show him where ancient relics lay dormant, hidden from the world. Joseph assumed that by contacting these unclean spirits; it led to the plague of Murkans that destroyed Malastay. On the map, there was a single circle around Avodah Mortis (Nation of the Dead) and an X on Continent's Peak, which was the highest mountain located in the west. Joseph grabbed his chest at the sight of what was said to be located inside of the mountain. He then fell to the floor in prayer. "Have you answered my prayers, oh merciful Lord?"

Next morning after everyone had awoken, Zacharias lay on the floor in a heavy sleep. A motherlike tap on his shoulder got his attention from Kelly. Slightly, his eyes peered open as she helped him to his feet. "Good morning," she vibrantly spoke. He gave her a dull wave as he proceeded down the corridor to grab Grear. They had brought their horses into the town hall last night after the snowy veil had faded. Joseph marched through the hall with the rest of the horses following behind. "Mornin."

"Uh, hi," he achingly replied.

"How do you feel?" Joseph asked.

"Fine, I'm doing fine," he lied, holding his lower back and side where the claw had pierced his skin. Still, a melancholy feel had found itself a home for everybody had lost someone in the curse of Malastay. Zacharias mounted his horse, Grear, and then extended his hand out to Kelly. "Would you care to ride with me?" Full of joy, she accepted and grabbed around his stomach. "Ow," he yelled as his body jerked. Joseph and many of the others laughed while she apologized then tossed her arms around his chest instead. Jokingly, she added, "I really can't win with you, can I?" Zacharias pulled the reins and gave Grear a slight kick, which set him into a run that surprised Kelly, knocking her into his back. He laughs to himself as they ride off ahead of the group. By the grace of the Lord, there were enough horses left in Malastay found at an old ranch the Murkans seemed to have missed for the women to carry the children on. For the rest of the day, they headed toward Salem and were forced to stay in the same cave they had on the way there. The worry and pain cast upon Joseph was present in his contemplation of the night; it was getting worse. Likewise, Zacharias struggled in the acceptance of Davidoff's sacrifice; he felt he should be alive instead of himself. They did not bury the bodies that were inside the governor's office for they were unsure whether curse or plague would be cast upon them if they were to undertake the endeavor. That same notion had resonated among the other twenty men of Salem after the battle that was remedied by both prayer and the baths found within the governor's personal quarters located below the library.

They arrived on the mountaintop village of Salem before sun or reason that morning unhindered by extreme weather this time. Although it was soon to be a tragic situation, Salem's beauty held strong for the emotions of renewal lingered within every breath of fresh morning air. Standing on the hilltop when they arrived was little Mariana who came running upon them with Penelope standing on a large rock waving from afar. *Who are all these women and children?* Penelope thought to herself. When they had entered the main square of the village, Joseph called a town meeting. Once gathered, he commenced with his speech. He called forth the families, eleven wives whose husbands had not returned. They had brought back their bodies in which they were going to bury in the village cemetery. The crowd silent before him, Joseph raised his Bible and began to speak loudly, "Malastay has been cursed and is now gone! Its governor sold his soul to the false gods Pheme 'Fame' and Mammon 'Greed' so that he could bask in his own glory! This I read in his personal memoirs, and for this deed, the city was cursed for their leaders sat idly by! These women and children you see before you are the only survivors!" Now Priscilla was the wife of Davidoff, who was an elderly woman, fell to her knees, pulling on Joseph's overcoat. "Tell me Davidoff isn't dead, not my husband, Joseph, where is my husband?" Priscilla begged him to tell her. Not a word was said by anyone as he alone had carried Davidoff's body on his horse that was wrapped in linen. Joseph walked over to his horse and grabbed the lifeless body lying him before her. The cries of Priscilla punctured everyone's heart as the other women from Malastay gathered around and mourned alongside her. Wailing overtook the square, but still, Joseph carried his message: "These men gave their lives for the cause of justice, and they will be remembered for eternity in the Book of Life." Zacharias went to speak, but Joseph knew that he was going to try and take responsibility for their deaths. Joseph gave a slight shake, telling Zacharias not to as Kelly put her arm on his shoulder. Drawing his sun-engraved sword, Joseph rested his forehead on the hilt. "If you must blame someone, then blame me, it was my idea to send the expedition, these men are dead because of me." They took the eleven bodies to the graveyard, all of which were wrapped for some were in pieces. Zacharias would carry Davidoff's body. Together, all the men dug the graves, and with each plunge of his spade, Joseph asked himself, "How many more are going to die like this because of others wrongdoings? How many more graves must I dig? God, please save us, save these cursed lands, please save my people!" Penelope could see the distress in him, so she kissed him on the cheek and held him close from behind. Whispering in his ear, she said, "Joseph, you are a strong man in the eyes of the Lord for He uses and blesses you profoundly, but you must be strong now for our people more than ever. Do it for all of us, show them how God works in all situations especially the hardest ones. Most of all, show them the love Christ showed for us while we were still blinded in sin." Joseph kissed his wife and felt his spirit able to stand the trial ahead if only barely. Zacharias helped carry the remaining bodies to their graves in which they marked with small wooden crosses with their names being etched into them. Well over three hundred men women and children stood before the cemetery as Joseph searched for the words to say. The eleven wives, some with children, then came out to the grave markers and Joseph presented them each with their husband's swords. He gave Priscilla her husband Davidoff's sword last, giving a silent stare reflecting to himself how he died. Zacharias stepped out in front of the large crowd. "Davidoff gave his life to save mine, he died to"—he then paused for a moment—"to protect me a man who didn't even know his name." Zacharias put his arm on Priscilla. "He did the best he could and that's all that a man can do. In the face of his destiny, he rose up and grasped truth, but most of all, he taught me the importance of sacrifice." As he was saying this face-to-face with the widow, he was desperately trying to keep his composure fighting back the tears of compassion. "Please forgive me," he begged quietly as Priscilla grabbed him close. One of the other hunters then proceeded before the crowd. "Zacharias saved our lives, if it wasn't for him, every single one of us would have died. Hail unto Zacharias and Joseph, glory forever to the fallen who have now risen up with the Lord!" Joseph had dropped his Bible by accident during this and it landed in the book of Isaiah. "Thank you, Lord," he said to himself as he picked it up, knowing the given sign. Zacharias had noticed the Good Book falling to that page Joseph was about to read. This was the first time Zacharias had heard a verse from the Bible read directly from the source. Joseph then reads out of Isaiah:

> The righteous perisheth, and no man layeth it to heart: and merciful men are taken away, none considering that the righteous is taken away from the evil to come. He shall enter into peace: they shall rest in their beds, each one walking in his uprightness.
>
> Isaiah 57:1–2 (KJV)

"I know this is hard to hear right now, but even in times of woe, especially times of woe, we must rejoice in the Lord for He has spared these men from evil. In this righteous act where few gave up their lives so that many could live, we have been brought together as one people, as one family. Do not forget the sacrifice they made for they shouldered their crosses at the end of their life just as our beloved savior did in the final sacrifice." Snow came down in excess as the clouds blocked out the now rising sun, but still, Joseph's words picked up the spirits of all those who listened, for even when light seems not visible, it always finds a way to reach us. *Never did I know such loving words were held within the Bible, always have I believed it to be a book of lies made to gain power for the malevolent, but then again even evil can masquerade as partial good,* Zacharias thought to himself. Finally, Kelly who was the leader of the refugees stepped forward. Personally, she thanked each and every wife along with their families before addressing the crowd. "Nothing we can give you will pay for all you've done for us. Please at least let us bless this village." Kelly and the other refugees prayed along with the children over the eleven wives and gave them all a mighty blessing of loyalty, honor, but above all else, love. This love was very special; this was the kind of shared love only shown between those who purely cared for their neighbor for this was unconditional love.

For the next three weeks, the citizens of Salem took in the refugees of Malastay. Zacharias and Joseph along with the other men were able to rest and recover their wounds. Kelly, in particular, took care of the young warrior she was fond of. That breakfast, Joseph, Penelope, Zacharias, and Mariana sat at the table as they normally would and a knock was heard at the door. "I'll get it," Penelope said as she was already up. Opening the door, the gentle voice of Kelly gave a gleeful bid good morning. "Oh come in, Kelly, how are you this morning?" Penelope asked as she invited her in for breakfast. Kelly sat at the table as Mariana who was pressed against Zacharias's arm smiled for she called her the new big sister. Today, Kelly was very well put together and had her hair and eyes beautifully arranged by makeup native to Calina. "You look so pretty today, you have to show me how to do my hair like that," Penelope exclaimed. "Ha," Joseph laughed, then added, "You're not twenty anymore, honey." Penelope flung a sweet roll against his mouth. Everyone laughed as Zacharias said in a shy tone, "You look very nice today, Kelly."

"I'm glad you noticed. It took you long enough," she said with wide eyes yet broadening. Joseph replied to him, "Loyal friend, expert swordsman, and Guardian of Salem, yet not one much for romancing," he stated, nudging his side. Zac gave him a monotone stare in return as Penelope and Kelly giggled. Together, they sat and conversed over a wide array of things just like a family until Joseph asked Kelly as to what the refugees' plans were long-term. "We're going to go to Evangela to the city of Antioch," she answered prominently. "Ah, Antioch where we were first called Christians, originally made to be a negative title if you did not know," Joseph chanted.

Penelope jumped in, "Joseph and I were born in Antioch, his family lineage dates all the way back to the times of Sir Abraham Desteeran and the holy knights." "Desteeran," Zacharias questioned.

"Yes, the first holy knight of the Gentiles. Sir Abraham's last name was Desteeran. Why, do you know someone by that name?" Joseph asked.

"I once knew a teacher by that name, but he's dead now."

No one presses the matter further.

"If only the holy knights had been around, perhaps the tragedy of my people could have been avoided," Kelly stated with a slight bit of anger.

"So what is Evangela like?" Zacharias asked to everyone at the table.

"Really big," Mariana exclaimed.

Joseph seeing opportunity rushed in, explaining, "Evangela or free nation is a wonderful place where people from all over the world live together unhindered by national identity. It is the only region in our world unaffected by the monsters of the earth. People often forget that since the majority of cultures had to fight to attain that peace. People from all walks of life live there together: white, black, Sceran, Cruatian, or even eastern, it does not matter all have the common dream of what some deem as equality and the pursuit of happiness. Alas, the once beautiful nation of the holy knights or Sword of the Cross has become a nation of man's law. The elite rule by a centralized judiciary or judges if that works better for ya."

"That's a bit too much for this breakfast table, dear, nobody wants to hear a rant this early," Penelope stated to her husband.

"Sorry, I went off on a tangent, didn't I?" Zacharias thought to himself as to just what this Evangela was really like if people from all walks of life really could live together in harmony. "Let me add though, the people there are good people, sorry to sound a bit cryptic with that message," Joseph stated.

"I understand," Kelly replied. Also, she included, "Well, I really must be going, if you have time later, I'd really like to go for a walk with you, Zacharias." After she had left, Penelope turned to him. "So are you going to start courting or what, you two would be so good together."

"I'm not much of the loving type at this stage in my life."

Penelope shook her head. "You're hopeless. A perfect woman for you falls in your lap and you."

Just then, a loud commotion was heard in town, everyone got bundled up and went out. A local celebrity had made his way back home surrounded by an entourage of guards. His name was Fanero Malchior, who was currently regarded as the most famous playwright in western Vulgata; he was born and raised right here in Salem. Fanero was a blond-haired man of average height, who was wearing an expensive violet wardrobe resembling royalty. He also had a large top hat and a black cane with an all silver handle in the shape of a frog. Looking to Joseph and his family on the hill, he called out his name. "Good friend, how are you?" Fanero said to him with his effeminate voice. Zacharias took one look at him and immediately did not like him. He hugged Joseph, and as he did, they could see rare gem and ring on his fingers. "Still living here, Joseph? When will you come and work for me in the limelight?" Now Joseph had been a friend of Fanero's family from when he was a young boy and grew up teaching the boy in his church. When Fanero's parents died of sickness, he was left alone in the world. Joseph and the village watched over him and raised him as the village did with any orphans. "It's good to see you, Fanero, how are you these days?" Joseph asked, happy by his presence but slightly troubled by his exalted appearance.

"Fantastic, I just finished yet another play, and now the Church of Law in Valencia has asked me to unveil it during the Week of Commemoration!"

"That's quite an honor, Fanero, your parents would be proud of that," Joseph told him. Joseph also could see in his mind that Fanero had fallen to the vile trap of fame and fortune. Zacharias attempted to walk down the hill past him to get on with his day, but he was stopped by one of the guard's spears. "Back up, commoner," the guard yelled in a snide tone. These soldiers are clad in a fine chainmail that rests underneath hardened leather. Zacharias drew his blade and cut the spear in half. "Draw another weapon on me and you'll mimic that spear!" The other guards were ready to attack him when Fanero calmed the situation. "Do you carry the large sword on your back for show or can you actually wield it, sir?"

"Zacharias," Joseph told him.

"That name suits you, do you have any idea what your name means?" Fanero asked him condescendingly. Penelope crossed her arms ready to fight herself.

"His name means God hath remembered," Penelope then yelled out.

"Precisely, you do well to remember that, young warrior, for God does remember our wrongdoings especially when common dogs oppose those of royal blood," Fanero added in a prideful tone, chin high leaning on his staff. But it was that grin that look of unadulterated supremacy, the one where every fiber of hair from the individual points to your disdain of them. Zacharias was about to shoot back a line that would have started a battle when

Joseph then stepped in. Sternly, he started in on him, "Fanero, what happened to change you so? Once you were a loving and kind person to all, do you not forget the humble upbringing you had here? Also do not ever misuse the word of God at my home again for in the eyes of the Lord, the saved are all His children!" Fanero put his hand over his mouth as if truly caught off guard.

"Joseph, I would have thought a poor man like yourself, would have been excited to see me rise to the next level in society. We all have to answer to money." He then gifted Joseph a small sack of gold coins to prove his point. Joseph took the bag and then tossed it on the ground.

"I take back my words of your parents being proud of you. They didn't die praying for their son to turn his back on what is righteous." Fanero then rolled his eyes, running his left hand across his mouth.

"Those weren't my parents, Joseph, for my mother is fame and my father fortune, and they have made a giant of me. All who raised me should be grateful to have held the honor and now prestige of having created another of high society's ruling class." Joseph and Penelope put their hands on Zacharias's shoulder as they stepped in front of him.

"Be gone from my house, Fanero, but know you may return if you ever decide to apologize not to me but to the Lord." Fanero brushed his coat where Joseph had touched it as one of the guards went to grab the bag of gold.

"Leave the scraps for the cur," Fanero commanded as he left.

"Sorry about that, he was once a better man," Joseph told him as Penelope acknowledged this as truth.

"Any man who needs others to guard him is a coward and he is no exception, it is that kind of elitist thinking that pollutes the success of man," Zacharias explained, now tromping away.

Once in the village, he was going to talk with Kelly about her plan to migrate to Evangela with the other refugees when he saw more of Fanero's guards around. "I wonder what they're up to," he pondered, watching them enter the art gallery followed by pursuing. Two of the guards had entered before him and gone into the back room; quickly, he darted back to see what they were doing because he heard arguing. Boom! He'd run directly into a young woman and knocked her over. Right away, he helped her up. "I am so sorry, that was entirely my fault, can you forgive me?" he told her as he frantically searched for other words to ease the situation. The woman was of exotic beauty for she was a Cruatian (people of the ocean); she had hair far more white than the snow outside and eyes of priceless emerald. In the most warm and serene voice he had ever heard, she replied, "It's all right," the glimmering pearl states from the calming ocean floor. His heart felt as though it was going to fail at the mere sight of this beautiful young woman. "What is your name?" she asked him.

"Why would you want to know my name?" She looked at him as if she was able to peer directly into his soul with her spectacular green eyes complimented with long black eyelashes. Then she stated to him, "Why do you not find self-worth? You're kind and very handsome." His lips and nose clench desperately searching for words to say. "My name is Zacharias and you are?" Giving off a masterpiece of a smile that carried the waves of a healing heart, she states, "Cordelia, my name is Cordelia Faverent."

"You have an enchanting name, Ms. Faverent." Cordelia, who was wearing a blue dress, bobbed a curtsy respectfully to him. At this moment, the guards came out of the back room carrying a strange painting as if it were a child. Cordelia rotated her head to the guards and her hair immediately turned dark blue like her dress. Zacharias's eyes expanded, resembling the feeding whale. "Hah, your face is priceless," she said to him. "What? Like that painting the guard is holding as if his life depends on it?" Cordelia let out the kind of laughter she would not have graced anyone else with and took interest in him; her hair then turned back to its white color, no blemish or defect. "So you're a warrior with a sense of humor, very rare indeed, but you're also good looking, you must have a woman in your life," she asked.

"Flattering, but no, I've never loved a woman before, and how did you know I was a warrior?"

"Perhaps the sword on your back, and has anyone ever told you that you have honest eyes," she said in a really animated voice.

"Wow, you flatter me more than I deserve," he answered.

"No, I really meant that, I find you to be genuine," Cordelia reinforced. Just then Fanero waltzed in with the rest of his guards. "Cordelia, we're leaving!" Zacharias turned and glared at Fanero, a wolf inside the gate an enemy of his home. "I'm glad we met, perhaps fate will bring us back together again one day," Cordelia sadly said. Cordelia strolled outside with the guards before quickly poking her head back in, asking one last question. "By the way, I didn't catch your last name?"

"Don't have one," he said with a wink.

"How can you not have a last name?" she asks.

"Why does your hair change color?" he counters.

"One day, when you give me your last name, I'll tell you why my hair changes color," she said, leaving with a bright grin. Cordelia left, Fanero entered, standing in the doorway tapping the wall with his cane. "Tsk, tsk, now you wouldn't be bothering my star attraction, now would you?" No reply is given. "What are you too good to speak to me or cannot a dog understand the pure language of an aristocrat?" Zacharias knew the game, trying to get him to strike him so his guards could justify a fight. "Let me make myself clear before I leave, if you ever talk to my star attraction again, I'll have you painfully murdered, understand?" Zacharias treads to the doorway and stops in front of Fanero face-to-face. "If you hate me so much, then why don't you do the honor yourself, you know like a man does, but if history has taught us anything, it is that men do not exist within aristocracy, only boys with power led by money unearned. Just as the silver frog on your cane implies greed, perhaps that's your real problem. Let me enlighten you, Fanero, greed is nothing more than a coward who must hide his infinite false pride behind mountains of material possession as a frog hides beneath a swamp fearful of predator. But who am I, but a common man of simple thought?" Zacharias explained, smirking at Fanero while also towering over him with a superb amount of physical stature. He then pushed him out of his way with his shoulder knocking Fanero flat on his behind. Fanero pointed his cane and yelled, "No one will remember your name, you're nothing, not even a scratch on a rock! As for me, I am a giant in the real world, and all know my name, Fanero Malchior!" Picking up his top hat and adjusting it, he met up with his guards and left the city with Cordelia.

When Fanero was yelling, many heard, but none as much as Kelly who watched the entire incident from the bakery. Zacharias proceeded onward as Kelly met up with him. "What did you do?" she asked.

"The self-proclaimed king barred my path, so in the game of chess, one must move pieces to secure victory."

"His tower will fall, he deserved it. Regardless, nobles have no power in these parts. I can't believe you met Cordelia Faverent, The Angel's Voice, they say she has the most beautiful voice heard in a century." Kelly then took his hands because she saw the stars in his eyes and knew instantly. "That's her, isn't it?"

He took a deep breath. "If only I was someone and could get a woman like that, Fanero's right, perhaps I am nothing, I don't even know my parents." He sank but Kelly wouldn't allow it. "You are something, you saved our lives, these people love you, Joseph and his family love you, any woman would be lucky to have a man half as good as you are."

"Thanks, Kelly, I needed to hear that." The two then went on a walk together. Sitting on the far hillside of the city, they watched the sun set that day.

"Zacharias, we're going to go to Evangela the day after tomorrow when the trade caravan arrives. If you want, you can come with us, it could be a new start."

"A new start sounds like a distant dream never leaving sight but just out of reach," he poetically stated.

Kelly coughed, asking, "You're still thinking about Cordelia?"

With a surprised look, he asked in return, "How did you know?"

She rolled her eyes. "A woman knows when a man has eyes for her or someone else."

"Kelly." He signals in facial expression before speech.

"Yes," she answered, grasping his hand all the more.

"Do you think a woman like that could ever fall for a man like me, someone who has never been at peace day to day?" Kelly's heart poured out to the gentle nature of Zacharias and laid a kiss unto his lips with everything that she was. He blinked for a few moments and thanked her.

"There, now you know how to kiss her when the right time comes," Kelly said as she helped him up. "Also Fanero claimed himself a giant but without the use of your heart, it all counts for nothing, you have a giant heart, Zacharias, never forget that for that is what makes one noble."

At dusk, he steps inside to Joseph who was sitting at the table with his pipe. Sitting beside him, he asks the pastor, "Love is tough. How do you know when a woman is the right one to marry?"

"I'm gonna need more tobacco for this conversation," Joseph jokingly says. "Honestly, you just know when you know."

"I see, I don't know anything about love between a man and a woman. I've never known a woman." Joseph inhaled his pipe to a level that made him cough.

"Sorry, I wasn't expecting you to say that. That's a good thing, keep that for when you get married."

"Why is that?" Zacharias asked with much interest.

"Well, when a husband and a wife lay with one another, that is a sacred act to be respected for that is the homage being paid of two becoming one flesh under God in the Holy Covenant of Marriage. It is how a man and a woman bond on the deepest of levels further bringing them together."

"Always am I intrigued at how you can relate all things to God, Joseph," Zacharias laughingly acknowledged. "Kelly asked me to go with her to Evangela the day after tomorrow," he told Joseph.

"Indeed, she did tell me that yesterday to see how Penelope and I would take it. You know we love you dearly, right?"

"Yes, you guys have done more for me than I could ever repay," as his inner being plunged to the dreadful thought of all this coming to an end.

"Well, I want you to go, I'm going to be going out on one last journey into the abyss." Joseph declares.

"I thought you were done with your journeys?"

"I was, but in the governor's memoirs, I've found something that could change everything."

Zacharias slightly stood up and hunched over closer. "What is it?"

"I believe I've found the location of the tomb of Sir Abraham Desteeran, firstborn of the holy knights. It is said that his legendary sword or the Sword of Abraham was buried with him. That sword is the one thing that could resurrect the holy knight's order and call forth the Twelve Exiles at the completion of the Trial of Kings." Forward, he inches more and more as Joseph began to say these things and his spirit was full of wonder and excitement.

"The ex what?" the clueless-to-the-issue swordsman replies with disarrayed word. Joseph in all seriousness revealed, "The Exiles are the twelve chosen to lead the world in the final days before the return of the savior before the holy judgment of God upon men and celestial being alike. The Seventh Exile will be the leader of the Exiles and he will bear what is known as the

Trinitarian Sword. The Trinitarian Sword is the final step for the Sword of Abraham and is the conclusion of the Trial of Kings." Zac's eyes gaped in disbelief.

"What does that even mean, what is the Sword of Abraham? I have no idea who these Exiles or what not's are, but if you're going on this adventure, then I am coming with you!"

Penelope came out from behind the living room. "I'm sorry I was eavesdropping, but let him go with you."

"I'm not blocking his choice," he argued.

"I've already made up my mind. I'm going with you with or without your permission, Joseph."

Penelope snickered as Joseph declared, "Get your things ready, then were leaving in two days for Avodah Mortis, nation of the dead."

"Nation of the dead?" Zac questioned, placing finger to ear.

"Yes, we're first exploring She'ol, the giant graveyard city. In the index of Codex Gigas I found the governor's notes. In those notes, he stated that the spirit of Pheme and Mammon came to him and revealed him this location. But it was by inviting that spirit into the city that drew the Murkans and destroyed it." Although Penelope was nervous for Joseph leaving on yet another journey, she was comforted that Zacharias would be going with him as she had stated. Still Joseph, Penelope, and especially Zacharias were all excited for the location of the blade that banished evil long ago from the lands had now been disclosed. Granted, they all understood that perhaps this location could be nothing but a fallacious assumption, but better to check and know than live in wonder. Unknown to our heroes, a far darker mystery lay brewing in the lands of the dead where even the mighty giants have all been but forgotten.

6

To Kindle a Dream

Part 1: Flint

The following morning was unusually orthodox; the refugees packed and spent their last day in Salem saying their good-byes. Joseph and Zacharias checked and rechecked to make sure they had everything they were going to need. Kelly made sure that all the widows and orphans were prepared to travel to Evangela the next day with the trade caravan. It was surmised that the journey would take less than a week on horseback with that many people. That night, Salem held a feast in honor of their friends who had blessed them by staying in the village. Although the refugees from Malastay didn't have much, they gave their tithes of 1/10 of what they owned to the families in their gratitude for everything they had done. They actually wanted to give the citizens more, but they would not allow them to bankrupt themselves before they were to start a new life. Minus Zacharias, they all prayed together that night for protection from dangers on the roads ahead. Everyone turned in early that night except Zacharias who sat on the edge of the city as the moonlight brought about its splendor on the mountainside. Filled with more stars in the twilight than he had ever seen, it was an astral masterpiece unmatched by any words Fanero could ever conjure. A piece of him wanted to live out his life here, but he knew it would kill him more not to go off on this adventure with Joseph. Deep in assessment, he wonders, "What kind of journey lies in wait, what kind of peril, what kind of rewards? Always have I wondered have I searched for my reason for my purpose, but always have I been left longing to know of why I even exist? These people showed me I was a person, that I wasn't alone, that we are all important. Never will I stop searching for that distant place the one said to only be in dream and star." Standing up, pointing his sword to the sky, a declaration is made: "God, if you are as merciful as Joseph claims, then reveal to me my destiny and make sense to me the riddle of Vulgata. Tell me why you took my grandfather and why you let this curse of death be bound to me. Do you hold the divine majesty to overcome death or does that only stop at mere words a storybook cannot fulfill? Whatever the truth may be, I am going to find it or die searching." After saying this, he sat back down, and Mariana joined, resting to his shoulder. "What are you doing up so late, little one?" he asked.

"I wanted to say good-bye to my big brother." His arm is placed around her as they sat watching the stars.

"You're my little sister, Mariana, and you know I love you."

"Why do you have to go?" she said with her lips curled and eyes that drew from a reservoir of immeasurable emotion often doubted in child.

"Your father has found something that could save a lot of people's lives, and I go to help him find this relic."

"What's a relic?"

Zac laughed. "Something from a long time ago that makes people remember things, things said to be lost forever."

Although a child, Mariana was remarkably intelligent and she reached in her rucksack, handing him her teddy bear, Mr.

Sebastian. "I want you to take him with you, so I don't become a relic and you forget."

He was stunned at the intellect of a child. "Mariana, I could never forget you, you saved my life." Mariana had a perplexed look, for suicide was one thing a child could not understand for it is not in a child's nature. "But, but you saved me from the green monster," she professed with all her blessed heart.

"You're right, Mariana, I did, but you showed me how to live." He then kissed her on the forehead. "Are you sure I can have Mr. Sebastian? He is your eldest friend," Zacharias stated while handing it back to her.

Mariana pushed the bear back to him. "No! He will protect you from being lonely because Jesus doesn't like anyone to be lonely." It was something he could not fully understand as of yet, but for some reason, the words "Faith of Child" kept ringing jubilantly. As he stood up and picked up Mariana to carry her home, she pointed to a shooting star that streamed across the night sky in all its celestial glory. Mariana hugged around his neck and lay her head down. "See, He did that to show you you're not alone."

The day of parting had arrived, and Penelope got up before dawn, cooking them a most grand breakfast. The merchants that had arrived conducted their trades honorably, exchanging gold and silver coin for lovely painting, song, and above all else, imaginative perspective. The wagons were many, and the guards well armed in steel weapon and armor, to travel Vulgata is no simple trek. Upon their armor, the symbol of man's law is present, for they were of Evangela, sent directly from Galatia. The city of Salem offered to pay these men to take the refugees, but their leader denied payment, he too was a believer in the Lord and pledged to take them there for free. This man, furthermore in his long speech with Joseph, discussed that he would carry the message of Malastay's fall unto the high courts of Evangela. Together, the Voltel family, Zacharias, and Kelly sat and broke bread one last time. Afterward, they gathered the townsfolk and refugees and everyone prepared to part ways. Joseph pulled out his world map from the attic and showed Zacharias their journey that would be taking them about a week's plus journey southeast. "All right, let's saddle up," Joseph yelled out to everyone. Kelly stood in front of the refugees of Malastay as Joseph and Zacharias stood in front of all the denizens of Salem.

"We wanted to thank you all for your kindness, hospitality, sacrifice, and love you've shown us," Kelly tearfully exclaimed. Penelope hugged her and said her good-byes.

"Don't you forget about us, okay," she said sniffling and handing her a single letter that she was not to read until she reached Evangela. Mariana was holding everything back and had become solely upset they had to leave again. She hugged her father Joseph as he said his good-byes, then Penelope gave Joseph a long lasting kiss, someone whistled. Most of all, everyone turned to Zacharias, the Guardian of Salem, who pulled out the teddy bear and got on his knee to thank Mariana for it. She crossed her tiny arms. "Daddy has to go because it is his job, but why can't you stay. You promised you wouldn't leave."

Speaking to her tenderly, he reveals, "Because I have to find out who I am. I'm sorry, I did make a promise, and I want to keep it more than anything, but it's just one of those things, you will understand when you're older." He then went to give her a hug, but she refused because she was mad. Joseph gave him a pat on the back. "Come on, friend, let's set off."

Zacharias then mounted the white stallion Grear and Kelly ran over. "Be careful out there, and remember, we'll be waiting to see you again one day in Antioch." He takes her hand and kisses it, then smiled at Mariana. "You know I could never forget any of you, and it is because of you why I must defend what I have come to love." Penelope gave him a silent nod, holding her right hand to her eyes, which were outlined in painful farewell. A sharp ray of light coats Salem. Zacharias glances over his shoulder at

Joseph who in return tightens the reigns of Jesibelle. They both gave a smirk as Joseph tipped his cavalier type hat and their horses reared up, launching them into a forceful charge down the mountain pass. Joseph drew his sword and pointed it forward, proclaiming for all to hear, "Never regret the past, always move forward, fighting to defend the truth that made you who you are, Atyrael be with you!" Mariana could be heard on the hill, yelling for them, but onward their horses rushed into the plains. Everyone watched this beginning as two heroes embarked on a quest unknown to them that would call forth their destiny, no matter how difficult the trials ahead. After they had left the lands of Calina, the air grew warm and the winter left not a single trace. This was the norm in Vulgata for only a day or two in any direction could yield extremely various weather conditions. It has always been like this in this world and has received an endless supply of fable and folklore to keep any guessing as to the actual nature of this matter. Regardless of legends yield, it seems at the roots of all understanding that interconnection always finds a home only revealed by the waters of sacrifice at the designated hour. Early on in the journey, they stopped at Hope's Lake where a miracle happened and Joseph was able to catch dozens of fish in just one afternoon. "You're one phenomenal fisherman," Zacharias said to him for he only caught one. Joseph shared his catch with him. "Eh, I'm more of a fisher of men really."

"Hmm, well, I can't believe you caught so many, I only got one," he slightly vented.

"It only takes one" Joseph reinforced.

That night, they slept by the lake, but Zac woke halfway through the night in a cold sweat. Joseph awoke startled. "What is it?"

"Nothing, just a bad nightmare, that's all, let's go back to sleep."

But it wasn't just a bad dream; he saw something in his nightmare within the lake. When Joseph had returned to his slumber, the curious young man tiptoed over to the lake and examined his reflection. His image began to move about on its own even though he was stationary. Faintly, his reflection spoke, but a single word repeatedly by inaudible syllable: "Manistof." A small splash was heard at the other end of the lake; frightened by this, he peered at what seemed to be a figure standing in one of the trees. Grear was also startled, staring in the same direction. Gently, a soothing gust exhibits, causing the branches to sway revealing no such intruder. He then returned to sleep, believing they were not alone, but nothing of the matter could be done.

For the rest of the week, the two headed southeast, passing through field, plain, stream, also seeing other monsters in the distance around unpopulated lands. Some stammer around scratching their living off the very rock as others can be heard screaming as terror in the night, hungry for the shadow within shadow. Twisted tails cursed in bloodied feather, tainted limbs protruding to biological impossibility, and claws as eyelids scraping the sight, it makes one wonder, where is God in this broken earth this cesspool of sin? The mission shouldered by our heroes although of good intent is hindered greatly by these many nightmares that scourge the lands. An even worse reality was that compared to the creatures such as those that dwelt within the days of old, these were nothing. Perhaps it was by the mercy of God man had survived this long. On this day, they passed through a series of geyser fields; the ground is a broken sort of clay for miles in every direction. "What is this?" Zacharias asked.

"I read in a book once that geysers were only around volcanoes. So I assume it's connected somehow to Continent's Peak, which is just a colossal volcano," Joseph explained.

"Something feels weird about this, I can't explain it but something just gives me a strange notion above my regular senses, like a message is written here from long ago."

"Perhaps your soul is speaking to you. In fact, that has to do with spirituality if it is indeed the soul speaking even past the mind." He disregarded the answer and the two trotted through on their horses, and all of a sudden, hundreds of geysers let loose. Water jetted forth over a hundred feet into the air. For a moment, they were frightened because the water could have been hot enough to scald them. As it came down, it was ice-cold, which actually felt amazing in the blazing sun. The sound of water bursting forth and raining onto the clay like ground made a song all of its own. Another traveler passed by them who was on foot. "Hello, how are you today, friend," Joseph asked in jovial voice. The man appeared to be all alone in the world and took no notice to Joseph at first. "Well, I'm hungry, let's sit and eat," Joseph told him as he went and sat in a dry spot where no water had fallen. Zac sat and began eating some bread with a fish cooked earlier as Joseph went and asked the man if he'd have lunch with them. The man was very old and disclosed that he had nothing to eat or drink. Joseph brought him over to sit with them and broke fish and bread, sharing it with him. The man ate with them that day and blessed them for sharing with him. When it was time for them to move on, Joseph gave him one of their leather canteens, the water was gathered from the flowing geysers birthing life. Saying good-bye, Joseph asked, "What is your name, traveler?"

In a caring voice, the man said, "Lazarus, my name is Lazarus, and today, you have honored the Lord in a mighty way. Is it She'ol you travel to?"

"Yes, it is our intent to enter Continent's Peak within the nation of the dead."

The man said his final words before leaving, "We all must sleep at some point, but only in Christ Jesus can we wake up and walk." The man laid hands upon them both, then left them as they marched through the geyser fields. Zacharias did not understand but noticed he felt raised in spirit.

Later that night, they approached the city of She'ol, meaning grave, pit, or abode of the dead. This city rested near the King's Highway, which was a road constructed connecting the outskirts of Valencia to Avodah Mortis, Athens, Bordeaux, Valinth, and the city of Grias. Tens of thousands of gravestones are seen as far as the eye can see as a full moon illuminates the lamented city. Great bones spiral out of the ground from an array of beasts whose time is long past. Another larger bone pathway holding the appearance of a massive and endless ribcage sits at the center of the decaying civilization, drowning in unnatural dirt. They stick out of the ground for miles, some fifty feet wide and more so high, leading to Avodah Mortis. Continent's Peak points up to the heavens, proving just how mighty Vulgata is. Around the base of the volcano, a gigantic city sits with buildings constructed into its sides. Wooden bridges connect the city built of rock among the peak that extends to an immeasurable height. Zacharias's hand sits over his mouth, looking at the endless series of graves.

"Joseph, why are all these here?"

"World War I," Joseph informs in a type of despondent voice as a single bolt of lightning prepares the coming storm. Joseph stared at the peak as thunder was heard in the distance. "In the year 2598, WWI broke out between east and west. Never had east and west engaged in worldwide conflict before that date. In the first months of the war, the casualties from both sides were so severe that getting all the bodies back home was impossible. Disease began to spread killing more and more, so finally, a plan was devised and Avodah Mortis was established. The ten-year war raged on and would become known as The Big 10. Well over a million gave their lives for the western alliance and each of these graves contains multiple bodies so it adds up fairly easily."

"Why is it I've never heard of this?" Zacharias asked.

Sliding down the damp hill to the city of She'ol, Joseph further informed him, "What happened in The Big 10 has left a remaining scar on the political landscape that may never fade, few talk about it, and it is well hidden from most history books. Much more than east versus west, the ten-year war was decided by the war of the three knighthoods that were armored in white, silver, and black. The black-armored Drudge Knights of eastern

Marduas were both without mercy and driven by hate for all things religious vowed to dismantle Valencia and her proclaimed holy institutions. This was not without purpose for Valencia had proclaimed Marduas unholy and placed a permanent embargo act against all trades to or from the east thus crippling their economy. Trade was prevalent in those days, especially for eastern export. The Silver Paladins vowed to protect the Church of Law in Valencia against all enemies foreign and domestic. At that time, the west was united, so an attack on one nation meant an attack on the entire west. Almost overnight, the world was pulled into the first ever world war over religion as the black knights set foot on western soil, assassinating a top chancellor of the Valencian Empire. Finally, the white-armored Holy Knights fought to end the war, but their motives were not of political or religious interest. The holy knights fought to defend those who could not defend themselves for Vendalas was the first nation to fall under the drudge knight's rule in which they massacred all its civilians, that's why it is in ruins to this day, which I'm sure you already knew. The silver paladins were outnumbered and decimated by the drudge knights they once deemed as weak pagans without purpose. Fact is, the drudge knights were also driven by a belief, they wanted to end all dogmatic rule in the world not just religious teachings. It would be the holy knights at the end of the day that defeated the drudge knights, but they would never fully join the silver paladins for they believed the Church of Law's hierarchy to be an organization fallen to hypocrisy and malevolence. It would be that public declaration that would forever split apart the holy knights of Evangela and the silver paladins of Valencia. Only thirty-two years after the war, in the year 2640, the holy knights were exiled from Evangela in which Valencia decreed them enemies of the western state for the destruction of the Devokian people. Finally, it was revealed to the world by both Evangela and Valencia that the holy knights had fallen to the will of the evil one using black magic and sorcery. The holy knights were never heard from again. So was the true conclusion of WWI in my opinion with those in black defeated, those in white exiled, and the victor bearing a false silver crown."

"I don't believe the holy knights would do such a thing as to resort to sorcery, Joseph, it just doesn't add up," Zac stated upset.

"I agree, my brother, and that is why we are going to find this sword and hopefully disprove what history has done to them."

"Joseph, why is this sword so important?" Zac asked. Joseph would then go on to explain to him about Abraham's long ten-year process of constructing the blade and his battle with the three sons of Satan that led to Evangela's and the orders' beginning.

After this conversation, large groups of people were seen waltzing from grave to grave. "How peculiar is that?" Zacharias said.

"Yes, those of Avodah Mortis worship the idea of death being humanities' purpose," Joseph told him. Rain then began to fall as they could see hundreds of people appearing out among the graves, worshiping them. Happily yet eerily, they danced and sang in a foreign language; Joseph noticed one man pretending to speak in tongues and rebuked him in thought. "So do you remember that bad feeling I had, Joseph, I think it's pretty self-evident right about now." Zac laughed, but Joseph did not; he is very bothered by this. Pulling their horses behind them as to give them a break, they began to walk on the long stretch of dirt road through the bone trenches. In all directions, it was a wasteland of graves with people not noticing their presence or perhaps just not caring. "Joseph, do you have any idea what these great bones are from?"

"I can't tell you why they're lined up like this, but I can tell you they're also from WWI. Back then, both east and west commanded powerful and immense fiends from all over the earth. A great deal were enslaved in the Valencian-deemed Holy Restoration War, then passed down from generation to generation with the offspring bred for war. They were to be kept as national defense only, but when WWI was not going as planned, the colossal devils were called in, man waged war with weapons he could not control." Zacharias glanced up at the curved and narrow bones that were seemingly sharpened to fashion some kind of royal pathway and tapped Titulus against it. "Don't you ever find it sad we as humans use even creatures for war? I mean, they don't know why we fight. Sometimes, I feel ashamed to be a human being." Joseph pondered for a minute on the statement. "Well, you're right in saying to use them for our plans can be selfish, but I would say if you're fighting for the right reasons, perhaps it's a blessing. Take the sword on your back for instance, it is not inherently good or evil, but one could argue it is a mere tool for he who wields it. Don't get me wrong. I love animals, but I hope you understand my point."

"I do, you make a good point, Joseph, this place is just depressing. Let's go find this tomb already, I've been excited over this for days." Further down the road, Zacharias noticed the appearance of a strange woman outside of the bone trenches, playing a harp transparent in appearance. Rain was now pounding on the ground, making visibility low, so they took refuge under a lumbering bone as if from an ancient dragon. The woman's face was painted in a ghastly fashion and she was in a jester outfit not seen for hundreds of years. The left shoulder of this outfit held the countenance of a smiling white mask while the right held the same, only it was sad. Playing the harp, she was also singing a dirge to the name of Lily; she was weeping in between notes. Emanating from the gravestone was a thick mist that began to fill the surrounding area. He called out, "Hey, what are you doing?" She began to play drastically faster the closer he got to her. "Are you okay?" he asked now soaked, touching her shoulder. When he did this, she turned around and gave a devilish smirk as her body fell apart. Her face melted before his very eyes in a graphic and acidic fashion, but as this was happening, she began to speak to him. In agony and sadness, she called out for help, but as he tried to console her, she grabbed his shoulders tightly. Holding her off, he was within inches of the grotesque face that was falling apart onto his arms. With her top layer of skin missing, she held a joyous grin as eyes and mouth opened to a point where her jaw ripped off and eyes fell out, hanging by optic nerve, but they did not stop staring at him. "Peekaboo! I have found you little bastard child of Manistof," she screamed, pulling him closer with demonic strength, then laughing hysterically. Joseph smashed her off him with a monstrous kick, which sent her body crumbling into a pile of mush; he then helped his friend to snap out of the fear. They return to the saddles of their horses.

In the distance, a pack of Alreeth is seen flying in the skies. Alreeth, which dwell within mountainous regions on average, is a creature the size of a large horse that has the appearance of a dragon but functions much like the hawk. Coated in a dark violet carapace, they are mildly armored, but this armor is made for offense for it comes to sharp points along the top portions of their long wingspans. The Alreeth normally wait upon the sides of cliffs and swoop down on their prey one at a time with their wings smashing into them like a storm of lance and spear. Having one large eye, which takes up their entire head, they can see perfectly over large distances. Their mouths are located where the stomach should be that opens horizontally with three rows of razor sharp teeth. At the edge of their wings, small talons sit for swiping when they reach the ground and walk on their two hind legs. As these beasts were swooping in and out of the crowds among the graves, Joseph and Zacharias saw one group of seven people's skulls and torsos get dismembered by the flying guillotines traveling at incredible speeds. The six Alreeth were flying in a clockwise circle, in the sky, taking turns diving into the crowds of people. Each time another rejoined the ranks of the other five, the blood coating was washed off by the thick rains. One of the Alreeth moves into attack position against the heroes and plunges down at them. They dive off their horses as its wings cut the very rain around them. The beast landed and began walking over to them, standing at about nine feet with its wings sprawled and its mouth on its stomach opening and closing without reason. Its wings were stained in the blood of those it had just killed; together, both of them grasped blade for battle. "Get back," Joseph screamed at Zacharias. The beast was locked onto Joseph, wobbling one step at a time with its massive red eye fixed on him. "Zacharias, get behind it, we'll use a pincer attack, it can't be easy for this thing to pivot!" He rushed behind it and cut the left wing off. The beast gave off a piercing deranged squawking noise that alerted the others. It turned with its other wing, knocking down Joseph with a loud smack, and began to hobble over to Zacharias. In this chaos, the crowds were running in their direction being chased by the rest of the pack. One man ran into Zacharias, knocking him to the ground. The beast with one wing swung it around the man and trapped him against the creature's stomach where its mouth was located. Desperately, he struggled to gain his freedom kicking and shrieking wildly, but it was hopeless. From the mouth, a sharpened tongue constricted his chest, pulling him into the mouth. Zac watched in horror as he could hear the bloodcurdling screams while bones crunched in its powerful jaws. Mangled pieces of the man fell to the ground along with half his face locked in terror, sticking to the leg of the Alreeth. With each bite continued more pieces of the mangled body fell mixed with cartilage, tendon, and sinew, the sight is unbearable the sight is a herald of the dreadful and endless tortures within hell. The rest of the pack then came swooping upon them and four more people were diced in half, and for a moment, their legs could be seen running without their torsos as they were in shock violently spewing gore in all direction. *This must be stopped. This has to end! Justice must stand. These people need help now! God, where are you?* Zacharias beckons in his fear whilst slipping in the mud, still reaching. When he looked back, the beast on the ground was charging him screeching with blood now covering its entire stomach and wing where the man was eaten alive. "Joseph," he calls desperately, swinging at the beast to keep it away, for it was trying to fall on him, meaning certain doom. Just then, a sword plunged out of the beast's red eye and a yellow mushy liquid gushed forth. "Have a nice journey to hell," Joseph yelled as the beast fell over him on the back.

Five more remained in the sky as they readied themselves for the real fight. "We have to get out of here, we can't beat that many," Joseph commanded. He then gave a loud whistle and their horses returned in which they then mounted and galloped into the bone trenches for cover. Hiding in the bone trenches, the other five Alreeth circled above, unable to swoop at the base where the bones were thick. Dozens of others hid also as Joseph stated, "Sulfur, I smell sulfur." Suddenly, the rain became warm and, soon after, slightly hot. A lightning bolt displays itself halfway between She'ol and Avodah Mortis in the shape of a demonic figure watching over them. Everyone saw this, and in horror, they fled, sticking to the overhanging walls for safety, but the Alreeth stayed. The sulfur smell continually grew increasingly potent as the rain's temperature rose. All five of the Alreeth burst into a transcendent flame and came crashing to the ground inside the bone trench. Screaming in pain, they went berserk, running into walls and even fighting each other; the flame would change from red to black every few seconds. "Now's our chance, let's go," Zacharias said to Joseph, ready to charge in on Grear.

"Wait," Joseph advised.

"What is it?"

Joseph then reached in to one of his packs on Jesibelle and pulled out a vial of holy water with a golden cross engraved on the bottle. "Hold out your sword." Joseph then poured the holy water on both their blades, then nodded to make the attack. Charging across the trenches, they advanced upon the balls of fire. "I have the right flank, you go left," Joseph ordered. Their swords easily slashed through the Alreeth's flesh, and in their frenzied state, they were able to catch four of them off guard. On the last one, the two of them converged, but it took off in flight inside of the trenches, hovering to the main city of Avodah Mortis. Galloping behind it, the two champions were unable to catch up but stayed in pursuit. Joseph grabbed his bow off the side of Jesibelle and readied his arrow with eyes of true sight. Carefully, he aimed the incredibly difficult shot while galloping at high speeds. A young woman had fallen and hurt her leg in the trench far ahead, and the winged abomination was soon to catch up to her. Fire from it swept backward, and all at once, all of the skin rolled away, flinging at Zacharias. Instinctually, Grear maneuvers out of the way; Titulus catches the blazing carapace, forcing it and him to the ground. Zacharias called on Joseph, "Shoot the damn thing now!" Joseph fires and hit the creature directly in the soft spot on its heel, which caused the fiery abomination to look back and run into the bone as it then crashed into the dirt path. As it was fighting to get back up with its dislocated neck, Joseph then rode by and slashed its skull clean off. Titulus remains one with the earth, wrapped in an inferno, Grear rests beside. Standing before his companion, Zac kneels to the horse, petting him then thanking him. The white stallion stands then bows to the claymore whose flame is purged. "How did you do that?" Touching the hilt, he realizes it is hot but not unbearable, so he draws Titulus from the grounds of the dead unto his right hand. Grear neighs upon his hind legs; the iron gates around Avodah Mortis open. "Are you okay?" Joseph began to ask the woman whose leg was injured he had just saved. She would not speak, but when she looked to the gates, she smiled. A group of people marched to them from the city; among them was a man who stood over seven feet tall. He wore a black overcoat with one long row of gray buttons and was completely bald; on his forehead rests a tattoo of a pyramid with a closed eye serving as the capstone. "Welcome, my friends," the man said in a deep yet kind voice with his arms held open. "Are you the ones I have prophesied about that are to enter into the mountain to complete the Trial of Kings?"

Joseph stood in front of the man, obviously wary of his intentions. "Hello, I am Joseph Voltel, and this is my friend Zacharias." The tall man pointed his hands at the fallen woman, and they picked her up and began carrying her into the city. "My name is Mortician, and I am the leader of this the people of the dead."

PART 2: TINDER

Mortician and everyone else returned to the city constructed of stone, asking the destined travelers to follow. "What of your people who lay fallen among the fields?" Joseph asked him.

Mortician laughed. "What of them? Is it not time we celebrate over their passing, yes?"

Utterly insulted, Zac stops Mortician grabbing his shoulder. "Are you inferring that we should celebrate the ordeal of slaughter that just happened?"

Mortician placed his oversized thumb over his chin and then smiled as he towered them. "I see you do not know our venerated customs, allow me to share our belief so perhaps you may reach a new degree of enlightenment. Death is the only thing that lasts forever, and one day, everything, including Vulgata, is going to fade away into stardust. All that will be left are memories of the earth and her inhabitant's eternal dreams. The people of Avodah Mortis have risen above meaningless cares such as terrestrial purpose. What matters is who we were, my son, nothing else, so depending on how you die, that is how you will be remembered. Those people who died in that field died in a glorious way, we all envy their finale, and by merit, they will never be forgotten for their loneliness was slaughtered and offered as sacrifice to the lunar gods above." Zacharias was so appalled by this he became furious, producing his claymore before Mortician, stating, "If you want your death of merit so bad, maybe I could give you that right now!" Joseph eased his wrath, asking him to put his sword down; he obeyed. Mortician smirked and closed his eyes, now looking at Zacharias with the all-seeing eye upon his forehead, which began to open. While his eyes remained closed, he said, "This is all just a misunderstanding, it's not as if we didn't care for them, they've just gone on ahead of us, that's all. But do know I would welcome death by a warrior of your status, oh, how that would honor me so and furthermore set me up as an oblation all my own." Mortician then pointed up to the sky. "Don't you see, young Zacharias, even now the souls of the deceased eternally rest among the stars, leaving clues of what was, what is, and what is to come forever outside the realm of time." Mortician attempts to spiritual dominate Zacharias but is countered in silent prayer by Joseph; spiritual battle takes place between the two with the third fully unaware. Joseph then asked him about the volcano. Mortician's eyes rolled open as if coming back into reality. "Yes, we were excavating around the peak to find new burial spots for those of royal lineage when we came upon an ancient doorway."

"Can you take us to it" Joseph asked. Mortician began to go toward the base of the peak at the eastern side of the city. He then put his hand on his sides, kneeling to Joseph, asking a single question, "So what do you think about death of merit, Mr. Voltel?" Joseph, who was deeply troubled by the question and the culture, fired back. "Do know it is my job in life to preach the word of God. Salvation cannot be earned by any kind of man's so-called merit, and living life with that ideology will only bring damnation. I say this as a friend bringing the truth, Jesus Christ died to forgive sins because no one can go to the Father but by the Son." Mortician, now serious, began to articulate his already planned-out rebuttal. "Did not Jesus earn his true merit after he died on the cross and his life came to an end?" Joseph was a phenomenal debater and did not get angry as he felt Mortician's plan was to make him look bad in front of his people but far more Zacharias. Perhaps that was even his plan all along in his connective speech to first gain the agnostics' attention, then attempt to falsely refute the gospel by the devil's eye of impure knowledge. Instead, Joseph pulled out his Holy Bible, remembering one of Jesus's I am statements, also allowing the Holy Spirit to command him as he had been from the start. Joseph glanced to Mortician and read:

> Je'-sus said unto her, I am the resurrection, and the life: he that believeth in me, though he were dead, yet shall he live: And whosoever liveth and believeth in me shall never die. Believest thou this?
>
> John 11:25–26 (kjv)

"So, Mortician, my question for you is simple if Jesus said I am the resurrection and the life, how can his life have ended on the cross? Now he did die on the cross, for all people face the first death, which is of flesh for the flesh must die for the spirit to live, but three days later, rose from the dead, the resurrection, and forty days later ascended to heaven to be seated on the right hand of God so in that he did not perish." Mortician then scrambled for an answer for many of his people had heard this.

"Our heaven is our name."

"What was that?" Joseph asked.

"Our heaven is our name so we reach for the means that is all, I am done with this conversation," Mortician told them as they had reached the door. Joseph winked at Zacharias, knowing he had stumped him. Pointing at the door, Mortician explained that none of them could enter and had been trying to open the door for weeks but were unable. They did not attempt to dig in from another route out of fear of causing a collapse. This was all a farce; the truth was this was a holy site, and they were unable to draw near. The door was two massive white stone tablets, a foot or more thick that stood with the legendary seal of the holy knights engraved into it half on each side. This seal is a grand golden cross that is also a sword; just as the holy knights' seal, the sword's hilt stands upward and the bottom is the point. "Let me try," Zacharias boldly stated.

"There is zero chance you're getting that door open," Joseph said, chuckling between them. He placed his hands inside the stone tablets' crack that went down the middle. Forcibly Zac pulled and pulled it didn't even budge. "Joseph, we have to get in there!" Out of breath, he stepped back and bumped into a tarp that caused him to trip and fall. "Be careful, young master, that's an artifact we found right there in front of that door," Mortician explained. Joseph then walked up to the door and noticed dirt covering a single engraved word at the foot of the cross; rubbing it off, he says aloud, "Genesis!" Joseph, being a godly man, searched through spiritual understanding on the subject. Joseph ponders to himself, "Genesis, meaning beginning or introduction, how does that correlate with this door? God being the beginning and Jesus being the light of truth perhaps a reference to alpha and omega. So if we speak through synonymous illustration, then that means end should be a factor. I've got it! Just like how Jesus returns!" Joseph then opened his Bible again:

> Ask, and it shall be given you; seek, and ye shall find; knock, and it shall be opened unto you: For every one that asketh receiveth; and he that seeketh findeth; and to him that knocketh it shall be opened.
>
> Mathew 7:7–8 (KJV)

After reading that, Joseph knocked on the door and backed up as it began to open. The two stone tablets opened up and then crashed to the ground. The one on the right fell on the tarp and ripped it off where Zacharias had tripped. Sitting there was a hole where a massive twenty-five foot tall skeleton of a humanistic corpse sat reaching for the door as if it were the last act of the giant. Zacharias, Joseph, and Mortician all stared at the skeleton with each of their minds concerned with a separate issue. Joseph worries "Nephilim" under his breath, Zacharias said "Manistof" in his mind, and Mortician also whispered to himself, "Master." Mortician stands beside Zacharias, "Allow me to lay my hands upon thee in this the revelation of your brother." The offer is dismissed frankly.

It was now morning, and regardless of the skeleton, the two heroes valiantly went forth into the deep dark tunnels of the mountain without thought or hesitation, only preparing two torches as to light the way. Behind them their horses follow after Joseph gives another whistle; they most certainly were not going to leave them with the people outside. For the next half of the day, they travel through the dark dry tomb until they enter a main chamber room where spots of sunlight are able to peak in. In the room stands a giant circular wooden cog with twelve points around it. On each of the points is a drawing of a zodiac sign. All twelve zodiac signs surround the wheel each thirty degrees apart, and in the core, a thirteenth sign is modeled. A man bearing the snake stands as the symbol known as the snake bearer or the great healer. To the right side, another stone door sits; Joseph attempts the same thing he did before, but nothing happens. For the next hour, they try everything to moving the cog, which will not budge, to prying the door, the result was the same. Joseph tries scripture after scripture and nothing happens. Tired and frustrated, the two take a nap and are awoken by Grear and Jesibelle hours later after nightfall. Joseph, thrilled by a glorious clue, yelled, "Zacharias, wake up, the door is open!" He wakes up and they can barely see a thing, so he lights his torch and the cog turns and the door slams to the ground. The zodiac signs glow with the moonlight. "Ha, that's it, Ophiuchus, the thirteenth zodiac." Joseph smacked himself in the noggin. "Ophiuchus." Zacharias held out his hands in rotated fashion.

"Yes, Ophiucus, the bearer of the snake, referring to Jesus being the light. Watch, put out your light, Zacharias." He did and the cog turned, making the door yet again open, but this time, a hint was left shining at the feet of Ophiuchus. It read:

(For we walk by faith, not by sight:)

2 Corinthians 5:7 (KJV)

"We have to traverse this final path by faith in Jesus not by our own rebellious sight." Joseph showed Zacharias his Bible to better prove it. Joseph then added, perhaps you should wait here. I don't know what will happen if a nonbeliever goes in there."

"I appreciate your sentiment, but regardless, I'm going in there."

"This is not a good idea. I don't like this," Joseph says to him, verily worried.

"I know how to get in there now, so I'm going in whether you allow it or not," Zac says back defiantly.

"Do you really feel it wise to test the Lord?" the pastor then throws in, knowing he will most likely be met with hostility. A deep breath is taken by the young man, who then runs his palms through his hair, exhaling loudly. Nothing else is said on the matter as they leave behind their horses. Joseph enters into the door and it was pitch-black; hearing his friend follow behind, he worries all the more. The path is narrow and they had to walk sideways at first just to squeeze through. Behind them, the door closed and Zacharias's fight or flight response began to take hold. "Are you all right?" Joseph asked, reaching for him.

"I'm fine. I just can't see a thing," as he ran into a wall. Joseph asked him to come over to him and keep his hand on his shoulder to help guide him. "You're as blind as I am in here," Zac stated dumbwittedly as he started to light his torch, ignoring the wisdom of the scripture out front.

"Don't light that torch!" It was too late, and as he did, the floor he was standing on opened up and swallowed him to a deep chamber within the tomb. Meanwhile, where Joseph was standing, the floor immediately closed back up and he began to yell but nothing was heard.

Alone in a pitch-black tomb, Zacharias calls out to Joseph repeatedly, but there is no reply. "Definitely should've listened, why do I always have to be so stubborn?" he states, patting his own skull where he fell on a rock. Then the voice of a little girl in the distance surprised him. Gradually, he crept to the sound. A melody is heard from the voice of a little girl drawing memories from his childhood as many things seemed to do. Following the tune, he passes around what was thought to be a corner. Beyond reach, the child stands illuminated in vibrant color and life even though everything else was dark. "Am I dreaming?" The little girl looks just like a young version of Cordelia whom he had met in Salem. "Cordelia," he called out. No reply was given as she danced in the shadows personifying love and laughter; her hair shone as the winter's flurry, still white like he had first seen her in the art shop. She began to dance along an even more blackened hallway. "Wait, wait," he calls out, chasing after her, running into each painful barrier. The further along she got, the older she became until he saw her as a teenager wailing over of a gravestone with her name upon it. "You're not alone, I'm here, please stop crying," he yelled out. She disappeared through a door that closed behind her and he knocked. Her voice yelled back, "Go away, I want to die!" Her request is denied while he infiltrates through the door. Grown to an adult, Cordelia was now chained to a statue of a strange woman clothed in the sun. Below her feet is the moon and atop her head a crown of twelve stars. In her arms, she is clinging to a newborn red dragon with seven heads and ten horns and seven crowns on its heads. Cordelia's exotic emerald eyes lit up the room, but as she cried, so did the room begin to be overtaken with the waters of sorrow in the form of rain. Higher the levels reached and larger does the size of the red dragon increase. Wary at first, Zacharias steps forward, noticing this vision pays him no attention. Desperately, he then tries to break the chains with his sword, but it had no effect. Cordelia began to drown as water reached the ceiling and her hair was now blue. "I'm not gonna let you go, Cordelia!" Zacharias reached for her hand, and she closed it, revealing to him that it was his fault she had died. Snapping back into reality, he finds himself alone in the dark, for he had hit his head on a rock and passed out momentarily from the initial fall. "It was just a nightmare, that's all," so he thinks. Suddenly, he heard Cordelia's voice say to him, "You killed me, why couldn't you save me?" Repeatedly, she screamed this at him. He fell over as his mind was in immense pain that was now shooting through his core. "Leave me be!" Seven spirits began to shout at him all at once that made his ears bleed. The PLAGGES speak, "Stand with us! Lay with us! Hate us! Steal us! Consume us! Become us! Cease with us!" He is powerless and must endure as this attack continues. Again, the attack comes full circle from the demonic spirits. "Belphegor! Leviathan! Beelzebub! Mammon! Amon! Asmodeus! Lucifer, chief liar, king of the damned, betrayer of God! You answer to death!" The insides of his very bones were in a pain that words can't describe; needless to say, he was close to being drained. Yet another dark spirit came to him and spoke to him even more directly, "Joseph can't save you here, Zacharias, neither can Alcus." He began to run to the best of his ability through the tomb to get away. "Joseph, help!" Screaming alone in the abyss, the spirits' faces began to appear on the walls silently staring at him without word. Some were missing facial pieces while others were the faces of terrible and grotesque demons. Others are sown together by bloodied chain, one is bound in knives protruding from inside the face. It was too much for him to handle, so he collapsed to the ground, hearing their footsteps all around him. Vulnerable to their will, he turned over on his back and tried to crawl away, but all the strength left his body. Standing around him in a circle were seven specific demonic spirits that he could physically see with an eighth that hovered above. These demonic faces constantly altered, never clearly revealing themselves, but instead, his attention is drawn to the terrible number eight descending to his body. They did nothing; they said nothing, they just stared at him as they knelt ever closer. Helpless, only tears came out of Zacharias's eyes as they attacked his soul directly. The unholy spirits all stood up, glaring at the other end of the hallway when Joseph appeared, holding out his Holy Bible. "In the name of Jesus Christ who was sent by God Almighty, I command you by the power of the Holy Spirit to return back to hell! Jesus does not abandon his flock nor does he forsake God's children! Leave now, Satan, I rebuke you!" The spirits feared Joseph and fled. Sitting curled up in the corner was Zacharias weeping and broken as Joseph came before him. It was hard to understand his words at first, but the meaning was clear for truthful tears are said to be the loudest; he had reached a level of sorrow Joseph had not experienced but could only sympathize. "I can't take it anymore. I can't deal with this for." Before he could say "years," Joseph knew and held him close as he continually wept in his shoulder. It was that moment when Joseph finally understood the hardships his friend had always seen and why believing in Jesus was so hard for him to do. Instead of throwing the gospel at him in words, Joseph knew to just love his friend who was hurting, and in that moment, his did ineed open that much more to the truth. Joseph knew it was only now a matter of time. Now regaining his composure, Zac asked for his forgiveness. Joseph helped him up. "It is not I you should ask for forgiveness, it is the one who holds the keys to the deepest of your inner desires known as dreams," Joseph solemnly explains.

7

Alpha and Omega

After Joseph had calmed his spiritually attacked friend, he reached into his rucksack and pulled out a small rope, tying it around their waists. This would be the second act in this ropes life to leading this individual. "There, this is so we won't get separated again," Joseph exclaims fumbling around in the dark, trying to complete the knot. Wiping away the last tears from his face, Zacharias apologizes for trying to light the torch. "It's all right, mistakes happen, all that matters is that you learned from that mistake, which I'm sure you did. But I do have a question if you don't mind me asking, how long have dark spirits been after you?"

"Since I was very young, after my grandfather Alcus passed away."

Joseph proceeded to navigate through the abyss by spiritual guidance from he that is Holy. "I've known dark spirits were with you from the first day I met you, but I just wasn't sure to what extent. I had meant to talk to you about this sooner, but out of respect, I waited to see if you would."

Zacharias sighed to himself then spoke, "Well, I wanted to bring it up for many weeks, but wasn't sure you'd understand. I felt ashamed by this curse, you're such a good person and me, this freak plagued by the shadow."

Joseph apprised him that it was nothing to be ashamed of. "Look, the thing is, forces are at work in the world. Most people will never understand until it is too late, they have eyes but they do not see and ears but they do not hear. It may sound strange, but what you have been going through is an amazing blessing." Greatly perplexed by this, the cursed man grew silent, pondering, *How in the hell is this, a blessing? I've suffered for years by my own guilty decisions bringing many to the grave. I thought a blessing was supposed to be a good thing?*

"Why so quiet all of a sudden?" Joseph asked, still marching on.

"Joseph, I don't understand. I've endured nothing but pain and sorrow, the mainstay of my life. To say this is proper would have to mean direct intercession from God and that I do not accept."

Joseph stopped and then spoke directly to him in the dark, "It's hard to see things for what they are in the present when you feel imprisoned by the unknowing, but when you begin to look at it from the long-term perspective, therein lies your key to freedom. God works in eternal absolutes and acts when He chooses not when we want Him to. Since the Lord looks at things outside of time, would He not then know what is best for us?" Thinking to himself, Zac began to scrutinize his past that had not yet been revealed to another living soul, it then dawned on him.

"Joseph!"

"Yes?"

"You're right, it's incredible. If I hadn't seen what I'd seen or dealt with certain things in my life, then your family and yourself wouldn't mean as much to me. I know that sounds weird, but all the bad made the good really something ya know."

Joseph smiled although it could not be seen. "Lovely, I'm delighted that made sense to you. Working as a pastor, I hear countless issues, which is fine, but one of the hardest things for me to get across is that going through tough things is designed to make people stronger. Much like the way a sword is forged so are we, a sword that is not forged or tempered properly cannot stand when the day of battle comes. So is it with a finely honed blade hammered out in the pains of fire and restored in the water of purification. Although a grueling and patient process swords like that are remarkably blessed for they yield a crop a hundred times their size on the Day of Judgment. These are dearly treasured by their Father who delivered the breath of creation because of his unrestrained love."

Zacharias began to laugh and give way to the last of his tears from the incident earlier. "I just can't believe how correct you are and that I've never realized these things. You've taught me much in such a short time, sometimes I feel like nothing more than a broken hilt who will be forgotten. Fanero told me that I was nothing on that day when I met The Angel's Voice, Cordelia Faverent. I felt the same way when those spirits had surrounded me, like I was nothing, like I was helpless and alone in the world, even more in my heart. You saved me, but that name you used, Jesus Christ, when you said that name, I felt the strength in my body begin to return and then they left as if banished. That name made me feel like I was someone, like I wasn't alone anymore, and I don't understand why." Zacharias asked if Joseph could share with him who that was and why it sent the demons away. For over fourteen years, he had lived with the demons haunting his every footstep cursed by the touch of death, and no matter where he ran or hid, they always found him.

Joseph then speaks with spirit ready to leap from skin. "Since I've met you, it's been my goal to teach you about Jesus Christ, but in all those moments, you did not want to hear it because you weren't ready. That is fine and all, it's just funny now here in this cramped abyss without sight, you want to learn about the light. Irony is not without personality, I suppose." Zacharias understood the joke reference to a certain extent and laughed with his friend. "Once again, I must ask you to listen to a story from my past, but I'll only tell it if you want to hear it." Joseph told him with all the hopes he'd say yes in the world. "Yes, yes, I'd love to hear this story, but after, can I still hear about this man named Jesus?"

"Of course, there's always time to talk about Jesus, but a lot of him will be explained in this story, I promise." Joseph then began to convey the message of just who he really was as they continually traversed the tomb, searching for the resting place of Sir Abraham Desteeran, firstborn of the holy knights.

The Story of Joseph Barnabas Voltel

Joseph was born and raised in Evangela among the capitol city of Antioch in the year 2932. His father, who was a prominent hunter, also worked in the ministry within the Church of Salvation. He worked among the youth, leading and guiding them into adulthood as students of Christ; this is known as discipleship. He dearly loved the children as did his wife, Joseph's mother. They were only able to have Joseph and would be unable to conceive anymore children within their lifetime. They loved him profoundly, but were heartbroken for having a large family had always been their dream especially his mother's. Joseph was very close with them and worked alongside his father in all things from hunting to the church ministry. Needless to say, when he became seventeen, he followed in his father's footsteps on the ministry path, the only difference being Joseph felt compelled by the Lord to become a full-time pastor. On the day he undertook the journey to becoming a pastor, an old evangelist took him under his wing. Joseph's father explained that he was now a man. That day, Joseph received the map now located with him taken from the attic of his home back in Salem. A promise was then made between father and son to remember wherever life's journey may course in Vulgata, so would God always lead. Joseph asked his father what a man exactly was and what he told him prevails in his heart still. He looked at Joseph and said, "Son, today thou art a man and new things shalt be brought to light in thine soul. Today, new responsibility shines on your path for a man is one who spiritually leads, protects, and provides for his family and the lost just as Christ did and does for the church. A man is one who composes thyself honorably in all situation, especially when no one is around. To be a man is to marry one woman as thy wife never breaking thy marriage vows and to respect and love her in every way one can as shown by Christ who leadeth that marriage. A man is to be always searching in his given task for how the Lord wants him to grow, adapt and change at a moment's notice. Most of all a man is to look over the fellowship with grace, dignity and compassion ready to lay down his life when called to battle. Can you accept this, my son?" Accept he did; afterward, his father pulled out his Holy Bible:

> But thou, O man of God, flee these things; and follow after righteousness, godliness, faith, love, patience, meekness. Fight the good fight of faith, lay hold on eternal life, whereunto thou art also called, and hast professed a good profession before many witnesses.

1 Timothy 6:11–12 (KJV)

This was spoken before the altar in the Church of Salvation where a great wooden cross stretches high above in constant reminder of the loving embrace the Lord offers freely by grace. Joseph really would never forget those words as he was handed over to the evangelist who would be the first of many mentors on his path. The next year, his father passed away and his mother was left alone; Joseph's life became her and the congregation. The church body blessed them financially, which eased the worldly burdens mightily. Joseph met Penelope, his now wife, when he was nineteen years of age in the COS during the delivery of his very first sermon that covered the finer details of a godly marriage. She approached after, infatuated with the way he had delivered the message for a godly woman is won over by a godly man as he is her. Joseph explained to her that it was the Lord's triumph, he just did what He asked. The next Sabbath while the main pastor was speaking, Penelope came and sat beside Joseph. To this day, he cannot explain how beautiful she was; her very soul brought forth a radiance that forced a blushing smile the entire service. When the communion plate was passed around with the bread and wine, she held it to him, and her hand brushed up against his. Already shy and now surprised, he dropped the plate, which in turn spilled over her dress. Everyone in the church witnessed as he leapt and ran to grab a cloth; the pastor couldn't continue with the sermon due to his endless laughter. Like fire, it spread around the church; both Penelope and him were beet red as the attempt to clean her dress was distressingly made. From there on, they had fallen in love; a year later, they were married. For years, they attempted to have children but were unable. Joseph eventually came to be the lead pastor of the Church of Salvation; it was such a blessing and more so responsibility that he did his best to honor properly. Together, Penelope and he lived in Antioch until the year 2964 when they moved to the small city of Salem in Calina. At that time, he received confirmation that he was supposed to go out into the world and preach the message of Jesus Christ. About once a year, Joseph would leave on a mission's trip and journey somewhere in Vulgata to begin what is known as church planting. He would spread the gospel and appoint elders as an apostle by the name of Paul did in the New Testament of the Bible. After that had begun, Joseph would move on to where his soul felt most compelled through guidance from the Holy Spirit. Mariana was not yet born, so it wasn't impossible for him to continue off into the world and preach the word. It would be the year 2970 that proved the greatest test of his faith when a religious war broke out to the east. The lands of Marduas had fought over religion since what most would surmise as the genesis of the clock. Thousands of refugees strived to gain political asylum in the west. Now there was only one land route into the west and that was through the defensive city known as Grias.

Grias began construction in 2608 after the results of The Big 10 as to secure western stability. Valencia undertook a massive project with the combined war funds from all over the west to block off the only stretch of land that connects east and west. The plan was simple: construct a massive walled-off defensive city, so at the most narrow portion of the Dolgorum Cliffs, an army's numbers would count for nothing against the mighty defenses of Grias. Combining the greatest military and architectural minds of the age with a seemingless endless supply of golden coin and labor, the west struggled for thirty agonizing years to finish the juggernaut Grias. The project was overseen by master architect Nehemiah from Maldecium. At the completion, Valencia overtook the reigns of the city proclaiming it as the holy embrace of God protecting the west from the vile sins of the east. It is that same spot where Sir Abraham Desteeran once defeated the demon Cerberus at what was known as hell's gate. The mammoth city of Grias is comprised of the three largest castles in the world of Vulgata, only second in size to the Church of Law. They are interconnected by a two hundred foot high wall stretching for miles to both sides of the cliffs. Each castle was named after an archangel from Valencian point of view, the left being Raphael, the right being Gabriel, and the median Michael with a golden statue of them atop each. The wings are so substantial, each castles side is wholly protected. The center castle, which is the largest of the three, contains Samson, the world's largest catapult that takes a hundred plus men to operate. Sitting atop such a high perch, it can hurl boulders and stone at a most devastating accuracy that can crush entire armies with a single shot. Behind the walls sits the main city, which is populated entirely by military personnel from Valencia. A grand army of multiple thousands of swordsmen, pike men, and shield men plus three times as many archers, crossbowmen, and now riflemen lie in wait to assist gatehouse and wall alike. Over two thousand silver paladins sent from the Church of Law herself remain stationed in command of the city backed by a never-ending mountain of provisions. All this just to cover the precautionary terms of pretended peace. In the core of this massive military network, a mysterious clock tower dictates the functionality of Grias by the hour. Atop this tower, a four-sided titanic shield with a grand cannon inside warns the city of coming assault. One side of the clock faces the west surrounded in a golden sun while the other side stares east locked in full moon. The north face is the clock itself as is the south, but unlike the north, the south counts backwards, the two sink three times a day at noon, evening, and midnight. Finally, a massive drawbridge located only on the middle castle serves entry between worlds. It lowers past a deep poisonous moat in front of the giant walls. A lone beast named Shamar tamed from the World War hides in wait as the bridge's sole guardian. He is a massive thirty foot high pure black tortoise with white lines across shell and body also having seven heads that hide within the thick plate. Additionally, all of the walls above contain hundreds of regular-sized catapults, trebuchets, and ballistae, many of which that have now been upgraded to cannon-based technology. To run such an armed complex, the innumerable engineers are led by a well-coordinated grouping of officers sent directly from top Valencian schools of war in Constantinople. The fact of the matter is that with this much firepower bolstered to a single chokepoint within the Dolgorum Cliffs, no army could ever pass.

Word would come from Valencian crown to refuse passage of all refugees at the border, and pressed with an impossible crossing into the west, these people were forced to turn back to their war-torn lands. As this message reached across the west, Joseph had a dream that told him to travel east to spread the gospel of Jesus Christ for all to hear. That same month, he traveled to Valencia and presented the case before King Avilius Voltoro in Alexandria because one could not cross into Marduas unless you received permission from Valencian royalty. Avilius granted Joseph audience then a royal seal of approval, and he was able to cross into Marduas through Grias. Passing the drawbridge into the east, the poisonous moat of a strange violet substance begins to foam and bubble vibrantly. The animal known as Shamar surfaces and one of its seven gigantic heads extends from the blackened shell on an even darker slimy neck. Twisting around Joseph, it examined him, blinking with ruby eyes dripping muck from a formidable snout seemingly sharpened. The intimidating guardian lowers its head, allowing Joseph to pet it as the rest retract into the carapace. Surprisingly gentle, it then allows him passage through the Dolgorum Cliffs. The overhanging ledges of Dolgorum protrude higher than the three castles, making one feel as though they are entering into the ethereal plain. After that, the Forlorn Gorge is another wonder to behold for this oasis stretched on for days showcasing the beauty of the east. For several weeks, he traveled around stopping in and out of cities attempting to spread the gospel but was shunned out of the majority of them. He came to learn that the ongoing religious war wasn't just a religious war as the west had been led to believe. Three major tribes: the Amerith of Israel, the Judeans of Volstrom, and the Samarians of Goleme, all demanded control over the east. The citizens explained to Joseph that those to the north fought with the harnessed powers of the very corrupted nature Vulgata had waged war against since the beginning. To the south terrible forms of technology had been created, utilizing both medieval and gunpowder-based technologies, some inventions even clung to the unutilized power of steam. Finally, they explained that the Amerith stood by the pretenses of their religious doctrine, which rallied the most men of any eastern cause. For thousands of years, Marduas had been fastened in fatal dance between nature, science, and religion, all vowing to use their ways to set forth a new unified Marduas under one of these ideologies. But there was a fourth variable that had been around since 1759, they were known as the drudge knights. These knights were currently in allegiance with the clandestine organization known as the NWF (New Way Forward) movement who originally united Marduas in WWI before its economic collapse that threw the region back into a perpetual state of war. The drudge knights, although completely loyal to Marduas, would only join one they could accept as king. These knights were different for they did not accept a man as king from lineage but from deeds from a merit that proved destiny had chosen him to lead. They believed the NWF could once again find such a man. In this day, their current leader, General Dante Vladimir Alexander XII who was the first to lead in all twelve generations of his family line, believed the day of Marduas's true king was soon to come.

Joseph would later travel to Jerusalem where he knew that it could potentially be dangerous due to a majority of the Amerith not believing in Jesus Christ for they did not believe He was the messiah. Great numbers of them followed the Law of Moses set forth in the Old Testament. A few days, he remained in Jerusalem, searching out any potential candidates to plant this church, but none were found. Every time he attempted to ease into foreign relations, he was countered by violent mobs quickly erupting in outbursts of dogmatic rage. Feeling as though a failure to the Lord, his spirits fell low and he considered returning home, abandoning the assignment. Later that night, a sign came to him: a group of drudge knights coated in their black plated armor with golden lining passed through the city riding south, mentioning the recapturing of stolen slave. The word "slave" pierces Joseph's being, and it is further revealed to him that they are who he is to share the message of salvation, the decision is made to tail these knights until situation escalates to action. For days, they traveled south through the endless desert complimented by clear blue sky. One night, they converged with hundreds of other knights and attacked a nameless city where tens of thousands of slaves were being held by the Judeans of Volstrom. Flintlock rifles and pistols erupt against the drudge knights who are mostly unaffected by their thick armor. The medieval tanks like coal in the night set forth the desolation of the city by fire, then laying claim to these thousands of slaves. The rest then merged alongside their brothers in black who waged further war to the south. It would be that night among the burning ruins where Joseph found a young boy of eleven left to die. Pushing the debris off his body, he was gravely injured. The boy pointed to the west of the city, and for days, they rode in that direction coming upon a far larger slave city in the desert. This setting was different; it was populated by tens of thousands of nothing but runaway slaves, a safe haven protected within a crater of sand. Hebron was the name of the city that sat by the coast of the Tarene Sea. They took in Joseph and the injured boy, allowing them to live with them. These exiles scattered and lost across the desert wasteland wanted nothing more than a place to call home. Even Hebron was not safe anymore as the three main factions continually warred for control over Marduas forcibly converting any of the slaves they could find to their banner. Many weeks later, the boy, close to complete recovery, returned accompanied by his mother. His name was Titus and his mother's Gabrielle; she was deaf and mute but could read lips. Titus was able to sign with her and tell Joseph of what she said. Titus followed him around everywhere, speaking of the hardships undeservingly sustained on a broken people. He was without father for his mother and self had been banished from their home some years ago because this certain culture would not accept her heritage. Young Titus one day asked about Jesus for Joseph spoke of him daily; he was finally able to convey the message as many sat around to hear.

Standing up and holding the Bible, Joseph shared the story of Jesus Christ, savior of mankind. Once upon a time lived a man whose name is Jesus, who is the Christ. He was conceived by the Holy Spirit and born of a virgin mother named Mary who was married to Joseph, the carpenter. Jesus Christ was equally God and equally man at the same time. Jesus had descended to men as a child by the Holy Spirit within the womb of Mary. He cried, laughed, and broke bread with us, he was one of us, but the miracle about this was that Jesus never once sinned. When he was (about) thirty, his ministry began in which he preached the coming kingdom of God and the repentance of sin in his name.

Most doubted the authenticity of his lineage and that he was in fact the son of God. The Pharisees in general attacked this claim bitterly as the Sadducees refused to believe that their was to be a resurrection of the dead in the last day. Jesus taught that none who testify of themselves does it for good cause, but that he did not testify of himself, but in fact, his witness was his Father who was God. Christ explained that nothing righteous comes from anyone except be it by the Father and that he was in Him and that God was in himself (Jesus). Throughout the next three years, Jesus performed many miracles ranging from curing the sick, giving sight to the blind, driving demons (unclean spirits) from people, and also raising the dead; he did these among many more. Jesus Christ called out twelve disciples, who later would become the twelve apostles, one of whom betrayed him: his name was Judas Iscariot. Jesus Christ, who was both man and God in the flesh, truly loved everyone and gave these two commands when asked which the greatest commandment was in the Law.

> Je'-sus said unto him, Thou shalt love the Lord thy God with all thy heart, and with all thy soul, and with all thy mind. This is the first and great commandment. And the second is like unto it, Thou shalt love thy neighbour as thyself. On these two commandments hang all the law and the prophets.
>
> Matthew 22:37–40 (KJV)

Jesus then later established the New Covenant, freeing us from the Old Testament chains of sin bound by the Law of Moses in which all men are enslaved to

> And he took bread, and gave thanks, and brake it, and gave unto them, saying, This is my body which is given for you: this do in remembrance of me. Likewise also the cup after supper, saying, This cup is the new testament in my blood, which is shed for you.
>
> Luke 22:19–20 (KJV)

Shortly after the last supper, Jesus Christ who led a sinless existence chose to lay down his life for the flock by shouldering the cross to his death. Holy, blameless, and pure was Jesus Christ, but still, they brutally beat, tortured, mocked, and crucified him on the very cross he carried to Cavalry because they believed that he was a blasphemer who was not the son of God. They fashioned a crown of thorns painfully to his head and a notice was fastened to the cross that read: JE'-SUS OF NAZ'-A-RETH THE KING OF THE JEWS. After dying on the cross and being laid to rest in the burial tomb, he was resurrected back to life on the third day just as he had promised. Forty days later, Jesus called the eleven apostles before ascending to heaven to sit at the right hand of God to forever watch over the flock. Jesus works as our great and only intercessor before God the Great Judge as Satan works as the terrible accuser. Do know that through belief in Christ, one is gifted with the Holy Spirit. He convicts you of sin through repentance in Jesus's name to live upright and righteous lives which honors the Lord thy God.

> For God so loved the world, that he gave his only begotten Son, that whosoever believeth in him should not perish, but have everlasting life.
>
> John 3:16 (KJV)

All who believe in the name of Jesus Christ will be saved by his mercy, grace, and love for eternity. Do not hate God for the things that happen in your life but know He's the only one who ever truly loved you and the only one who can. All that is good in the world is of God and that is confirmed in the testimony of Jesus Christ. Never believe you are alone for you are not and the greatest part about God's grace is that eternal salvation in heaven is free, one must only accept God's son Jesus and repent of your sins in his name. You see, when Jesus Christ died, he was a sinless man, which gave him authority over sin and sin being death gave him authority over death in which he was resurrected, proving complete victory over it. Jesus Christ, who now resides in heaven before the throne of God, can forgive your sins on the Day of Judgment, which we will all stand before. Only through Jesus Christ can you be forgiven your sins and the only way he can help you is if you believe in him. First by your profession of faith in his name, then by baptism which is commonly done by being submerged but let he who can understand know that the main baptism takes place within the heart of the individual that is made new in Christ. Faith meaning believing in what you cannot see may sound hard at first, but if you truly look at it, he wants you to seek with your heart and soul. By looking faithfully, you can see Jesus for who he really is and that is love. Each and every person alive was made by God to glorify Him for that is the purpose of humanity! Never forget your Father knows even the number of hairs upon your head and wants nothing more than a relationship with you His child! Amen!

After Joseph gave this message, it spread among the slaves for weeks and a great multitude came to faith in Christ. For that time being, he was baptizing them in the name of the Father, the Son, and the Holy Ghost, which are the three persons of God, all different yet all the same. Although Titus and Gabrielle were already believers in the Lord, no one wanted to listen to the mute woman or the child. Gabrielle thanked Joseph for spreading the message to them, but he thanked her more because her faith in the Lord was what allowed him to speak that day for she had prayed diligently for the slaves to receive that message. Titus, also full of spirit, revealed that far to the eastern coast, there was a secret village of over two thousand orphans hiding away from national conflict. He informed that among them was his brother Saul and that he was attempting to find him when he was trapped in the battle. Titus had wanted to tell him that for a long time but did not want to burden the man who pulled him from destruction. Hebron knew of this but would not make the journey out of fear of being captured. Early one morning after days in prayer, Joseph decided that visiting these children was what he had to do; Titus inevitably joined his side. Gabrielle wanted to go, but Joseph asked her to stay with the newfound believers in the Lord, praying over their safety for dark spirits always come to break those newly risen in the faith. Together, the missionary and the boy quest through the wilderness of the desert for a couple of weeks. One evening at dusk, they came across the hidden village by the coast where orphans lived alone. Abandoned babies, children, and teenagers were scattered across the city, taking care of each other without the need of adults. At first, they hid from Joseph, but soon peered out with curious delight at Titus who stood beside him. Children came out of the framework, holding even smaller children in their arms. Among them, there was one little boy in particular of only about four years old who stood pointing at the only intact building in the destroyed city. The child dashes to Joseph, grabbing his leg, looking up to him, stating, "God has come! God has come!" Eyebrows raised, Joseph explains he is not God, but he had come in His name. All the little ones cheered and wept because someone had cared enough to come for them after the world had forsaken them. The little boy around his leg ran up the stairs of the decrepit inn to the top floor where one hundred and fifty children lay in beds. Some were mortally wounded, others with life-threatening illness and leprosy. Titus found his brother Saul in this room who was very sick and could barely see. The dying children turned to Joseph with eyes that brought forth mercy. The missionary at first feels that this task is too big, that how can one man save all these children? Then realization sets in that these young ones have nothing, that God has led him here because their prayers have been heard, his strength is renewed knowing the Lord will deliver them.

Walking outside, he asked the children to get ready to leave with him the next morning for the journey to Hebron. The young boy who had hugged his leg from earlier asked about the hurt children. Joseph explains that God had a way, followed by asking what the child's name was; the boy confessed he did not have a name. After, he went back into the inn and talked among the dying children over the course of the night. To most, the gift of speech to another human being is often disregarded as a common practice, but to these young ones who could see the truth, it meant the world. Joseph stayed with them in that room all night, praying over each and every one, the last being Titus's brother Saul. Resting on the floor, Joseph fervently prayed for God to save them until he fell asleep hours later.

The waves of the Trelsch Ocean can be heard crashing onto the beach, but are quickly muddled by the cries of Saul, the thirteen-year-old brother to Titus. Joseph awakens with Titus to the graphic scene displayed; every child had passed away in their sleep except for Saul. Excitedly rushing upstairs, the boy with no name enters, full of joy ready to leave to Hebron. The golden smile turns to horror, sniffles, then sobs that alert the rest outside. Joseph is unable to comfort the boy for he runs off and is then taken by immense grief himself. That morning, the pastor carried all 149 bodies outside and began to dig one massive grave. The older children helped, which took half the day. It would be the child without a name that would bring out a small wooden cross that would mark the bodies' resting place. On that day, he named the little boy Simon Peter.

For weeks, the over eighteen hundred orphans followed him through the desert, trusting the Lord the entire way. Each morning, they awoke blessed with manna, white bread-like sweet-tasting food on the ground. Also along the way, they ran into the occasional oasis, but one day, when the sun was blazing worse than ever, one was not found. Together, they prayed and begged the merciful Lord, and before them was a rock, and from it, water burst from the earth for all of them. Upon drinking it, Simon Peter was the first to give thanks to Jesus, who was the rock upon which waters of life were freely given. Titus's older brother

Saul who was the only one who lived from the inn traveled in the rear of the group the entire journey watching over all the children, making sure none were left behind. Day in and out, Saul carried the youngest ones until he had no strength left. God had clearly kept him alive for a specific reason: the boy was a leader at heart and the most blessed. After weeks of travel, the journey to Hebron was completed, slave and child were reunited. Gabrielle had gotten her lost son Saul back, who signed with her constantly after the first loving embrace.

By night, Simon Peter slept at Joseph's side and by day was his shadow. Sadly, Joseph's time with them was coming to a close for word came that the King of the Amerith Dominic Falscious had dispatched troops to find and kill him. A lone traveler who witnessed Joseph burying the children believed it to be work of sorcery from the House of Magus and had brought it to the crown in Jerusalem. A potent mix had now been concocted out of a cauldron of rumor of a man trying to spread the gospel around a month earlier. These two were coined as one, so needless to say, the pastor from Salem knew his company drew danger to the people of Hebron. None of the slaves wanted to turn him in. Instead, they devised a plan of escape from Marduas by raft to sail across the Tarene Sea. Now it was impossible to get to the other side without being deported back for the seven lighthouses of Valencia also stretched along the coastline all the way to the lower part of the west in Athens. These garrisons known as The Seven Lights served three functions: (1) to guide Valencian ships in and out of the Tarene safely that could also transfer to the Euphrates River; (2) to defend and coordinate against all creatures, refugees, or eastern attack by sea; (3) to bolster naval superiority in the Tarene by assisting the fleets of Valencia with additional supplies, maintenance and sailors if the need should present. Any refugees who ever crossed were immediately deported back into Marduas by ship or land through Grias. Joseph was able to get across due to the royal seal given him by King Avilius, but that was it, no others could join. Over the course of the next day, hundreds constructed a small but sturdy raft capable of withstanding the Tarene, and by nightfall, it was prepared. As a dozen men dragged it down the sandy hill to the coastline from the city, thousands and thousands of slaves stood around outside in the night, saying their good-byes. Gabrielle would convey their final words to Joseph. She signed and Saul spake, "We thank you for everything, messenger of God, you are truly a one who walks with Christ and we could never repay you for what you've done. Please, Joseph, carry the message of what is happening here in Marduas home. We are sorry to ask this one final message of you, but millions are suffering across the east and you alone can save us for Valencia holds these travesties in secret from the western nations." Gabrielle then hugged him one last time and a single tear fell as she then signed something Saul became infuriated by. Gabrielle demanded that Titus and Simon Peter and Saul go with him.

Before he can even consider, arrows rained in, killing hundreds of slaves from all direction. Chaos ensued as drudge knights charged down the sand-ridden dunes, gashing and dismembering any in their way; defeat is absolute. Gabrielle grabbed Joseph's shoulder and forced out the only words she could. She screamed, "Save sons! Find Holy Knights!" These words brought about by a woman incapable of speech out of desperation to save her sons forced Joseph's decision; it was nothing short of a miracle. Holding Simon Peter in his arms, Joseph grabs Titus and screamed for Saul to follow. The slaves gather together by the thousand, trying to protect them. Exalted lances rippled in chaotic spike impale or shred most. The drudge knights are fierce and without mercy, stampeding through the crowds on the heaviest of cavalry. Specially bred for war, these horses fear not death; their armor is legendary with specially designed blades coating the hooves as to ensure those trampled upon and missed by the first wave do not rise. Every horse and knight of the first contact wave is drenched in bloody sacrifice with patches of flesh stuck to their weapons. Reinforcements then take the field on foot with finely crafted and masterfully honed steel weapons that decimate slave from limb. Commanders survey the battle from atop the dune, but in front of them, their general whose armor is glorious holds true the sight of the night's hubris; it is General Alexander. Approaching the raft, Joseph sees it is not immersed in the Tarene. Together with Saul and Titus, they push with all their might impeded by the wet sands, but young Simon Peter stands atop the hill, unable to understand the sight of this slaughter. Saul with foot ripping apart the sands plows to Simon Peter before he himself is captured. "Go, take care of my brother, Joseph!" Saul continued to holler as the vessel had now entered the water. Saul's cries could be heard further and further away as the knight takes him with the rest of those captured. Titus went running after his brother whom Joseph now had to chase after. The pastor's arms seize Titus forcibly, but before he returns to their escape route, a single arrow that was meant for Joseph strikes the back of the child's head, killing him instantly. Murder of a child streaks Joseph's countenance in unjust stain. The last image Saul witnesses of his brother was Joseph holding him against himself in the appearance of a shield when in reality he was trying to protect him. With the body of the boy and Simon Peter, they got away in the raft but the shrieks of Saul brought a disturbing silence even among the drudge knights.

BACKSTORY END

Joseph finished his story, but his eyes carry on in the darkness of the abyss plagued by the sight of Titus's murder and Saul's cries. "Zacharias, I'm afraid I haven't always been entirely honest with you. Fact is, I've been looking for the Sword of Abraham for many years. Now on this day, I believe we've found it and I can fulfill Gabrielle's prayer for I failed saving both of her sons."

Zacharias put his arm on Joseph's shoulder "I never knew you carried that kind of weight, my friend."

Joseph then revealed. "Simon Peter lived with us until two years ago when he died. He saved Mariana from drowning in a sheet of ice that broke loose when she was dancing on a frozen lake. That was Hope's Lake, the same place where we rested and you awoke late at night. Simon Peter pushed her off a piece of ice that was cracking, and in turn, he fell in. He was able to pull himself out and get Mariana off the ice, but when I had returned, it was too late. He had already died of hypothermia." Joseph began to tremble, mentioning how he died, but then stopped, stating, "Then two years later, you came along and saved her again, you saved her from a second death." At that second, Joseph touched a wall and its torches lit up the room; it contained the holy knight's seal upon it. "We've found it, Joseph, it's the tomb of Abraham," Zacharias whispers in admiration. The door began to open, and Joseph's awestruck face was slowly revealed in the light, top to bottom. "Zac, all those children who died in the inn they went to heaven. I prayed for them to make it home, and years later, I finally realized they all went back home to Jesus." Zacharias looks to him intently. "You're the most amazing man I've ever met, you make me truly believe that this Jesus really could have lived." Joseph's heart was filled with happiness for he knew the story had planted the seed of understanding within his friend that would soon germinate in his soul to a tree of rebirth. "Joseph, should we bow or something before we enter this place?"

"I'd say that sounds like the right thing to do, Zacharias." The two of them drew their swords and bowed as they held them to the door for two very different reasons. Finally, after over a dozen centuries, the sword holding the name of justice was once again to be found.

8

The Sapphire Finger

Entering the burial site of Abraham, four torches lit up around the room. Each torch was sitting in the left hands of ancient statues of holy knights; there were four in all. Together, they encircle a grave multiple feet away with each statue being ninety degrees apart. In their right hands, they all held out their swords also pointing to the ceiling at an ancient portrait. Atop the ceiling was the same zodiac formed that was located on the wooden cog that had allowed them into the abyss. The twelve zodiac signs surrounded an image of Christ Jesus, but this portrait was not what most were used to in Vulgata for the Prince of Peace was of his proper Hebrew appearance. Success is found, movement is not, as the two could feel time and space around them come to a most grinding halt. Together, their thoughts focused on the stone sarcophagus shaped like the majestic armor of a holy knight. In front of it sat a stand with a message inscribed on it. Joseph stepped forward. "We've done it, this is happening." The two were positively manic over the legendary find for Abraham had been buried for over thirteen hundred years. Zacharias reviews the inscription on the stone made tablet which readeth:

May the purity of light bear His testimony sounding unto all never to be forsaken. Only shalt the vindicated set forth upon this holy realm. Thy word blameless and thine heart true know all shalt be judged by thine intent. Forever shalt the four winds of heaven protect the Lord's flock and whomsoever seeketh out company of the fallen be purged in the fires of eternal damnation, such is justice. Here slumbereth Sir Abraham Desteeran, firstborn of the holy knights of the Gentiles, whom even asleep guards thine celestial torch to light the way for the returning savior on man's account to man not heavens. Blessed is the Herald of the Spirit whom shalt grasp thy holy sword to thine heart for his name is the VII Exile. So shall it be as it was in The Age of the Lost the holy knights shalt gather in the deep by council of the XII Exiles who receive counsel from the Holy Ghost to glorify the Father who gifted us with the blameless lamb Christ Jesus. Amen.

Signed, SOC

After reading this, Zacharias looked to Joseph and announced, "I think you should open it. This is your find." Joseph nodded as his heart was pounding out of control, standing before the sarcophagus, slowly pressing against it. Joseph wonders to himself, *Titus, Saul, Gabrielle, can I now finally fulfill my promise?* Joseph began to open up the seven latches on the side, and as each one was opened, images of holy knights flashed within abstract thought. He could see great victories from the War of the Fell Dragons–1925 to skirmishes across the battlefields of The Big 10–2598, and so many more. Now opening the final latch, he could see Abraham standing in Evangela by Covenant's Bell Tower with hundreds of other holy knights raising their swords to God. Still imagining this, Joseph then spoke, "Finally, the holy knights are going to gather as they once were, finally, all things will be made new, finally, the purpose of those I have buried is revealed." Zacharias stood outside of the circle, peering into the grave as Joseph used the hilt of his sword to pry it. Joseph blankly stared for a few minutes and said nothing. "What is it? What does it look like?" Zac asked earnestly now on his tiptoes. Joseph dropped his sword and slumped to the floor, shielding himself regretfully, pressing against the stone casket. Silence was second to the loss in Joseph's concealed word. Glancing into the coffin, the vagabond sees no body and no sword; it was empty. All but a pure sapphire finger pointing to the isolation of the grave. Reaching in and snatching it, he then began to study it, not yet comforting his friend. "I've failed them, I've failed the little one who died for me," Joseph told him in a petrified voice. "I brought you all this way and now I've failed you too." Zacharias had never seen him act like this; it was hard to look at a man of such profound love and confidence toward others break down. But continually, he examines the sapphire finger. "Joseph, where would we be able to find statues made of sapphire?"

"What do you mean?" Joseph was so focused on finding the Sword of Abraham that when it was not there, he completely overlooked the sapphire finger. Standing before his broken-down friend, he taps him with the finger. "Look, don't you see, it's a clue." Zacharias was not hindered by this in the least; instead, he just saw an extended adventure. "Joseph, this is just another piece to the puzzle. That's all, don't give up just yet, you're my brother, and without you, I hold a trivial amount of hope to finding this blade." He then yielded Joseph the sapphire finger and he inspected it. "Athens, minerals such as this exist only in Athens, most likely mined in Ephesus." Zacharias stood up and helped him up with a mighty grin. As they began to leave the tomb, the warrior laughed. "You cannot deny it is kind of funny that we came all the way down here and the tomb was empty. Did you see the look on your face?" Joseph was able to laugh it off with him, but more so, he was glad he had lifted his spirits. Joseph then considered to himself, *This time, he has enhanced my morale. My prayers are happening, praise be to you, oh heavenly Father.* Light filled the tunnels as torches across the abyss ignited, making their exit unchallenging.

Now entering back into the first room with the zodiac cog, their horses lay in patient wait. Grear rises, being petted by his master, who asks, "So what do you think the sapphire finger could mean? I mean it's blue and pretty for whatever that means but definitely part of a statue of some sort."

"Well, our best lead as I said will definitely be in Athens' capital, Ephesus. Athens is a nation that believes there to be many gods and goddesses watching and warring over Vulgata, and they believe in sacrificing to them to curry favor." He tosses the sapphire finger back to Joseph, stating, "It's pointing also so that should help us find the statue if only slightly easier. But why would the finger of a statue be lying inside of Abraham's coffin and his body gone?"

"I don't know, but what I can say is that I don't expect to find safe results because of this. The Athenians have been known to also dabble among occult traditions, even directly worshiping Baal or Molech chthonic deities, patriarchs of idolatry. Just be prepared for whatever we find. Everything we've seen thus far is elementary in comparison to what we may discover there." Hearing those words of the potential danger, the man unprotected to dark spirits plummets to the very bottom of a fissured ego, trying to climb out. *Can I do this? Can I encounter Manistof if he is to find me directly? I cannot bear it, oh, please don't take me back to hell. Save me.* Shaking his head, he attempted to knock away the rogue thought. "What is it?" Joseph asks, hopping on Jesibelle.

"Nothing, just forgotten scars trying to reopen." The two then proceeded to exit the tombs the way they entered.

Close to the exit, a foul odor occupied the air. "This is the smell of decay," Zacharias exclaims. They drew their blades and marched unto daylight that blinded them until their eyes could adjust. As sight returned to them Mortician the leader of the city, sat on a throne of bone and skull surrounded by hundreds of citizens, lying around him who died in worship. "What is this witchcraft?" Joseph yelled out. Zacharias carefully stepped forward as Joseph glanced to the hole where the giant skeleton was lying earlier. The giant skeleton is gone. Zacharias, now atop the throne of demise, poked Mortician with Titulus. "Are you alive?" Mortician's head lay on his shoulder with a golden chalice in his lifeless grasp. Zacharias picked up the golden chalice and smelled it. "Poison, they drank poison!" Joseph walked over and confirmed that it was poison, implying that this was a ritual suicide. Joseph studied the look of Mortician and the all-seeing eye on his skull was now open. After this, they searched the city, and it was completely abandoned, not a soul remained. Repeatedly, they called out for survivors for over an hour, but were met with only the wind's chilling response of change. "Just like in Malastay," they say together.

"Absolutely, it's become a ghost town all over again," the pastor says.

"We should go, Joseph, Avodah Mortis has fallen."

"I hate to say it, but I think it already was, let's see what lies in wait in Athens." Zacharias accidentally dropped the sapphire finger, which pointed to Continent's Peak. Unknown to them, the finger pointed out a most dangerous and cunning spy that sat high above the many bridges, watching their every move. He picked up the finger and mounted Grear, riding out of the city with Jesibelle and her master. Now moving further southeast to the nation of Athens, the two could see a dust storm swirling about Avodah Mortis just as the snowy tornado had overtaken Malastay. A sense of urgency grew stronger as they rode on to the next step of their journey toward finding the fabled blade. Little did they know they were now not the only ones in search of the blade.

They traveled along the King's Highway beside the great aqueduct, which brought water all the way from the defensive city of Grias which drew from the Euphrates. As they neared closer to Athens by the day, they could see the long Taurus mountain ranges stretching across the land. Between them and the massive aqueduct that sat over a hundred feet high, it really gave the impression of just how small we as human beings really are. The morning before entering this new nation Zacharias, asked Joseph how God could care for us so much when we are so minuscule. Joseph explained that we are God's most beautiful creation and that we are cherished by Him deeply. He told him that we were made in His image from the dust of the ground and that He breathed life into us. The explanation is finished off by telling him of how a mother or a father loves their child even though they are tiny to them. Later that morning, they came before the Gates of Minos leading into Athens. These gates were bronze and contained all there words within Greek text, which neither of them were capable of reading. Regardless, the two passed into an entirely new world of its own. The weather was warm and the breeze serene, for it came in from a combination of both the Treslch and Clyptic Oceans. On the ground, soothing warm sand draws hopes of recreation all the way to the shorelines that are not yet visible. They had entered a small city known as Crete, which held lavish temples fashioned in the architecture of the Doric order. Also in sight was a bronze fountain staging a dozen graven images that were statues of Greek gods: Zeus, Hera, Poseidon, Hades, Hestia, Athena, Artemis, Apollo, Aphrodite, Hephaestus, Ares, and Hermes. In particular, two stood out more than any: Athena who was propped up higher than the rest, but what caught their eye even more was the false goddess Artemis who stood pointing her bow to the moon. Her statue was made completely of sapphire. "Joseph, that's it, she's made out of the same thing as the finger." Joseph first stepped in the fountain, trudging through the water, comparing the sapphire finger and it was a perfect match. The only problem being is that it did not go to this statue, for this statue was whole. "Well, at least we know now were in the right place," Joseph explained. Town guards rush out from behind the temple's pillars dressed as Roman legionaries; they ran over and demanded they exit the fountain before they arrested them. "We messed up," Joseph joked as they left the fountain confronted by dozens of iron-tipped spears and wide rectangular shields. The captain of the guards whom they called Centurion screamed, "How dare you desecrate the image of our gods and goddesses! Do you not know they command all things on earth and in the heavens?" Joseph, who had his hands in the air, apologized. "Regardless if you know or not, you've broken a sacred law here not to defy the gods, no entry in that fountain is permitted!" Centurion proclaimed for everyone to hear, drawing his gladius from his left side; his subordinates carried theirs on the right sides to indicate rank. As they began to arrest them, an oriental man about the age of Joseph hurried over; he was wearing a white tunic with a strange seal upon it. "Leave these men be, they most likely were unable to read the laws at the gate," the man explained to Centurion with a highly educated tone. Centurion stared at him and the metallic seal. "Sire, I beg your forgiveness. This was my order, allow me to house the retribution of my folly." The oriental man laughed loudly for all the crowd to hear, but instantly, his eye turned to severity, preceding, "It is okay, but leave us be, now." Zacharias and Joseph thanked the man and asked for his name.

"Terrick Feradin," he replied.

"This is Zacharias and I am Joseph Voltel," he introduced then shook Terrick's hand that was rough and worn. More noticeable is his gaze, he appears exhausted from mental toil.

"I see you were admiring the statues in the fountain, have you come to learn of them?" Terrick questioned. Joseph told him that he was a pastor and that he followed the Lord Jesus Christ. Terrick smirked, then gave Joseph a nod of approval. "Ah, another Christian, seems to be becoming more of a rarity this decade. I too believe in Jesus the Christ, what of you, young warrior?" Grabbing a fistful of sand, Zac let it sift between the cracks. "I don't know what I believe in, but I'm trying to keep an open mind for when I do decide." Terrick tossed his metallic seal to him that had the symbol of the inventor's guild from Maldecium (Nation of Science) inscribed on it. He then explained, "This was once my original calling, I am an inventor. I've traveled years across east and west seeing many a wondrous thing created by man. Keeping an open mind to things is an amazing trait to have, never forget that. But what I can tell you is keeping an open mind doesn't mean accepting everything presented, but instead seeing what something is then concluding yourself whether it is right or wrong, you must discern. Knowledge is important, but without wisdom, knowledge counts for nothing." Zacharias remained intrigued by the statement of knowledge and wisdom being used separately.

"Wait, I always thought that knowledge and wisdom were one and the same," he said to Terrick.

Terrick then began to explain, "Intelligence is the realm of thought, but you can break that bread into two variables. Knowledge being the ability to retain information, and wisdom, its application. My point being knowledge without wisdom to apply it becomes useless as most of our inventions have become overtime." Terrick then bent over, picking up a grain of sand. "But you see, young swordsman, if you are wise, then even this single grain can be used in a beneficial way for in the eyes of the Lord especially the smallest things are important. For using things so tiny deemed as weak show how mighty He is. Much like children, did you know the kingdom of God is ran by those with a childlike faith?" Zacharias really liked what Terrick had to say for he was a master inventor. It was immensely profound to him to hear a lot of the same words as he did from Joseph from a man in such an opposite field of study. Joseph surveyed the metallic seal and asked, "So how long have you been a master inventor, Terrick?"

"Long enough to see the pluses and minuses of scientific exploration."

"Rights and wrongs of science," Zacharias asked.

Terrick answered, "Yes, science as all things much like the sword is not inherently good or evil but is yet another tool man can use for what is right and what is wrong."

"Perfect answer," Joseph added. Joseph also began to urge that they really had to move on because they were searching for the home of the sapphire finger. Terrick examined the finger carefully. "Hmm, this is very interesting, Mr. Voltel, where did you find this?"

"I'm sorry I can't disclose that information at this time. I don't mean to offend thee," Joseph told him, feeling poorly about it.

"Well, I'll tell you what, you look as though the two of you have traveled a long way. If you can help me with something, then I shall help you with this treasure's origin, which I may add is a sacred relic to these parts."

"A relic, you say, how so?" Zacharias asked emphatically.

Terrick withdrew his facial exterior jokingly like he was frightened at the tone presented. "Come, I will explain on the way to Ephesus." Together, they set out for the city of Ephesus many miles south.

For the next few days, they traveled through Athens, staying at various inns together. Terrick explained to his newfound friends much of Athens and their history with the Greek gods and goddesses. Most importantly, Terrick would explain to them that the statue of Artemis was not the only one created out of sapphire that there used to be one located in Ephesus. Legend depicts that Artemis would return once every hundred years for the hunt. They learned that Terrick lived among the Athenians as a shipbuilder, helping them to construct larger vessels for fishing operations off their local shores. Terrick also explained that he had only been here for a few months and was soon to return to Marduas in the east to finish his most important project. When Joseph asked him about this project, he respectfully told him that it was classified for the time being, but soon, word would spread in castle and hovel alike.

Early one morning, they arrived in Ephesus where they would hope to achieve the goal to be set forth by the inventor. The structures here are more elegant made having pillars of the Ionic Order, and more homage is seemingly paid to Artemis. Entering the city of Ephesus, Terrick explained the other part of his deal. Stepping around the local markets, which were packed with all kinds of people ranging from exotic Greek women to strong Greek warrior men, Terrick went into a tattered antique shop selling antiquity. "Good morning, can I help you find anything in particular?" a charismatic vendor said to the three of them. Terrick marched over and picked up a bronze compass that was relatively expensive. "You help me purchase this, and I'll help you find the information you're looking for." The compass beheld the portrait of a fearsome sea serpent engraved on the back of it. Zacharias took a look, "What is that sea monster?"

Terrick announced, "The Failiff, Guardian of the Oceans." The shopkeeper told him that he would not part with it for cheap. Joseph asked him how much he wanted for it and the vendor asked for two hundred pieces of gold.

"That's outrageous," Zacharias stated.

Joseph then jumped in, "I'm sorry, good vendor, but we do not have that kind of money."

"Well, I'm always willing to trade," the vendor proclaimed with a devious grin. Outside shuffling through the packs sitting on Grear, Zac pulls out something wrapped in cloth. As he unwrapped it, the vendor's excitement grows for it was the golden chalice from Avodah Mortis. The trade is carried out, and in return, he selects a brass handheld telescope. Zacharias bestowed Terrick the bronze compass with the Failiff on the back. Joseph peered over, exclaiming, "I can't believe you took that."

"Well, it's not like they were going to need it anymore, no offense to them. I just assumed something like that could help us along the way, which it just did." Terrick laughed as he thanked them for helping him purchase the compass. "You have no idea what this means to me, it was once mine, but I had no way to purchase something this expensive at this time. This was the final piece I needed for the project located in Marduas." Terrick then began to journey to the main library in Ephesus as the two of them followed in eager hope.

They then entered the library where they were greeted by a kind elderly woman. She was very far along in years and could not walk without her cane, but still insisted to show them around. Terrick had known her for some time since he had been living among the Athenians. "Will you be needing your key, Mr. Feradin?" the old woman asked.

"Yes, I'm on an important mission today, these are new friends of mine." Terrick then leaned in and whispered to her. The old woman smiled at the two of them and gave Terrick a fairly large key containing the image of pelican vulning itself. As they were walking with Terrick, she told them not to get lost. They wondered how they were going to get lost in this place for it was only a two-story building with a few dozen shelves of books. Together, they wandered to a black gothic door in the back that had the frame of a gargoyle with the handle inside the mouth. Terrick pulled out the large key and inserted it where the hidden lock was. "Wisdom always prevails," he informed them in a quirky manner and an awkward laugh. Joseph found it to be comical; his friend did not. Entering into the room, it was an old supply closet with nothing special until Terrick moved over an old suit of centurion armor. On the floor sat a hidden floor compartment which he lifted. A long ladder led to a secret library thirty times as large as the one upstairs. "What exactly is this area?" Joseph asked.

"This is the secret library of the holy knights left here from before their days of permanent exile." Zacharias and Joseph gape at the hidden study, but neither said a word, not at first. "What is it? Surely you know about the holy knights, and even more so you, Joseph, if you're really a pastor," Terrick inquired. Joseph began to bring to light why they were there. "Mr. Feradin, the truth is we're in search of the Sword of Abraham. We found his tomb in Continent's Peak from the notes I found in the index portion of Codex Gigas in Malastay. In Abraham's tomb, we found this sapphire finger and that was all." Terrick rubbed his chin, slightly shocked by this revelation, first questioning the authenticity of the claim made. "I see so you came here to ascertain whether or not that sapphire finger will reveal the truth and if it points to Abraham's lost blade?"

"Yes, we have to find out, we're on the brink of discovery on our mission of reuniting the holy knights," Zacharias adds in a dire voice.

Terrick took a long deep breath. "Listen, I'll help you find your clue, but do not trust to find a hope in the holy knights. They're never going to return to these cursed lands."

"What is it?" Joseph asked his new friend. Terrick revealed on his forearm a brand, and immediately, he knew what it was.

"I was wrongly accused of this act, and because of this false accusation, I to was exiled from Maldecium by the Church of Law. They took my daughter who was only an infant away from me and my wife left me, not believing I was an innocent man." Terrick was choked up over this, and Zacharias did not understand what the brand had meant. Joseph explained to him that the brand was symbolizing he was both banished from the western lands and the charge was pedophilia.

"When lies like that can be given in groups like the New Way Forward movement or the Church of Law, then the time of the holy knights is sure to never return, Joseph, they're not coming back. I don't want to sound mean to either one of you, but the fact of the matter is justice will not happen till Jesus returns, and until then, nothing will ever change, all we can do is wait."

Joseph patted Terrick on the back. "I believe you to be an innocent man, and like Jesus, you were wrongly accused. Now we're going to find this clue so we can continue our search for Abraham's sword." Terrick is profoundly touched by the empathy from him and a burden buried long ago lightens, if only slightly. For the rest of the day, they searched throughout thousands of ancient tomes. Tons of lore surrounding Vulgata were found but none on the other statue of Artemis. They found many a magnificent thing about the holy knights and books upon their ancient tactics once deployed. Granted, Terrick was already well informed on ample amounts of this information, he always enjoyed learning more.

Toward the end of the night, they began falling asleep in the library, but Zacharias read and read with all his mental capacity, not wanting to waste time learning this precious knowledge. The spirit of excitement kept him going as he was surrounded by an endless series of books. One book contained a seal just like the one on his beer stein, which was given him by Davidoff who sacrificed his life for him in Malastay. As he studied the cover and opened it, the old woman slowly came down the ladder, tossing three blankets down. She wobbled over on her cane. "What are you still doing up, young man?" Resting by the Book of the Guardians, he peered up to her eyes only. "How long have you known about all these things? Do you know much about the holy knights?" The old woman smiled back at him. "Oh, since I was a little girl, my grandfather used to tell me magnificent stories of the once legendary white knights bordered in gold who gave all at the Lord's order. But those days are long past and now nights grow long as the shadows return to their former fraudulent and, may I say, unholy majesty. That book you hold speaks of a black dragon turned red out of his hatred for mankind and all of God's creation. An ancient serpent known as the Devil, he throws the world into confusion and chaos. Lucifer, Satan, and the evil one are just some of his many names."

"Really, you say his name is Satan?" Zacharias asked.

"Yes, he was once an archangel of light who lived in heaven with God, but he decided to rebel because Lucifer held an infinite pride wanting to become as great as God. With Satan fell 1/3 of all the angels in heaven who decided to join in his rebellion. Once fallen from heaven, they became demons and dark spirits to plague the world of mankind."

"What chance could we ever stand to something like that? How is that fair of God to let that kind of evil pour onto us?" He questioned with an upset tone. The old woman placed the blanket around him. "With no dark, could we understand light?" She then laid blankets over Terrick and Joseph who were both lying asleep around piles of books. Joseph was plopped in the middle of one book as a pillow. After that, she began to leave and bid a good night. "Thank you," he said to her.

The old woman replied, "You have honest eyes and so handsome, you're going to make a special girl a perfect husband one day." After she left, he glanced upon the cover of the guardian's book one more time, wondering, "Satan. I did not know evil had a name or a king all its own. Could Manistof be linked to this Satan? Perhaps, that is the master he speaks of. Could all this evil and dark spirits that haunt my footsteps or even the curse of death upon me, is it all connected to a single infrastructure? I've always believed evil existed and lived through it if only barely, but never could I have fathomed a possibility of it being so cut and dry. That only good and evil exist that can't be right, it just can't be. There's too much gray area, too many factors and underlying facets at play. Perhaps if we find this sword, things will finally make more sense. Mostly, I just don't understand that there was a man named Jesus Christ who was both fully God and fully man and that he died for our sins. Why would he have to die for sins because of some nonsense law, and is sin considered what God deems it? If so, why does He get to be the judge what makes Him so special, I just don't understand, but at the same token, if He created us would not the Creator be good at least from our perspective? But then again, as Terrick is an inventor, could not the one creating do it for purpose of evil or good, which means what if Satan wasn't evil, he just disagreed? But then again, if demons and dark spirits are his followers, I don't believe he would be good for a second. He is clearly evil. Why doesn't God just destroy Satan once and for all? Why the wait? Why must we suffer like this?" He wrestled over this for an hour before he fell asleep.

They awoke to breakfast and a letter for Terrick all lowered by basket by the old woman. He opened the letter and read it to himself, holding a slightly disturbed expression. "Joseph, Zacharias, I'm sorry I must go, something of the utmost importance has been brought to my attention." Terrick then relinquished the bronze compass, apologizing that he could help them no longer, but they told him to keep it that it was a gift for helping them with the guards. "I couldn't accept something like this when I haven't completed what I promised," Terrick added, feeling terrible.

"Go, my friend in the faith, do what you are called to do, you honored us by taking us this far. In no way shall we impede what God has called you to do," Joseph praised. Terrick prayed over them then said his good-byes. "Perhaps fate will bring us together again, my friends," as he then began to ascend the ladder.

"Where is it you're going anyways?" Joseph asked.

"To Babylon, a city located deep within the lands of the Amerith. It's not far by trade ship, but you need a special seal of approval from Valencia. This medallion I carry around was mine from when I worked for the NWF. I don't work for them anymore but I keep this handy so I can get around easier, you know like a renegade."

"So you live among the Amerith? I take it you sympathize with them," Joseph implied.

"Yes, and the rumors are true, they have been exiled to the desert under the order of the New Kings of Marduas. Just know, the reason I tell you the holy knights will never return is from many dark truths learned from the east and there is no stopping the coming tides of bloodshed. Like a beast, it rises to the heavens and will destroy whatever resists the coming change of ideology. The three kings of Marduas will spread their dominion across the west, and not Evangela, Bordeaux, or even Valencia can do a thing about it, millions are going to die very soon." Joseph nodded and Terrick also added, "Also stay away from Sodom and Gomorrah, which is not far from here resting on the coastline for it is damned, good-bye, my friends, heaven's wisdom be with thee." Terrick then went away in haste. After this, the old woman returned one final time with an ancient tome wrapped within tattered garment. Zacharias asked, "I'm sorry, but I never asked your name?"

"My name is Martha," she replied as she gave him the tome. She then went on to notify them, "For years, I had forgotten about this, but talking to you last night made me remember of my family's late treasure. It was this book in which my grandfather used to read me the stories of the holy knights. How about you keep it? I think it will serve you well. I have a positive inclination about you." The book was opened, and it was of the complete accounts of both the rise and fall of the holy knights all the way up to their demise. Joseph let out the loudest sigh of appreciation. Zacharias rotated to Martha, "Are you sure, this is legendary, this is, well, I could never repay you for something like this, it's priceless."

Martha hugged him, stating, "God is going to use you in mighty ways, but you better promise me, you'll find a good woman who will treat you right."

Joseph chuckled, "I'll make sure he does, Martha." She then strolled over to Joseph to the best of her ability and whispered something into his ear. "Come on, let us rent out a room and review this book," Joseph said, releasing all of his inner emotions like a child. Zacharias looked over at him as if he were crazy. "Joseph, I don't know about you sometimes," he said, grabbing the ladder. Joseph, who is rather frenzied, pulled him off onto the ground as another joke. "You're too slow," Joseph then yells as he sped up the ladder with the tome like a young man himself. "Not to humble a pastor!" he yelled, jumping up and chasing after him.

Ephesus had an inn at the edge of the city where the coast could be seen from the balcony only hundreds of feet away. Entering the room, Zacharias exclaimed, "I can't believe that Martha gave us this."

Joseph put the book on one of the beds. "She did a great thing for us. I definitely believe that her lineage traces back to the holy knights' origins."

Zacharias began to open it. "I'm grateful for this gift, Joseph, but how is this going to help us find out where the other statue of Artemis is for this sapphire finger? Even at that, how do we still know Artemis is the right statue for us to find just because the other statue in Crete was made of sapphire?" Joseph sat down on the other bed that was separated by a cabinet.

"If this book contains the holy knights reign in entirety, then how they ended will also be of answer. Perhaps in how they fell will shed some light on what happened to the Sword of Abraham even if it does not coincide with the sapphire finger or this city of Ephesus." A knock at the door was heard.

"Come in," Joseph replied. The innkeeper entered with lunch for the two of them. "Joseph, eat, we have a lot of studying to do," Zacharias attempted to blurt out, almost choking on the meal. Joseph then placed the sapphire finger on the mantle and broke bread with his brother. A bit later, the innkeeper returned with some wine, which they did not yet drink as they tore into the book for the duration of the day. When night had fallen, the innkeeper returned a third time with a candlelit lamp for them to use, for he knew they were studying diligently. Everything in the book was rather straightforward about the wars the holy knights had fought, the generals who commanded them, and the tactics they used and those who served. Finally after skimming through this book, they had reached the final chapter. After this, the two ate supper and consumed some wine.

9

Avarice of the Ancient Serpent

Joseph began praying in silence so that he could understand what they were about to read to the highest degree. "This is it, Zacharias, the words we read here are going to reveal how they fell. All the major details have been correct thus far, so I don't see why the fall will be any different, these records are indeed authentic."

Zacharias took a long deep breath and cracked his knuckles. "Let's do this," he stated, ready for mental combat.

Joseph then said, "For years and years, the Valencian Empire has deemed the holy knights traitorous heretics for destroying the nation of Devok and unleashing the mighty Hilaris. Now we learn what really happened, I always believed it to be a lie that they turned to sorcery as Valencia claims in the history books. The holy knights served for some thousand years by faith in Jesus Christ. They wouldn't have thrown that all away to unholy necromancy that is from the Devil. I just wanted to thank you for everything, we've been through a lot of horrific events thus far, but it was all worth it for this. I wouldn't change it for anything." Zacharias picked up the book and pulled out the medallion from around his neck of the Voltel family. Grabbing the insignia, he boldly stated, "This crest testifies to the bonds of family, just like

Martha gave us this tome that was a part of her family. The holy knights fought and sacrificed their lives for those who could not defend themselves. They believed all to be welcome into their family, and now, their downfall is revealed to us. If we never take another step after reading this, we've still gone further than what I could have ever imagined. May this lead us to what you seek, Joseph, you deserve it more than anyone." Joseph then began to read the final pages of the holy knight's most tragic ending.

ACCOUNT OF THE DOWNFALL
LETTER FROM GENERAL BETHERION

Fallen, fallen is man's sense of justice in the year of our Lord 2640. It has been thirty-two years since the fated destruction of WWI, but a new foe swells fresh. For two years, the defensive city Grias stands proud, granting Valencia western dominance with their ever-encroaching military prowess. The west is held in trap, all commerce is forced to go through the Valencian Empire. Trade and travel routes remain closed off from the east as to deny outside influence. Displeased with the results of the war, Valencia, drunk with vainglory, mocks them with false propaganda directly from the Church of Law herself. They have deemed the easterners as forgotten and damned to the ways of pagan culture. For the past many years, we, the Sword of the Cross has politically stood against the once true nation of Valencia. Jesus Christ gave his life for all to hear so that through his name all could come to be saved, and we shall never turn from that foundational truth preordained since before Vulgata, our somatic residence. Our order remains at saber's edge soon to be overtaken by the maelstrom of legislative initiative. Evangela turns her back on the teachings of the Lord's name upon which her foundation rests. Here we wait in Antioch underneath the Church of Salvation for we know that our days are few. The government has fallen to Luciferian elitists spewing lies and malevolence across the land by means of devious propaganda. Where, oh, where are the patriots, once vast was our force now whittled to a mere five hundred holy capes. For centuries did the Ten Commandments dictate law justly in our capital now demolished in the name of a leadership poisoned to the deception of secularism. Evangela, now a nation of man's law, has declared the church unfit to serve and any who refuse will be deemed enemies of the state. For over a thousand years have our brothers bled on the battlefield for the freedoms all share only for it to be forgotten and dishonored because the false promises of moral relativity. Clad in the full armor of God, we persist in watching over Evangela, but laws have now been emplaced, making any mention or teaching of Jesus outside of church illegal. To enforce the law of the land, a new weapon has been brought to the forefront; these men are known as the Judges. The Judges are known as the new domestic guardians of the state and we, an extremist threat. Political steps have already been taken against us to force a complete voluntarily disbandment. Woe to this nation who is turning from the Lord for He will lift the veil of protection that has always safeguarded Evangela from the corrupted nature of Vulgata. Still in His glory and splendor, the Lord shows mercy for those who hold steadfast believing in His name, and they are many within our borders. May His light forever shine upon all who believe even when national pride blasphemes the Holy Bible openly. Sword of the Cross is soon to be forgotten, but let not any believe that we did not love our nation, our people, and most of all the God of Abraham, Isaac, and Jacob. Signed, First Commandant General Moses Betherion.

ACCOUNT OF THE DOWNFALL (CONTINUED)

Early in the same year, Valencia would demand all sacred relics from each nation in payment for their protection from the eastern lands. One nation in particular would refuse, and that was the nation of Devok (Forest Nation). In those days, two forest nations stood: Scera and Devok. Both denizens of major forests, they were considered family to one another with Scera being the younger sister to Devok. These two forests along with Cruatia existed in the west long before any nation was ever established in the journey to the west. Those of Sceran heritage were prone to the peaceful nature of the forest, whereas those of Devokian blood were said to be the very wrath of nature. Scera gave up numerous holy relics to Valencia as most nations did out of fear of retaliation. Devok would not give up their sacred relics regardless of the might possessed by the crown and church. Once every five years, the nations of the world would confront each other in the Coliseum of Vindication in Valencia to serve national matters. One warrior from every nation would compete over international dispute in order to avoid major bloodshed in war. It would be this year that Devok would openly mock Valencia in their capital city of Alexandria in front of the west and call out their church as the embodiment of hypocrisy and greed to deem war over relics. The Devokians witnessed to the world that Jesus would not do such a thing; the Sword of the Cross would stand by them in this most essential political declaration. The Valencian king had both the Devokians and the SOC removed from Alexandria by threat of death, but it wouldn't stop there. Upon return to Evangela, the holy knights would rest in the forests of Scera, they had long been allies since the founding for Sir Abraham Deesteran was originally a Sceran himself. The Scerans were fellow brothers and sisters to the order, many of which believed and followed the word of God. Only days after the Devokians had returned to their forest lands also Valencia launched a massive crusade of eighty thousand strong to the forest. Both Scera and the order did not hear of this until they had marched past Eregia into Devok, and by then, it would be too late to avoid the coming genocide.

At the breaking of dawn, the army of crusaders could be heard approaching Devok for their steps shook the very ground in metallic piety. Thousands of Devokians gathered along the tree lines looking into the muddy fields of the clamoring army soon to alter history substantially. Their armor thick and steel weapons shining in the light, the Devokians stood no chance against an armored force of this magnitude. The boldest knight rode out covered in ceremonial red armor with a white cross embedded on his chest plate to the tree line, holding a royal parchment in shield hand. His helmet had an arrangement of white and red feathers that flowed down to his legs. He held a fearsome lance in the shape of a cross forged for the upheaval of the forest roots. In the other hand, a broad shield holds high the twin griffons of Valencia, Castor, and Pollux. Looking to the forest, the knight plunged the cross into the ground, absolving his mind of sin. Then reading the parchment he decreed, "By order of the king and the holy Church of Law, you have been deemed heretics of the alliance and are to offer all holy relics contained within your homeland! You are then to guide this crusade through your lands into the holy site of the Veeran swamp! If these demands are not met or military action is taken against this crusade, then it shall be the same as an assault upon crown and church! Obey these commands and thou shalt be liberated from thine charge! What say you?" No answer is given, no parley is made. The lone knight then grabbed his lance and returned to his commanders. The crusade was formed into three major ranks: the first being the cavalry corps. which were five thousand heavy armored cavalry ridden by steel-plated warrior. Their lances are far longer than the eastern knights, but are made to strike a single foe instead of the mass. The second was the infantry corps, which were sixty-five thousand heavily armored soldiers carrying variations of sword, shield, mace, and axe. Finally, the archery corps, which were ten thousand lightly armored soldiers carrying longbows accompanied by daggers at the hip. There were no silver paladins within this force for their primarily role was the defense of the church; they remained in Alexandria. Seeing this vast army, all the cities within Devok began to evacuate deep within the forest as warriors of the forest gathered around the front for two days.

Finally, the king of the forest, whose name was Midbar, rode out onto the battlefield on a Yijarii to discuss terms. The Yijarii is a massive green fox the size of a horse with folded-up flesh like praying mantis arms resting on its back that extend for either climbing or combative purposes. He was clothed in an emerald cape and wore a crown made of special branch, and in his right hand, he carried a large two-handed staff bearing the image of a wolf with angelic wings. The knight who had decreed Valencia's message two days prior rode out to negotiate. The king of Devok asked the knight his name; he responded that it was Polemeo. Now the king of Devok was multiple hundreds of years in age and his wisdom superbly more profound than most alive asked the young knight, "Why war with us, is there such a need to quarrel? The Valencian Church of Law is taken by their avarice over these holy relics, which were passed on to us by our forefathers." The king of Devok, Midbar, dismounted the tamed beast and bowed on his knees in the mud holding up his staff presenting it as a gift and token of friendship. "Please, good knight, take this and leave us in peace," King Midbar both humbly and desperately begged for the safety of his people. Sir Polemeo, without clemency or compassion, draws his specially crafted bastard sword and beheads the king right there in front of every eye of Devok. His horse rears up, knocking the Yijarii over, which the knight then cut its head off also after plunging his blade through spine and earth. Polemeo jams the staff into the ground, mounting the Yijarii's then Midbar's decapitated skulls upon it. Red and green blood of man and beast mix as a violent gale ruffles the feathers on the knight's smeared helmet. He declares, "No pagan shall ever live by their blasphemous words of trying to befriend the holy Church of Law!" The crusader army began to hit their shields and weapons against their chest plates to taunt the forest further. The Valencian crusaders' arrogance ran so deep they truly believed that their means would please God, that the means would justify the end result. From the tree lines of the forest, over ten thousand

Devokian warriors screamed out in a flawless wrath as Polemeo rode back to his fellow crusaders certain of rapid triumph. The Devokians entered a frenzied state, then firing a massive volley of arrows unto the Valencians out of retaliation for their fallen king. Their thick armor and shields were unaffected by the thousands of arrows, and the crusade marched forward slowed by the fields of sludge. The Devokians launched an endless series of volleys, but the advancing force would block every attempt, only taking minimal casualty. To the right of the crusade, all five thousand cavalry stormed across the plains assailing straight for the defending force of Devok. The Devokians took to the treetops where they retreated into the heart of the forest. For days, the Devokians retreated deeper into the wilderness as the crusaders' vicious hammer of religion crushed every city in their path. It didn't matter to them; they killed everyone and everything. In their deceived hearts, they believed they were under the authority of God.

The further the Valencians pushed, the more they learned just how mystical Devok actually was. The sun did not penetrate through the trees entirely nor did sound seem to carry as the wilderness sang its own song. Covered in dense vegetation and insects, no one had ever seen the crusaders grew nervous. Never before had war or men not of the forest touched these lands and the crusaders knew of this. In the soul of the forest, thirty thousand Devokians descended upon them from the treetops in a massive ambush late at night. This was of great advantage for the people of the forest can see at night better than regular people can during the day. The Yijarii had been clinging to the sides of trees and camouflaged by their green fur dove into the hordes of crusaders. Their eyes scowled in neon blaze as forest and man stood united in reprisal for king and blessed fauna. Furious mantis scythes of the Yijarii sink into the flesh and armor of men. Devokian warriors shower arrows with precision through the darkness. Elaborate traps entangle and impale crusaders to the sides of trees who are then shredded by throngs of forest soldiers, their weapons are sharpened branch and poisonous vine. The initial skirmish of three thousand crusaders were crushed in the slaughter of the night, fertilizing the ground with their sin. The following morning, the crusaders would gather and attack the force absent of hesitation. Between their thick armor and steel weapons, the crusaders annihilated the Devokian forces of thirty thousand in only two hours, losing only another two thousand themselves. Unshaken and bolstered with an army of seventy-five thousand, the Valencians advanced fully into the forest, butchering over a hundred thousand of innocent civilians including women and children. The crusaders had justified their actions from their religion for what holds a man's heart more than a justified belief? Their genocide of the Devokians was a clear violation of human rights and something was soon to be done.

Word had reached Scera by raven before the crusaders entered Devok. Knowing this, the holy knights rode to Devok's aid, and it was then that the last five hundred holy knights were prepared to lay down their lives. A ten-thousand man archery corps had formed a blockade barring any refugees from escape. Steel arrow falls from the clouds much like the loss of every feather upon Satan's damned wings. The holy knights charge through the loosed flurry, shields towering, faith unto war, and blades ravenous for the divinity of justice. The holy weapons lacerate bone and sinew with ease as the horses themselves thrash about in a controlled fury sided with the raped wilderness begging for liberation. Every knight participates, every knight slays those of yet another false holy war. One, two, even three are killed by every swipe and stab of the sword, foul tongue is bashed into submission by the golden cross ever present on celestial shields. It was a battle that could not be avoided, the slaughter of innocent civilians had to stop, and it was the only way to secure an escape route. Decimated, the few hundred from the archery corps left alive disband, gore blends with the plains of mud. The white knights roar across the forest, encountering refugees across the fallen kingdom. The Devokian people help them to their main city so they are able to organize a mass exodus; word is spread by the whispers of tree and men alike for days. Under every rock, leaf, and root, people gather from nature's realm.

Meanwhile, the Valencian crusaders had split into two major groups. The first which was comprised of twenty thousand men entered into the sacred ground known as the Veeran swamp. The second which was forty-five thousand found out from their scouts that the archery corps was demolished. An expeditious counter attack is planned before the migration can begin. First Commandant General Moses Betherion III leads this exodus as forty-five thousand crusaders converged on their position with unprecedented haste. General Moses lifts his titanic and illustrious axe, calling upon the Lord to pull them through. As he did, the forest spread apart, giving a clear path for the next day so they could escape, but as it opened up, it closed behind, trapping the crusaders within the wilderness. In all reality, it was a prison for the very vines of the forest barred their paths, but who was the jailer? The Valencians had murdered well over a third of the Devokian race and would soon pay with their blood. For only days later, the remaining crusaders from the Veeran swamp emerged without relic and without reason. Of the twenty thousand that entered the swamp, only one thousand came out, but far worse, they had awoken the wrath of the Devokian forest, the mother.

As the knights lead the exodus to Scera, few remain behind in the stained fields before the trees running reconnaissance in case any attempted to pursue. Something had happened in that swamp deep within the labyrinth of anguish, something had caused a reaction never seen. From the Veeran bogs, a dreadful atrocity is awoken, screeches of a colossal and ancient monster carry for miles. Inside the forest, the Hilaris had revived and the now forty-six thousand remaining crusaders attempted to escape the coming sacrifice of themselves. Toward the main tree line, a blackened tree that appeared to have been tossed into the fire sprouts and grows in seconds with a width well over a hundred trees; the final height is five hundred and fifty five feet. Its massive branches were the heads of monstrous hydras. A dozen plus reach high above before they began crashing down into the forest, slaughtering thousands of crusaders. They devoured dozens at a time and simply smashed others, but each time, another rose, blood, body, and limb poured forth from their mouths soaking the treetops. After the carnage had splashed and leaked down the sides of the blackened tree, the very roots from the ground opened up and began to swallow the bodies into the earth. The holy knights watching, weep for the thousands who reached out their arms screaming in agony trapped within biblical pools of condemnation. Once the Valencians had retreated from the forest, not even five thousand remain of the initial army of eighty thousand strong. The holy knights do not attack or provoke for enough blood had been shed over this pointless war. The hydra's heads hovered above as an eternal sentinel bearing testimony to the blatant avarice and hubris from those who had raped its mother. The broken Valencian crusade trembled in fear and would return home in shame being the parents of this monstrocity born of sin, the Hilaris.

Two hundred thousand Devokians enter Scera, but their home was gone. That day, the Scerans took in the Devokians to live among them forever and looked to the white knights as saviors. The holy knights rebuke the statement and then explained to them that it was not them but Jesus who had saved them. Together, the Scerans and Devokians were united as a one people of the forest who would now be known as the Alkirum. The Alkirum together demanded war against Valencia, but it would have been lunacy seeing as the crusade was but a shadow of Valencia's power. United as the Alkirum, those of the Devokian royal family handed over to General Moses Betherion III a piece of sacred cloth. This was no ordinary piece of cloth for this was the cloth that contained the blood of Christ. It was this final piece that was to be assembled to the Sword of Abraham, which would advance it to the Trinitarian Blade. When this happened, it would usher in the time of the Exiles to rise and light the celestial beacons of the earth to bear testimony to the return of our savior on man's account to man. That week, both the knights and the Alkirum mourned and rejoiced over events finalized. After that, the order planned to return home to report on what had happened as to rally a political response against the injustices of Valencia. Good-byes are said to the Alkirum who honor the holy knights by establishing a covenant; it states that the holy knights are welcomed as family to any of the forest. This was to be passed generation to generation.

One final return is made to Antioch. Rain fell that afternoon as clouds blocked out all traces of the sun. Standing with heavenly tears dripping down their white-plated armor, they watch in disbelief as the remaining crusader army stands by the Ten Commandments. Behind, the Judges are accompanied with Evangela's own military equipped with thousands of already aimed crossbows. The Judges demand the legendary arms of the SOC, the Valencian crusaders slowly advance. Refusal to give up their weapons is shown as every holy knight sheaths weapon and does not surrender it for the right to bear arms had been with Evangela since the founding. Innumerable citizens watch from the Church of Salvation and the city in horror. A lone pastor passes the crowds from the doors of the church. He then proceeds through the ranks of the five hundred and stands before General Moses demanding the cloth piece. He had betrayed them and claimed to the government they were heretics who turned to sorcery. The Valencian crusaders testified, stating the holy knights had unleashed the Hilaris by these means. Never before had a foreign military set foot in the Kingdom of Evangela. In front of everyone, the pastor opened his mouth and consumed the cloth. "Today, I will live forever for the blood of the messiah now flows within my veins," he whispered to the holy knights. General Moses Betherion was then shot to death by hundreds of crossbow bolts, his armor withstood inhuman punishment, but even this grand armor is not invincible to earthly demise. The Judges of Evangela ordered the myriad of crossbowmen to fire as the Valencian crusaders blocked all other forms of retreat. Together, these men shared the ups and downs of life, they and their families lived as one, their church stood united as one, and now they died as one. A lifetime of sacrifice and servitude did these patriots give to a nation undeserving. In the end, the brothers of the faith stood honorably saluting the church and were carried home by a tempest of swift demise.

ACCOUNT OF THE DOWNFALL
THE FINAL HOLY KNIGHT

After the slaughter of the holy knights had come to an end, I would awake that night buried beneath my brothers. I had been shielded by the bodies of my dearest friends who sacrificed themselves to save me. Pushing them off, I arose to the darkness of the night surrounded by the dead bodies of the patriots who gave their lives for one another and a country blinded by vainglory. Thousands of members from the church held a candlelight vigil as they wept and wailed over the fallen, the carnage was total, the nation lost was soon to see murky days turn black. A few saw me stand up in what they called patriot-stained armor and rushed me into the church as to hide me. We traveled to headquarters underneath where they mended my wounds.

Later that night, I awoke to a frightful screaming above, I went to investigate. The pastor who had betrayed us stood at the altar, yelling out in pain and agony, ripping out patches of skin and hair. Continually, he profaned the name of God and began to call out the name of Manistof. Soon, a dark spirit appeared in shadow, trying to help him endure the pain. Just then, his skin began to split open and his legs snapped in the opposite direction falling off. Ripping out of his skin, a massive half-man half-snake was born, standing twelve feet tall. The dark spirit deemed him the immortal betrayer for the spirit of Judas Iscariot was with him and he named him Ephestus. The lower half of his body was of a massive snake, but his top half was that of a man with blackened scales and a snake's countenance. The dark spirit commanded him to bow and accept allegiance with Lucifer, and as Ephestus lowered himself to the spirit named Manistof, the shadow placed a crown of iron thorns upon his skull. Oil flowed staining the altar and then Manistof commanded Ephestus to wait for him in the church of Sodom in the city of Gomorrah located at the southern tip of Athens. Ephestus revealed to Manistof the burial site of Sir Abraham Desteeran, which is where his sword was located. Pleased by this, Manistof explained to Ephestus that he had devised a plan to get the Sword of Abraham so that he could destroy it. He also added that Ephestus was to hide in Sodom so that the cloth piece he had consumed could never be found so the Sword of Abraham could not be completed. Manistof feared this weapon and stated that if the Trial of Kings was to be accomplished, then the Trinitarian Sword would rise and bind the twelve Exiles who could ruin everything. Ephestus, in a snake-like voice, asked him exactly how he would enter into such holy ground for a dark spirit even as strong as Manistof would be stopped by angels of God. Manistof disclosed to him that his agents were many.

Hearing all of this, I knew I had to get to the sword before he did. I had to make sure the Exiles could one day obtain the sword. Injured, I traveled by horse for days, only stopping in Scera to gather supply. I could not tell them my mission, but I did inform them that I was the last of the holy knights and that it was now up to them to wait for the Exiles. When I had finally reached Avodah Mortis, I entered in through the mountain through the spiritually protected doors bearing our seal. I traveled past zodiac's hour and the abyss, finally entering Abraham's burial site. Unknown to me, I had let in a dark spirit known as Artemis. In the abyss, she came to life through the power of the moonlight, and because I had opened the doorway, she was able to enter his tomb. Made completely of sapphire, she was a statue more real than the earth, I attempted to combat her, but my mace held no effect on the statue. One strike sent me crashing into the wall as she began to open Abraham's grave. I lay there disoriented and I could see the spirit of Abraham hovering above his grave as he slashed at the statue with the legendary sword knocking off her finger and causing her to disappear. Walking over to the grave, I peered inside and his body and sword were gone; all that was left was the sapphire finger, which I dared not touch. Leaving Avodah Mortis, a rockslide crashed down in front of the entranceway, hiding it deep within the earth.

I traveled to Athens to find and destroy Ephestus who betrayed us into death. Stopping in Ephesus, there was a library where the order had moved a plethora of secret knowledge for it was not safe in Evangela from years prior; it is one of two. I filled the last of this book with my own words of how our downfall happened entrusting this truth to a dear relative. May whoever reads this know the holy knights died with faith, love, and honor for God, family, and country. I go now to Sodom and Gomorrah to face the demon Ephestus. Know that the last of us remained fighting till the very end, and may the light of heaven forever shine upon your path no matter the struggle. Atyrael be with you! Signed, Sir Joshua Desteeran.

END OF THE ACCOUNT

Zacharias and Joseph both glanced over to the sapphire finger and not a word was said. Zac extends his arm carefully, taking it. "So this belongs to the hand of a demon?"

"Yes, I believe that to be so, and now, we finally know how the holy knights were betrayed by one of their own," Joseph reiterated from the story. Now standing up Joseph began to brief him on the plan. "I'm going to go to Sodom and Gomorrah in the morning, and this time, you cannot go with me."

"What do you mean?" he declared angrily with his eyebrows scrunched up and mouth open.

Joseph pulled out a wooden cross within his rucksack and sat beside his brother. "Do you remember what happened in the abyss in Avodah Mortis?"

"Yes, but what does that have to do with this?"

Joseph sighed. "What Terrick said about this place being damned was in absolute truth, it is a city fallen to depravity and sin. In the abyss, you were spiritually attacked, it will be tenfold in a city home to unclean spirits. They're going to try and get you if you enter this place, and this time may kill you." Zacharias ate his words feeling upset for he knew Joseph was correct. "I want you to wait for me at this inn. I shall leave in the morning and return before or by nightfall." The young man obeyed Joseph's command, but by no means does he agree. "Everything's going to be all right. I'm sure Ephestus died some three hundred years ago. I'm just going to check his gravesite just like Abraham's."

"But the sword, Joseph, the sword is gone like the story said, it disappeared," Zacharias conveyed this message with deep conviction, trying to sway his decision. He then added "You don't have to do this, let's just go home back to Salem where it's peaceful. Penelope loves you as does Mariana, hell, the entire city loves you and needs you, Joseph!" Joseph gave a half smile for the other half of his emotions were focused on the task ahead with those holy knights left to die so humiliatingly in front of their very church.

"It is because I love them I must do this. The thing is even if the sword is not present, the cloth piece should be to the Sword of Abraham, perhaps that will cause the sword to reappear. If not, we then would still have a piece of the puzzle at least. We owe it to them for everything they did and this knowledge we have just received is yet more proof this journey was meant to be." Joseph then put out the candle and each of them rest in their beds, talking in the moonlit room. Zacharias turned his head away, upset, covering his eyes, quietly saying, "If you don't come back, I'll kill you myself." The words float to the bowels of his heart, echoing the pains of loss, but Joseph begins to laugh. This is not the reaction he was expecting. "Why are you laughing? I don't want you to die!"

"You want to kill me if I die, that's not even possible." Joseph returns with a solemn voice, "Do you remember when we entered Malastay and you ran into the snow veil before any of us?"

"Yes, that was painful how it tossed us on the other side, but there was no way I was letting you try it out, you have a family to go back to."

Joseph stated, "That day, I learned something from you. I learned that no matter what, you would never give up on my family or I. I don't know what happened in your past, but I know it must have been pretty horrible. I can see it in your eyes when you speak. You taught me what it means to never stop fighting, to always take one more step. Without you as a friend, I'd have given up on this journey by now." Joseph then additionally stated:

> Iron sharpeneth iron; so a man sharpeneth the countenance of his friend.
>
> Proverbs 27:17 (KJV)

"Just be careful tomorrow. Penelope made me promise I'd bring you home alive. You cannot let me go back to her having failed that mission, she may kill me too." "Understood. I assure you I will be in and out of the city as fast as I can, believe me, I don't want to be there." Joseph then also revealed, "Mariana really does love you as a brother, did you know that?" Zacharias pulled out the teddy bear Mr. Sebastian out of his pack and smiled.

"If anything should happen to me, it's up to you to take care of them, do you understand?" Joseph tells him in an unconventional dejected tone. Zacharias is unable to see this, but multiple tears run down the face of his friend. Both of them lay there for a minute, staring at the ceiling, until Zacharias revealed, "Manistof is the name of the dark spirit that primarily follows me around."

"The same name of the spirit Sir Joshua Desteeran spoke of?"

"Yes, that's him. He's the same one who approached me the day you were able to send him away in your household with Penelope."

"Only what is holy and just can drive away what is wicked," Joseph told him. "You see, that's what I don't understand, what does the word *holy* even mean? In fact, I don't understand what the word *holy knights* mean, I mean, why couldn't they bear another name? I looked over that entire book Martha gave us and saw no mention as to why they have that title."

Joseph answered, "I'll tell you what. You wait here for me to complete our mission tomorrow and I'll tell you what it means upon my return."

Zacharias smirked in the dark, replying, "All right, you tell me that tomorrow and I'll share with you my testimony."

"It's a deal," Joseph said.

Both of them contemplate on the others promise made.

"Do you really believe in the Exiles, Joseph?"

In his last words, he states, "As much as I do that the son hath risen."

10

Blazing Pestilence

Late does the hero rise at the appointed hour, following a nightmare that felt more real than a woman's touch. Thinking to himself, he began to dwell on the seemingly celestial experience where he witnessed Penelope tell him not to let her husband die on this journey. Continuously, her words imprinted his every connective thought, her begs and pleas only increase. Battle of intellect ensues, he is unsure whether or not to intervene to alter the course. On one side, Penelope made him promise, but on the other, Joseph had given direct command not to enter Sodom and Gommorah. Ever since he had started to live with the Voltels, he let them make most of his decisions. Trust had not yet been regained of his personal judgment since he had taken a dip in the River Styx by mode of attempted suicide. After a man comes face-to-face with death especially by his own hands, something changes in that man. When peering unto death's mirror and the reflection is thyself, a person is forced to confront who they are at the basest of levels, but when it is by your own hand, everything changes on an even further scale. For how can a man trust the world when he cannot trust himself? Zacharias trusted the Voltel family with his life, but had not yet overcome the fear of trusting himself once more. Without stop or relief, the thought of Joseph going to this city clouded his logic. Never before had he felt a feeling like this, this was different, this was a calling. Try as he may, he is unable to force further sleep to shake the feeling, but the more he resists, the stronger it becomes. For over an hour, these thoughts bombarded his psyche until he turned over to his pack and could see Mr. Sebastian sticking out, staring right at him. Tender memories of Mariana stirred and consequently the thoughts of her without a father are delivered. Leaning up out of bed, speaking quietly, he says to himself, "I can't let this happen, this is my family and families lay down their lives for one another." Now picking up the teddy bear, Mr. Sebastian, he held it close to his chest. He whispered, "God, if you are as real as Joseph says, then show me. Reveal to me the reality of all things and why I am to live a cursed life, what is the purpose? More importantly, let me find this Ephestus, regardless of his current state. Let me find him or his resting place so that Joseph does not get hurt." Fist is clenched, resolution is absolute. He placed Mr. Sebastian on the bed beside him and then thought to himself in all certainty, "I'm sorry, Joseph, but this I have to do whether you come to understand why is not of my concern. I have to do this for me. I have to learn to trust myself again or I will never be able to recover from these scars. I made a promise to your family and I intend to keep that promise." Zacharias then tiptoed over, grabbing both his pack and sword in all silence, knowing there was no turning back. Stepping outside, he began to prepare Grear as he could hear the waves crashing along the coast unhindered by societies clatter. He trotted off onto the coastline where he then galloped with the stars as his guide. Miles away from the city of Ephesus, he rode beside a strange and disturbing sight. A pack of wandering Clariad trudge along the sands, wailing in pain and sorrow. These shape-shifting creatures were unlike any he had ever seen. Dozens of them began surfacing out of the ocean, adding to the confusion, but they were not hostile. They had four legs and moved about much like a small bear, swaying their heads from side to side. The face continually morphed, never assuming a definitive shape in the night. Clariad are also known as water elementals. They are polymorph types of monsters with water flowing around their bodies, which is the only element they are known to be composed of. Every area of sand in which the liquid feet touched turned black as if polluted. "Come on, Grear, let us ride around these monsters and pay them no heed," Zacharias said while patting Grear's neck. Riding around the pack of Clariad, they began to die one at a time, studying him. As they died, their water-like bodies deconstructed and only a puddle of black wet outline remained. This sand was then washed back into the ocean by the coming tides. He stopped Grear for just another second, peering out into the ocean, stating, "So many things I will never understand about Vulgata." He then went on, dwelling upon the potential anger of Joseph for the decision he'd made to disobey. The Clariad continued to rise out of the ocean and die after they had gone. One in particular is different for it does not come ashore; instead, this Clariad takes on the shape of a man swimming to the city impure.

A mile away, the massive city of Gommorah could be seen in the distance and the church of Sodom to the rear climbs far higher. Surrounded by a formidable bronze wall around the city and a gate built for giants, he began to slightly regret the decision. Hundreds of braziers lit the tops of the fortress. Now only a quarter mile from it standing on a fairly high sand dune, Zacharias dismounted his white horse. "Grear, I need you to wait for me, okay, I don't want to put you in any more danger than you have to be." He attempts to push forward, but Grear rubbed his nose to his back. "Grear, I have to go just wait for me." Again, he started to walk away and Grear bit his pack and pulled him. Zacharias turned around and sat and Grear sat beside, resting his head on his lap. Petting his head, he could feel the nervous heartbeat of the horse who was spooked. "Grear, you're a good horse and the best gift anyone could ever ask for. Please do this one deed for me and I promise I'll return to you, okay, boy." Again he stands and Grear remains lying, watching him on his descent to the fallen city. Two rows of long iron torches paved the sandy path all the way to the gate. Now standing before the gates of Gommorah, Titulus shows purity shining in the moonlight. "Please, Grandfather, watch over me, for I can feel a dark presence unlike anything I've felt before." A loud crack was heard that tore through the haunted coast and the gates began to open. Gaze fixated on the entrance, peripherals check the watchtowers that remain empty. He begins to shake but not from fear, instead, from adrenaline. Knowing Ephestus was here in this city alive or deceased, he wanted the demon's head that brought the holy knights to an end. The gates were now wide, but still, he stood outside the portal, slowly inspecting the surrounding area in case of trap. Not a person is around, yet he knows he is not alone. It was not a bad presence, but instead, something strangely familiar, something noble and just. "What is this feeling within, who is there?" he declared. Beside him stood a ghost clouded by a dim light. Catching Zac off guard, he stood frightened, also jumping backward. "Who are you?" he asked. The apparition did not answer nor did it acknowledge that he was standing beside him; instead, the ghost floated into the city and then vanished at the slight sound of a faint ringing bell. Zacharias advanced past the gates and was surrounded by the entirety of its structures. Old claylike buildings stood around the interior, and in the distance, a single torch could be seen approaching. "Who goes there?" Zacharias proclaimed with his sword diagonal to hairline. Creeping along, he could see a figure with a long crimson cloak approaching him with his face secluded by hood. The figure held a long staff with a bell attached to the top of it that rang with each threatening step. Only a few feet from him, the figure removed his hood, declaring in a depressed tone, "Late is the night, traveler, declare thy intent?"

"I've come to find Ephestus."

The man in red cloak inched closer, bowing to him. "Master, you have come as you said you would," he said to Zacharias, morbidly excited. Although the dialogue is directed at him, the true recipient is Titulus. Instead of questioning why the man was calling him master, Zac saw opportunity to find Ephestus and went along with it. "What is your name, servant, I have forgotten," he asked.

"Surely my name is not of importance for the master is all that matters, have you come to deliver us our earned salvation? Please, my master, come with me, I wish to show you of the glory we do in your name," the cloaked man spoke in a voice now mixed with fear and concern.

"I'll go with you, but it is my intent to see Ephestus, will you do that for me?" Zacharias questioned him again.

"Yes, yes, my master, but we must first see the others?" He knew that it could be potentially devastating to follow this man, but it was his only lead at finding Ephestus and to break away now could be more so detrimental. The man leads and he follows past the narrow alleys and corridors of the city by the blackened bay. All the while, Joseph lay sleeping, not knowing his friend had left for the area he had warned him to avoid.

The man in red plowed through thick sands as they became higher deeper within this discreet world. With each step, the bell could be heard ringing on the staff, increasing in pitch. Zacharias looked around for any citizens, but saw nothing. "Something isn't right, I can feel it in the very air I breathe," he began to tell himself. The man disappeared behind another alleyway and only the bell served as guide. Turning into the same corridor behind the hovels, there was a long iron stairwell leading to a secret spot by the coastline. The path down is lined with cage extending from the railings. He could hear the vague sounds of noises that did not sound right, and with each step, his heart began to race faster until it physically hurt. Every fiber of his being told him to leave this place, to run away, but he had to proceed for the Voltels sake. The bell suddenly stopped and he could see the lone torch sitting by a hidden group of buildings below the main city and between a lone snake-coiled obelisk erected. Chains hang from a ceiling unseen. Walking forth into this underground portion, he was locked in place by the sight he saw. The man in red stood holding a bizarre pitcher of wine. "Master, are you pleased with us?" In a flush of embarrassment and disgust, he bars sight to ground. Barely did the torch light the area, but what it did light was more than any sane man should ever have to witness. In alleys, corners, and everything in between, he could see men laying with men, holding not an ounce of shame. Hundreds looked over to him without stopping their inhuman orgy, and Zacharias turned to the man in red, refusing to directly acknowledge such vile acts. As this was happening, he could hear the sexually charged noises of men and women fornicating together all around as if his presence threw them into a frenzied state. These people had forfeited their souls for the lowest of carnal desire, and although the love of Christ could still save them, they chose to remain in rebellion.

> For the invisible things of him from the creation of the world are clearly seen, being understood by the things that are made, even his eternal power and Godhead; so that they are without excuse: Because that, when they knew God, they glorified him not as God, neither were thankful; but became vain in their imaginations, and their foolish heart was darkened. Professing themselves to be wise, they became fools, And changed the glory of the un-corruptible God into an image made like to corruptible man, and to birds, and fourfooted beasts, and creeping things. Wherefore God also gave them up to uncleanness through the lusts of their own hearts, to dishonour their own bodies between themselves: Who changed the truth of God into a lie, and worshipped and served the creature more than the Creator, who is blessed for ever. A'-men. For this cause God gave them up unto vile affections: for even

their women did change the natural use into that which is against nature: And likewise also the men, leaving the natural use of the woman, burned in their lust one toward another; men with men working that which is unseemly, and receiving in themselves that recompence of their error which was meet.

Romans 1:20–27 (KJV)

"Take me to Ephestus now!" Zacharias said full of disgust and rage.

"Yes, my master, you are free to join if you wish" the man in red explained with a dim smile drunk from the wine he offered. He gave no answer as the man in red proceeded back up the stairs into the main city. Alas, it was even worse at the top of the city, for somehow, him being there had alerted everyone. Following the cloaked red figure, he noticed in the distance that people were now sodomizing (lying with animals). "Truly beautiful the union of man and beast, the very harmony of the world, wouldn't you say? It's a shame the rest of Vulgata cannot understand our bliss," the cloaked figure stated with joyous pride. Zacharias grabbed his red cloak, pulling him face-to-face. "You listen here, you conniving bastard, take me to Ephestus now or I'll kill you where you stand!"

"I am sorry, my master, I will take you to the Church of Sodom, it is there Ephestus slumbers." Ripe with ire, the young warrior felt overwhelmed by levels of sin and finally understood what Joseph had meant by fallen and that some things really were as simple as black and white.

Joseph awoke from his sleep and noticed the teddy bear beside him. Sitting up out of bed, he could see that his friend had gone. Joseph slammed his fist on the desk. "You fool!" Joseph then immediately readied himself for departure.

The man in red had now brought Zacharias forth to the Church of Sodom. The dock is well aged, extending out to the church in the bay. Gargantuan is the structure standing dozens of stories high covered in windows from a numberless amount of rooms. The dull night sky compliments each uncaring stone placed to perfection. "Once were these called the twin cities Sodom and Gommorah, but now a relic of the past for all to remember the glory of the master," the guide yelled, holding his staff up to the church. What made this cathedral turned church so impressive from an architectural standpoint wasn't just the sheer grandeur of it, but the spire resting upon the northern parapet. A smoky spire extended hundreds of feet surrounded by masterfully designed stained glass portraits facing each of the four winds. Each portrait contained a season of death, the man in red explained, "One by man, another by nature, another by self, and the last by heavenly judgment!"

"Is this is a church or a cathedral?" he asked him.

"Once was it a cathedral when the bishop of lustful desire ruled, but now a lonely and forgotten church where the ancient serpent yearns to shed new skin." Zacharias noticed the drawbridge was already lowered to the dock and could see the ghost covered in dim light crossing, the man in red did not see this. He then followed the ghost who had gone through the grand church's doors. Standing on the drawbridge, he could see other large stained glass windows that were shaded in orange to green colors. In the waters below, thousands of snakes slither through the waves, inching up the structure all the way to the top. Walking to the doors, he thought to himself, "The ghost is not my enemy, I believe it is guiding me." Zacharias pulled open the left door slowly as to not make noise, but it inevitably made a loud creaking noise that echoed about every inch of the vast structure .

Standing in the main lobby, there was a long and narrow staircase lined with red carpet and the armor of knights on either side reaching the top. Each knight stood holding heavy stone axes to chest, but these were not of any knighthoods yet seen. They were not holy or drudge or even silver paladins. Zacharias stepped over to one and ran his hand across the statue, finding a single emblem. The emblem rested upon their chest and was of a snake wrapped around a tree. "The snake and the tree, what does that have to do with a knighthood?" He then headed up the stairwell as the eyes of the statues watched him behind his back. At the top of the stairs, it opened up into an extensive room only held in broken fairytale. The ceiling reached hundreds of feet high with a great row of illustrious antique chandeliers extending across in a single straight line. Hundreds of church pews lined the room, to the sides, wooden confessionals showcased blood-stained guillotines inside. Various levels of the church ran alongside magnificent balconies as if once made for all of Vulgata's royalty. The red carpet extended from the stairs and opened up down the middle aisle of the pews, leading all the way to the main altar. High above the altar sat a massive stained glass portrait of Eve reaching for the fruit at the tree of life with the snake in its branches. Surrounded by a half-circular marble staircase, the red carpet reached to the top where it stopped before the massive statue of half-man, half-snake. This snake statue stood twelve feet high and the snake's head rose upward to the ceiling. "What is this place really?" Zacharias said to himself as he walked along the carpet to the altar glimpsing at the classic design. Glancing up, he noticed that the chandeliers were all lit, which he had not initially paid attention to. Above the lit candles was a painting across the entirety of the chapel. This painting was of an uncountable number of fallen angels dressed in stars of their own, praising a figure that was one with darkness descending upon the nations of the earth. Now walking up the altar, the skeptic noticed the statue was looking directly to the black figure.

Just then, at the other end of the church, a great pipe organ began to play, resonating throughout the building in the sound of an old Gregorian chant. Surveying the room at the main balcony above the entranceway was a man in a beautifully decorated violet robe mixed with silver lining. The man held open his arms as if before an audience, shouting, "Welcome, my son!" High above the man sat yet another large round stained glass window that was golden orange like the sun. By this stained glass window, a catwalk connected entrance and altar passing slightly above the chandeliers. Zacharias felt nothing, but the presence of evil from this man and pointed his sword as he came out one of the side stairwells into the main room. "Who are you?" Zacharias yelled out.

"I am both priest and caretaker of this magnificent archetype for the coming revelations of mankind," he explained in a pretentious voice. The priest then rested his hands inside of each of the sleeves as he crossed them together, strolling past the main aisle. Now standing at the first stair of the altar, he glanced up and sighed, "Alas, if you must call me something, Pontifex will have to do."

Still pointing his sword at Pontifex, he demanded, "Tell me where Ephestus is!" Pontifex laughed while shaking his head and removing hand from sleeve. "Young man, do you not know unbridled wrath will not get you what you seek in this world." He waved his finger in a no motion; his fingers are unusually long. Titulus is lowered but not summoned to sheath.

"I've traveled a long way, what is it you ask of me, priest?"

Pontifex stares with a sinister eye. "It is not what you can do for me, but what I can do for you, for it is the job of a priest to heal the sick."

"Am I so sick?" Zac replied.

Pontifex tilted slightly. "Do you not hold to your soul the touch of death? Is not the print of Manistof seared to your back?" His eyes widen as Pontifex climbs the stairs. With each step, he spoke another word, "I cannot take your pain away, child, but the one who can stands behind you." Zacharias glared at the statue he knew represented Ephestus and rotated back as Pontifex stood within arm's reach. "How did you know that I have the curse of death bound to me, Pontifex?"

"Because it is my job to know for god discloses all spiritual matters to me," Pontifex exclaims. The priest then also adds, "The pain you feel is unbearable, my son, if you will allow me to remove it, I will then show you where Ephestus waits. But I cannot show you the true nature of Ephestus until your plight is removed for you are unclean in the eyes of god."

"To remove this curse I had never thought possible. My dreams, my eternal wants gifted before me and to find Ephestus all together." Zacharias walked over to the statue of the snake and exclaimed to Pontifex, "I don't understand what it is you want from me, truthfully?" Pontifex relocated behind the statue and pulled out a block in which opened a passageway down into the cellars of the church. Carefully stepping down the pathway, he stated, "What I want is for you to meet our god." Pontifex then disappeared as Zacharias thought to himself, *How does he know everything about me?* He could see the same ghost standing before the statue and it also followed the twisting stairwell. Looking to the floor, he pulled out the Voltel family crest, stating, "Joseph, I'm sorry, but this is something you could never understand. I know that this is a trap, but I must trust myself again even if it is the wrong decision." He then copied the ghost's path, thinking of Cordelia's tender voice; even the thought of her fair skin and gentle tone brings him at least limited peace.

Entering into the cellars, a few torches line the walls in which a surplus of barrels can be seen. At the end of the long cobwebbed cellar sits a large wooden catwalk with stairs leading to a stone-made floor. Pontifex stands at the bottom, lighting a chandelier that he then began to raise up by rope that was rigged to a pulley system. At the edge of the room sat a large piece of cloth covering over some type of fairly large figure.

"Are you ready, Zacharias? Are you ready to meet our living goddess?"

"I thought you said god, not goddess," he replied.

Pontifex smiled as he grabbed the cloth. "Depends on the form our master chooses." Pontifex then pulled the cloth off of the figure and an enormous statue made completely of sapphire stood with a bow pointing directly at Zacharias. "This is the master's current form. Her name is Artemis, virgin goddess of the hunt and the moon." The room filled with the splendor of the sapphire's midnight blue color and Zacharias was mesmerized by it. "Come, come and revere the living goddess for only she can heal you," Pontifex stated as he bowed to Artemis. Zacharias inched down the steps as his heart was fixed upon the idea of being free of his curse. Standing before the statue whose eyes were closed, he remembered the sapphire finger within his pocket. Carefully, he removed it before the statue and its eyes opened and were a ruby red. The statue came alive, moving, absent of our understanding of space and time. She began to speak into his soul with a serene and loving celestial voice. "I am Artemis, goddess of both the hunt and the moon. The pain you feel in your heart is more than I have seen and it saddens me. Pledge your allegiance to me and I will hold you to my bosom, healing your curse of death. I wish for this, my greatest hunt in the destruction of death, so that I may be known as the messiah." Zacharias's eyes stared into the scarlet eyes of Artemis whose arms were now open with her bow in the left arm. Overcome by emotion, he falls into her for the chance to be free of loneliness, his destroyer. Gradually, her arms close, his face leaned down pressing up against her chest, but the feeling is not of stone but of flesh. "Take me as your goddess, Zacharias, and not only will I heal you, but I will show you my true form and love you all the days of a shared immortality. I know how lonely you are and I too am lonely for I am trapped within this statue. Let us free each other." Artemis then brought forth her right hand that was missing the pointer finger. "Return my finger and seal this covenant of marriage with me, young warrior of endured trial, and we shall be joined in eternal matrimony. I have saved my virginity for countless millenniums and you are worthy of that gift. Join me and we shall rule our own kingdom for mine is that of the Gentiles and I her queen." The red eyes of Artemis pierce his unprotected soul; no longer is he in control of his actions. Artemis brushed the broken hand against his cheek and began to rub her statue-like face over his also giving him a makeshift kiss upon the cheek. His entire body trembles, cognitive response is lost, and his vision is entranced. "Yes, I will take you as my bride," he states in a monotone voice stripped of emotion while he held out the sapphire finger much like a stringed puppet. Pontifex could be heard giving praise beside them, "Revere her, revere, and save the one who loves you, become one with us, and never be alone again." In the mind of Zacharias, images of everyone he ever knew and loved flashed before him. Sad and tragic ways they all died played again and again projected by Artemis. "I can end all this if you will restore me with my finger, sealing night's bond by slaughtering any notion of that blameless lamb of day," Artemis added in a compassionate voice. In the midst of all this, Penelope's voice is heard asking if she could sit beside him just like when she had first met him after the knock at the door in the Voltel household. "No, this can't be the truth, this can't be the way, the Voltels showed me what love of others meant and this is not it," Zacharias screamed in his soul. Artemis attempted to distract him with various other things, but he was focused on the Voltel family and their bonds. "Joseph, Penelope, Mariana, Alcus, Kelly, Davidoff, Terrick, all of you and so many more have shown me what love is and everyone of you spoke of Jesus Christ in some way." At that very moment, the mention of the name Jesus made Artemis completely return back to her normal statue-like state and close her eyes.

Meanwhile at the gates of Gommorah, a figure covered in strange garb and hood entered into the city. The same man in red with the bell staff met him and bowed in pure fear, stating, "Finally, my god has arrived, please take mercy upon me, oh sovereign lord!"

In a voice of single motive, the man stated, "Tell me where Zacharias is!"

The guide in red stated that he was inside the church of Sodom. "Can you please bless me, oh mighty lord?" The figure steps forward, overtaking him with his cloth. A loud crunch is made and the guide's throat is smashed by grip.

"Artemis will pay with her blood for this," he said to himself as he stomped toward the church of Sodom.

Standing in front of the statue of Artemis, Zacharias was trying to regain his breath. "What the hell was that, Pontifex?"

Pontifex swells with malice. "How dare you insult our goddess, Artemis! Do you know what you have done, boy?" Pontifex shouted back, pointing at him with such ferocity that his finger dislocates. Pontifex quickly regained his composure as he set the bone back into place and then apologized for the outburst. "You can still apologize to her and still return the sapphire finger, she will forgive you. This is your last chance to accept her as your goddess and be cleansed of death's curse before he finds you!" Pontifex is now on his knees rocking back and forth.

Zacharias, glaring at Pontifex, remembered the story of Joseph's past and stated, "You speak of her being a living god, but what has she sacrificed, nothing! I have learned of one who did one who gave up all for everyone, what about Jesus?" Pontifex stood staring as his countenance began to turn far more red than the eyes of Artemis. His body began shaking violently, but most of all his head. In a sinister and nefarious voice, Pontifex asked, "What about Jesus?" as his body began to split apart and bones snap in various directions. Zacharias, now shaking in fear, began to fall back up the stairs as he saw his head twist forcibly backward until it snapped. Holding his sword in his direction, he worked up the courage to make a run for it. Panicking in his mind, he dashed through the dark cellars as the torches began to go out one by one. Frightened, he ran into one of the barrels, cutting it with his sword, knocking him down. Wine poured forth running across the floor flowing down the way he came. He could hear the sinister laughter of Pontifex as he was morphing into something else entirely. "Get me out of here, not like this, I can't die like this!" Zacharias became lost deep within the cellars that had advanced to a jailer's paradise. Minutes went by as he crept around, praying that the monster would not find him. Loud hissing noises paint the walls as he hid behind hundreds of barrels. Looking around, he realized he was within a massive warehouse of these barrels of wine for Sodom and Gommorah was drunk in the pleasures of their sin. "That thing is going to find me," he said to himself as he shook so incredibly hard; he could barely control his breathing. At that moment, Zacharias remembered Mariana and how sweet she was playing hide and seek with him the day she had snuck out of church to find him by the bridge. "That's it. I'll hide," he thought as he plunged a hole in the backside of dozens of barrels thus draining them. He hid inside one, but the pure smell of this heavily fermented wine made him cough. The monster heard this and could be heard slithering its way through the room, tossing barrels everywhere. It was now beside his barrel, he could hear depraved hissing but could see nothing. Grasping the family crest of the Voltels around his neck, the barrel he was in, along with many others, was launched like the rest. Zacharias lay in a motionless state of shock covered in debris and wine. In a snakelike and hate-filled voice, the snake yelled out, "I will find you, phantom of Desteeran, and I'll kill you just like I killed the holy knights, your brothers, I am Ephestus, herald of betrayal!" Deeper into the cellars, Ephestus wandered and could be heard screaming in the dark. Scared, Zac slowly rose and could see the ghost waving for him to follow. He crept toward the ghost who led him to the main stairwell. "Thank you, Mr. Desteeran, I take it," he quietly whispered, nodding his head with deep admiration. The ghost whose face could faintly be seen in the light smiled at him and pointed up the stairs then disappeared. Zacharias made his way out to the main altar of the church.

Hiding behind the statue, he knew the real Ephestus was on his trail. "I'm not ready for something like this, when he gets close to me, my heart feels like it is going to explode." Not a sound was heard as he peered out from behind the statue with his brass telescope. Examining the balconies, he made sure no other snare is set. "This is nothing like the beasts I've battled before, Ephestus's presence places a fear that binds me by unexplainable paralysis." Valor pushes him to inch his way to the altar's stairs, preparing to make a run for it. In the silence, a muffled breathing noise was heard behind him so he turned, striking the statue with his sword, knocking off the tongue. "Phew, just the statue," he said, taking a deep breath. At that moment, the shaking tongue of Ephestus licked his neck from behind him. Taken with fear, Zacharias dropped his blade, turning to the real Ephestus sitting directly in front of him. Ephestus constricted him with his tail and slammed him against the statue. "Where is the Sword of Abraham?" Ephestus demanded as his face came closer and his tail rattled violently. Atop Ephestus's skull sat a crown of iron-made thorns, digging into his brain, driving him mad. His powerful tail squeezed around his body tighter and tighter. "Where is the sword?" Ephestus screamed louder, shaking uncontrollably. Saliva dripped down Zacharias's shoulders as he was full of fear to a level he could not speak. He struggled to break free, but it was useless. Ephestus began to laugh at the pain delivered; it brought him great pleasure. His voice is the solid unification of both a man's and a woman's to turn to the lowest pitch. "Do you think for a single moment you are going to get loose? I'm going to continually torture you until you reveal to me where the sword is!" Zacharias knew that there was no answer he could give that would save him. Instead, he yelled out, "Why did you betray the holy knights? They trusted you!"

Ephestus laughed in murderous joy. "They died because they were weak, putting others ahead of themselves, they died because it was my choice to betray them, but most of all, they died because their God is dead!" Desperate and out of air, Zacharias spit in Ephestus's face and cried the name of God.

A bright flash of light pierces the entire church. Ephestus is caught off guard as the stained glass behind the altar shatters and a figure with a black cape drops down, smashing into him sword first. Ephestus raised his arm to defend himself and the sword cut it off as the white shield of the individual bashed his false crown, sending him flying down the altar, crashing into the pews. The statue had fallen over, pinning Zacharias to the ground but not injuring him gravely. Zacharias covered himself from the rest of the falling glass that struck all around, but as he looked up, the black cape flowed to the floor as the individual stood tall. White celestial armor with golden lining around the crevices covered the figure for it was a holy knight and a ray of light penetrated through the stained glass at the other end of the church onto the altar upon him. Upon the holy knight's head sat a helmet wrapped in the wings of a golden eagle that held a lowered head within the wings, protecting something also jetting out to a sharp point. On the chest plate, the brilliant image of the sun pronounced daybreak neighbored by broad pauldrons of an advancing cause. Pointing his sword toward Ephestus, the holy knight shouted in a deep voice:

> Behold, I give unto you power to tread on serpents and scorpions, and over all the power of the enemy: and nothing shall by any means hurt you.
>
> Luke 10:19 (KJV)

Ephestus ascended, swaying on his tail with the spirit of revenge, and pointed to the holy knight with his other arm, shouting in demonic fury, "Alpha!" The holy knight leaped down the altar and engaged in combat with Ephestus. Ephestus's tail wildly flung around, crashing pews as the holy knight dove and ducked from each incoming lethal strike. His sword strikes Ephestus repeatedly with devastating blows, knocking off scales and patches of flesh. Blood from Ephestus spattered the marble floors as he retreated slashing and biting at the holy knight. "Die, die, die, I will not rest, I will not slumber until all of you are dead, until I preach unto you the message of my father who art in hell" Ephestus yelled out. The holy knight did not speak, but with each attack, block, and parry, his just war cry overtook the church of Sodom. They battled back through the stairwells, out of the sight of Zacharias who was desperately trying to get out from under the statue that had him pinned. "Come on," he yelled, pushing with all his might for several minutes, and finally, the statue began to budge. Still, the conflict could be heard echoing as Ephestus yelled out blasphemies against God and the holy knight declared the Lord's holiness and judgment of all things evil. Once free, he could see them engaged in melee combat on the catwalk by the stained glass window above the entrance. The holy knight slashed off the tip of his tail, throwing Ephestus into a squeal of pain while darkened blood gave an all new meaning to stained glass window. Ephestus grabbed him with the remainder of his tail, trying to coil advantage. He then ferociously slashed the holy knight's armor while biting upon the unbreakable surface, but he could not break the full armor of God. The great fangs of the beast shatter from this action. Ephestus clenches his tail all the more; his chipped fangs rip apart the already mortal wound. Like a dam, black liquid severely gushes on to the knight attempting to drown him. The holy knight called upon the name of Jesus Christ and the window that did not retain portrait now contained the portrait of Jesus Christ being raised upon the cross looking up to heaven. This sight stirs the Holy Spirit inside the knight, reminding him that the Lord is the head of the church. Following in suit, the holy knight begins to smash his head into Ephestus with the sharp wings of the eagle atop his helmet, piercing his skull further than the iron crown. This frees the warrior. The holy knight who had dropped his sword scales Ephestus's back and began to smash his head with his shield, hitting him repeatedly with the force of heaven behind it. The crown of iron thorns dug deeper with each powerful blow, causing him to lose all concentration. Ephestus reached out and wrapped his tail around the chandelier as the holy knight regains his sword, jumping onto it beside him. Out of desperation, Ephestus, who was near death, tried to cut the chandelier and drop the both of them, but the holy knight lopped off his other arm. Ephestus, now an absolute serpent, lunged forward to bite him, but the agile knight leapt across grabbing the railing of the catwalk and Ephestus fell through the chandelier. Zacharias, who was standing only feet away from below the chandelier, witnessed Ephestus's head fall directly onto a ceremonial candle holder that jammed through his chin out his skull. The holy knight who had stepped back onto the catwalk stared at Ephestus, whose body hung from the chandelier, holding to disbelief of the loss. Attempting to say a last word, he is unable; a volcano of pain erupts from the pierced head, then killing him. A waterfall of black blood and guts collect below in a heap of slop as it rained from the chopped-off edge of his tail, arms and crown of weakness. Zacharias glanced up and saw the holy knight looking directly back at him from the visor of his helmet. Before either could say anything a long dove-like cloth from the tail of Ephestus glides down followed by the light. Unstained, it appeared as though it had never been inside of him in the first place. "The final piece to the Sword of Abraham," he said to himself. Zacharias then held it up to the holy knight. "It's the final piece to the sword, this is yours!" Zac then jumps up victoriously. The holy knight nodded and then bowed on his knee, holding his sword up to the Lord in triumphant prayer, giving Him the day's glory.

Just then, standing at the main stairwell into the church were four elite mercenaries. Each one was uniquely different for the one in the center had thick red armor covering his body and face with a two-handed mace so immense no normal human being could have wielded it; this man looked as though he was a standing battleship. Most peculiar was that the bulb of this appeared as a bell yoked with six trumpets. To his left stood a remarkably tall man with a long bow just as big and two sets of arrows: one giant, the other regular; he appeared to be an elite ranger of some sorts, wearing a lighter armor of the same coloration. Behind him, a man held tight the reins of a slim yet powerful gray stallion coated in rare plate that his armor was connected, but in his other hand, a long-chained whip brushed the floor littered in fabricated thorn. Finally to the right of all three stood a man dressed in an overcoat indicating nobility held a flintlock rifle with bayonet to his chest. On his coat a detailed map was pinned and atop his head was a tricorn accompanied by his silent salute to Ephestus. Zacharias stuffed the cloth into his pocket and was about to speak before the holy knight interrupted. He slashes the chandelier's main line and sent it plummeting almost crushing the four men. The man on the horse could not move back as fast as the others, so when Ephestus smashed onto the ground, the puddle of blood coated his armor and horse. In a dire heavenly voice, the holy knight commanded Zacharias to run as he pointed his sword to the altar. Zacharias began to sprint to the altar as to retreat past the wine cellars. Behind him, the ironclad red mercenary with mace smashed through the chandelier and grand arrows meant for a dragon began to fly from the other mercenary, barring the altar path. He took cover behind the pews as the man with the flintlock rifle began to fire upon him. The holy knight flung his sword from the balcony, which would have hit the man, but the one in thick armor blocked with his superb gauntlets, knocking over both the great archer and the clever rifleman. This gave Zacharias the second he needed to escape. As he was running, the horsemen trampled Ephestus's body and began to gain speed quickly. The holy knight who had run out onto the catwalk only seconds before began cutting the rest of the chandeliers, with a dagger of blazing topaz and an onyx hilt. The horsemen began to leap over each crashing chandelier, readying his whip to grab the target now almost up the stairs. Humble to the Holy Spirit, the knight waited to cut the last chandelier and let the horsemen run past it; as he cut it, the horsemen reared back his chained whip. At that moment, the chained whip caught with chandelier and pulled the weapon from his hand, gashing it considerably. Zacharias entered into the cellar, desperately sprinting past the same room where the statue of Artemis was. Unsure or not whether the sapphire finger held evil properties, he flings it at the statue. The apparition could be seen waving down the corridor and, in a fading voice, yelled at him to follow. The ghost took him all the way to a secret exit out of the church under the wave that was connected right into the city. Zacharias opened the cellar doors and ran out, then stopping for only a second. "Who are you?"

The ghost said in all haste with a profound voice, "Sir Joshua Desteeran, and I'm not a ghost, I'm a spirit. I was the final holy knight of my age, I was ordered to wait here to help the one who would defeat Ephestus for I was unable. Be strong, Zacharias, we are with you, now go!" He complied to the command given and began to rush in the sands. Passing through back alleys, every step was potentially dangerous. A mob of the townsfolk had formed and attempted to bar his path, but a bright light blinded and threw them to the ground. It was the holy knight; he waved Zacharias toward him as the citizens cried out for they had lost their sight from looking upon the armor of God. Bolting through Gommorah, the holy knight pulls out a horn, which fits into the visor of his helmet, and he blows into it seven times loudly. The holy knight's long black cape flows with each turn until they reach the main square; two horses can be seen galloping across the sand dunes toward them. Out of breath, the two stop as Zacharias sees both Grear and Jesibelle, but before he says anything, the knight removes his helmet and it is Joseph.

"Joseph, you're a holy knight," Zacharias yelled in profound confused happiness. Joseph rested his helmet at his leg, pressing his forehead to the friend almost lost.

"Next time, just listen to what I say, got it!" Gasping for air, the two of them laughed slightly, waiting for the horses.

"No time for talk, we have to go, the Black Hand folds upon us!" The two horses were nearing in heavy gallop, splitting the earth around them, but before they could exit the square, a man covered in black garb appearing from shadow emerged. Removing his hood and cloak, he held a large black tome in his left hand and his body was covered in a scale-type of armor made from the fires of a black dragon scorched in crimson apocalypse. "Who is greater than death?" the man roars, raising his left hand to the sky. Joseph, who had grabbed his Bible from behind the Belt of Truth, slams it to the ground, shouting once, "Veil!" His Bible sparks profusely, drawing a cross in the ground around them. Out of retaliation, the mutinous book begins to chant as the pages open on their own flipping wildly. Sand and debris begin to lift and hover around the battleground. This leader began to scream out speaking backward, and as he did, a demonic set of robust wings could be seen within his shadow weighted in blazing shackle. "Behold the spectacle of my glory for I am Veil, necromancer of fire and plague, and today, achievement is attained!" Shockwaves and tremors explode, sending an indescribable boom to all of Athens. Flames swell over ten feet, engulfing the heart of Sodom and Gommorah, but they are not natural flames; these were flames bearing the coloration of red, orange, and black far more powerful than its relative of regular flame. All the plaza burns, blocking Grear and Jesibelle from their masters. Although strong, the fire does not overtake the cross drawn by the Holy Bible. Veil stands among the inferno with piercing yellow eyes wet from flowing magma. Joseph removed his cape. "Zacharias, this cape is heat resistant and it can only cover one of us. This armor will not save me from flames pulled from the spiritual realm," Joseph told him as he wrapped it around his body.

"Joseph, no you can't make this kind of decision, you're my brother. I can't do this. I promised Penelope!" Zacharias begged him in desperation personified.

"You be strong, my friend," Joseph said, reaching for his helmet. He then placed it over Zacharias, grasping his arms and looking at his face. The end of this companionship is realized by both. "Now you are a holy knight, rise, Sir Zacharias," Joseph yelled in his final proclamation, launching him with all his might past the fires to the horses. Falling to the other side of the flame, the cape had disintegrated, which made him unable to cross back. "Joseph, not like this, don't you do this to me," Zacharias shrieked with all his being shedding multiple undeniable tears that ran down on their own accord. The Bible that was sparking begins to project a sword made of sunlight that Joseph waits to draw for the Spirit is preparing him to do so. "Zacharias, remember the things I have taught you, but most of all, do not forget that you are never alone in this world for you always have your heavenly Father! Now go unto the forests of Sccra and find Aurelius Garlen, you tell him to converge at the sign of the eagle! Protect the cloth piece, finish the mission we started, this I order you! Now go and do not look back!" Zacharias mounted Grear, and as he leaves, Joseph pulls the sword of the Spirit from the Bible. He is encased by the light and blazes far more brilliantly than the fires surround. Valiantly, he charges through the inferno, clashing with Veil who conjures the claws of the last dragon to pull the city into hellfire. Every structure burns as does every person who made this their home partaking in its iniquity. A single talon surges from the warden below, claiming the church of Sodom and the city of Gommorah as his own. The prize is the souls of those now damned and the punishment is damnation. Another nightmarish boom rings across the sea louder than any cannon created, perhaps the venomous language of the prideful. Ground, shore, and coast begin to spill into the earth with the city held in the dragon's grasp. The ocean flooding the sinkhole attempts to douse the old serpent's breath but is unable. Amidst the destruction, Joseph begins to overtake Veil as the talon comes to a close, leaving only a crater that does not fill with the surrounding waters from the Trelsch. Not once did Zacharias look back, hearing all of this.

11

The Sower and the Wolf

Zacharias rode for miles as fast as he could with Jesibelle behind. Running on pure adrenaline, he could not let Joseph's sacrifice go in vain. Stopping in Ephesus, there was no sign of the mercenary group that had followed him inside the church of Sodom. He purchased the supplies he would need for the journey home in haste and then set off to Salem. People were out in force that day, wondering as to the great sounds heard; they did not yet know Sodom and Gommorah were gone. Holding the emotion of Joseph's death back, he refused to confront it. The journey out of Athens is a rushed silence pushed harder by the swarming reminder of curious rumor of the twin noises. Passing by the fountain of false gods, he could see the statue of Artemis that Joseph had studied only days prior. He glared at the statue, his heart demanded vengeance, but not just for Artemis, it was to all things able to usher chaos on a whim. Riding past the Gates of Minos, he is plagued by the constraints of his curse, the touch of death. "I did this, they were searching for me because of Manistof." For slightly less than two weeks, Zacharias pushed Grear and Jesibelle hard to return home to Salem, only resting a few hours a night. Every day, he switches horse, but one is always without a rider, a cruel reminder that Joseph was never coming back. He pieced together that the horses must have been special horses of some kind given to Joseph for he was indeed a holy knight.

Finally, Zacharias reached back to Hope's Lake where they had once rested. He stood in front of the lake, remembering that Joseph's taken-in son Simon Peter had died here saving Mariana. He gripped his heart as his inner being intensely pounded, making it impossible for him to stand; He splashed into the lake. Slowly, sinking to the bottom, fighting himself. "Joseph, I'm sorry I've failed you, I can't go on. I can't tell Penelope that you are dead. How much longer will the world kill the good men? How much longer must I see everyone I love die because of me?" Right there, he hit the bottom of the lake and sat. An image of Joseph taking Simon Peter and Titus who had died crossing the Tarene flashed in memory. As the last of his air ran out, he knew Joseph would never forgive him if he did not protect his family. Zacharias pushed off hard with his legs and surfaced, seeing the two horses standing by the lake peering down. Grear bit on his shirt and helped to pull him out. Petting both Grear and Jesibelle, he explained to them that soon they were to return home to Salem and he needed them to comfort Penelope and Mariana for Joseph was not returning. At the mention of Joseph's name, the two horses lowered their heads as if paying homage to him. A fire is started that night after he changes into dry clothes. Turning to an empty log, his emotions ran heavier. "I'm not going to cry over your death, I have to be stronger than that for your family, for myself. No more sorrow, only the mission matters now." Zacharias lay awake that night, dreading the deed of telling his family he had died to save him and that it was his fault. "Joseph was a holy knight and I never even saw it. Time and again, he spoke of them and I just didn't piece it together. Why did he not tell me?" It was too much for him to handle at this time so he forced himself to sleep.

Two days later, he had arrived to the base of the mountainside where Salem rests. Zacharias dismounted Grear and began his sad walk up the trail, carrying Joseph's pack. The snows had already melted away. Clouds began to set in and a light downpour fell as he swept his hands between his dark hair, preparing himself, desperately seeking out words of comfort if only for himself. Reaching the top of the trail that overlooked all of Salem, he dropped Joseph's pack as he stared. He doesn't move for several minutes nor does his brain, but his spirit receives the final push of horror. Salem was burnt to the ground. His facial expression is panicked, his body in shock. He wants to run but cannot; he can only take compact steps, it seems he just can't wake up. "Penelope, Mariana," he said unable to yell. "God, no, not my family, please give me the strength to do something, anything." Motor functions return and he sprints up the hill toward the destroyed red cottage. Grear watches as his master slips by the mud on the slope. He punches the ground, then picks himself back up. Entering what is left of the cottage, the walls, floor, and roof are all gone except part of the main staircase. Only a partial amount of the upstairs had endured. "Penelope," he called out of a slight hope that they were alive. Slowly, he climbed, not wanting to know the truth yet having to, and when he reached the top, the visual broke him. Penelope lay against a single wooden beam with little Mariana in her left arm; they too were dead. A massive arrow sat piercing Mariana's back out into Penelope's, connecting the two of them even in death. Zacharias fell to his hands and knees on the charred floor, trembling, crawling forward unable to cope. The mother's long brunette hair covers her daughter, and in Penelope's right hand, she grasped a blood-stained Bible clinging to the Lord's call home. Zacharias reached down and grabbed Penelope's cold and lifeless hand with both of his, holding it to his face resting his head, but refusing to cry. This action is his apology; he is not ready to let go and what is now empathy ascends to anger. Infuriated by the arrow connecting them, he cut it so he could easily pull the disgrace from both of their bodies. On the front of the arrow stuck out a haunting piece of parchment. Grabbing this, it read:

> It has come to our attention that both the Voltel household and the citizens of Salem have been harboring the one we seek. In Salem's refusal to explain your location, we have been forced to take necessary action as to obtain your whereabouts. If you are reading this, Zacharias, know that you have caused this in your refusal to acknowledge the harbinger of the black rose, you signed the contract with initial sin and the wage is death. You are the lost property of Manistof, and until that payment is made, everyone you ever come to love shall painfully suffer, then die because of you. The master has been forced to take drastic action in deploying us as a final resort. Why continually let others suffer because you are too fearful to face your destiny? Should you not grow beyond the realm of the selfish and join your father? Alas, we are only servants to the master, and in his infinite knowledge, he has granted you a reprieve. Present yourself in the Tree of Lament and all shall be finished in our little game of The Trial of Kings. Until this demand is met, do not trust to find a hope in a world already damned.
>
> Signed, Veil, leader of the Black Hand.
>
> PS: It was oh, such a simplistic joy butchering Salem, but none was as sweet as Mariana who called out your name in the end and you never came. Not a greater pleasure exists in Vulgata than the screams of a child soon to die.

For a moment, he sat there in silence as the rain pounded against the floorboards without care just as it had when he was in the ruined playhouse. Zacharias dropped the parchment to the burnt floor, slamming his head painfully. It is the loss of innocent little Mariana that drives him over that edge. "Damn you, Manistof, I'm going to find a way to kill you if it's the last thing I do. I won't stop, I won't rest until I pull the beating heart from your fucking chest. Everyone involved will pay in pain, I will break bones and tear flesh. I will crush the eyes within your skulls, trapping you within the agony of darkness. I will drag you to Hades, and when you are helpless and beg for mercy, you will be met with further discomfort as long as it can be drawn, that I will savor dearly." Then repeatedly, his hands violently hit the floor as he cried out the name of the Father. Penelope's body fell over from all the shaking, and Mariana's small body rolled out of her arms in front of him. In her arms, she held her bear, Mrs. Elysia. Barely able to view her face, Zacharias picked her up and held her close to his chest. Her body is spiritless, and not an ounce of understanding is drawn only lament surfaces. "I'm sorry, I was too weak to protect you. I have failed you my little sister." Rocking her back and forth, he began to sing her an old lullaby that his grandfather used to sing when he was very young. He attempts to look up and speak to heaven, but words are silenced before birth. The feeling is sickening it is the paralyzed state of loss still being identified. Zacharias carried their bodies out to the graveyard and set them beside Simon Peter's grave. After he had placed them, he walked into town absent of hope to obtain a spade in which he knew would be in Mr. Royalton's blacksmith stable. In the plaza, the bodies of the mangled villagers were piled, some of which were pinned to the walls of buildings by giant arrows. Grear poked his nose into his back as he, without breaking eye contact to the heap, stated, "Some Guardian of Salem I am." Reaching into one of the pouches on Grear's saddle, he pulled out the beer stein with the symbol of the primordial guardians. "Here's to you," Zac said in pure sorrow, placing it atop the bodies after tilting it to the side and emptying the collected rain. With the spade slung over his shoulder, he returned to the graveyard. On the right side of Simon Peter's grave, he began to dig with only the sound of nature's uncaring shower to mock him. After the hole was dug, he gently placed Penelope inside with Mariana in her arms. A feeling of regret overtook him all the more when he remembered the one thing he had not told them when they were alive. Pulling out the medallion around his neck, fighting back untold weight, he stated, "My name is Zacharias John Desteeran. I promise by all that I am, you shall be avenged or I'll die trying. Rest now forever, my friends, my family, my saintly liberators." Exiting the hole, he checked Joseph's horse for anything to put into the grave with them. Mr. Sebastian was sticking out the side of one of the pouches. Staring at it, he was reminded of the sacred memories spent with the Voltel family that would never return. Gripping the bear tightly, he looked to the sky, scrunching his face tightly as to not weep, desperately looking among the clouds for just one single answer. "Why did you not stop this God?" Placing Mr. Sebastian on Penelope beside Mrs. Elysia on Mariana, the two bears that were once married would now sleep forever with the family he so dearly loved. He began to bury them, and with each plunge of the spade, he was pushed further to the point of madness. "Why must these things happen? They didn't deserve this, these were good people! Look what I have done, what I have brought upon these people, God, just kill me please kill me and end all of this! Barely can I understand the cruelty of my own affliction, but others that did not deserve this punishment, how is that right? They killed a mother holding her child, an innocent helpless child, and where was God? God did nothing because He does not exist!" Once the graves are filled, Joseph's horse Jesibelle sat on top as if blocking the incoming rains. "Come on, we have to get going now," Zacharias said to her. The horse remains in the mud, refusing to move. Slightly, he tugged on her reins, but she would not budge. Looking at the horse in admiration, he understood that her place was with her family, so he removed the saddle and reins. He hopped on Grear and turned back only once at the scorched village where he had regained his humanity now taken once more. One last time, he remembered all the love that was shared to him regardless of who he was and one final time he spoke to them. "Joseph, Penelope, Mariana, Salem, thank you for everything. I will never forget you for you loved me even when I did not love myself. I will find the Sword of Abraham and destroy Manistof along with his agents. Oh, Salem, one with song and praise may your songs carry an eternity for whatever precedes this life." Zacharias then began riding through the windy grasslands to reach Scera so that he could find Aurelius Garlen whom he knew had to be another holy knight. Although he'd already left Salem, one final song would be sung for in the debris of the Voltel household; the music box given to Penelope by Joseph lay atop her novel, *Faith of a Child*, testifying to the love held in a home absent of loneliness.

For well over a day and a half, he rode with everything Grear could offer until they reached the tree lines of Scera. The forest was gigantic, just as the map had said it would be. Each tree reached well over a hundred feet from the surface with their branches and leaves shining most magnificently. Smiling at this sight, he collapsed onto the grass. Physical and emotional exhaustion had taken their toll on him, but none worse than bottled-up pain, the stumbling block of many a male. Alas by no means would that be the end of his plight, for now another nightmare would find its way to the broken swordsman. Now asleep, he began to dream of being home with the Voltels sitting at the kitchen table. Penelope, Joseph, and Mariana were laughing and conversing among themselves, the sun shone through the window perfectly. Suddenly, everything changed for the worse as the home burst into flame and Joseph was nowhere to be seen. Penelope ran upstairs to grab Mariana, and as she did, a great arrow pierced through her body and her daughter's. Lying there, bleeding out, Veil advanced up the stairs, standing before them. "Now I'll ask one last time: where is Zacharias?" Penelope sobbingly told him they had gone to Avodah Mortis as he threatened Mariana's remaining life. Zacharias tried to kill Veil, but he disappeared as he could then see Joseph lying dead in the crater of Gommorah, reaching for his family. Then Penelope stood before him alive.

"Why did you let us die? You were a part of our family, why did you not protect us from the dragon?" Joseph stood beside him without his armor, stating, "After all we've done for you, you failed my family, to think, we trusted you," he said while shaking his head. Mariana then stood before him covered in her and her mother's death. "You're not my big brother anymore."

"I didn't mean to let this happen, please forgive me," Zacharias begged. The three of them stood disowning him as he pleaded for forgiveness. "Someone, help, I can't handle this anymore, where are you, Jesus?" he yelled out. At that moment, they went away and standing before him was his grandfather Alcus. Alcus smiled to him and spoke in such a voice that it touched his heart to a forgotten realm, "Don't give up, you're not alone. Manistof is using everything against you to try and defeat you, but you are meant for so much more than you know, you cannot give up." Right there, he lifted up his grandson to what seemed another dreamlike dimension where it was far too bright for him to see properly. Joseph stood there beside his family, Penelope, Mariana, and even Simon Peter whom he had never met. All of them smiled in purity, Joseph walked over to him. He was wearing the same celestial armor slightly brighter that he had died in and his family was adorned in elegant white robes. Joseph then spoke as a crown of glory was atop his head, "Zacharias, you know we love you. Don't let the evil one use us against you for you already know the rock that we stand upon. You must call upon your Father, it is the only way to defeat Manistof, better yet the only way you're going to survive. Know as much as we care for you, it doesn't even shadow in comparison to how much your Father cares for you, now go complete the mission we started together. I know you can do it." Joseph walked back, standing with his family, and put his arms around them as they began to float away into the light. Zacharias chased after them, but was stuck on the ground. "Joseph, don't go, please, I'm not ready to say good-bye!" The last thing he heard from them was Penelope's gentle voice telling him they'd always be in his heart. An unexplainable voice then lovingly declares, "Good morning." He then awoke to a sharp gust of wind in the grasslands and the warm sun which breathed life into him. "Zacharias, come out," the voice of Alcus called out from the tree lines of Scera. "Grandfather, is it you?" he yelled out while running into the forest. A shadow that looked like his grandfather was moving from tree to tree. "Wait, please wait for me. I need you!" The shadow continually called out to him and bounced from tree to tree until it stopped. "He's come back. I'm not alone anymore," he yelled in a pure joy of relief only given over by Christ. Standing before the tree where the shadow had stopped, he excitedly brushed his hand against it. "I've missed you for so long, Grandfather." His face like a dam ready to buckle, he noticed the shadow was no longer talking or moving. Looking back, he saw that the shape was only an image from the radiant light through the tree branches. After all these years, he had just now hit the bottom of his emotional journey; he truly was alone. Slowly, he slumped into the tree with his face against it and knees to the ground. Beside him, he sees a flower wilted; that is the only witness at his broken heart. Ashamed that even a flower witnessed him so vulnerable, he hid himself within his palms. A statement plays again and again, but until he says it, the toll is not paid. "I don't have anyone to call a friend." The floodgates are open. Silently, he wept and gnashed his teeth alone in the world as the final hope he had of his beloved grandfather was now also gone. "My family is all dead, there's no one left, Father, help me please." Soaked in confession, he was forced to once and for all confront the Almighty. Reaching out a single hand above him and covering his wailing persona with the other, he spoke, "Father, I am sorry for everything I have done, please help me I cannot take another step. I have doubted you, mocked, and discredited you for everything wrong in my life when it was never you. Please, Lord, forgive me, please reveal to me truth. It hurts knowing you are real and yet I know nothing of your nature." After several minutes of letting everything out, Grear trotted over and rubbed his head against Zacharias. He stood up and wiped his wet face dry; Grear began to stroll deeper into the forest where Zac could see him lie down. Walking over, he saw a rabbit keel over and Grear was sitting right in front of a stream. Beside the stream was a hollowed-out tree. Renewed by the sight this site had snatched him from the depths, he then spoke to Grear, "Food, water, and shelter, God, does exist. Thank you, Father." Humbled before the stream, he scooped up the water and lapped it and then felt rejuvenated. Long missed from the past few weeks, he began to laugh wholeheartedly with this new revelation in his life that God was in fact there and had always been with him. That He loved him and had carried him this far, that He had never given up on the child He so loved. Later, Zac began a fire by the stream and began to cook the rabbit when all of a sudden, a couple of fish also leapt out of the water and died beside him. "God has provided even more food, our first feast!" he yelled out and began to rejoice in His name for the first time in his life. Grear entered the pond and also began to jump around as if giving thanks alongside. That night, he rested inside the hollowed-out tree and reflected cheerfully that he was no longer alone in the world. "God, thank you for everything, although I still do not understand the complete concept of you and I'm sorry for that. Please just tell me what you want me to know." He fell asleep that night, still fresh with the sting of loss, and even though he did weep further for a family moved on, this time he did so, eased by the Lord who allowed him to let go. The Voltel family crest was held tightly to his bosom this night.

Fresh is the air of daybreak, greatly lessened is the weary soul. Grabbing his gear, he prepared to set off into the forest, but instead of riding his horse, he decided to walk as Grear followed closely behind. The forest was magnificent in all ways, reflecting the pristine majesty of the Creator who is synonymous with nature. Densely covered in vegetation of all shades of green, this was indeed a grand setting for renewal. The trees are as humanity in all shapes and sizes, standing over rocks that are endorsed by endless fields of moss clouding the shell. Occasionally, a waterfall graces the perfect landscape drinking from one of the four great rivers. "Grear, isn't this fantastic? Look at all the beauty here. It was all planned made by Him, the master gardener, just as Joseph said," he stated examining a grouping of lilies of all colors. Picking one and smelling it, a storm of butterflies shone throughout the forest, it is one being. Mesmerized by the flash of this divine haven, he knew that it was God calling to him that He was right there. Fourteen years, a shattered self was now mending. A jolt of holy lightning sends tingles to the body, creating a happiness not yet known or understood. This rapture plows the fields of despair. Something stirs ever deeper ready for freedom, but the day of rebirth is set to a later date. In the distance, dozens of deer could be seen traveling together. Thinking to himself, *Where am I going to find Garlen in this the forest of forests?* For two more days, he traversed Scera and had become completely lost by his captivation for the surroundings. Stumbling upon a hidden grouping of fallen trees that created a bridge over a steep gorge Zacharias decided to cross. Grear waited on the other side as he carefully went along the trees smeared in moss making them quite slippery. The drop to the bottom was well over two hundred feet. Once reaching the other side, there was a dense thicket in which he entered to find an isolated pond overtaken by multicolored dragonfly. Entering the pond, a single tree sat to the northern edge, but this tree was different for its leaves were all violet wrapped around twelve branches shaping into a goblet. "What kind of tree is this? I guess it won't hurt to check it out, perhaps one of the Alkirum live inside." He stepped out into the shallow pond and the tree opened up, creating a hollowed-out doorway. Drawing his sword and stepping back, he at first believed the tree was going to attack him, but after a few seconds, he realized nothing was going to happen. "I'm trusting in you, Father, please let this lead me to the Alkirum so that I may continue the mission." Mustering up his courage, he entered into the tree and was met with a long path leading underneath the pond. Scores of ants descend in a crowded straight line. "Perhaps I should follow these ants and see where it leads," Zacharias said, examining the ants climbing over one another.

Dark yet peaceful was the journey into the hollowed-out tree where he was met by another magnificent sight. A narrow dirt path stretched out and resting on either side was a line of trees all with leaves made of solid ice. Night had risen once again on the region and traces of moonlight could be seen reflecting off the ice. Walking down the illuminated path, he was careful not to step on the ants that stopped at the edge of the road where a tiny hole sit. It went straight down and the bottom could not been seen, so he was unable to proceed; meanwhile, the ants could be seen traveling downwards together. Standing there, peering in, a piece of the ground broke around his legs. Sliding down the steep hole, he fell into another grand chamber. A gigantic circular clear blue lake sat in an area without covering and the full scope of the moon was seen in this the forest's theater. Behind, in front, and across him, he could see that the room was surrounded by the same trees bearing leaves made of pure ice yet they did not melt. In the middle of the lake sat a single island and in the center of that island, there was a series of large thorn bushes surrounding something. As the auditorium, the lake, and the island itself, the thorn bushes lay arcing inward forming a type of ring around something. "What could be inside of that? Something feels familiar to me as if I've been here before," he said to himself remembering other times this same emotion had rippled. The moonlight which bounced off the ice leaves all pointed to the island resting on the lake, which only furthered his resolve to investigate. Stepping into the lake, he noticed it was no deeper than his ankles so he began to push forward, Titulus in hands. Twenty feet away from the island, the lake had a drop-off, forcing a swim to the goal. Sheathing his sword, he began to swim, and with each stroke, he could feel the chill of the frozen leaves alert his senses of danger to come. Stepping onto land formed of a clay-type substance, he searched around for any potential danger. In seeing none, he warily advanced the unusual formation of barbs. "Marvelous but is it alive?" he spoke in awe, glancing inside the barrier. A single glowing block of ice sat with the body of a wolf cub encased inside. Reaching in to grab it, a miniature black rose popped out and began to dance around. This surprised him, so he reached in and plucked the flower, which bit his finger. "Ow, what the hell is this?" he yelled, throwing it to the ground and smashing it with his boot. A green puddle of what seemed to be chlorophyll lay where he crushed the carnivorous little flower, and looking back, he could see another one growing exponentially. The thorn swallowed the block of ice then rose up for they were the teeth of a far greater black rose. Already bigger than him, the flower kept on growing and large sharp vines began to surface around the lake swaying to the tune of the black rose. Holding his sword dual-handed, he stepped back as the rose only grew larger swaying in the luminescence. It's dozens of vine-like arms twisted and swirled in the water until the black rose reached adulthood at over thirty feet high. Along the edges of the lake, an ethereal type of emerald flame erupted, imprisoning Zacharias. "You've got to be kidding me, this again, just like in Sodom and Gommorah, where are you, Veil!" he yelled out, wanting the Black Hand for himself, but they did not appear. The rose opened its massive black bulb with the jaws of a shark and teeth of thorns. Its multitude of vines began to whip down, cracking across the arena. Each one hits closer in the hurricane's chorus of vertical, horizontal, and diagonal strikes, pushing Zacharias into a fortified stance. One barely misses the kill, but a thorn cuts deeply into his forehead, his own blood trickles in front of the iris, causing much pain. "Come on, you bastard, if you want to dance with the devil in the pale moonlight, I'll show you how!" Defense shifts to offense, and with each bass note played by Titulus, another vine falls rolling across the island. Green goop sprayed out from them, drenching the landscape. Where the liquid fell, more vines began to grow until hundreds of vines came crashing in around Zacharias. Blocking with his sword, one of the creepers unleashes the orchestra, sending Titulus flying into the water, sinking to the bottom. Diving into the water, he reclaims his sword, followed by a lone vine living underneath the island. It sprouts additional spines before grabbing hold of him, gashing his body extremely. The clear water begins to turn red before it lifts him out of it. Able to breathe, he cuts it off him and lands into the shallow portion of the lake. Standing up, he grabs hold of his sword that has a stream of his own watery blood pouring from hilt to blade. All around the island, the vines create an impossible barricade of water and thorn splashing in constant succession. "I have to get the bulb, it's the only way this thing is going to die," Zacharias yells to self before he charges the island again. Cutting through the wall, he dives back into the deep, then impeded by makeshift tidal waves. When he made amphibious landfall, the massive black bulb lowered to the ground, reaching out for him with its wide jaws preparing to consume. His charge to the target is terminated by the innermost vines. This legion of them tears open his anatomy. Gravely injured, he cries out in pain as they begin to pull him toward the jaws of the demonic flower. Zacharias plants his titled claymore into the ground and holds on for dear life, pulling away from the creature with all his might. "Not here. I'm not going to die here, too many people died to get me to this point, I can't let their sacrifices be in vain!" Upon that statement, his pocket rips open and the cloth piece from Ephestus's body fell out. It shone a bright light, the vines released him, and the monster retreated backward, defending the bulb with its rotating phalanx. The light from the cloth piece reflected on the ice-like leaves and the lake turned dark except for the deep part surrounding the island. Noticing this, Desteeran grabbed the cloth and jumped back into the water, leaving Titulus to stand guard. Diving many feet underneath the island, the cloth piece illuminates the block of ice containing the wolf cub. It was wrapped in a strange wire not of this world in which Zacharias cut with his side dagger. Now snatching the cub petrified, he surfaced and saw the defending choir lose voice, only the rose remained. Retrieving his blade, he waited a moment to see if the monster would die like the rest, but it did not. "Now this ends," he yelled, charging forward in newfound courage of the second act. The massive bulb began to smash to the ground like the mallet of a court fertilized in broken law. But his case is tried and true, bringing him to the stem of the trial ready to nip it in the bud. Zacharias cocks back his two-handed verdict against the adjudicator but one juror is not pleased. Two anthropomorphic arms cloaked in shadowy vegetation of their own sprung forth grabbing his shoulders. The face of Manistof appears, holding a fiendish childlike grimace. He is of the stem, yet the coloration moves about like a shadow within flame. "Let us finish the Trial of Kings," Manistof screamed in a cacophony of human and animalistic mixed tone while biting deep upon Zacharias's neck. Unable to move, he could only yell as Manistof's indescribably sharp teeth burrowed further toward his spirit. His arms were locked in place, unable to swing or move, so he began to kick the stem. The bulb begins to lower itself and the shark-type jaws plummet. "God, no," he screamed out as he tried to pull away from the devilish arms and mouth restraining him. The cloth piece flew like a dove out of his pocket and wrapped around the neck of Manistof so tightly that he was beheaded. Then in one violent jerk, Zacharias twisted his body, freeing himself but pulling his left shoulder out the socket. As the bulb bit upon him, he was able to plunge the blade into the roof of its mouth. It crunched down with all its might, sprouting the blade out the top of itself. Two glowing orange eyes opened up on the side of the bulb as it cried out in pain before dying itself and crashing onto the island. Court is adjourned.

Lying on the ground in pain from the many wounds around his body, he bled out, holding the cloth piece out in front of him. The emerald fires around the lake fade away and the ice shards melted among the trees, raising the lake slightly. Turning around, a staircase made of white bark stretches up out of the pit. Looking around, the block of ice containing the wolf cub is gone so he began to exit. Proceeding up the unnatural staircase, the endless cuts and tears weep for the body. Every step of freedom holds the blood of his sacrifice. Zacharias enters into a realm of the forest not like the rest. This was a sacred garden, one of which he could feel within his soul from first glance. The moon and the sun coincided with one another as the left half of this realm is one shrouded in sorrowful night and the right side blanketed in dazzling sunlight. A line of incorporeal separation is formed, leading in a straight path all the way to a great tree. The moon's half is decayed and barren, sitting in a river of sludge. But the sun's side is full of celestial fruit, the bark is pure white, and a river full of life flows unto eternity. The cloth in his pocket began to vibrate wildly, and it shook more the longer he stared at the tree and its fruit. "What is this? Joseph would never believe me if I told him. Then again, this may be where he already lives." Standing hundreds of feet away, he attempts to take a step forward and out of the brush beside him emerged the titanic face of a red-eyed black wolf. Struck with fear, Zacharias remained perfectly still as it leapt in front of him. This black wolf was roughly the size of ten men, and upon its back, four massive wings littered in eyes sprawled open, causing Zacharias to take a few steps back. One set of the wings was used for flight while the other concealed the majority of the wolf's body. The wolf spoke to him telepathically as every eye bled ferociously, staining its white wings. "I am Algeron and you must leave now or die by the jaws of hellfire." As this was happening, another regular-sized wolf appeared from the tree embraced by the purest of sunshine. It too had four wings around it, but this one's body was wholly engulfed in a circulating flame far brighter than that of worldly flame. Marching down the bright path, the wolf's head and blue eyes held high, holding the block of ice in its most majestic jaws containing the wolf cub. Its paws do not burn the ground, but what is burnt is the sight of Algeron who cannot look upon him, he fears it. The intensity of the angelic flame sends Algeron running, but when this wolf howls, the moon's side of the realm is annihilated. Stars crash from the heavens; the ferocity of the divine flame is so intense that the moon and Algeron are obliterated in their crops yield of destruction. The blood of the righteous first martyr and Zacharias remain perished between the altar and the temple.

A warm nose then presses up against Desteeran's fallen body and he rises to the wolf dressed in ember. The secondary realm is gone, and now everything is as the sun's side. Standing before Zacharias, he spoke into his mind also with eyes covering its wings staring in unison. "I am Rayus, Protector of the Tree of Life, you have arrived at the appointed time, Sir Zacharias John Desteeran." The block of ice continued to melt within his mouth as Zacharias asked in his mind back to Rayus, "What is happening? I'm sorry that I do not understand. I died, and now, I'm not dead?" He is fearful of this heavenly entity. Rayus placed the thawed-out wolf cub in front of him. "The Almighty Father has answered your prayers, John, rejoice and give thanks for you were chosen before the earth itself to join your brothers of the cross." Pressing his fiery nose against the cub, Rayus spoke one last time, "Tala shall assist you on your long journey ahead as will the others. Know that the Almighty is with you, Zacharias, and He has remembered your name as he remembers all His children. I must bid you farewell for the days grow short and the unification of beginning and end is soon to accompany the revelation of God unto mankind. Now go and meet the Alkirum, this He commands, Atyrael shall guide your path!" Rayus did not speak again and his blazing wings vibrantly opened up pointing to the exit. Zacharias obeyed and picked up little Tala and held her to his chest, giving thanks to the Lord as he proceeded to the stairs. Turning around, Zac asks in genuine expression, "How is the Voltel family?" Rayus does not answer, but instead rests upon the ground with head in paw and wings folded back, and for that brief second, Zacharias can almost make out a smile before he leaves.

The stairs brought him back to where Grear was standing by the gorge. With one eyebrow raised, he states, "Thank you, Father, truly you are amazing." Bending down to pick up Tala, he noticed his shoulder was fixed and his cuts healed but the scars remained. Tala, who was a tiny female wolf cub, rolled around in the plants, then stared. Her fur was a light blue, but her eyes were a darker blue and atop her forehead sat a strange symbol. Holding Tala out, she licked his nose. Squinting his eyes, surprised, Zacharias said, "Your tongue, it's so cold." He places Tala back on the ground and she begins to take off, and for the rest of the day, he chases behind the forest guide. Running with all her little legs could offer, she eventually gets tired and lies on a log. Desteeran scoops her up and puts her inside his rucksack as he mounts Grear and continues in that direction until nightfall. All the while Tala's tiny black wet and frigid nose can be felt pressing up against his neck from time to time as she peers out. Making a fire that night, Zacharias grows sleepy with Tala resting on his chest. He remembers how Joseph always knew what something or someone was, how he always knew to look further than outer appearance. "I suppose appearance could be a root of deception, perhaps that's why we are to reach out to Jesus by faith and not by sight alone. Even among this the garden of God's people, perversions such as the black rose yet sprout. To the eyes of the world, Satan is guised as a sower, and friends are sometimes presented as wolves. If a man reaps what he sows, then surely Joseph and his family have gone to heaven for the love of Christ, their crop, and paradise the harvest."

And no marvel; for Sa'-tan himself is transformed into an angel of light. Therefore it is no great thing if his ministers also be transformed as the ministers of righteousness; whose end shall be according to their works.

2 Corinthians 11:14–15 (KJV)

12

Royal Promise Kept

Part 1: Recollection

At first light, the rest is disrupted by Tala yelping into the ear. Opening his eyes, she began to lick into the ear, sending a wintry chill down the spine. Playfully, Zac pushed her off and she plopped onto her behind, staring back at him. Gathering their equipment, Tala then wanders off far ahead. "Well, she's off to a bright start, isn't she, Grear?" Grear snorts and began to follow, leaving their master to be last in line for another adventure. Jogging after them for several minutes, he noticed the two of his animal companions stopped before a strange formation of rocks. Seven peculiar-looking stones sat behind a wooden arch of some kind. Tala sat directly in front of the gate, looking up to its center, which contained a carved-out symbol of the winged wolf which he had seen yesterday. "Could that be Rayus or Algeron or another?" Zacharias pondered. Touching the arch, Tala began to give a slight howl to the best of her ability. Still investigating, Zac walked through to better view the seven boulders bearing the faces of very unique wolves. Each was special in its own way, holding various markings while some were high in length and short in width, others followed the opposite pattern. The middle boulder was by far the most intriguing for it was shielded in nothing but moss, yet the face of it appeared to be the leader for the mouth was ajar. Glancing back, he noticed that Tala was gone as was Grear. Calling out to them, nothing is heard. "That's just great, now I have to find them," Zac said to himself while rolling his eyes to the stones. Then a powerful gust of wind flowed into the forest and the leaves from all over could be seen falling to the ground in every shade possible. Harder and harder it blew as additional leaves rush behind him. Some passed over the arch and some under it, but the ones that went under it did not come out the other side. "They've disappeared, ah, I see." He ran through the arch diving in head first and fell on the ground, but nothing had happened. "Always," he yelled out, also laughing that his plan had failed. Multiple times he attempted to leap back and forth into the arch, but nothing would happen; all the while he could still see leaves occasionally flowing inside of it. "Okay, this is getting ridiculous, why can't I go to the other side?" He sat in front of the seven stones council seeking counsel and noticed leaves were flowing out of the alpha's mouth. "Hmm, how strange the leaves are flowing from inside that boulder, perhaps there is something inside. I swear this forest plays nothing but silly games." Peeking inside, he was blasted with another wave of leaves. When the wind died down, he was able to look around; it was barren. Pulling himself out his mind was filled with a type of knowledge he had not yet come to know. Images, conversations, and everything in between that Joseph had taught him flooded his understanding. The multitude of things spoken to him from Joseph began to make a strange sort of sense like it was all interconnected somehow. In particular, one memory stood out among the rest from when Joseph had knocked on the door in Avodah Mortis to gain entry into Abraham's tomb. Swiftly returning to the arch, he knocked on the side of it with his chest held high. After, an image of another realm of Scera appeared. Zacharias looked back to the boulder, then to the sky, and nodded. "Well, here we go," he stated, shrugging his shoulders and waltzing into the gateway.

Passing it, he became enormously light headed and fell on the ground. Before him, as far as the eye could see sat structures one with nature. There appears to be three stages to this society. The first remains as any city would on the land itself; the second, inside of the very trees; and the third remains high above in the branches of the treetops. Zacharias had finally entered the realm of the Alkirum. Branches guarded the majority of sky over the kingdom and the sun's glow illuminated the forest in a different kind of dimmed shine. This light was somewhat darker but brought forth peaceful feelings most society does not know. With great wonder, he looked around, remembering his greatest childhood memories with his grandfather Alcus. Nearby, Tala and Grear sat overlooking the dominion of Scera. He then picked up Tala, holding her in his arms, and proceeded to the city below. Voices of its denizens could be heard, and as he passed a bit of brush, he entered into what seemed to be a market. Hundreds of people were bustling about in daily activity as one woman holding a pot of flowers stopped in front of him. "Who are you?" she asked surprised. She then walked up to him and set her pot down with a smile. "My name is Lindsay Stirling," she said while performing a curtsy. She was in her thirties and had long braided violet hair with a lovely summer dress on. Her smile held true to what Zac perceived as a humble character rich in spirit. "Oh, hi, I'm Zacharias," he awkwardly said holding out his hand. Lindsay giggled to herself and asked, "Where do you hail, sir, surely, you are not one of the Alkirum?" The Alkirum are different from the appearance of regular people; they are keen in eyes that slant upward to a slight degree. Every member of their people has long hair, but more than anything, an Alkirum is identified in the actions of the mind. They rationalize differently than most, where the average person sees advancement they see only stability with all things grown naturally.

"I've come bearing a message for a man whom I was told lived here."

"What is his name?" she asked. Just then, some of the local forest guards paraded over to Zacharias, pointing and cheering.

"It's him, the protector of the forest! He has come," one guard yelled out.

"Protector of the forest?" Zac asked Lindsay who was an Alkirum herself. Lindsay put her hand over her mouth for she had not noticed Tala in his arms.

"Will you please come with us? You're to stand before the king and queen of Scera," one of the guards said to him. The guards were nothing short of ecstatic as the citizens also became when they saw the wolf he was holding in his arms. "Tala, looks to me like you're a celebrity here," Zac said to her. He spoke to Lindsay, adding that it was nice to meet her, and she waved a good-bye to him and little Tala as they were escorted by the guards. Grear stood by Lindsay as this was happening, and Zacharias yelled back, "Would you mind caring for my horse until I come back? I'll pay you!" She knelt picking up her pot of flowers, shouting back, "Yes, be sure to meet my husband when you come back!" Each guard was equipped with a massive wooden spear and armor of ceremonially engraved wood. Underneath the armor, they wore various colored tunics, which were to indicate rank. Soon, they approached a vast bridge made of a peculiar glass type of substance that suspended over a lake coated in branch and flower. On the other side of the bridge sat a grand stone castle built into a massive tree, which was suspended over top of the lake, the top of the tree extended above the castle. Behind the tree castle sat multiple waterfalls collecting into the same lake, which ran throughout the city. Escorting Zacharias on the path was a man who stated he was captain of the local guard wearing a wooden helmet made to appear as a hawk. Walking over the bridge, Zacharias could see giant multicolored fish through the glass within the water. When they had reached the other side, water ran from the tree's large branches and leaves creating a veil encircling the castle. The guard waved some sort of glowing root in front of it, creating an entrance, and they proceeded onto a massive stone-made courtyard surrounding the castle. "This is amazing, how do you even build things like this?" he asked the guard. "Tenacity, young lad, tenacity," the guard said while laughing at his excitement. Hanging from all the sides of the castle branches hundreds of Yijarii are cradled by this their mother. Each of the countless foxes watch his every move. The captain stood by the main entrance and pointed his spear inside. "The king and queen will be very glad to see you, just remember your manners." Zacharias nodded and strolled inside, holding Tala within his arms.

A pathway decorated in rare vegetation escorts, sounds of rushing water could be heard ahead. Every corridor is taken by flower, insect, but most of all thriving colonies of Buzzies. A Buzzy is a creature native to Scera that appears as tiny living teddy bear without ears or nose. Unable to really defend themselves, they band together in large quantities, creating cities among Buzzy kind. Their homes are made of pinecones and twigs where they pack together tightly at night for warmth. These are friendly creatures, living a life of tending to the forest. Most of all, they love flowers in which they pick often; to every Buzzy is a special flower they carry with them. It is said that if a Buzzy favors someone, they will part with it in an exchange for friendship. Zacharias stares at them for a few moments as some climb up to the windowsills and others play among the flowers. "I'm not really sure what they're doing, but they are cute." Reaching the throne room, he was met by a flood of water pouring out from the ceiling that was composed entirely of violet mushrooms. The water flushed into a single hole in the room and began to swirl to its depths. As for the hole, it was surrounded by shining silver gates with large spikes atop them resembling butterflies. To the sides of the room, stone statues of forest warriors riding unique

Yijarii sat as if guarding the monarch. Twin broad staircases span from them met into a single set of stairs, which sat only steps away from the waterfall. Upon walking further into the room, a throne built of emerald and oak overlooked from atop a high balcony. A single branch jetted outward forming the symbol of the winged wolf. "Hello," he called out to the throne. From the balcony, the fair appearance of a young and beautiful blonde girl appears. Displayed in an elegant dress with a silver tiara around her head the girl yells down "Who are you and what are you doing in my castle!" Zacharias blinks several times before answering jokingly, "I'm here to save the forest of course." The girl frowns before disappearing from the balcony. Just then, the king and the queen of Scera enter the room with their many escorts gazing at Tala. "My boy, you have done well," the king states, rushing over to him with arms open and cape flowing. He was well aged in years as was his wife, but they were quite lively and kind for royalty. "I am Drake Amerius, King of Scera, and over there is my wife, Queen Salene Amerius." Zacharias shook his hand, forgetting to bow, but the king did not mind; in fact, he was ecstatic. "Ahh, finally a man who knows how to shake a hand" he said in a jovial voice, chuckling loudly.

"I'm sorry to ask, but why have I been brought here? Are you upset I've trespassed onto your land?" Zacharias asked. The escorts laughed as did the king and the queen who explained to him that he was the long-awaited warrior of the forest. "Warrior of the forest, what do you mean?"

Drake then said, "Have you not come to redeem the cursed forest of Devok?"

He takes a deep breath before answering the question. "King Drake, Queen Salene, I'm not who you think I am. I've come here not to redeem Devok, but I've come to find a man by the name Aurelius Garlen. I'm to deliver an important message from a dear friend who was killed not long ago." Drake looked at Zacharias with a sort of sadness and soon apologized for his assumption and for the death of his friend. He then added in a concerned voice, "How is it you obtained the celestial cub? You must have stood before the tree of life as our prophecy states? Did you not defeat the paradox of nature Feeñera? That cub you have is divine proof. Are you not the sign of the eagle?" Looking to Drake, Zacharias stated, "I am actually in search of the sign of the eagle myself. It is the message I am to deliver to Garlen."

Drake glanced to Salene who, in turn, replied, "It is said that the first chosen of God shall be united under the sign of the eagle. We the Gentiles await this sign for when it comes to pass Christ will unite both the eternal forest and the faithful church, ushering in His return."

Drake then answered, "Yes, she's right, I know of one man who may be able to help you find this Garlen character. Search in town for a man known as the Large Painter, he is friend to most." Footsteps could be heard gracefully approaching from the stairs behind them. "Afternoon, my dear sweet daughter, how are you today" Drake yelled out. Holding up her long dress as she waltzed down the stairs, she looked over to Zacharias and gave a sweet smile. Thinking to himself yet again, he wondered, *"Was this not the girl who just yelled at me?"*

"He is handsome, is he not, young Alveria?" the queen stated. She nodded a profound yes and rushed to Zacharias. "Awww, isn't the cub just adorable? May I hold her?" she asked. Handing Tala over, Alveria held her in her arms like a baby. Her eyes alluring, she introduced herself in a romantic and sweet feminine voice, "Greetings, it is so nice to meet you. I am Princess Alveria Amerius, the only child of the royal family and you are?"

He began to answer, captivated by the lashes batting like the wings of a butterfly. "My name is Zacharias but if you choose you can call me Zac."

"My favorite name, you must have a wife, you're far too handsome and strong to be alone," Alveria stated, moving closer to him.

"Uhmm no, it's just me," he said embarrassed. Partially paralyzed by her charm, he took a few steps back attempting to regain composure. He did this not out of cowardice, but the fear of a woman getting close to him for he did not want to brew anymore hurt. "Come over here, silly, I don't bite," Alveria said in front of everyone, grabbing his arm. She then whispered into his ear, "Unless you ask." Zac's face turned beet red as he swallowed his thoughts before bidding everyone a farewell and vacating the premises. Tala jumped out of Alveria's arms and ran after him. Salene walked over to her daughter. "Why doesn't he like me like all the rest?" Alveria asked.

"Not all men are the same, dear, but he's a good man. His expression testifies that men like that know how to treat a woman properly." Alveria smirked to herself, excited that she has found the man she had been waiting for. Drake thought to himself, "He is a holy knight that I am positive, we shall stand by him as they once stood by us in our late hour. I will not see that promise forsaken even though the whole of Vulgata has. Scera shalt not recant! The Hilaris is soon to be slain."

Zacharias went back out into the realm of the Alkirum, passing by the captain of the guard who stopped him momentarily. "Were all of your questions answered, young warrior?"

"Somewhat. I need to find a man known as the Large Painter, do you know of him?"

"Indeed, that woman you met earlier was his wife."

Zacharias exhaled slightly. "Of course."

"You'll find the Stirling home at the end of the market by the flower shop resting inside an old oak." The guard then let him pass as Tala ran by. "What is your name, captain?"

"Prey," he says, removing the hawk helmet. Zacharias then returned back to the market that was overtaken by well over a thousand people who began to cheer at his return. "Hail the forest warrior," one man yelled out. Another screamed, "Redeemer, the redeemer has come!"

Putting up his hands, Zacharias yelled out, "I hate to ruin the party, but I am no redeemer of the forest!" After saying that, the crowds began to dissipate and leave in a melancholy atmosphere. Searching the market, he said to himself, "What is going on with these people? Are they so desperate for a messiah? All I did was kill some giant plant, but that doesn't make me someone of worth not after the hurt I've caused." As he was arguing with himself, he walked right past the flower shop where Lindsay was working. She noticed him and called out, waving a bouquet of flowers "Hey, how did it go?" He snaps back into it in the flower shop. "This is a magnificent place you have here, was it always like this?"

"Yes, but it used to be vacant until my husband and I came here and set up shop," Lindsay said while trimming a few flowers.

"I hate to bother you again, but is your husband nicknamed the Large Painter?" Lindsay smirked at him and gave yet another laugh. "You're far too formal for my humble little flower shop, you're not in the Amerius castle anymore."

"I guess you're right," he replied, smelling a bouquet of flowers. A fuzzy palm presses against his nose.

Lindsay snatches the Buzzy and sets it outside, stating, "These Buzzies, I swear, they never let me get any work done in peace. But yes, he is my husband. His name is Malfius, but just call him Beck. He is below the castle painting the waterfalls. I'll tell you where he is, but you have to promise to have lunch with us, okay."

"Ya, sure thing," he said to her unsurely.

"Your horse is out back, just fetch him when you return." Before Zac could leave, Lindsay brought him out a fresh glass of lemonade, handing it to him in a maternal manner. Receiving the glass, he was reminded of the same kindness shown to him by Penelope and knew at that moment he could not get close to them or history would be soon to repeat itself. Tala then runs into the flower shop and rests on the main counter, curling up into a fury light blue ball. "She is so precious, can she stay here for a short while?" Lindsay asked.

"Doesn't bother me, she seems to do what she wants anyways, no use trying to control her," he replied while leaving.

"That's all women," Lindsay replied, petting Tala.

Carrying on in the city of foliage, he found his way to the lower levels crossing ever twisting vines down a type of ravine. A solitary piece of land lay stretching out into the lake resting below the castle tree. On this piece of a land, a literal giant painter sat with canvas creating a portrait of the waterfalls. "Are you the one by the name of Malfius Stirling?" Zacharias calls out. Turning around, the man replies in a deeply masculine yet kind voice, "Yes, that would be me, and who are you, friend?" He had a hard look to him and his hair was dark and cropped, but his eyes embodied the meek nature of Christ. Blue paint dripped off of his brush and stained his pants. Zacharias apologized for distracting the man for he was so incredibly big that he felt he might fight him for causing him to do that. His biceps alone were larger than cannonballs and his shoulders thrice the size. He walked over to Zacharias, and standing before him, his massive chest protruding, he held out his monster of a hand. "Call me Beck," he said in the utmost joyous way. Zac shook his hand, introducing himself also, and Beck was surprised. "Heck of a shake you got there, and by the looks and size of the sword on your back, you must be a formidable warrior, are you not?" Zacharias began laughing for the bear of a man was complimenting him on his power. "I am a warrior, but you must be kidding, you're many times myself a man." Malfius gave out a laugh that echoed within the ravine with his hands on his stomach "Oh, I'm no warrior, just a painter, that's all."

"I'm sorry to bother you, Beck, but I've traveled a long way to find a man by the name of Aurelius Garlen. My friend Joseph Voltel died protecting me and, in his final words, charged me to find this man and deliver the message for him to converge on the sign of the eagle." Malfius stepped back for a minute with a heavy look in his eyes. "Joseph is dead?"

"Did you know him?" Zac asked.

"Yes, I have delivered paintings and portraits to Salem for years. Joseph was a dear friend as was his family. Are they all right?"

"Malfius, I'm sorry, they are all dead as is Salem." Biting his tongue, Malfius stepped over and sat beside the lake with his feet in the water, stating, "I am ashamed I was not there to help them."

Zac went and sat beside him, explaining, "There's nothing to feel ashamed about, there's nothing anyone could've done. What happened to them was unjust and I'm going to kill the ones responsible. Beck, did you know Joseph was a holy knight?" Malfius put his robust palm into the water, splashing himself with it, "The man you seek, Aurelius Garlen, did live among the Alkirum here for some time, but he is gone now. Very few knew his name for he went by the pseudonym of Silent Night." Zacharias reached into his pocket and pulled out the cloth piece that contained the blood of Jesus Christ. "Joseph, in his final moments, killed Ephestus and from the snake's body fell this. This is the final piece to the Sword of Abraham. I have to find that sword because only with that can I kill the ones who killed him. Joseph and his family took me in and saved my life and the ones responsible for all of this are known as the Black Hand, they are led by a man named Veil."

Malfius's eyes glanced over at the cloth and his jaw dropped. "This is the sacred final piece to the sword, your words are truth." Malfius then held up his hands and praised the Lord, saying, "Blessed be thy name for the time of the Exiles is soon!" Standing up, Malfius helped Zacharias to his feet. "Come, my new friend, we shall talk more over lunch."

"Malfius, wait, you should know something about me. I am cursed by the touch of death by a demon known as Manistof, and whomsoever I get close to will die because of my intervention. The same thing happened to the Voltel family and Salem. I don't want to bring that plague upon your household."

Filling his lungs with fresh air, Malfius replied, "You say Manistof did this to you, correct?"

"Yes, and I am now forever cursed by the flight of destruction for my decision I paid by the fledgling of sin."

"Do you believe in Jesus?" Beck asked in all seriousness.

"Honestly I've denied the idea of God my entire life until only days ago. I'm not really even to sure who Jesus Christ is as a person. Joseph once explained to me of how he died on the cross for the sins of mankind, but I didn't understand why he had to do that, why he had to suffer. God does exist that I am sure of, but I do not know how so, what I can say is that I believe that Jesus did live and is connected but I have yet to 100 percent follow. And until I commit, I don't want to say that I do out of respect for those who do believe such as the Voltels and Salem."

Malfius nodded and smiled at the same time. "Your eyes state of the hardships you've experienced in your lifetime, young swordsman, but did you know that Jesus Christ overcame death and was resurrected on the third day? With that being said, even the chains of death cannot bind you, if you ask your Father to save you by accepting his only begotten son. So come and have lunch with my wife and I, please honor our household with your presence." Thoughts raced in Zac's consciousness. "What if I get close and they also die because of me? How could I live with that again? Maybe he's correct, what if this time it is different? Will God protect me? Will He protect His children? Oh, I hope that this is true. Could I finally be free from the clutches of Manistof?"

Malfius tapped Zacharias. "Are you there?" He then added, "Here, let me pray over you, the Lord will not allow harm outside of His will, trust me."

"All right," Zac answered nervously. Beck laid his hands on Zac and prayed over him; after that, the two returned back to the flower shop inside of the old oak tree.

Lindsay had lunch prepared, and they all sat and broke bread together. Malfius and Lindsay prayed and gave thanks for the meal in front of them. Although Zac had abstained from this, it was not because he did not believe, but it was because he did not yet feel ready to partake; he did not feel worthy. After the meal had been consumed, Zacharias began to tell Lindsay and Malfius the entire story from when he was introduced to the Voltels all the way up to him entering into the realm of the Alkirum. This story went on into nightfall and they were intrigued by it greatly. Malfius began to speak, "Zacharias, thank you for sharing with us this information. As you know, many things are happening in our world that we can't explain by written word or scientific exploit. With that being said, something profound is going to happen, can you feel it?"

Zac licked his lips and replied, "My entire life I was never able to fit in with regular people, and the older I get, the more I understand as to why. Even from when I was a child, I instinctively knew things that others did not. I knew that monsters beyond our comprehension existed in the world far worse than those even in nature. Always have I felt a force of pure good and absolute evil pulling everything in either direction, but I did not want to believe it was that simple. From what I've taken in within my short life, I've noticed that it doesn't just affect people but, in fact, all things. The knowledge of science, the innate sense of nature, and the philosophies of religion all pulled to do good or evil."

Malfius smirked, "You're more spot on than you know. I would challenge you with another question if that would be all right?" Raising an eyebrow, Zacharias signaled that it was. "If you really sit and objectively think about it, the statement you just made really does explain the world. Everyone falls under one of those three categories as their foundational belief structure. Those of science believe in man's ability to always search for answers to always find a logical, rational truth and advance technology for our use, the science nation of Maldecium can attest to that. Places like Scera and Cruatia fall under the category of letting nature take its course, and we as humans live among it, respecting it always. Those who believe in nature know that the habitats of animals will sustain themselves as long as we do not interfere. Lastly in this three-handed deck of conviction, we draw the belief of religion. Those of religion believe in both scriptures and holy writ from long ago while some for preconceived dogmatic behaviors such as sacramentalism," Malfius explained.

Zacharias, who was very happy to hear this, replied, "Not to sound offensive, Malfius, but you're quite intelligent."

Malfius laughed. "I understand what I look like and I get that said a lot." Lindsay also laughed carefully, listening to their conversation. She kissed her husband on the cheek, embracing his arms, then sitting in his lap. She then lovingly stated, "Like my husband was getting at all those three types of foundational beliefs are interconnected."

"By what?" Zac asked.

"By faith, dear, each one of them lives by faith, even if they do not know it."

"I don't understand. Isn't faith only for those who believe in religion?"

Malfius chimed back into the conversation. "The term faith means believing in what one cannot see. With that being said, we can concur that in all walks of life, we all have faith in some way. Those of science believe in the ideas they have not fully developed, they believe that the universe holds the answers, even though they do not see them much like invisible air. Those of nature who believe in the instinctive order of the world know that the sun will continually rise and that nature shall sustain itself although they cannot see the reason why the plants grow and wilt. Finally, those of religion hold faith in the church and in God, depending on what religion you speak of even though they cannot see Him. These people do not see the spiritual force inside or outside of them, but they believe all is composed of this. So if you really look at it, God is in all things and He is the good pull in the world that you spoke of. In retrospect, the fallen evil one, the Devil, is the paradoxical counterpart and negative pull in the world. So science, nature, and religion are all double-edged swords capable of being used for right or wrong. Even the Holy Bible, which is good, can be used for evil if taken out of context or added to as in apocrypha or also by watering down what the word really means. Those are the primary reasons why we see an overabundance of Bible translations. People are far more connected than what they choose to believe, but that's why Jesus taught us how to love so that we could break down those barriers and pierce the heart with his everlasting truth."

Zacharias listens carefully and Lindsay stated, "Don't let the tragic things of your past prevent you from living your life, Jesus doesn't want you to hurt alone anymore." That night, Malfius and Lindsay offered for him to sleep in their home, which was located not far from there.

When they had reached their home, Malfius sat outside with Zacharias as the stars held partial face among the great trees of Scera. "You said it was the Black Hand who killed the Voltel family and Salem, correct?" Malfius reiterated.

"Precisely, do you know anything about them?"

"I've talked a lot tonight already. I hope I am not boring you," Malfius answered, crossing his arms.

"No, it's fine. I want to talk, I've missed out on it for far too long," Zac replied. Malfius closed his eyes, gathering his thoughts as he prepared to explain. "Well, here it goes," Malfius said sarcastically. "Long story short, I do paintings and portraits for a playwright by the name of Fanero Malchior. In working on his large-scale plays and productions presented to royalty, you hear a lot of things, including about the Black Hand. I've only heard it spoken in rumor among certain high up nobles, but it seems they were frightened of this group. They explained that the Black Hand was led by a man by the name of Veil, a self-proclaimed necromancer of fire and plague. He is surrounded by four other elite mercenaries who make up the Black Hand. They are known as: The Mace–Gravus Delerian, The Bow–Falus Delerian, The Horse–Derrigan, The Mind–Maystrick. Together, they combine a most deadly elite form of military prowess combining Power and Armor, Range, Speed, and Intelligence all united by the perfect Leadership of Veil. This group is made to be the perfect assassination squad to target high-end political officials."

Zac then asked, "Do you believe they work for Manistof as the parchment in Salem read?"

"Believe it or not, it is said they answer to another, the Slave King to the east, Victor Carthright. It is believed that Victor Carthright is using them as a fear tactic for the coming war of east and west just like in the Big 10 (WWI). Carthright holds the keys to the gates of war some even say the very spirit of the phoenix of Marduas lives within his soul, soon to be reborn."

"Victor Carthright, you say he's responsible for all of this?" Zacharias asked concerned.

"I'm not saying Manistof is not a part of this, perhaps Carthright is in allegiance with him as the united eastern front does have many allies."

Grasping Titulus, he exclaimed, "Then my fight is with Carthright also."

"Let not rage consume you, it is how the evil one lures us in, we have to learn to let go and forgive as Jesus did for us. Don't let hate rule over you."

"I'm sorry, Malfius, I'm just not ready to accept that," Zac said, gazing at the tip of the blade imagining his enemies falling before him.

"These are dark times, and more than ever, friends will need each other for the advancing waves that will crash against all. You've arrived here at an opportune time, in two days, we ride to Valencia for the Week of Commemoration, you should come with me. I'm sure we can find Garlen there."

"Are you sure, Beck? I really hate to get in your way," Zac replied, sinking at the idea of saying good-bye.

Beck patted him on the back. "Oh, trust me, it's a grand occasion, you're going to love it." After that, they went to bed and Zacharias slept in their guestroom.

After he had fallen asleep, Malfius and Lindsay whispered among themselves. "Lindsay, he is the one, he is the one Joseph promised would come," Beck said. Malfius then lowered, resting into his wife's embrace. "Joseph and his family are dead, how could this have happened," he added sadly.

She comforts him by rubbing his hair. "Joseph and his beautiful family are home in heaven with the Lord, he gave his life for what he knew to be true, we will never forget them. Joseph said many things would happen, and they all did, perhaps he did not receive his final vision until his last day."

Malfius whispered, "We're going to set off to Valencia in two days with the rest. I want you to join the next caravan to Evangela and wait for me there." Lindsay nodded yes as the both of them peered through the doorway watching him peacefully sleep. "He looks so tired and hurt," Lindsay whispered into his ear.

Beck, holding her waist, whispered in return, "He has been well prepared for the trial ahead. When I met him this afternoon, I felt the Holy Spirit all around him in a way I have never felt before. The Spirit then reached out and grabbed my own heart, and at that moment, I knew even before language confirmed. Soon, the veil shall be raised in Valencia and all things presented true." The two of them left the doorway with a smile and, together, prayed in their room, giving thanks to the Lord for the mighty blessing received.

PART 2: ASSURANCE

Waking to the smell of a magnificent breakfast, Zac steps out to Malfius and Lindsay, giving final preparations to meal. "Good morning," they both say to him with delight as Malfius wears a ridiculous chef hat looking as a king's chef. Zacharias then sat with them and they ate together. "So you met the royal family yesterday. What did you think of Princess Alveria, did you know she's said to be the fairest beauty in all the forests of Scera, if not all the west?" Beck said, nudging Zacharias.

Lindsay presses her cheek. "It hadn't crossed my mind, do you have someone special?"

Deeply, Zac sighed out loud, "Me, no, I prefer to be alone, it's how I've always lived."

"Well, I heard she's taken quite a fancy toward you," Lindsay threw in, broadening thrill.

"Ha, I had forgotten to ask if you had a lady," Malfius yelled out. Lindsay and himself began to chuckle. A knock is heard at the door, and Lindsay goes to answer. "Sorry, we're kind of a quirky married couple at times, we find comedy in most things."

"I like to see people laugh, but I'm slightly lost at the joke here," he said back, squinting.

"Because if you really wanted, you could get a good woman, you're not a dimwit, plus you're a warrior, that helps a lot," Beck stated, flexing his right arm.

"He's also very handsome," Lindsay added, strolling happily back.

"Oh, uh, thanks, I guess. I'm not that great at accepting compliments if you hadn't noticed," he told them. Lindsay brushed aside her violet braided hair, placing her elbows on the table and her head cupped within her hands, also leaning forward on the chair. Continually, she smiled at him as Zac questioned, "Why are you doing that?" Malfius started to laugh to himself slightly, and it grew more when she spoke to him. "It seems you've been invited to participate on a date with young Princess Alveria Amerius this afternoon." Zacharias staring back at Lindsay without emotion made the two of them give in to comedy. Malfius laughed so loud that Lindsay began to do the same, Zac stayed in the same blank state, which only fueled the experience. "Looks like he's gonna have to deal with it now," Malfius yelled out to Lindsay, slapping his friend's back. Silently, Zac took a bite of bread with honey on it and held the rest to Tala. He then spoke on the matter, "Okay, here's the deal. I've never done this before, what do I do?" Lindsay gave him an angry look. "This is no time for lies!" Malfius who hadn't stopped chuckling at the last joke was joined by Zacharias but not Lindsay. "Okay, okay, we have to be serious to this matter now," Beck sarcastically added. At the end of that, they all had to catch their breath and get a drink of water to recover. Lindsay left the room and grabbed a pot of flowers first checking for the infernal Buzzies. "Take a look at these flowers, are they lovely?"

"Without question," Zac replied.

Lindsay then told him, "In terms of marriage, a woman is like the gentle flower: if a good man cultivates her and treats her right, she will grow. But if you do not pay her the attention she needs, the flower will wilt and die. A man is made to spiritually lead his family with the word of God. These seeds are planted early in a relationship by being upfront of both yourself and intention. Just follow the example of Jesus and how he died for the church, his bride. The Lord will give you what your heart desires for He put those desires within you to seek Him out. Do remember that your heart can be deceived and that's why you don't just follow but lead your heart."

Zacharias raised his glass of water to them. "Thank you both for your kindness and generosity, my new friends, the Stirlings." Malfius and Lindsay raised their glasses in return and clashed them against his. "I can drink to that," Malfius profoundly stated.

A few hours later after he had gotten cleaned up, Zacharias went off to meet Princess Alveria. Tala and Grear remained at the Stirling household. Malfius and Lindsay loved precious little Tala and spent the morning playing with her, but Tala favored playing in the garden out back, searching out Buzzies, which warded her off with petal attacks. Malfius began his preparations for the journey to Valencia the next day. When Zac arrived at the castle, Captain Prey grants him entry past the watery veil.

Entering back into the main chambers, Alveria sits even more fair than the day before, wearing a lovely pink dress with umbrella and white gloves. This was one of the few times Zacharias did not have his sword on him and was given a nice-looking azure overcoat to wear that was Beck's. It was a bit big on him, but it was from when he was younger so it wasn't too terrible. Zacharias walked over to Princess Alveria and held out his hand. "Do you need help up?" Alveria giggled and accepted. "You're a funny one, and I'm so glad that you came!" Blushing at the simplest touch, he replies, "Well, it would have been rude for me not to accept an invitation, I suppose, but minus that," he then stopped his statement by the waterfall rushing down the room. Grasping the silver railings barring the way to the depths, he glanced back at Alveria over his shoulder. "You look very beautiful today." Alveria lit up like the summer's glow, then trotting over, she closed up the umbrella and grabbed his left hand with both of hers. Her voice was young and naïve, backed by infatuation. Also her blue eyes mixed with blonde hair were difficult for Zacharias not to look into, for it spoke of a loving peace he had never known. "Come with me. I have a surprise for you," she said to him with a facial expression made of fascination. Dragging him out of the castle, passing Prey, they stroll to the rear of the courtyard. Alveria stood scanning the waterfalls. Around her neck was a silver necklace with a pure emerald inside. Alveria held it up, and before them, another glass-like bridge appeared, extending over the waterfalls.

"How did you do that?"

"I'm a princess, silly, there's many secrets I won't tell you," she said, covering her mouth and strolling across the span. Following her, it is noticed that it connects to another series of bridges that lay atop the waterfall. These are made of thick intertwining vines with branches sprawling out the sides, holding various colors of anemone flowers. This vine-made path led unto an exalted oak tablet carved with many names.

"This place is magnificent, but what is it?" Zac asked.

"These are the names of all the fallen royalty of Scera. This isn't the surprise, close your eyes."

Zacharias listened for only a moment, then gave in to curiosity, surveying the setting. Alveria stood in front of him and leaned in close, whispering, "Please do it for me," as her lips gave him a kiss on the cheek quickly. He did as she asked and she led him past another series of trails for several minutes. "Okay, we're here!" Opening his eyes, an illustrious garden sat with an interlocking hedge maze behind it for well over two miles. "Welcome to my secret garden, will you be my chaperone?" Alveria said, holding her umbrella over her head and extending out her right hand palm down. Grabbing Alveria's hand, he felt kind of uncomfortable fighting over his self-worth. Together, they walked into the maze, but Zacharias did not speak at first because he was falling apart inside. Duality had taken its course as the storm in his persona raged. "No woman can love you, look at the things you've done to others, you struggle just to be yourself day to day. Manistof, be gone. Malfius said you could be free of this, remember? Don't for one second believe that someone as beautiful as a princess could ever love you, a man who can't even protect his family. What would Alcus think of me now, better yet Joseph and Penelope? I should be out finding the Sword of Abraham to get those back who killed you, but instead, I'm here, have I dishonored you further? Mariana is dead, she is dead, do you even understand, that innocent little girl suffered a painful death because of you! Zacharias, go find Garlen, tell him to follow the sign of the eagle! You're a holy knight now."

"Hey, what's the matter, are you feeling okay?" Alveria asked him, snapping him back into reality. Zacharias pinched the top of his nose, followed by rubbing his scalp. "Yes, I'm sorry, there's a lot on my mind, and I should be paying more attention to you. Can I be honest here?"

Alveria put the umbrella over him, blocking out the sun. "Of course you can!"

"I've never really done this before and you're so pretty, and I'm just, I don't know how to say, a mess," he said to her, feeling like he was nothing, then looking away humiliated. Alveria put her arms around his back and gazed directly into his eyes for he was quite taller than she. "You're such a sweetheart. I just want to kiss you," she stated in all desire. Alveria's eyes closed; dropping her umbrella, she gently ran her fingers down his neck, which shot a pleasurable tingle within his body. Her other hand sat behind his head as Zac then also closed his eyes and moved his face in by slight tremble. Their lips pressed up against each other, and he gave her a long passionate kiss with all of his heart. While this was happening, his right hand sat on her back, his left on her arm. After the kiss had ended, Alveria pressed his tender yet meaningful smile, his eyes are genuinely lost in hers. "You see that wasn't so bad, you're an amazing kisser, I knew you'd be." Zacharias gave a smile that no one had ever seen containing his utmost confidence, stating, "Oh, thank you very much. I've never kissed a woman like that before." But he did indeed remember when Kelly had kissed him, he does hope she is doing well. Alveria wrapped her arms around his, leaving the umbrella as they sauntered deeper into the maze that held walls over ten feet high and stone path.

Traveling for some time, they then reached the middle portion of the maze where a cabin and fountain sat. "This is my secret hiding spot to get away from the rest of the world and I want to share it with you." Alveria grasped him tightly and studied his eyes vicariously. Before he could speak, a rustling noise was heard in one of the trees above. Rotating to the tree, he heard Alveria scream out. Behind them sat a Yijarii, which was a giant green fox with flesh like mantis arms upon its back that could extend and retract on command. A girl stood with long fiery orange hair; she was dressed in a far more ceremonial type of wooden armor that custom fit her athletic body. Atop her head is a string of charming forest beads. She held the center of a long double-bladed sword made from fine steel crafted from a master blacksmith not of these parts. Pointing it at Zacharias as she circled around him, she yelled out, "Who is it you think you are, imposter! I know you are no hero of our people, now speak before I cut you down where you stand!"

Zacharias kept his wits about him, staring at the stone pathway, but his tone spoke in controlled aggression, "No claim to that matter was made in seriousness."

"You will look at me when I speak, what is it you plan to do with our princess?" He stares the young woman down now, refusing speech. Alveria began screaming at her to drop her weapon immediately, but the woman would not listen.

"Stay out of this, Alveria, he is not one of us!" Angrier she became, the more Zacharias stood scowling silently. The woman then twirls the weapon before launching a powerful strike to kill, but he stood as a statue of war, not yielding an inch. She stopped her blade against him just below his eye; Zacharias grabbed the blade with his hand, cutting it moderately. His blood winds down her sword as he peered into her orange eyes that matched her hair with a red trail also streaming down his cheek. "When you swing your sword, you better kill your opponent, for they will show no mercy in retaliation." She gasped at the sight of his blood cascading down her double-bladed sword and let go of her weapon that clang loudly as both sides bounced upon the rock repeatedly. Zacharias gave it back to her. "This is a fine blade, it's obviously sharp but must have cost a fortune, was it purchased from Valencia or Bordeaux?" She snatched the sword back, soaking her own hand in the crimson reminder of a lineage long past upon the hilt. She hopped on the Yijarii completely caught off guard. "I'm sorry, Alveria," she said in a soft voice before jumping on top of the hedges and running off. Alveria ran over to him. "Are you okay? I am so sorry and even more embarrassed!" Alveria took off her gloves and wrapped them around his wound.

"Who was that?" he asked curiously.

"Her name is Joan, she is the guardian of the royal family, please don't take it personally, she is of the Devokian line. She is my dearest friend whom I regard as sister."

"Devokian blood?" Zac asked as his own could be seen stained on the road.

"Yes, she is a pure Devokian and I am pure Sceran. Those native to Scera are much more peaceful as those of Devokian descent are far more aggressive. You've heard the story of how Devok was destroyed by the Valencian crusade hundreds of years ago, right?"

"Yes, but many still believe it was the holy knights who destroyed Devok."

"Well, we don't, we have always been friends to the holy knights for Sir Abraham Desteeran, being the first holy knight, was Sceran born and raised. Also, the holy knights saved the peoples of Devok, leading them here to live with us. It is because of that act graced from up high that the Alkirum have been united. Albeit, after years of passed down rumor, exactly how that story happened, we are not sure." Zacharias went and washed off his cut in the fountain and Alveria sat beside him. The sun began to set. "Should we start to return home? It's getting late out and I don't want to get killed for having not returned you unto your father," Zac jokingly said.

Her feet resting in the water, Alveria replied in a depressed way he did not expect, "Will you stay with me here tonight?"

"Uhm, are you sure that's a good idea?"

Alveria thought to herself, *I don't want to be lonely anymore, I like him, I really like him, and I don't want him to leave. Have I come on too strong? Will I chase him away this way?*

"Hey, I'm the only one who can get lost in thought around here, Alveria," Zac said, poking her shoulder.

"You're a riot," she replied.

"If you want me to, I'll stay here with you tonight." Alveria leapt into him with a hug, and at that point, little Tala came running up to Zacharias.

"Tala, how did you get here?" he said surprised. Tala hopped up and licked the wound that then became cold and slightly froze over which in turn stopped the bleeding. She rolled about in his lap as he petted her. Alveria went to pet Tala, but she dove into the fountain and all the water turned into a sheet of ice. She was seen running around under the ice unaffected and then smashed through a thin piece as if nothing had happened. "Woah, did you see that?" he yelled out to Alveria.

Picking up Tala and holding her in her arms, Alveria replied, "It's amazing really, and the older this celestial cub gets, the more her powers are going to grow. I'm happy that you have received such a delightful blessing. I could think of no one more deserving." Together, they sat on the fountain until nightfall.

Hundreds of fireflies lit up the area and the ice had melted, so the sounds of the fountain returned. Zac had his arm around Alveria who rested against him. "I wish it could be like this forever," Alveria whispered.

Tala had fallen asleep on the pathway as Zac answered, "She came all the way, knowing I was injured." Then standing up, he grabbed Tala as Alveria signaled for him to come inside the cabin. Inside, she appealingly went into her bedroom, calling his name. Setting Tala down in the main room, he followed her in, taken by racing emotion. Alveria was lying on a single bed as Zac thought to himself, *I believe she wants to lay with me. I'm not sure I'm ready for this. What do I do, make up an excuse, but then again, she is beautiful.* Zac's foot was tapping on the floor and his hands slightly trembled much like earlier. "I'm not going to make you sleep with me. I know you're a virgin, just from your actions," Alveria said playfully.

"Are you not a virgin?" he asked her in return.

"Yes, I was just teasing, you're no fun," she said with a passionate smile. She then added, patting the bed, "Come sit beside me." He sat beside her on the bed and she rubbed his shoulders. Alveria pressed her body up against his, putting her mouth to his ear, "My real surprise for you is I want to give you my virginity, let's share that with each other." Desteeran stood up as if infuriated by the statement with his fists clenched. "Did I say something wrong?" Alveria asked concerned. Zac, whose back was facing her, spoke with his eyes closed, "No, not at all, I apologize. It's just I'm supposed to be finishing the mission Joseph gave his life for, and here I am, only caring about my own wants. I mean no disrespect, Your Highness, but what kind of friend would I be if that's the action I chose?"

"No, it's just fine. I was actually scared myself," Alveria said, exhaling.

Zacharias smiled, asking, "May I share this bed with you? I'm tired of being alone." Alveria made room for him and cuddled with him as he lay. Both of them locked eyes and said thank you to each other at the same time. Their hearts pounded heavily as they gave one more passionate kiss. "Will you come with me to Valencia tomorrow for the Week of Commemoration? I have no one to escort me to the royal ball on the fifth day," she added with a sad face.

"I promise I'll go with you. I'd be honored," Zac responded. Also he stated, "But I already told my new friend Malfius, the Large Painter, that I'd go with him because we have to locate a man by the name of Aurelius Garlen."

"That's just fine, when you're free, I'd like to spend as much time together there as we can if that's all right. I'll help you on your mission if I can," Alveria asked, rubbing her nose to his.

"Sounds like a plan." The two then fell asleep fastened as one accompanied by the serenade of the fountain.

After they had returned to the castle the next day, Alveria met with her parents and Zacharias returned to the Stirling household.

He explained what had happened the night before, so they knew why he hadn't returned. Lindsay also had her things packed, but she would not be going with them to Valencia, she would be returning to Evangela with another caravan. After saying their good-byes to Lindsay, Zacharias and Malfius met up with the Amerius family escort that was preparing to make the journey to Valencia. Only Desteeran and Stirling rode horses, the escort was made up of a multitude of Yijarii with Joan's being beside the royal carriage. Alveria waved to Zacharias as Malfius smirked and jokingly punched him in the shoulder. "Looks like you have a lady now, my friend." Joan, on the other hand, gave him a stern glare, pointing her double-bladed sword to the sun. The king and queen gave a respectful wave good-bye to their people as Prey led the convoy. At that time, the escort moved out as the Alkirum cheered them on to represent all of Scera before the infamous Church of Law.

ACT II
GRIFFON'S CROSS

13

Wings of the Vindicated

The royal Sceran escort traveled for ten days, and during this, Malfius and Zacharias grew closer as did his relationship with Princess Alveria and her family. The journey should've taken no more than a week, but royalty tends to take its time, a luxury most of us will never know. But Joan was the opposite; instead, she withdrew more by the day, never speaking a single word to him or anyone for that matter. Together, they passed over the Euphrates River, followed by the Valencian line through the famous bridge city of Romulus. The sites of Valencia were breathtaking from all of Southcross, which was the bottom half of the nation divided. Decorated with cities of white cobblestone and golden statue of heroes long past, it was said to be the land of milk and honey in the west. In the world of Vulgata, there was no greater nation of castle for the glorious architecture kissed by garish light spoke of a divine constitution, setting it apart anything less than the highest of noble society. Early that morning, the royal escort reached the capital city of Alexandria, which rested between Southcross and Northcross. Six legendary white gothic castles capped with pitch-black rooftops reached to the heavens encircling the deemed holy Church of Law safeguarding the heart of Alexandria, bride of Valencia. If one was to view the church from overhead, then it would be noticed that each served as the point of a hexagon with its northern and southern tips being directly in front and behind the Church of Law, perfectly defending it within this radiant diamond. Although hundreds if not more feet from each other, three vast levels of bridges connected each castle overhead, making one solid trinity between the six. Alongside this, from the plateau of each citadel, one additional bridge ascended to the higher balconies of the grand church, merging the six into a seventh. Much like the rest of Alexandria, a plaza of colorless cobblestone sat in front of the Church of Law, but among these, darker stones formed the image of an interlinked rosary. As for the great house of worship herself, she stretched far higher than the mighty castles. The city went on as far as the eye could see in every direction and its chalky and golden grandeur second to none. Hundreds of smaller villages and cities lay scattered across the endless stone pathways, creating one mega city that was Alexandria. Throughout the region, the vast yet peaceful Keystone River ran with canals built to intersect all of the castles along with the Church of Law and her magnificent courtyard. Peaceful and extensive covered bridges high above the river guided each entrance before the Church of Law, allowing ships to pass underneath. The Church of Law in fact rested on a man-made island that had harnessed the power of the healing waters to protect them. Tremendous warships could be seen arriving from the river by the hour docking underneath castle and church. The Amerius family was met by bishops dressed in green and white robes wearing silver crosses around their necks. Zacharias and Malfius sat on their horses in the back of this caravan, studying the monstrous city.

"How are we ever going to find Garlen in all of this?" Zac asked.

Beck dismounted his horse, viewing the Church of Law. "You know this is one of the largest structures in our world. Zac, before we get too involved here in searching for Garlen, remember this place is littered with both ally and enemy, discernment is key. Above all else, show no one the piece of cloth Joseph died for, certain clergy will have you killed or arrested just for holding such a relic," Beck told him in whisper.

Zacharias replied, "I understand, this structure is incredible even compared to how immense the church of Sodom was."

Malfius replied, "It is a magnificent feat, but only to those who fear the Lord, there are some who sit on thrones of their own glory here."

"Zacharias, come, the royal church service is about to begin. I want you to sit beside me," Alveria yelled out, dashing over to him.

"Well, go ahead, I'm going to have a look around myself," Malfius stated, urging him to go. Alveria grabbed Zacharias's hand as Malfius smiled, walking away, also taking Grear and Tala with him. A prodigious marble staircase ascended easily a hundred feet to the great gates of the church. It was the largest church ever built by man, and within a profound multileveled white spire that outreached to paradise, a grand silver bell is protected. Above that, two griffons with matching crowns held high in talons, a colossal shield augmented with a diamond and mystical rose attesting to the Virgin Mother Mary. Their wings sprawled and beaks in everlasting screech, these twin sentinels infinitely proclaimed their names that were Castor and Pollux, who make up Dioskouri if the call of war should arise. Below the silver bell, six additional bell towers surround, each being placed around the main corresponding in direct path of one of the six surrounding castles. The doors reach twenty feet high and span ten in width, also bearing the same symbol of the twin griffons. By the door, multiple silver statues of paladins sat as

Zacharias inched beside, admiring the pristine artistry. When his finger touched the statue, it spoke, "Welcome to the holy realm of Valencia where angels live among men, please proceed into the womb of our mother, the church." It was in fact not a statue but one of the ancient silver paladins, and at that moment, the rest came to life, embodying a statue like faith frozen to law. They pressed open the door and stood at attention, holding their swords to their chests, paying homage to the Amerius family who was close behind. Entering the church, it was entirely made of marble, marvelous tapestries lined the floors, and stained glass of biblical truths upon the walls. In the main lobby, they were greeted by another bishop who guided them into the main chapel where worship was ready to commence. Thousands of nobles lined the pews surrounded by red carpets. Atop the countless balconies, princes, kings, and their counterparts all awaited the ceremony. Much like the church of Sodom, this to had a massive altar in front with angelic paintings hovering over the ceiling, but this time, it was angels around the earth with a figure of light overtop. Alveria took Zacharias's arm and began to sashay down the aisle. As they entered thousands of nobles turn gasping at her elegant beauty, and whispers among them resonated. No one knew who the young man was or if he was even of noble lineage. Alveria had them travel all the way to the front as organs began to play echoing throughout the church sorrowfully. A special pew was reserved in front, for the Valencians always attempted to curry favor as their atonement for the sins against the forest long ago. "Everyone's staring," Zac whispered to Alveria.

"I know, isn't it just marvelous?" Alveria whispered back.

Not so much, he thought to himself. Then, multiple bishops were seen trooping past the aisles, carrying large crucifixes to the altar. Together, they began to chant in Latin. Then an old man walked out from behind the altar wearing a black, red, and white robe decorated with precious gem assisted by a grand mitre atop his head. In his hands, he carried a large staff made of solid gold, bearing a red cardinal that held a bent cross within beak. The elderly man who held a most protruding white beard stood before the church with a somber gaze. He placed the staff into a slot so it remains propped up beside his podium. "Welcome, my brothers and sisters, to another glorious Week of Commemoration the Lord hath graced," he says but does not yell for voices carry easily here. He then continued, "I would like to thank you all for making the journey here to worship with us as family. Long ago did we fight among ourselves, but it is here this very week we pay our respects to all those who have died in the alliance defending our freedoms yet underserved. I would like to take a moment to confirm rumor that the Voltoro family has indeed fallen to an unknown culprit who shalt be found by the Lord's divine retribution. Long have I served the Voltoro family and the loss of the sons, Eurus and Coprulus deeply wounds my heart, may they rest forever in the holy kingdom by the grace of the merciful mother." As he said "mother," a majority of nobles stated in dejected unison, "Praise be to Mary, holy mother of God." The priest leans up to the staff placed firm and slightly cries, rubbing his face around it. Zac's eyes began to glance around with an uncomfortable feeling, also tapping his foot without control.

"What is it?" Alveria questioned, poking his arm.

"I don't like this place, something isn't right with these people," he said back. A single feather then fell in front of the elderly man speaking and he bent down to pick it up, carefully. Everyone's attention is to the rafters, but they are unsure of what they are seeing as many of the women scream pointing and nobles begin stand in fear. It had the body of a man but the traits of an eagle. With an alarming wingspan, it descends before the statues of the saints behind the old man, holding a finely crafted war halberd. Its face was of a white bald eagle and its body was pitched in brown feather; it also had thick leather armor with slots cut out for the wings. In a loud aggressive voice combined of both man and eagle, he spoke, pointing his halberd to the priest's heart.

"You, betrayer of pulpit and liberty, how dare you stand where my father Avilius stood! Let all of Valencia know it was you who had my family murdered as to gain control over this disillusioned state! I am Prince Eurus Voltoro, heir to the kingdom of Valencia, and I charge you, Caiaphas, with heresy against the monarch, the punishment is death!" The priest known as Caiaphas pulls his staff from socket. "You do not behold the appearance of a man let alone prince, what vice has called you forth, demon?"

"If I am such a devil, then why not cast me out if thou claimest to be chosen?" Eurus's fingers that are large talons grasp his weapon all the more as his eagle eyes stared down Caiaphas in the spirit of vengeance. Caiaphas stands fearless in return as the silver paladins, clad heavy, rush in by the dozens all with gleaming weapons verily drawn. "Leave the patriarch," one of the paladins yelled out, slamming his mace to shield.

"Imposter, you are not Eurus for he is dead along with his brother Coprulus, you dare dishonor this holy place by the sacrilege of your fell tongue!" Eurus launched his weapon at them and grabbed Caiaphas by his robe, knocking off his cap and disarming his golden staff, which in turn fell before Zacharias. Holding his face against Caiaphas, his wings unfurl and he screeches powerfully, deafening the church. His trenchant talons tear the ornate robe as he asked a lone question. "Why did you do this to us, Avilius trusted you!" Caiaphas smirked, no one notices. "The only one of a foul nature here is yourself, do you not see what your ideals of paganism have done to your body?" Caiaphas then whispers to him with his back to the congregation. "Avilius chose to worship outside the church, he joined the reformation, and for that, he was cursed to the path of the fallen. And that is all you'll ever be, just an animal feeding from the scraps of Lucifer's table, always hungry, never fulfilled." Eurus harshly smacked Caiaphas and then threw him down the altar while his wings returned alongside his armor. The silver paladins stormed the altar and arrested him, for they did not want bloodshed nor uncontrolled martyrdom within the church. Taking him away, Alveria felt a sharp pain of sorrow and believed the words he had spoken, knowing he would die for them. One of the silver paladins helped Caiaphas up and back to the altar. Caiaphas smiled with blood staining his robe from his nose and beard. "As I said, the imposters among the church today are many, but the Lord shall protect those holy in his sight. It pains me to add that as there is no line left of the Voltoro family, the Church of Law has assumed temporary command over the whole of Valencia until a more permanent solution is presented. I had intended to confirm this to you on the last day, but in light of certain grotesque accusations, I am forced to show the church's loving hand stolen of surprise." Zacharias grabbed the golden staff and brought it up to the altar before the church, handing it to Caiaphas for Alveria had urged him to do so. In returning it to him, the old man replied, "Thank you, my son. Who are you, I have not seen your face before?" All eyes remain on his introduction of only first name. Caiaphas then asked, "Doth thou hath a last name?" Although wary of the priest's intent, something clutches the depths. "Desteeran," he replied. Ominous is the introduction. Caiaphas stares directly, "Blessed is he who loves his father." Zacharias took notice of a ring on his finger, but this ring was strange indeed for it was of a lord resembling a godlike image with angelic wings sprouting out of his ears.

Later that night, Zacharias met up with Malfius and told him everything that had happened. They were put up in a local inn as Alveria and her family stayed within the castle north of the church. "Beck, that was the sign of the eagle, it must have been," he exclaimed.

Beck then stated, "I believe you to be right, we have to find where they are holding him in order to learn more. Perhaps finding the eagle man claiming to be Prince Eurus will guide us to Garlen or better yet find out what Garlen was supposed to move on."

"That man, the one named Caiaphas, there's something not right about him, Beck, there's something I don't trust about this entire church setup. I felt an aura around him, it made me want to say things about myself that I pray not share with friend," Zac said in a dark tone.

Malfius was doing pushups and replied a few words after each rep, "There is much more at work here than just the death of the royal family. It's far too great a coincidence that the entire royal family would just die all at once and the church gains control over the entire territory. All this happening right when the three kings of the east begin to press against the western alliance." Finishing his pushups and catching his breath, Malfius then added, "Finding either Garlen or the eagle man will yield us our answers, don't fret, we will fulfill Joseph's final wishes, he was my friend too, you know."

"You're right, it will be fine," he said as they went to sleep.

Day 2 (Monday):
Military Review and Ceremonial Parade

Early the next morning, the streets were filled with tens of thousands of citizens as new arrivals poured in constantly, both national and international. Royal trumpets, large bells atop castles, and cannons from battleships were this day's anthem. Meanwhile, the castle Alveria was staying in with her family fell to utter madness as everyone prepared for the military review only hours away. Zacharias and Malfius went to the main square together where they were to meet the princess.

At this time, Joan, the fiery orange-haired protector of the royal family, sits with her Yijarii atop a flourishing baker's roof that is preparing fresh bread for the day. Joan said to her Yijarii, "Valencia, nation of the false church, oh, how I loathe this place. It's a shame that eagle man didn't kill Caiaphas in the very place he weaves the mirage of haven." She then stroked her Yijarii's head. "Isn't that right, Devoss, you understand more than most, myself included." Joan then held her double-bladed sword out in front to the distinguished bell tower, looking to Zacharias in the crowd who was standing beside Malfius watching the incoming parade. "I was wrong to have attacked and ignored that man, but apology must not come now, not when so much is at stake. For what it means, young swordsman, I was wrong, my emotions got the better of me. It won't happen again. I mustn't let the rage of my ancestors dominate my conscious," Joan added as Devoss bowed, stretching and yawning, also showcasing the mantis-like arms. Joan means well but for a Devokian to apologize to one not born of the forest, that is another argument entirely. Although loyal and caring, they are not ones to see outside the ideology of nature: if it is not grown and cultivated, then it is not pertinent to the culture.

The royal choir begins to play as the deafening sounds of thousands roar across Alexandria. Valencia's first three generals came out with thousands representing their mighty force. The infantry, archery, and soon cavalry general all marched through the city being cheered, wearing their ceremonial coat of arms while raising steel unto church. "Sword and church seems to be the theme of the day," Zac said to Malfius who returns with a pretended grin. From the Keystone River, Admiral Jake Conway led the seventh fleet (Levi) with his capital ship, *The Briton*, in which a single volley is fired from the main deck. The great banner, the griffons bearing twin cannons to one another, reaching north with dominate talon, shone brilliantly to all signaling their military prowess, they are the only nation in the world with a naval fleet. Also cannon technology had newly come to power only very recently, and aside from Maldecium, no others command such awesome militaristic advantage especially by the high seas. Then came the silver paladins clamoring proudly with General Zaccheaus Carlyle leading his elite knights all decorated in with scarlet image of Castor and Pollux on chest plate and shield. To each knight red and white cloth embraces the pristine craftsmanship of their armor. These were the best of all Valencia's weapons for they had defended her since the founding. After the fall of the holy knights, they were the only knighthood left within the western lands to lead the campaigns against the monstrous wilderness. General Carlyle held his marvelous falchion out to the Church of Law and his silver paladins lined the violet carpet up the stairs to the structure. The grand doors opened and standing in the entrance was a lone warrior, a man who looked as though a giant from the days of old. "Behold the Hero of Valencia, Fearstein Damascus!" Caiaphas yelled out. Damascus, girded in the heaviest thick plated golden in appearance armor engraved in blue markings, descended down the marble staircase into the square. With each step from his profound armor, the seven bells atop the Church of Law chimed like a fable come to fruition. Slung over his shoulder, he held the largest ball and chain ever wielded by mortal man, the weapon's name is Votum. His back contained a large steel shield cluttered in wrought spike, guarding him like the shell of a warring tortoise. On his sides, two bastard swords sit accompanied by long flowing white threads carried in the wind that connect to his armor. Zacharias poked Malfius. "Who is that monster?"

"Damascus, they say he is the greatest hunter alive, that he has triumphed over many a warped fiend. The church uses him as their main warrior in the Coliseum of Vindication as to ensure victory ever fifth year. Don't let his appearance fool you, he's arrogant and foolhardy, he'd rather take ten thousand with him against a legendary kill and lose than live a common life."

At that time, a few spectators sitting by the Keystone River watching the seventh fleet passing by noticed masses of bubbles forming in the water as torn fins rose. They attempted to signal to the ships, but they were preoccupied with the military review. In the rear of the fleet line, a hideous undead whale's immense head with black soulless eyes and body stripped of flesh split apart the river. Its prodigious jaws open around one of the ships, biting off the stern. Dozens of sailors slide into the razor-sharp teeth and are eaten alive by the terrible beast known as a Storfas. Another surfaced and leapt onto the main deck of a ship, causing it to break in half and sink. The sailor's screams alerted the fleet and the lake began to turn red as other Storfas feasted on the men of the sea. On each of the sinking ship's sails, the opposite griffon is seen reaching for freedom but unable. Admiral Conway, seeing this, signals the fleet and turned his massive capital ship, *The Briton*, around into firing position. Conway turned to his first mate, stating calmly, "Let us show the world the righteous firepower gifted to Valencia from heaven." Conways then screamed, "Take aim, fire," as the grand cannons roared into the river, tearing apart the Storfas. Guts and gore floated in the harbor from men and monster alike as the seventh fleet entered full engagement. Dozens of Storfas began to surface as hundreds of technologically advanced cannons went to war with those swept in from the ocean impure.

Back by the main parade, the cannons echoed with black smoke looming above, and throughout the city, citizens panicked running in all direction. Mayhem had erupted among the crowds as the screams of monster attack were heard in all direction. The silver paladins rushed to the harbor led by Damascus and Carlyle while others grabbed the clergy rushing them up the stairs into the church then barring the doors. From the western causeway, Clariad began to also surface, attempting to enter the city. Much like the ones by the shores of Gommorah, the water flowed as their bodies while they continually shifted in shape, but these were different, they held a lime type of coloration. The silver paladins clustered in the hundreds, preparing their advance as town guards failed to combat the Clariad. A few guards who struck the water elemental creatures with their spears found it to be of no effect and were engulfed by their bodies. The water from the Clariad flowed around their bodies, melting away skin and bone, only leaving a dark blood-red color, making them even more terrifying. Their faces began to shift into the faces of the men they had killed, capturing their final painful photograph. General Zacchaeus Carlyle stood in front of his silver paladins with Damascus at his side. Thousands of the four-legged Clariad march along the causeway nearing the general populace. "Prepare phalanx!" Carlyle commanded his hundreds of silver paladins. "You hold the damn causeway, I'll get the stragglers!" Damascus screamed out to him as they all dumped holy water onto their weapons blessing them. "Bastard never listens," Carlyle yells in his mind, clenching his falchion and shield stiffly. Damascus smashed Clariad with his mighty ball and chain and one of them filled with the blood of a guard exploded onto his golden armor; inside the helmet, Damascus laughed in freakish delight. Admiral Conway and his fleet still engaging the Storfas held their position as additional fleets were seen fighting further down river. "Charge," Carlyle screamed out as the silver paladins took the fight to the Clariad in a single unit. Paladin and ship were now joined in this the harbor defense. The clashing and clanging of their silver armor took second to the war bound yells of a believed religious war. Masses could not help but abandon their retreat to the awesome sight of blade, mace, axe, and especially hammer tearing apart the sin-stained beasts that had interrupted this sacred day of honor. Along the shore, multiple Storfas that had broken past the blockade rose to the sides of the central causeway. Their flesh began to fall off in large patches, giving birth to multifarious grouping of deranged tentacle. Dozens of paladins were tossed into the river where their armor only served as a slower death for it took the undead whales longer to chew through. One paladin shredded apart the roof of the beast's mouth, killing it, but was in turn caught inside and drowned by the sinking corpse. Escalated to frenzy, the paladins' charge ever hastened. Thousands of Clariad began to bind into one another forming a single colossus that took up the entire end of the causeway. The silver paladins then split into two teams, one on each side of the wide causeway that stretched out halfway into the Keystone River stopping at a lone shipyard. At that time, the giant Clariad moved against the shipyard, sucking up hundreds of its workers into itself, as they disintegrated among its acidic body. Their fear-stricken images begin to quickly appear all over the monster one after another. The Briton, seeing this, switched the main load out to high yielding explosive rounds and then began a merciless bombardment blowing it apart as to assist the paladins readying vengeance. With each blast, it became smaller, but the regular Clariad continually marched onward as if possessed. "All right, boys, time to kick some corrupted nature's ass," Carlyle yelled. They stormed the shipyard slashing and hacking away at the fallen creatures. They were no match for the silver paladins, and when they were all defeated, Carlyle stood atop the shipyard, holding his unique falchion to Admiral Conway who in turn fired his flintlock pistol fiercely into the air, tipping his admiral's hat. The paladins cheered in victory, but at that moment, dozens of the undead whales dove out of the water into the main support beams of the dock, bringing it down. Carlyle was launched into the river along a multitude of other paladins. Wreckage and men impact with such force that those ashore can see the eruption of water clearly. The Storfas beached in the harbor's debris were ripped to shreds by the brothers-in-arms. Conway rotated his ship to grab those barely able to stay afloat. Half a fin could be seen behind Carlyle. "Help, there's one behind me!" Hundreds of silver paladins sat on shore, some shooting arrows, but it was ineffective to the one with voracious appetite. It began to surface as Carlyle desperately reached to his men, and as one of his faithful knights grabbed him, the beast's jaws came out of the water. A loud war cry was heard, every link of Damascus's weapon floats, resembling the protection of the rosary. The boulder of a steel ball presents, crushing the beast's face inward to incredible degree. The Storfas lay on the ground crying out in pain. Damascus began to smash its face all the more; he is without mercy or humanity, he is vengeance. "Consume it now, eat the steel, I will crush you and every one of your kind back to hell where you were devised! From the days of Adam to the return of Christ, you are to obey men and men alone!"

Carlyle yelled out to him, "Damascus, Thank you!" The golden man stopped striking the carcass of pulp. "I didn't do it for you, Carlyle, all will know I am the greatest warrior of beasts, no matter the cost." Damascus's voice was hard and spoke of countless battles waged in a lifetime. Holding to a disdainful look, he turned from the paladins, taking a bastard sword from his side and cut out what was left of the eye. Then he removed the groin piece of his armor and urinated into the wound of the beast; he was taken by a maddened laughter, held high on a pedestal of insecurity. The paladins are uncomfortable by this state of Damascus.

After the attack had been suppressed, order was restored to Alexandria by vast military intervention. Later that night, Zacharias and Malfius stopped at a local tavern that had a man sitting at a piano, generating merriment to the room with his passion of fast-paced music. The two of them grabbed a pint and sat, discussing the events of the day. "I'm a little unhappy they wouldn't let me pass into that battle today," Zacharias stated.

"What did you expect? These Valencian types don't want any outside help. They do guard both Grias and Hagan alone. I will give it to them, they did suppress an attack of that size fairly well," Malfius replied.

"Why do you think they came here like that? I heard some of the paladins and clergy saying they have never seen an attack like that all at once at least not in the capital," Zac added. Malfius took a drink of his ale and then set his elbows on the table, looking around, making sure no one was listening, "Something is drawing them here, I can sense a foul spiritual sense in the air. I'm going to search more tomorrow for any whereabouts of Garlen or the eagle man."

Zac also grabbed a drink of his ale. "Do you want me to go with you?" he asked while belching accidentally.

Malfius replied, "I want you to stick with the Amerius family tomorrow see if you can hear anything from them, they are royalty, of course."

Zac smiled. "Good idea, I hadn't thought about that." Meanwhile by the bar, Joan, the woman who had brought her sword against Zacharias, was also there, enjoying a beverage as a few of the locals sat beside her uninvited. "What do you want?" she said to them. These men were low-life pirates and talked in only foul language to her for they were drunkards; Joan got fed up instantly. "Oh, come on, just one kiss, you're such a pretty little forest gem," one of men said, rubbing his leg.

"Back off or you won't have a leg left to rub," Joan replied in a serious tone, not breaking eye contact with a single strand of fiery hair over her hardened yet soft skin. The men began laughing together, all pounding the rest of their ales empty. One man was so drunk, he tripped over a stool and fell over, which caused Zacharias and Malfius to turn around. Another pirate put his hands on Joan's chin and tried to force a kiss, but she punched him square in the jaw and he stumbled and fell over onto his friend. Many patrons laughed hysterically whistling to her. The other pirates got up to fight Joan as Malfius and Zacharias stepped in front of her. Malfius rolled up his sleeves, showing his bulging arms as Zacharias prepared to back him up. The men were in a group of five and the one who got punched in the jaw pointed, "Get out of our way, that little bitch is gonna pay in pain!" He attempted to push past and Malfius blasted him, knocking him out cold. The others ran off as the bar cheered them on, then Beck turned around to Joan, "You all right?"

"I could have handled them myself," she replied indignantly. As soon as she said that, she then apologized in an even harder spoken voice, "I'm sorry it's not you. I do appreciate what you did for me. I'm just nervous about the race tomorrow, that's all." Joan put her hands on her hips and took a deep breath, only glancing at Zac for a moment before leaving instantly. "She really isn't giving you a chance, what is that about? She's not normally like this," Malfius said to him.

"Ha, you're asking me about women, that's a good one, Beck." The bartender laughed along with Beck and the music returned.

"Pirates, all the same, all thieves, barbarians and cowards" the bartender adds. Before this counter remains one final pirate, he is black, rugged, far past intoxicated, and passed out under his tricorne decorated in symbol from the high seas.

"Oh, Demetrius," a barmaid says as she wakes him. He looks to Malfius and Zacharias who in turn think he may try to fight them. Attempting to stand, he about falls himself but instead smirks to them and chugs the rest of yet another beer. Then, stumbling out of the bar, Zacharias offers him assistance to walk. The pirate slurs his words, but they are strangely kind.

"Set me over there." Leaning him to the wall outside his noggin sways back and forth.

"Are you all right?" Zac asks. One last smile is given as he mumbles trying to tell him something. Before he can get it across, he passes out; a drunken thanks is given.

Zacharias and Malfius left returning back to the same inn from the night before. Lying in their beds, they talked for a while longer as Zac added, "You should've seen the way that man Damascus fought today, it was like nothing I've ever seen." Beck sat up fluffing his pillow, replying, "If a man saves the world and yet is not humble to the Lord giving Him the victory, then it counts for nothing. I've seen that man for years fight like no other, but he fights for his own fame, much like Fanero writes plays to bring glory unto himself."

Zac closed his eyes and put his pillow over his face but still spoke, "Why do you work for Fanero?"

Beck paused before answering, "It's a long story, but what I can say is sometimes we have to be in bad company to spread the gospel, perhaps he's even the one that's supposed to hear the message as does Damascus."

"I'm surprised you'd say that about Fanero, he's a sad pathetic boy," Zac stated angrily.

"Perhaps you're right, but all men are pathetic in the eyes of law. Jesus asks for us to love even our enemies, for do not even the lawless love their families? I know my words are harder on Damascus, but there is a difference when talking to one who claims to be a Christian and even more within leadership." Zacharias then walked over to his pack and pulled out something he had not yet shown Beck; it was Joseph's legendary holy knight helmet. Holding it to his chest, Zac's face emanated a feeling of sorrow as his fingers tapped on the celestial helmet of salvation. "Before Joseph died, he gave this to me and told me I was a holy knight and then he gave his life fighting for me as I explained. How are we supposed to love all of our enemies?" Beck held out his arm and Zac placed the helmet in his grip. Beck then stood up, also declaring, "Times of peace and times of war are far different. In the spiritual realm, warfare never stops, not over men's souls. We are to love our enemies, but when the ones we love are threatened, we are to lay down our lives for the flock."

Gazing upon the helmet, Zac replied, "So what is the love of Jesus like, Beck? I don't understand." Malfius smiled as he felt the Spirit giving the words he needed to say. "Learning what His love is like is something we all have to choose whether to accept or not. What I can say is Lindsay is my wife, my best friend, and my life, but as much as I love even her, it compares not to the love I feel toward Jesus Christ who showed me how to love."

DAY 3 (TUESDAY):
THE GREAT RACE AND FEAST

Three distinct knocks were heard at their door that morning.

"Who's there?" Malfius called out, throwing his pillow at the door.

"It's me Alveria, of course!"

Malfius reached over and gave Zac a flick on the head, waking him up.

"Hey, what was that for?" he replied with a sour expression.

"It's your wench, she's at the door," Malfius stated obnoxiously.

"I'll be right there," Zac said, getting himself ready. Meeting her outside, they went off into this the day of the great feast where the finest chefs in all the land would compete in multinational tastebud. Cultures from all over the world had come together for the taste of food, which is something all have in common in the general sense. "I love it, this is one of my favorite holidays of the year," Alveria gleefully pronounced, hopping in the air.

"How is Joan?" Zac asked unexpectedly.

Alveria moved her face back, perplexed, "Joan, why do you want to know about Joan?"

"Beck and I stopped at the pub last night as she was getting hassled by a few drunken pirates."

Alveria giggled. "Oh, I see, well, Joan's tough for a girl, but that's the way she's always been." Alveria then tilted slightly. "I assume she got into fight, is that correct?"

Zac found it to be comical that she knew this and told her, "She knocked a guy flat on his butt, it was actually pretty funny, then Malfius stood up for her."

Alveria tasted a sample of Cruatian oyster, which was one of their finest delicacies. Her mouth lit in a satisfaction as she answered, "Your friend Malfius is a good man, Joan has always spoken well of him."

"They know each other well?"

"Malfius is not native to the lands of Scera, but Lindsay, his wife, she is one of us." Then Alveria said something far more profound that was not in her normal character. "Zac, do you believe in God?"

"What makes you ask that, Alveria? I'm just curious is all. I have yet to hear you ask anything along those lines."

Alveria gave a serious tone. "These people, the ones running the church, they are not good people, Zacharias. I noticed in the church service the look on your face, you were so troubled. I must be honest, Malfius, Lindsay, and Joan have been friends for a long while and they have all recently met you. There's something special about you, you're a noble man. Not like the nobles in court, you are different from them, you care for all people beyond social class. Truly, you are a rare breed, a virtuous man of great spiritual worth, Tala can attest to that." Zac smiles greatly, answering, "Thank you for another wonderful compliment, you make me feel good about myself, did you know that?" Alveria blushed, pulling on her dress and slightly biting her lip as her heart moved another stage closer to his. "To answer your question, yes, I do believe there is a God as of recent, but I'm unsure to what extent yet. I've seen things I dare not tell you or anyone else. You're right, there's something wrong in this place and something drew those creatures here yesterday."

Alveria then told him, "I think God has brought Malfius, Lindsay, and Joan into your life for a special reason, and it's going to be revealed here in Alexandria."

"One can only hope, but I cannot tell you what I search for, please forgive my rudeness. I must find where they're holding Eurus."

That statement rushed through Alveria's mind as the wheels began to turn. "Joan can help , she's good at finding things out. I cannot ask my parents, they're under surveillance, Valencian eyes are a dangerous legion," she whispered. "Oh dear, Joan's race is about to start hurry, let's get to the track!"

Zacharias and Alveria rushed a half mile into Alexandria, stopping at a giant artificial race course set up with all kinds of obstacles and hurdles. It winded around long narrow hills, holding dozens of the most superb horsemen the west had to offer. Just then, Joan rode out onto the field atop her Yijarii named Devoss, the green fox stood toe to toe with the thoroughbreds.

Her head held high and faced painted with symbols representing the old forest of Devok long ago destroyed by the Valencians. The majority of the crowd gasped at the sight as the Valencian natives of Southcross glared in malcontent. Those of Northcross however did not take offense; in fact, they gave her a standing ovation, which only further agitated those of Southcross. Alveria and Zacharias ran out to meet Joan, passing by other contestants.

"Joan, I have to talk to you," Alveria yelled out, almost tripping on her summer dress.

"What do you want? This is very important, Alveria," Joan stated earnestly whilst glancing at Zacharias. Joan then dismounted Devoss who was dressed in native cloth and began checking her own formal armor. Alveria moved in close and whispered to Joan about Eurus. Joan brushed aside her ember-like hair and signaled for Zacharias to walk over to her with her pointer finger. He was cautious, coming beside Devoss as he stretched out his flesh like mantis claws. "Oh, he won't hurt you, the Yijarii know friend from foe and Devoss is the finest, she trained him," Alveria says. Joan then whispered back into Zac's ear, telling him that he would find Eurus in the dungeon of the castle southeast from the Church of Law. She explained that she had overheard certain Valencian guards discussing him that morning and that Zac would need Malfius in order to gain entry to the lower levels. Joan also explained that she would be joining them after the race; she too intended an audience with the one claiming to be Eurus. It seems this plan was prepared even before they had questioned Joan about it. Joan gave a final message for them to wait in the courtyard of that castle. Zacharias wished her luck for her race as he left to retrieve Malfius; Alveria stayed to watch the race.

After he had located Malfius and conveyed the message in which he knew already, they did as Joan had asked and waited in the castle's main stone courtyard filled with tourist and native alike. A half hour passed and Joan arrived with yet another shocking revelation forwarded by a shimmering smile. "I've never seen that woman break character," Zac whispered to Beck as they rest against the gatehouse wall. "I know that look, congratulations, Joan, you're positively glowing," Malfius said to her, extending his hand in gratitude, then pulling her into a bear hug. "Oh, you know I'm no good at these things, but thanks," Joan answered, then tried to hide her emotions of happiness. Joan then reinstituted her serious demeanor, quietly explaining, "All right, here's the plan, Alveria is going to distract the guards so we can gain entry and we'll do the rest, it's as simple as that."

"How is this going to work?" Zac asked.

Malfius crossed his arms, stating, "Well, the city's in military lockdown ever since the attack, most of the guards are out and about, so I doubt there's too many guards past the rear gate. Everyone's out getting ready for the feast tonight, so our odds shouldn't be impossible." Alveria then was seen gallivanting to the tag end of the castle as Joan, Zac, and Malfius followed in a nonchalant manner as to remain incognito. Four guards stood by the gate, which was open; Alveria dashed out in front of them, crying, "I-I've lost my brooch," she said, pretending to wail by the garden. The guards ran over to her in sympathy for she was the Princess of Scera after all. Alveria played her part perfectly, luring them away with her clever ploy. Malfius led the way into the gates as Joan and Zacharias followed. Alveria kept the guards busy by using her alluring charm to distract them further. Running through the gates, little Tala poked her nose out of Zacharias's pack, peering back to Alveria who in turn noticed over the guard's shoulder.

Entering into the castle, they are met with a lovely mixture of both gothic and classic medieval architecture. The castle itself is a living portrait of the lives of those deemed royal and noble. Red and violet velvet tapestries with amber fringe decorate the vertical and floor looms by every route. Marble staircase and floor sat as the mainstay in which small ornate chairs, tables, and paintings also match the tapestries. All this serving to enhance the decor of what the Valencian hierarchy would deem the ordained. To them, this meant that certain elite members of society were born bearing divine sovereignty over the impoverished masses by rule of monetary and administrative enslavement through the medium of religion; at least, that's how Southcross saw things. Standing in reverence of the fortress' artistry, Zacharias stated, "Everything I see here is so beautiful and colossal, what is it they hope to create?" Joan, searching around on her toes for any guards in sight, disappeared into the next room. "They believe this place to be a chosen holy ground, but let us find this Eurus first," Malfius said, brushing his shoulder against his pursuing Joan. Together, the three of them weaved in and out of the castle of antiquity that hosted ancient tapestries, telling a forgotten story of their own. Images of demons and knights paved the way along with others pertaining to apocryphal text not of biblical canon. Joan, Malfius, and Zacharias searched the decorative yet eerie hallways of the stronghold made lavish. They then passed through a great banquet hall where a splendid table stretched across the room, prepared for the night's coming feast. Plates of gold and silver along with glorious candles serve as a phenomenal backdrop to an already meritorious sight. At the wall behind the table, a grandfather clock made of pure amethyst rang for it was the end of the hour. Voices could be heard as they ran and hid along a flight of stairs into the cellars. Royal chefs could be heard frantically trying to get things ready for the night's banquet, arguing among themselves over the amount of wine that would be needed. "Do you hear that?" Malfius said to them.

"No, what?" Zac asked.

"I hear the faint sound of flowing water coming from the end of the cellar," Beck continued.

"But it's so dark down here, I'm not sure how we are to navigate," Zac added.

"Just follow me," Joan told them as she traversed the dark without problem.

"How is she able to do that?" Zac asked Beck.

"I am a native of the forest, an Alkirum, we don't need the light in order to see as most do," Joan proudly answered, tossing her hair to the side.

"That's amazing. I had no idea the Alkirum were so naturally gifted, what else can you do?" he asked with excitement.

Joan laughed to herself, "You're a strange one, but we can see without light, alongside hearing the whispers of all things natural and untarnished by curse." At the end of the cellar sat a massive boulder blocking an entryway. Malfius stepped forward, rolling up his sleeves. "Let me show you ladies how it's done." Malfius with his inhuman raw power was able to push the boulder enough to create a space for them to squeeze past. Behind it was a prison-type door with an iron padlock. Malfius pulled out a single steel gauntlet, and equipping it, he winked, placing a piece of straw in his mouth.

"No key necessary," he stated as he crushed the padlock with a single strike.

"Do you always carry around loose straw?" Joan asked, making fun of him.

"I guess the days of being a rancher's son linger still," Malfius answered. Passing the door, they could see water flowing down handrails shaped as tiny aqueducts on either side sloping to a cold and damp river within the dungeon. Zacharias crept down the flight of stairs reaching a narrow dirt path to yet another door as the river followed in various routes. An iron door locked from the other side stood in their way, and they were forced to follow the murky sewers. Splashing into the water, Joan pointed to the rats, explaining that they would show them the proper route. Joan spoke in a tongue not of human language and they followed a large group of these rats through a series of channels until they were led to a hidden chamber. This chamber descended to a grouping of iron cages where skeletons remain chained across floor and wall. "Look," Zac said, pointing to the edge of the room. A moat surrounding what appeared to be a stone jailhouse rests on secluded island. A venomous smell engulfed their lungs as they approached. Joan got on her knees, peering into the lake. "Acid!" Desteeran picked up an old sword hilt resting inside a skeleton's corpse and dipped it in the liquid. The sword hilt melted completely as they plotted to find a way across the acidic lake. "Well, we can't jump, it's too wide," Malfius stated. Joan searched around the room for some kind of mechanism or crank. Zacharias, who was skipping rocks at the jailhouse, had not noticed Tala who jumped out of his pack when he grabbed the sword hilt. Tala headed right up to the edge with her nose about touching. "Tala, no," he screamed, running over. Joan and Malfius also ran over as Tala sneezed from the venomous smell filling her nostrils. The entire moat turned into a solid block of green ice, which they were able to cross one by one. He held Tala in his arms, thankful that she was all right. "Tala, I swear, don't scare me like that again, I couldn't handle losing you."

Joan thought to herself, "He's loving and compassionate to animals to, I was incredibly wrong to have misjudged him. If only I was strong enough to apologize." Malfius had already gone on into the room, which was unlocked as Zac saw Joan with an upset illustration. "Joan, what's wrong?" he asked in a caring voice. Snapping back, Joan said in a forced positive demeanor "Let's see if this is the man you've been searching for." Joan then gave him a half smile, which still made him happy to see, she was coming around.

Entering the cell, it is lit up and decorated just like the castle above, a blood-stained blade marked table sits at the midpoint with two shackles connected most likely for torture. To the far end of the room, prison bars hold a figure who silently watches. Enveloped in grand eagle wings folded across body, yellow glowing eyes penetrate the darkness. "Why have you come?" he speaks in a disturbingly villainous tone not of his persona. All three of them are first frightened, then awestruck by this visual. "We've come in search of the sign of the eagle, do you know of a man by the name of Joseph Voltel?" Malfius asked. The eagle-like man's wings opened up, revealing his despair, which appeared as the face of a bald eagle just as before. Naked of armor but clothed in feather, he states, "I do not know the name."

Joan then questioned him "Who are you, man or beast?" His left talon tapped the bars, then scratched down gradually, the right opened in front of him like a spider resurrected. "I am Prince Eurus David Voltoro V, heir to the kingdom of Valencia." The voice remained rather daunting to them for it was a mixture of a human's tone and an eagle's. The way he verbalizes works very peculiar, for he lingers upon the end of many words spoken longer than need be. Joan and Malfius rotated to one another, unsure of the authenticity of his statement, but Zacharias presented himself before the cage cautiously.

"I believe you," he stated in high esteem.

He beheld him with his golden yellow eyes. "Tell me your name, warrior."

"How do you know I'm a warrior, and it's Zacharias."

Eurus slightly twitched in a bird-like mannerism, explaining, "I have seen you in a dream raised in glory bound by the most virtuous harbinger. A man's eyes speak the truths of who he is, and you, sir, are no exception."

"Where is the lock to this cage? We're going to break you out of here," he stated.

"There is none, this cage is sealed by dark magic, only a god token may open such heresy."

"god token?" Joan asked Malfius.

"Yes, much like the one Caiaphas wears on his finger, one must sell the seeds of many souls to obtain and in the end your own," Eurus answered, but when he mentioned the name of the cardinal, his voice answered in far more animalistic anger. Zac pulled on the bars, desperately attempting to find some sort of weak point.

"Forget it, young warrior, there is no way out of this, but let me ask, why is it you search the sign of the eagle?"

"A friend of mine gave his life and in his final words commanded I tell Aurelius Garlen to follow that sign, my friend was a holy knight, and I believe Garlen to be also," he told him man-to-man.

Eurus lowered his head, pressing against the thick iron bars with his beak almost touching Zacharias for he was taller. "I know of this Garlen, yes, we remember clearly now." His talons run from neck to beak, his speech confuses singular for plural. "This Garlen you speak of is no holy knight, but instead a misguided fanatic given over to murderous ways." Joan gasped, denying the statement, for Malfius had explained to her everything from the first day of commemoration. The feathers on his entire body rose and his wings began to flutter more ferociously each passing word, "Garlen spent years sealed away within the Wardens Keep for his crimes against the empire, vowing to one day dismantle the Voltoro kingship. He was once the greatest of the silver paladins, but instead chose to defect to foreign ideology from the east. After twenty years of imprisonment, he escaped and exacted his revenge against the crown. Garlen assassinated my mother and father, taking Coprulus and myself to the Tartarus Wasteland. By dumping us there among the blighted ground, we became twisted monsters ourselves. It is because of him my brother and I remain tethered to the hideous appearance of mere beast, truly the paradox of royalty. As for Garlen, I do not know his whereabouts, but what I do know is Caiaphas freed him to do his bidding by cloak and dagger."

"What of your brother?" Malfius asked.

"The last I saw of Coprulus, he was a monster far more dishonored than I, to him, my burden pales in comparison." Zac's face dropped as his mission from Joseph was now perhaps, a failure. Thinking to himself, he felt a sharp pain in the pit of his stomach. *"Joseph, did you know who Garlen was, has all been lost?"*

Eurus placed a talon on Zacharias's shoulder. "Listen to me, all of you, there isn't much time left." Joan, Malfius, and Zac stood before him, listening intently. Eurus then explained to them, "I too traveled far to deliver a message, which I have already given to General Zacchaeus Carlyle. The Church of Law is nearing completion of a sinister plot set in motion long before the founding of my homeland. I am not sure of the intent behind, but what I can share is that unless something is done soon, this nation will fall under martial law followed by a vast change in doctrine toward the general populace. I can only speculate, but growing up in Valencia as a prince, I believe they're going to use some kind of major political deterrent to unite the split nation into a most cunning trap. Perhaps, a false declaration, the end of the reformation could be the plan. Although a merger between Northcross and Southcross sounds promising, uniting my people under a rule like this will only lead to a complete loss of personal freedoms. What I do not know is whether this unification is to bring war of us or slaughter of others." All of their eyes were focused upon every word from the eagle's mouth.

"What are we to do?" Zac asked in serious manner.

Eurus answered, "Rebellion will come to Valencia very soon if the truth is revealed, those of Northcross stay only in hopes to restore this nation their home. They rightfully follow salvation through faith in Jesus Christ along with biblical canon, while those of Southcross cling to the chains of Law, now tainted by apocryphal text displayed as revelation. Seemingly, the separation draws from the Vulgate, from either the foundation of Antioch or Alexandria. A nation divided cannot stand, it will only take a single spark to ignite this civil war. My father, King Avilius, was an advocate against the breaking Church of Law along with Carlyle. Know that there are good people here in Valencia, most of which live across the farmlands of Northcross. Even within the church itself a few good men of the cloth remain fighting to restore what was lost in the great schism."

Joan put her hand upon Eurus, pitying him. "I'm sorry that I did not believe who you are."

Eurus slowly pulled away. "You must go, Maiden of the Forest, they are coming," Eurus demanded respectfully.

"Wait, we can't just leave him here," Zacharias begged them.

"Go, my friends, soon I shall join my (F)father in the next life. I'm glad I was able to talk with good people one final time," Eurus thanked them, pointing to the door. Before they left, Eurus blessed them, stating,

> But they that wait upon the LORD shall renew their strength; they shall mount up with wings as eagles; they shall run, and not be weary; and they shall walk, and not faint.
>
> Isaiah 40:31 (KJV)

Joan put her arm around Zac and forced him out past the frozen acidic lake. Malfius stood in the room for only another minute alongside Eurus.

"Does he know?" Eurus asked Malfius in a despondent voice.

Staring right back, Malfius answered in humorless tone, "Not yet, but he will at the designated hour, I take it you are the ninth, are you not?"

Eurus twitched again like a bird as he turned away from Malfius cloaking himself within his sturdy wings. "Protect him, my friend, he embodies hope ever present yet returning, Carlyle will guide you to the next step." Malfius proceeds to the door and Eurus asked one final question, "What is yours and the maiden's names?"

"She is known as Joan and myself, Malfius Stirling, I will see you again very soon, my brother in Christ." Malfius then left, catching up to his friends as Eurus was left alone contemplating his coming end. After they had passed the lake, the ice melted instantaneously, and it was restored back to its original state; this was after Tala was a certain amount of feet away.

Joan who led them back to the waterways was able to get the rats to show them the nearest exit. Whilst leaving, they saw a lone torch-lit ferry dock by the chamber where Eurus was located. To the side of the castle, they dashed out of a sewer pipe and ran into Alveria who was waiting in the courtyard.

"Oh, Zacharias, you're all right," she yelled out, tossing her arms around him.

"Joan and I are just fine, thanks for asking," Malfius stated as Joan giggled.

That night, Zac and Joan attended dinner with Alveria and her royal family in one of the great banquet halls in the northern castle. Malfius searched high and low for General Carlyle as the city of Alexandria shared multicultural food. People from all over the world broke bread together that night, dining together in happiness, both royal and common. Zacharias could not omit the thought of Eurus as he pondered on the revelation of Garlen and the coming doom of the melancholy eagle. "Joseph and his family are gone, and now Garlen is said to be a traitor. Salem, Malastay, She'ol, Avodah Mortis, Sodom and Gommorah all destroyed, and now even Valencia under polluted assault. Could this all be linked somehow? Is this within the will of God? What are you planning, Lord, is this how things are to be? Please tell me what it is I'm supposed to do? I cannot believe all of this would happen without reason, please reveal that I am not the cause." He conversed with the royal family for the rest of the night, enjoying wonderful and assorted dishes. Alveria talked about the royal ball to be held in two days with pure delight, and Joan, who had now taken a liking to him, began to open up to him as friend. This surprised the royal family as King Drake Amerius said to Zac, "If even Joan has taken a liking to you, then truly, fate holds a special quest for you." Together they laughed as Joan fought to keep serious demeanor; it was a night to remember of solid-tasting comedy.

14

Ecumenical Proclamation

Day 4 (Wednesday): Trials of the Warrior

Late into the next morning, Zacharias was spectating throughout the streets of Alexandria as warriors from all over the world faced off in respectful competition. Whomsoever won these events would be rewarded in gold medal and honored at the royal ball the following night. The events ranged from jousting, dueling, archery, strength, poise, tactics, to a great deal more. He watched as the land's most prominent archers challenged one another by dignity and hair-splitting accuracy. Malfius appeared in the crowds, rushing over to grab sight. "You seem remarkably excited to watch this," Zac said to him. Malfius pointed his finger at a young woman with long brunette hair and blue eyes. Her appearance held the most gentle touch, which some of the crowd began to mock. A black raven rested upon her shoulder, watching every arrow loosed. With each shot from her long bow, she hit the bullseye with deadly aim. This prompted veracity of a chronicled saga that was the Restoration War. Not since that century-long war had man united for a common cause for in those days, the legendary archery legions of Valencia were driven by the exactness of their faith. Alas, faith, as great as it can be from initial path is not void of sinister sibling. As all men can be deceived by even their own hearts, especially their own hearts, there serves a very exceptional blessing often missed. That is the remarkable gift that is woman, and through these trails of life fired for many reasons, it is woman's amazing faith that helps keep men on track. Women are not far different from the bow, for a woman is graced by humble beauty and hair that is the string. Men are like the piercing arrow, ready for the hunt to feed or protect their families. Not unlike a godly marriage between a man and a woman, the arrow cleaves unto the bow, helping to guide the direction in accordance with faith, always putting the bow first even if it is to be loosed unto death. This woman who was now winning over the crowds would go on to win both of the archery tests of range and accuracy by long bow and speed by composite. After she had taken her prize, she modestly strides over to Malfius. He picked her up in the air and spun her around before giving a notable hug. "I'm so proud of you, Stephanie, I knew you would win." She said nothing but had a joyous face as he placed her down. "Zac, this is my baby sister, Stephanie Stirling," he explained. The raven on her shoulder flew away, and he extended his hand. He delightfully introduces himself then adds, "You're a phenomenal archer. I'm honored to have witnessed that. Where did you learn to shoot like that?" Stephanie said nothing but smiled, then turning to Malfius with a merry twinkle in her eye. Stephanie kissed Zacharias on the cheek with a quick peck and then walked away as her raven landed back to her. Confused, he stood blushing as Malfius winked, stating, "She likes you, isn't that just grand. Oh, I should've mentioned Stephanie is both deaf and mute, but what she lacks in audio, she makes up for in sight kinda like Joan." Malfius then left to search out Carlyle, and Zacharias went off to meet Princess Alveria.

Alveria sat on the stairs leading to the Church of Law, crying alone. Noticing this, he rushed over to cure the ordeal. Kneeling before her, he attempts to comfort by gently grasping her palm. "What's wrong?" Altering between sniffle and speech, Alveria conveyed that he would be unable to escort her into the royal ball tomorrow because he was not of nobility. Instead of becoming upset over this, he grinned which Alveria did not understand. "What is there to be happy about here? This was really important to me," Alveria yelled, slapping his hand away.

"I'll just have to win my way in then," he explained. He'd been considering whether to compete in the dueling competition and now he would be granted answer. Alveria's spirits were raised as she then stopped her tears, transferring to joy.

"Well, let's go before you miss the challenge, which one are you going to do?"

"Dueling, I can handle myself with a sword," he stated, mentally drawing Titulus from his scabbard confidently. He had to keep his weapons within the inn since the Storfas and Clariad attack as did any armed individual. The two of them traveled to the dueling arena located not far from the castle they had broken into the day before.

Arriving at the arena, they initially would not accept his application due to it being late, but Alveria was able to get him in with her royal title and a little fuss. He left Tala in Alveria's care as he readied himself to duel by wooden sword. Desteeran would go on to battle four opponents with a two-handed wooden sword as others used other forms of wooden medieval weaponry. His last opponent was a swordsman holding a serious outlook who hailed from the lands of Evangela. Zacharias would go on to barely defeat the man by catching him off guard with a well-placed parry followed by a sweeping of his legs. He would shake his hand in defeat and introduce himself as Vargas before he bid him a farewell. *He hesitated*, Zac thought to himself as he watched the man leave pondering why he allowed him the win. Now having won his spot back into the royal ball, he would watch other great warriors win and lose grand challenges for the duration of the day.

All was well that day as tens of thousands reveled in the spirit of the warriors trials. New and old heroes rose and fell, but none would compare to the final event of the day. Fearstein Damascus was seen advancing through the crowds with dozens of silver paladins. Everyone parted ways as he strutted with momentous purpose, but what was he advancing toward? Zacharias, seeing this, began to follow, and as they approached the strength competition, gasps of wonder and fear echo collectively. Standing alone in the arena was a knight with the largest sword anyone had ever seen. His armor is thick yet forming to his physique; it is black plated with golden trim along the edges along a slightly raised guard on half of the neck piece. His black stechhelm inscribed in marvelous design held a curved slit that the top edges sloped downward valiantly. Around his neck, a royal scarf streams down the left shoulder, indicating the completion of a vowed conquest. A grand golden crown signifying kingship connected to the helmet, atop the middle of the crown was a breathtaking ruby in the image of a rising phoenix demanding vengeance. A cape of heavy white fabric decorated in magnificent golden artistry hide his back. The left shoulder plate is a mighty shield, the right side is three spikes awaiting impalement. Resembling a solid block of perfectly crafted glimmering metal unknown, the sword stood thrice as thick and seven times as sharp than any weapon forged west. He raised the equitable sword, smashing a boulder in two and then stared at the ground by risen dust. Behind him stood over a hundred drudge knights also encased in armor of similar but slightly less extravagant design saluting their king by drawing blade from sheath pressing it to chest vertically. Damascus entered the arena, dragging his ball and chain, Votum, around the king. The silver paladins stood toe to toe with the drudge knights neither speaking nor yielding an inch. Damascus, who takes off his golden helmet, speaks in complete pride, "It's nice to see a king finally showing face long garrisoned within eastern fortress, was thou afraid?" The king removes his helmet also, revealing a handsome dark-haired man, half-eastern and half-Caucasian with an immensely somber face taken from emotion. Silently, he judges Damascus but says not a word. Damascus becomes infuriated and demands an answer; the silver paladins ready steel. The king walks over to Damascus, sheathing his sword of giants in a rare scabbard behind his cape. The arena trembles in trepidation as he moves without hesitation. Damascus grasps the mighty chains of his weapon, but the king advances. "What the hell is he doing? Is he crazy? I am the greatest, people fear me, yet he holds none. I swear I'll kill him now and start a world war, my honor must be upheld!" Damascus worries to self. Now placed only two steps in front of Damascus, he raises his eyes to him and speaks in a calm yet more so sonorous voice, "To speak of fear, one must prove thyself worthy, has thou done this more so than the beginning of thy name unmerited? My most loyal servant Veritas who now slumbers within scabbard testifies to the deed of beheading the last fell dragon, Vishnu, son of Brahma. The west may know the name of Damascus, but Vulgata does not. It is the name of Carthright that men speak in shadow that nobles atop thrones high whisper in shame, it is the name of Carthright, not Damascus, that nations mobilize entire armies out of fright. Fear is a title only bestowed upon those of us who fear ourselves the most." The drudge knights who exercised extreme discipline followed behind their king as Zacharias stepped aside. He noticed that on their blackened chest plates a disturbing snowy image of a phoenix stood on a throne of scorched skull, but it was not fire that came out of the mouth, but instead shards of ice. Damascus yells back as the king leaves:

"You peasant swain! You whoreson malt-horse drudge!
The Taming of the Shrew (Act 4, Scene 1, Page 6, Line 58–59)

"That's all you'll ever be, Carthright, a slave risen to the status of a lowly drudge just like your sad excuse for a knighthood that follows by blind eyes yet snatched!" Still they move onward, uncaring of his tantrum, but the fact was Damascus had no idea how wrong he really was. He, as most westerners, did not understand that this order of black knights held the title of drudge not to dishonor but to humble themselves before the king as to exalt him. Word spread amongst the crowds of the king of the east and his exploits. Rumor held that he had alone vanquished Vishnu years prior and even that held not a comparison to how he led Marduas into a unified state. Carthright begins the ascent to the Church of Law. Zacharias flips to rage as he watches him out of sight. Screaming in his mind, he begins to lose it, "Carthright, that's Carthright, that's the son of a bitch who had Joseph and his family killed by the Black Hand and that monster Veil. No, I won't endure this!" Malfius grabs his friend who began to hurdle the stairs, then dragging him out of sight from the drudge knights. "Zacharias, no, you cannot do this, they will kill you," he yelled in his ear.

"Let me go dammit, he took my family away. I have to kill him even if I only have my fists," Zac screamed back with the utmost ferocity.

"Joseph wouldn't want you to do this, you can't. I won't let you die like this. He was my friend too," Malfius stated, trying to calm him. Pinned on the ground restrained by Malfius, Zacharias watched Carthright enter the Church of Law. As strong as Malfius was, he could feel such a power from Desteeran who was then able to break free from his fearsome grip. A face of utter distress overtook him as he then fell back down. "Why did God let Joseph and family die like that? How can this go unpunished! Where was God to save them? Joseph preached in His name and He did nothing when they needed Him most! There must be justice even if it is by our own hands. Joseph was burned alive. I could hear him being pulled to the depths for Christ's sake!" Zac bellowed as his face darkened with adrenaline.

Malfius who was startled by his strength knelt in front of him, speaking in all the truth he knew with his voice raising in pitch, "You're right, it wasn't fair in our eyes that he had to go, it wasn't right that his family died, they did nothing wrong." Malfius then yelled, shoving his friend into the wall, "Don't you give up here, you started a mission with Joseph, you must see it done!" People passing by began to gawk, but none intervened. Malfius bars him still. "Don't you blame God for Joseph's death. God used Joseph to glorify Himself and that was of a righteous and just purpose! You are my friend and I won't let you sit here and destroy yourself! Justice does not belong to us, do you not see it is that very thinking that drowns us in the tides of the coming Leviathan, just look at the Church of Law that believes justice is theirs to administer, is that right? Has it solved anything in almost two-thousand years? Was nothing learned in the Black Halo incident that took the other six continents of Vulgata unto the void of Cain?" Malfius then let him go, speaking calmly, "I'm sorry that I yelled, but God loves you more than you know, don't let the world take you away from Him. Also you have to stay alive or we won't be able to save Eurus or complete the Sword of Abraham." Zac let go of his fist, looking up to the church as he dwelt on the image of Penelope holding Mariana in the burnt-down cottage. Remembering the blood-stained Bible within her lifeless grasp, he exhales deeply, knowing Malfius is right. He then slung his arm around Malfius, and the two began to return back to the inn. "Thank you, my friend," Zac said, feeling embarrassed.

"It's not a big deal. You really did love Joseph and his family, didn't you?" Malfius asked.

"They were all I had left in this world and I don't understand why someone as high up as Carthright would have them, Salem, and so many others so far from the east murdered. Was it because he was a holy knight or something deeper than that?"

Zacharias bid Alveria a good night soon after and walked back to the inn with Malfius. "So how were you to defeat Carthright, his drudge knights, and the mythical blade Veritas?" Malfius stated sarcastically. The response is a chuckle from both before they turn in for the night.

DAY 5 (THURSDAY):
DAY OF THE ARTS AND THE ROYAL BALL

The sound of music vibrated through Alexandria this day as artists take to the streets presenting masterpiece and hope alike. Human expression is presented in the forms of painting, music, and play in every facet of the city. Malfius was out showcasing his piece of the Sceran waterfalls, which would go on to win the painting competition, earning him a spot at the royal ball. In a nearby royal court, Fanero's new play was debuting, crowds gathered in the thousands. Noticing this, Zacharias speculated for an hour hoping to catch a glimpse of Cordelia, the Angel's Voice, but she would not be seen. Later, he met up with Joan and traveled back to the castle where Alveria was preparing. Entering the castle gates, Joan gave Zac an honest glance. "I'm sorry about your friend and I'm sorry about how I've treated you. I was wrong to have misjudged you. I'm not a very pleasant woman, and it is hard for me to share how I feel."

He was surprised by this and answered happily, "Thank you, Joan, that means a lot, I'm glad we are becoming friends. Don't be so down on yourself, it just shows you care more than most." Joan nudged him on the shoulder with a smile as they strolled up a spiral stairwell. Zac stopped her for a moment and stated in all seriousness, "Joan."

"What is it?" she asked curiously.

"I have to be honest with you. I am cursed by the touch of death. I don't know if even God can save me from it, but before you get too close, I don't want you or Alveria to die because of me,

I haven't told her yet." Zac had a depressed facial expression, but Joan in turn stated in rare form:

> There is therefore now no condemnation to them which are in Christ Je'-sus, who walk not after the flesh, but after the Spir'-it. For the law of the Spir'-it of life in Christ Je'-sus hath made me free from the law of sin and death.
>
> Romans 8:1–2 (KJV)

Joan then tapped his noggin with her finger, adding, "You worry too much and search too hard for answers that are already planted within your inner being. Jesus can set you free, but it's up to you to make the decision to call on His name."

Zac thanked Joan and then asked, "How can he set me free?"

Joan lit up, being asked this, "By a profession of faith in the name of Jesus Christ, get baptized in his name. Most are done with water alongside accepting his name, but the truth is about accepting him within your heart by faith in him; that's where the real work is done." We can do it right now if you feel ready.

"I appreciate the insight, but I don't know about all that, it sounds, well, I'm just not ready." Joan understands, but still, he is held back by the feeling of being unworthy due to his sins; he is being convicted.

Passing through corridor and hallway, they reached the upper levels of the castle, finding Alveria. Joan knocked at the door and Alveria's hair flung out, and seeing Zacharias, she shut the door. "I'm sorry, I'm trying on dresses at the moment. Joan, can you help in here?" Alveria asked. Joan entered and he was asked to wait outside. Passing by was King Drake Amerius, Zac stood up, explaining his command to wait. Drake laughed loudly and Joan peeks out. The king places his arm on him, escorting him to his room. "Let the women play dress up, but let us find some fitting attire for you, my boy. You are in fact taking my precious daughter to the royal ball tonight." Once they reached his room, Zacharias explained that because he'd won the dueling competition, they had a designated wardrobe already prepared for him. Drake understood, opening an armoire made of pine. Inside was a royal seal of Scera on a patch that he handed over to him. Humbled by such a gift, he tried to give it back, stating, "I am not worthy of such an honor, great king."

"Oh, nonsense, you've done well by Scera, and tonight, you will be representing us along with my daughter Alveria", the king said gladly. "I want you to take my daughter in marriage, and when I pass, to rule the kingdom of Scera."

It was overwhelming for him to hear this and he humbly declined, "Sir, I, I apologize, but I've already undertaken a mission. I cannot let my friend's sacrifice go in vain."

Drake nodded, replying, "I can accept what you have said, but please consider the offer when your journey is complete. Alveria is our only child, and even though I love her with all my heart, she is not ready to rule. Things are not right in Vulgata and I fear for my people's safety is all. You are noble in nature, young swordsman, never forget that, but you are also friend of a holy knight, perhaps you are one yourself?"

He shook the king's hand, remembering Joseph knighting him before death. "Noble King Amerius, may I ask why do you think a king would have someone and their family murdered from so far away?"

"Who is it you speak of?"

"I believe Carthright sent the Black Hand to kill Joseph personally," Zac answers.

"Yes, one hears much of this wretched Black Hand, destroyer of lineage. I suppose King Victor Carthright foresaw Joseph as an imminent threat. If he was a holy knight and was targeted by such a squad, then perhaps he was a general. I believe the Sword of the Cross has already returned, and if Carthright knows this, he will do all in his power to stop them. He is different, he is a man born of slavery, reborn a king. I doubt anything will change whatever his resolve may be. Wars will never end as long as man holds dominion over the earth."

Later, the anticipated night had finally arrived, and Zacharias, dressed up in flawless white Valencian attire, knocked on Alveria's door. First, Joan stepped out in an all black dress complementing her orange flowing hair and said sternly, "Not a word, I never wear dresses, I don't like them, I'm only doing it because Alveria asked."

With care, he replied, "Joan, you look positively enchanting, any man would be lucky to hold you before this night's moon." Joan did her best not to smile but was unable to, for she had never been called anything like that by a man before. Blushing back, Joan told him how handsome he was dressed in white. After Joan left, Alveria came to the door and opened it. Standing before him in a ruby red dress with her face and blonde hair curled to perfection, he lovingly gazes with the beauty of what could be his wife. Zac's entire body was disarmed by the ravishing radiance of her appearance. With genuine eyes and tender speech, he said to her, "Alveria, in all my days could I have not wished for someone as flawless as you." He then reached out his hand, taking hers and kissed it softly, his eyes never left hers. Alveria blushed and curled her lips as she tilts. Butterflies awoke in her stomach as she blinked into a wide grin. Alveria slowly pushed him up against the wall with palm to chest and closed her eyes as she lay a deep romantic kiss on his lips. Their hearts pounded together as they held the kiss for some time. Zac thought to himself in satisfaction, "How long have I waited for another to love me? Is this it? Can dreams actually come to life?"

Alveria worried to herself while holding the kiss of infatuation. "I'm falling for this man, but it's happening so fast. I just can't help myself, he's so irresistible and charming, he likes me for me, not title." After it had ended, they held hands and began to leave the castle, holding a tight grip to one another. Going down an arduous flight of stairs, Alveria said to him, resting on his arm, looking up to him, "Zacharias, you are so handsome, you look gorgeous tonight."

He replied with a smirk on his face, "Oh, so I don't look handsome other days." Together, they howled with laughter all the way out the main gate to a Victorian carriage. Two white horses sit in front with blue feathers attached from ear to ground; they are joined by a coachman dressed for the ball. The chaperone tipped his hat to Zacharias and removed it for Alveria as they stepped inside the carriage that he opened.

Inside the carriage was Joan with arms crossed. "What took you so long?" she stated in a pretended voice. The carriage began to move and Alveria rests herself onto Zacharias with her long black eyelashes opening and closing. Joan shook her head. "Oh, brother," and Zac began to laugh mirthfully. The more Joan and Zacharias glanced at each other, the greater the laugh. "What is so funny, I don't understand?" Alveria obliviously asks.

"It's nothing, just an inside joke from Joan, that's all," he explained, trying to remain composed. Joan rolled her eyes as they passed through the city. Every alley, street, and sidewalk was packed with commoners dancing among the festivities, numerous amounts of them drunkenly cheered toward their carriage. "You know what, that appears to be a good time, perhaps we should stop by after the royal ball," Zac excitedly stated. Joan nodded in approval as Alveria gave a sour roll of eye.

After about a half an hour, they arrived to the royal banquet hall where royalty from all over the west was seen collaborating in a fairytale type courtyard. Stone pathways ran parallel along the perfectly cut grass with pillared columns extending to the main door. Bouquets of all arrays line these also as torch street lights illuminated the entirety of the courtyard. The most notable thing in this courtyard was the pool of the clearest blue water taken by a plethora of statues. Each resembles nobility holding strong to a ranging set of hyperemotional expressions. The carriage stopped in front of the path as the coachman opened the door for them, waving them on with a bow. "Well, here we go," Zac says to himself for he was worried to have to mingle amongst the so-called chosen. As they got out, Joan whispered to him, "Don't pay these people any mind, they don't live real lives, just hold your fight back, trust me. I have to constantly." Royal strings began to leisurely play as Alveria jumped right in, speaking among the nobles who all complimented her dress and stunning development into a young woman. Zacharias began to search around at the palace type of banquet hall, which was marvelous in its artistic Gothic backdrop. Facing the north facade, he notices even more nobles in the windows chatting the night away. An older nobleman steps behind him with a long decorative pipe in his mouth and monocle in his left eye. "Good evening, sir," he says, puffing out smoke away from him.

"Hello," Zac said caught off guard, shaking hands with the gentleman.

"Fine evening, isn't it," the noble said.

"Yes, and this is a remarkable place, not just this banquet hall, but all of Valencia. I've never seen a society structured like this," Zac replied enthusiastically. The noble removed his top hat, revealing dark gray hair taking a glimpse at the party. With a sigh, the older man states, "It's a real shame you weren't alive back when Valencia was really something. I'm afraid she's not what she used to be."

Zacharias replied, "It seems many things aren't what they once were, so I hear." The man took another long inhale of his tobacco, and when he exhaled, he complimented him, "I saw you fight yesterday in the dueling arena, it was brilliant. I have only ever seen one other like it. I'd like to extend invitation for you to join our ranks and begin the journey to becoming a silver paladin." Before he could answer, another gentleman tapped the noble he was talking to on the shoulder. "Good evening, General, it's not often you dress for such occasion." The noble who said this was wearing his ceremonial blue uniform that held badges of honor, which spoke of his lifetime of service to the Valencian Empire. He then introduced himself, removing his admiral's cap, "Greetings, I am Fleet Admiral Jake Conway, it's good to finally meet you."

"Finally?" Zacharias asked perplexed.

Conway laughed. "Carlyle told me about your fighting spirit, we hope that you will join the silver paladins, that is unless you feel compelled to give the navy a chance." Immediately, the words of Eurus found their way back to him as he realized this was the Carlyle he needed to speak to. Carlyle jumped into the conversation, speaking to Conway by dry humor, "He's made to be a loyal knight, not a foul-mouthed sailor." He found it funny that these two great military leaders were fighting over him, but he knew he had to speak to Carlyle alone. At that point, Alveria ran over, hugging him with a sweet face. "Oh, there you are, my love!"

Love? he thinks to himself. Carlyle and then Conway smirked and nodded at Zacharias as they complimented Alveria's looks. "Thank you, but what are you doing talking to my handsome man this night? I hope you're not trying to recruit him for war. He's a lover, not a fighter." Fleet Admiral Conway bid them a farewell with a wink, stating, "Perhaps a fighter for love." Trumpets then began to go off as fireworks twinkle above, and everyone went inside.

"Well, I guess we better attend this party," Carlyle said to them.

As he began to walk away, Zacharias spoke, "Excuse me, sir." Turning around and fixing his monocle, he replied, "Yes, my boy?"

"I need to speak with you again after the ceremony if that would be all right?"

"That would be just fine. I'll wait out here for a short while after the party," Carlyle stated. It was Zac's intent to speak to him about Eurus and ask for his help to save him with the additional hope of finding out more of Garlen, the Black Hand, and even the Church of Law. Alveria drags him to the decorated hall behind hundreds of other nobles. "Even the Duke Carlyle and the Barron Conway have taken a liking to you, how impressive," Alveria whispers to him, tickling the ear.

Violins began to play more steadily as nobles and their couples rushed inside two by two. They passed underneath a delightful archway into the main room where over a thousand nobles and their conversations evoked feelings of elitism but not necessarily deplorable, just sophisticated. Royal tables, chairs, along a grand violet and amber carpet supplied the room in first-rate decor. White balconies surrounded every side of the hall wrapped in precious scarlet cloth with a priceless chandelier built from the dawn of Valencia surveying the room. Paintings of notable nobles, statesmen, and heroes paste the walls, but one does stand more than the rest, somehow the blood of the Desteeran line draws young Zacharias unto it. This is the portrait of Aurelius Garlcn; his armor is so beautiful in all its make and deed that it is the epitome of chivalry. His appearance is locked underneath the visor of his helmet. Yet if he is a traitor, why does his picture stand in this hall of honor? Out in front of the dining hall, a grand stage sat with a mass amount of open space for the waltz after dinner. On the stage, lovely red velvet curtains remained closed with a single small balcony above shaped as a lion's head slightly opened. Together, the young couple steps into the room and gasps were heard from all over at her classic elegance and her handsome escort. Alveria had never appeared before the royal world as a grown woman, and tons of eyes were locked on both her and the crown of Scera. Although there were good nobles among these people, the majority had lost themselves in their quests for power. "Everyone's staring just like in the church," he whispered.

"Let them stare. I'm just happy to be here with you," Alveria stated, then hugged him in front of everyone. They found Joan among the crowded room, glass of champagne half drunk, and sat with her at the reserved Amerius table. As they joined, nobles continually strutted to the table introducing themselves.

Constantly, Alveria was blitzed by compliment as did her parents and Joan. Zacharias and Joan could see in a large number of the noble's expressions that they didn't care to speak to him for he was not of royalty. The attire they'd given him revealed that he had won his way into the ball. It really was meant to honor the deed accomplished; it's just some people didn't see it that way. It was funny, a society based upon merit could not respect what it meant to earn something; hypocrites were out in force this night. Regardless, a faction of nobles who resided in Northcross talked to him and loved that he had won his way; if it were up to these few, they would have Valencia embrace the ideals of a society stripped of social hierarchy. This in turn built his confidence greatly.

At that time, the playwright Fanero Malchior stepped out onto the stage and the room and music was rendered inaudible. "Good evening, ladies and gentleman, I welcome you to another special Week of Commemoration!" Holding his cane with the silver image of the frog on the end, Fanero removed his hat and bowed to the audience, who applauded him. Zacharias crossed his arms, remembering how Fanero had disrespected Joseph and him not long ago. Fanero brushed the long blonde hair out of his eyes and then continued his speech, "After tonight's show, it will be my honor to introduce to you the winners of this year's competitions!"

Zac whispers to Joan, "We have to go up there?"

"Ha, oh ya, forgot to tell you that," Joan whispered back, snickering, pouring a second glass of champagne to the brim. His body fidgets greatly; Alveria asks if he's all right. "I'm not one much for social gatherings, that's all," he said. Alveria moves her chair to his and leans on him to ease his nervousness. "You are so adorable, do you know that?" Her mother, Queen Salene, leers. "So without further ado, I've been asked to show the play that got me to where I am today, The Inlet's Dream!" Fanero yelled out.

The room storms with applause as the torches and chandelier were unlit in unison. Only the moon gave the room light along with hidden torches within the apron downstage. High above the stage on the lion's crown sat the narrator, and to the left and right below stage was the orchestra with a large piano where the audience could not see. The curtains slowly opened, and out walked the singer known as the Angel's Voice with a dispirited appearance. Zac remembers her from Salem in Calina and how she drew feelings of endearment not understood. Her hair was winter's white as she walked out and the piano then began to play a surreal melody in down tempo. Wearing a violet gown, she reached the end of the stage and her hair cried blue in front of all the audience. Everyone gasped for they were unsure whether it was a stage prop or not, even though some had seen it before. Behind her, the backdrop was lowered with an exceptional painting of a mountain splitting both sea and ocean. Cordelia began to sing, touching the hearts of everyone in the hall; she sang a song of memories not yet made. But Alveria did not like this; she noticed Zac intrigued by her and grew jealous. The piano synced up perfectly with every word, telling the story of a lone sea without a name who always wanted to become one with mother ocean. A tale of a forgotten body of water longing to return, but try as the inlet might it could never reach home. The play would go on for far longer, and Cordelia would give only one other solo performance. Antediluvian sea creatures made the inlet their home and would remind the sea of oceanic truths whenever they would venture out and return. At the end when the final backdrop had fallen, it was of Noah's Ark for the flood had come and overtaken the earth. Cordelia would sing her last song of the allegory of mother-ocean once again, reaching out to her lost child, the sea.

After the play had ended, Fanero, along with Cordelia and the other actors, bowed to the audience. This time, they gave a standing ovation along with piercing whistles. Joan crosses her arms in disgust. "What a joke these so-called believers are. They applaud that which makes a mockery of sacred scripture. A nation built upon the Holy Bible, and yet none seem to read it. Just Valencia, or all professors of faith by speech alone?" Royal chefs began to serve dinner, which everyone ate for the next hour. Alveria had noticed Zacharias's attention held purely to Cordelia; she secretly grew resentful of her unique beauty. Once everyone had eaten, Fanero took the stage yet again and the conversations sank low. "I hope everyone is still enjoying themselves tonight please let's give an applause to the Valencians for hosting such an event!" Yet again, the audiences rose in a standing ovation as many of the clergy from the Church of Law took the stage.

"Where's the leader?" Zac asked Joan.

"Knowing them, he'll wait till the end to make his grand entrance, they're notorious for drawing praise to themselves."

Fanero signaled for the applause to cease and then proclaimed, "Let's now introduce our winners from this Week of Commemoration!" Multiple handheld bags of gold with medals were brought out as Fanero began to call out the names. "Winner of the great race, Joan of Scera," Fanero called out first. Joan stood up from the table slightly tipsy, then strutting to the stage with head high, meeting Fanero and shaking his hand along with many of the clergy. The entire time, she battled for composure holding a deep-rooted hatred for the many liars present. Joan faced the audience with medal and smiled as Fanero called out the next three names of the winners from the great cook-off. Zacharias began to tremble slightly again, but this time out of anger, knowing he'd have to shake that man's hand. Fanero would call out these winners: Poise–Donovan Malborne, Archery–Stephanie Stirling, Jousting–Cedrick Elstrome, followed by Dueling–Zacharias. He marched across the room with a pretended smile as he then stood before Fanero. Fanero's eyes widened for he had undoubtedly remembered him. Without verbal acknowledgement, Fanero had one of the clergy give him his earned gold and medallion. Neither moved as the other winning contestants watched diligently.

Fanero whispered to him, "How sweet, you believe you can play royalty," followed by giving a smug glare.

He smiled back and tossed the bag of gold at Fanero's feet, stating without care, "Guess I've earned my way as you have. Don't forget scraps are for the dogs." He then strolled over by Joan as Fanero turned red before forcing himself to relinquish any action in front of the audience, as the show must go on. Fanero then read off the name of the tactics winner, his name was Abner Purecrest. Although not present, he had submitted a tactics manifesto prior that year, he was a Valencian defensive general and strategist currently overseeing the grand ballista city of Hagan, which defended western holy ground. After other musicians and a new playwright were called forward, then was Malfius Stirling by best painting. Malfius appeared from one of the main balconies and did this ridiculous waltz to the stage. Joan and the other winners burst out laughing as Stephanie, his sister, hid her face. Most of the nobles in the room found this unamusing, but good old Malfius was having the time of his life. Fanero shook his head, giving him the medallion. "Why?" Malfius pats Fanero, his boss, on the shoulder. "Why not?" Malfius replies. Parading over to the others, Malfius began to make absurd faces at his sister who was doing her best to hold a respectable demeanor. Stephanie turned red, as the other winners, Donovan, who was unbelievably tall, and Cedrick, who held a perceptive eye, introduced themselves. One of the clergy tapped Fanero on the back, whispering into his ear. Fanero looked back, noticing one additional bag of gold he had forgotten to mention a winner, the most important notably. "Excuse me, everyone, I apologize. I have forgotten the final winner of the general strength competition! For the first time in centuries, the Valencian nation is proud to host our brothers from the east! Long have we looked to each other with heated minds of war, but now, it is our hope as the entirety of Marduas stands united as a one nation we can learn to live together! I give you the man who has united the east, King Victor Carthright!" It would be that moment when everything stopped when storm balanced with serenity capable of tipping at the slightest shift of situation. Carthright, who was also dressed for the occasion, appeared from behind the stage with a formal cape swaying diligently. Wearing the same crown from his stechhelm, he emotionlessly stepped in front of Fanero, who was shaking. His robust build pushed tightly against his attire for even as huge as Malfius was, Carthright was on an entirely new level. Carthright's countenance held the most stern and terrifying look anyone had ever seen, but his words were unbelievably soft spoken, his dialogue well articulated. "Thank you, master playwright, it was an enjoyable performance. You are one of the finest." Carthright sat back on the stage, crossing his arms, sweeping the nobles with an authentic unsettling stare, much like one seeing his enemy before battle. Carthright then spoke for the hall to hear as he removed his crown, holding it out to them, "Shall we as human beings continue to be subverted by the doctrinaire of man-made throne? Or shall we one day come to realize that a crown is nothing more than something we choose to bow before. I was born a slave, yet here I sit wearing a crown, commanding the largest nation in Vulgata. Is this not proof of the true Trial of Kings? All men are capable of obtaining this, for a crown at the foundation is nothing more than a capstone for the cause presented to oneself." Peacefully, he touches the ruby phoenix and then returns title to throne, taking one glance at the lion above him. All the while, Malfius can see Zacharias desperately trying to hold himself together.

The music begins to return as Carthright congratulates the other winners in his serious demeanor, but the words he chooses to say to each is "Honor unto you." Hundreds of nobles take to the dance floor in a charming slow dance as Alveria meets her romance in the winner's circle. Malfius was standing by Stephanie when he noticed she walked over to Carthright. Stephanie gazes softly into his eyes whilst giving an adorable smile for a few moments. Carthright, holding a soulless temporal stare, speaks calmly, "Your eyes judge me, yet I am at peace with that for you are an angel." Stephanie calls him "handsome" in sign language, and Carthright is unbothered by the fact that she is deaf and mute, although he does not acknowledge what she stated, but how could he? Carthright takes her hand, and together, they begin to dance as Malfius glares at Stephanie. Meanwhile, Zacharias continually looks over Alveria's shoulder at Carthright. Malfius turns to Joan, and they begin to dance, intentionally blocking his view. As this is happening, Alveria slaps his shoulder to gain Zac's attention who apologizes. Malfius unsure as to why his sister is dancing with Carthright notices they dance almost instinctively. Placing his head onto Alveria's shoulder, Zacharias exhales a long warm breath into her neck. She places her hand on the back of his head, knowing that something is wrong. The music picks up to a fast-paced dance and then things became interesting.

An enormous golden goblet is lugged out and placed underneath the lion's mouth. Champagne begins to flow rapidly that is then placed into decorative glass for all the attendants, Joan slams her third. During this, Zacharias attempts to get closer to Carthright because he is going to ask him why he had Joseph and Salem murdered by the Black Hand. At this point, Fearstein Damascus is seen taking the stage while additional clergy enter around him. The music begins to dissipate as Zacharias stands beside Carthright at last. Malfius grabs Stephanie, berating her in sign language, which she does back too him far worse. Joan further feels the affects of the alcohol. Desteeran stares at Carthright, trying to find the words to say; Victor is fixed on the stage, but he sees him by peripheral vision. "Do you wish to speak to me?" Carthright asks him. Malfius, Joan, and Alveria watch nervously, praying this doesn't escalate into bloodshed. A trap door on the stage opens beside Damascus, and something begins to rise with a black velvet sheet concealing it. "Why did you order the Black Hand to kill Joseph and Salem?" Zac demands in a serious tone for only Carthright to hear. Victor turns slowly to him, but before he can speak, Damascus pulls off the cloth, revealing a giant aviary with Eurus inside. Everything stops, Damascus proclaims for all to hear, "Behold the traitor, one of multiple who murdered the Voltoro family!" Most of the nobles went berserk, clutching scornful obscenity alongside casting personal judgment. "Death by pain," they began to chant in unison, shaking their fists.

Damascus then spoke, adding, "On Saturday, before I am to face Carthright in the Coliseum of Vindication to see who the better man is, this imposter claiming to be Eurus shall be put to death by me in honor of the Voltoro family, this a gift from Caiaphas, the patriarch!" They cheered him in a boisterous ensemble of their own.

"So is the dirge of Valencia," Malfius stated to Joan. Alveria was clenching mouth for she could feel the uneasy energy of conflict to come. Zacharias felt a pull he had never felt before and jumped onto the stage as all eyes shifted to him.

"I challenge you for this man's life, Damascus," he screamed out charging in as Sir Galahad. Staggered by this, no Valencian intervened as Carthright then joined the stage in his own form of dark enthusiasm. Desteeran stared at Eurus who was beaten so badly, his grievous wounds would have killed a lesser man. Damascus held a dumbfounded appearance for he didn't understand a mere commoner challenging him. Carthright crossed his arms and spoke, "Well, Damascus, what are you going to do? It is my wish to face the best Valencia or better yet the west has to offer, so let me fight the successor of your bout." Carthright then examines the cage as Eurus's talons held out to Zac, shaking in pain, wanting to deny his help but was unable. His wings jetted out the sides and eagle eyes struck fear into the hearts of the nobles, but his friend the one who believed in him felt a deep pity. His heart sank, wanting to help him with all his soul for he did not just see only Eurus in that humiliating cage but remembered Joseph, Penelope, Mariana, and Salem. Just as he was able to do nothing then he had to do it now. The animalistic traits of the eagle gained control over Eurus's carnal instincts and he began to screech and smash into the cage savagely from his imprisonment, injuring himself further. Wanting to sway the hero's decision, ire was besting him, making him unable to speak in human language. He took a brave step toward Eurus and then the Valencian Patriarch, Caiaphas Caligula Vondorelan stepped out from behind the stage's darkness. First his golden staff with the bent cross in the cardinal's beak appeared as he would come to stand in front of Eurus's cage. Tense is the situation and two whole agonizing minutes pass. Joan, just shy of being drunk, blinks multiple times, raising her pointer finger. She points to Caiaphas and shouts, "Whited Sepulcher!" Malfius covers her mouth as she starts laughing, but luckily, no one reacts. Carthright then stares at his bent cross as Caiaphas spoke, "Are you sure of this, King of Slave?" Carthright nodded in approval as Caiaphas then went to the challenger. "I will ask only once, young swordsman, for all to hear are you sure you wish to challenge Damascus for the life of this grotesque imposter?"

Feeling the eyes of a nation, he stood his ground. "Yes, I am sure."

Caiaphas gave a wide grin and touched him on the shoulder with his staff, whispering, "Then may you find your answers in hell along with the Desteeran name." Caiaphas then made his proclamation, "In light of this new challenge and the acceptance of Carthright to face the victor, I am inclined to overrule and accept! If this commoner is to win, then the life of this fraud shall be given to him!" The lumbering giant Damascus held his hand out to Zacharias to seal the agreement, and as they shook, Caiaphas finished his order. "By the divine rules of the Coliseum of Vindication, you are bound by nationality! Since you have been brought here by the Amerius family and entered into the dueling competition by Princess Alveria, you are hereby assigned to the representation of Scera! With that being said, since you are to represent Scera who had no competitors this year in the coliseum, if Damascus is to win, then the Church of Law wagers the rights to enter Scera at my divine proclamation!" Caiaphas left as the Amerius family and Joan were overtaken by dread. All of the nobles of Southcross stared in devilish delight as the rest of the nobles turned to each other uneasy of the decree.

Before the aviary lowered, Carthright murmured something to him that made Eurus stare, ready to take his prey. Carthright smirked at Damascus as he walked away, bumping his shoulder into him, the cage then disappeared and the trap door closed. Damascus left the stage, following Caiaphas. Zacharias who was trapped inside a prison of insulting conscious contemplated over the rash decision finalized. "What have I done, have I now brought death to the household of the forest?" He pulls hair as he feels the weight of this looming catastrophe. Peering back, he speaks with a voice of fright to Drake, Salene, and Alveria, "I'm sorry, please forgive me." All of them leave without saying a word, but Alveria holds strong a heartbroken gaze, pulling to the decision of disappointment. Joan takes the stage, putting her arm on his shoulder, as Malfius stands behind him. "I didn't mean for this to happen," Zac said, pressing fingers harder.

Joan rubbed his shoulders, whispering to him, "It's all right, you did the right thing that needed to happen."

"She's right, you did what Valencia has needed for a long time, but we have to go, the fallen one watches us intently now." Joan motioned for them to leave. The nobles whispered among themselves as some of them began to cheer him on. Others began to curse his name, and soon, a riot broke out between royal families divided over a commoner facing Damascus. One man yells out, "We have not been disgraced like this since the days of the reformation!" Alone, the sleeping lion above stage vigilantly surveys the room, but none are to notice the last drop of wine drip from a held tongue soon to enunciate a newly awakened child predestined before man ever set foot upon the earth. "As Eurus had stated, it would only take a spark to kindle a nationwide fire in Valencia, but let us hope this does not also spread unto the forest," Malfius exclaimed as they passed the doors outside.

"This is going to change everything," Joan added with a smile that only Malfius could see who winked in return. That night, Joan, Malfius, and Zacharias would stay together at a secluded inn on the outskirts of Alexandria.

15

Divine Providence

DAY 6 (FRIDAY): THE CALM

No competitions are held within Valencia; she rests in preparation for the day of the vindicated nativity. Talk of a commoner challenging the legendary Damascus swept between royal court and common marketplace alike. Not a household went unhearing and not a person was left without opinion. Overnight, two factions sown in prior revolution arose within the state. Most from Northcross sided with Zacharias, who was a man of common birth to stand up to their fallen church and broken rule of Valencia. They saw him a champion sent by the Lord from their prayers to save Valencia from false religious rule. Opposing them would be the majority of Southcross, who branded him a false prophet sent by Lucifer to test their loyalty to the church. Those of Southcross held their foundation to the Law of Moses, believing that only through following the original 613 commandments could one reach the gates to heaven alongside worldly penance through the priesthood who stood on men's behalf before God. For centuries, Valencia waged political war over the issue with those of

Northcross explaining the Law of Moses was made to make man slaves to sin in order to understand sins power over us and in that Jesus Christ would break those chains thus saving us, showing God's holy love. The citizens of Southcross believed that Jesus, although the Christ, was not the end of God's plan for humanity. Their piety immense and course unwavering, this explicit majority would prove unyielding to the brothers and sisters of the cross just north. Recently discovered in apocrypha disclosed to the general public, they were attempting to advance scripture and saintliness. The mechanism used was that Mary was soon to return with Jesus's true form. That he had returned after the crucifixion not to the right hand of God, but to her womb and this rebirth was the second coming. Everyone in Valencia fitted by the sight of spiritual discernment gifted from the Holy Spirit knew of this most foul and wretched deception, but like a plague, this cult of rats infiltrated church and state. When the Voltoro family led Valencia, they sided with the northern subcapital Philippi along with their beliefs in order to unify the nation, but the Church of Law would act as the herald of Southcross' ideologies originating from the subcapital, Constantinople. For centuries, the church and kingships would flip sides, always trying to rule by dominant sect, but none would since the chaotic days of the great schism kindled by the Ninety-Five Theses. Leaving a permanent divide over the now ministerial administration, Valencia would never be the same, and during this time, tensions had reached the apex of both legislative and civil conflict, the pendulum is soon to write history in bias stroke. As Eurus had explained, civil war was soon to come for the Empire of Valencia. Northcross was left in the dark without the Voltoro family clinging to the shortening days of Phillipi. Yet they saw Zacharias as the warrior who would pick up that torch even though he had not intentionally asked for it. In only one night, the royal Amerius family of Scera was forced to rest the life of their nation on the shoulders of this young man. Valencia who had destroyed the sister forest of Devok long ago did so because of their greed for what they deemed as holy restitution. Scera, which was divided into what is known as the three rings of fate, held the most sacred site of all. They believed Zacharias had entered Eden as none were able; Tala was the proof of the venture to the denizens of the forest. Unknown to any of them was that as they believed he had stood in Eden, he had just as equally not for it was a vision, nothing more. The Church of Law knew of this sacred land and now wished to enter into Scera in search, hoping to find Mary divinely parturient. After what they had done to the Devokians, the Alkirum never let go of their resentment of organized religion and, further more, the Church of Law. Now for the church to have found a loophole into the forest, Scera would be forced to abide by the ancient western treaty written in subtext of bylaws of the Coliseum of Vindication. For when all the nations signed the treaty, they were bound to follow whatever terms were set forth as to prevent western collapse. The intent was to hold an infinite united front if another Big 10 (WWI) would ever break out. The terms of the coliseum were simple: one warrior from every nation would face off every five years to prevent war between two nations as to settle dispute instead of armies. To the victor, their terms would be upheld by the western alliance. If Scera would back out now when Zacharias signed the contract with handshake, the national backlash would leave Scera worse off than if the Valencians were given right to enter.

Alveria came for Zacharias that afternoon, but he was gone. No one could find him that day as they searched high and low. Malfius and Joan checked around the civilian districts while Alveria took to the castle she was staying at. As they searched for the missing warrior, Damascus put on a show of his own in the main square of Alexandria. Presenting his physical prowess and perfectly honed skills with his weapons, he warmed up throughout the day drawing much attention. Damascus took the challenge as nil a threat, but he was doing this more as a scare tactic to Carthright. King Victor Carthright would pass by that day, but would pay little mind to Damascus in his sad attempt to exploit himself. Victor, although the most feared world leader at the time, still exercised extreme discipline for him and his loyal drudge knights. As Damascus was foolhardy and arrogant, Carthright was what most westerners would deem as lawful evil. Carthright held the winds of change and could, by immediate choice, enable the next world war or work to unify the hemispheres. The Church of Law knew this too much degree, and none more than Caiaphas, who was attempting to befriend him. This would be the reason he catered to Carthright's wish to let Zacharias face Damascus for the life of Eurus.

Alveria had now searched the entire day and would eventually come to rest in a royal garden. She felt nothing but remorse for putting him through that last night and not standing by his side. "I'm a stupid girl to have blamed him for that, he was doing the right thing," she told herself repeatedly, scarring blame further. Joan and Malfius were unable to find him, but would run into Zacchaeus Carlyle, also known as The Duke, in the main square. He would ask them where Zac was, but they only shrugged in worry. Carlyle took Joan and Malfius to a secret place he had intended to show the young warrior far to the east of the city. Later that night, when Alveria was about to give up her search, she heard Tala's howls carried by the Keystone River. Zacharias was sitting at the end of the causeway where the shipyard was destroyed only days before. His feet submerged in the water as he watched moon and star with a melancholy spirit. "Zac," Alveria calmly spoke. He grasped around his body as if in pain. Alveria sat beside and his eyes remained closed. "I was wrong for how I treated you last night, can you please forgive me?" Alveria asked as a sole tear surfaces. Zac rested his head on her shoulder and she embraced him tightly. A freezing gust of wind sent ripples down the river and he then spoke, the voice is broken, "Will you take care of Tala if doom's spade is to bury me forgotten, Alveria?"

The princess rebuked the statement. "You must not say that!"

He stood up angrily, stating, "How am I supposed to defeat such an opponent? What chance do I have?" Alveria could not look at him at first for she knew there was a part of his words that were correct. She picked up Tala and glanced up to the radiant heavens display and spoke in her mind, *"Oh, please, God, be with him, don't let him die tomorrow, I, I love him."* Alveria then asked him to spend the night with her and the two of them traveled to an inn located by the river.

As they entered the room, they noticed Tala had fallen asleep in his pack. The room was pitch-black and he rest on the bed as Alveria sat behind him with her arms around his stomach and head resting on his neck. Alveria gently spoke, kissing his neck repeatedly, trying to comfort him, "There's something I have to tell you, but I don't know if you want to hear it." He turned around with an emotionally hurt appearance emerged in curiosity. "Zacharias, I've fallen in love with you. I just can't help it anymore. I left last night because I couldn't stand the sight of losing you. You did the right thing, defending noble Prince Eurus." Alveria began to cry once she said this and he held her close, running his hand through her hair and the other down her fragile back. "Alveria, I've waited my entire life to hear those words," he then whispered, choked up as he said it. "I'm a wicked man, Alveria, so many have died because of me, even children are dead on my account, how can you love someone like me, a killer?" Eyes watering, she pressed her lips and body against his as they fell onto the bed. Their bodies held tightly against one another as an erotic jolt shot through the both of them. They began kissing each other in various ways while rubbing their hands all over each other. Alveria said to him passionately that she wanted to give him something to live for as she then gave him an enduring kiss outside of time. Their hearts pounding in the quiet of the room, Alveria began to remove her dress by her right shoulder. Before her body was revealed, Zacharias sat up and stopped her.

With one hand on her cheek and the other pulling her dress back on her shoulder, he looked at her like she was the world. Caringly, he whispered, "Not yet. I care for you to much to waste your virginity outside of marriage, Alveria. After all this, I want to go away together where the problems of the world can't find us." Alveria, at that moment, fell even more in love with him, and together, they fell asleep tightly bound to one another. Although he had only told a half truth to Alveria, a piece of his inner being longed for Cordelia. He also felt that to sleep with her then and there would not honor God, just as Joseph had explained to him in his own kitchen.

Day 7 (Saturday): The Day of Vindication

The sun rose accompanied by great trumpets that proclaim the finale of the Week of Commemoration. Alexandria is covered in the amber glow that reflects perfectly off the white structures and the Keystone. They awake together, holding each other still as the sun illuminates the room. Zacharias stands up and prepares to leave as Alveria sits up woken in tears. "Please don't go. I'm not ready."

His spirits are far better off than the night before as he smiles and states, "Neither am I, but Eurus is counting on me. God is with me, Alveria, I can feel it."

Before he leaves, Alveria kisses him one final time. "I love you." He grabs his pack and opens the door, Tala's head pokes out panting.

"Wait," Alveria asks.

"Yes," he states, popping his head back in.

"What is the rest of your name? I never thought to ask."

"Desteeran," he states, pulling the door closed.

Alveria puts her hands to her mouth in amazement, thinking, "The descendant of Sir Abraham Desteeran returns before the vindicated, then that must mean."

Passing road and spectator, he can hear the royal trumpets all over Alexandria. Citizens and visitors are seen as far as the eye can see, all heading east to the coliseum, hoping to catch a glimpse of the heroes before they go in for only nobility enters this site alone. In the midst of this, he finds Malfius sitting alone on the bottom stair to the Church of Law, praying. He sits beside and says nothing at first, but instead watches the crowds surge. "A tragic beauty," Zac says aloud. Malfius opens his eyes and, renewed by the sight of his answered prayer, hugs him with all his strength, squeezing the life out of him. "I was so worried you have no idea," Malfius yelled out.

"Please forgive me for everything, Beck, it's just been a lot lately, but I feel good now, this is right, this is the will of the Lord," Zac answered.

"Glory be. He has opened your heart," Malfius stated in a jovial manner. Malfius then threw in, "You have to come with me, there's something of the utmost importance I have to show you!" Malfius then took him to the same secret spot Carlyle had brought Joan and him to yesterday.

Meanwhile, towering atop the city within the highest spire of the Church of Law, Caiaphas sat in a gold and silver throne cased in precious jewel. Beside him, two sacred guards stood over seven feet tall, holding massive pitch-black scythes also outlined in silver. Each guard was encased in a flowing white robe that had golden metallic lines running throughout; this cloth hid every inch of their bodies. Their shoulders were ancient white shields signed in Latin text and their plated helmets held a golden spire crowned with ten points. Lastly, where the mouth should be and only darkness dwelt, seven identical golden knives representing teeth jetted out in horizontal fashion, alternating, creating a solid cage of fang. Stretching across the middle of this illustrious room, an azure carpet connected both throne and ingress, which was guarded by a sight most would never see. A mystical door of tanzanite gemstone praises a lone angelic visage whose eyes are closed wide. Opposing each side of this stairwell were fifty royal guards adjacent from one another. These were silver paladins of the highest achievement and to signify that their helmets held long black feathers and armor and weapons were of the highest quality Valencia could forge. A figure scales past the twenty-five sets of guards, the gem's eyes open, and the door evaporates. Cloaked in a white robe, which was reversed to black on the inside, she had the appearance of one of the clergy, the young oriental girl of only seventeen bowed before Caiaphas. Holding the iron scepter of Valencia, Caiaphas tapped her shoulder, and she looked up in reverence. Caiaphas stood up, caressing her chin, speaking in a loving voice, "Dear sweet Amaralda, you're growing into such a beautiful woman of God, you do us all proud. What have you to report to your father?" Her demeanor is blank, but her eyes a calm and dangerous portrait. She then acknowledged him in a cold and calculated voice far more aged than her, "Patriarch, I have tracked the challenger of Damascus since Alpha escorted him to Avodah Mortis where they located the tomb of Abraham. The Black Hand was spotted, their leader put Alpha to death. Veil could not overcome the first Exile, and in the engagement, he successfully summoned a fell dragon, pulling all into the earth except Zacharias." Caiaphas signaled for Amaralda to stand, as he himself stood before a mostly rebuilt wooden cross. Caiaphas began to speak in a darkened tone, "Alpha is dead, the Black Hand on the run, and the Marduas triumvirate within our grasp as confirmed in the actions of Carthright. All is according to the word of the supreme delegates of York. Very soon, the whole of Vulgata shall bow to the holy Church of Law for their pagan beliefs." He then placed his left hand on the partial cross. "Once True Cross is completed, we will be able to prepare Alexandria for the final sacrifice and be freed from mankind's initial sin. Then we shall be able to place the capstone from the womb of the resurrected mother during the Second Nativity. The sign will be marked by the marriage of Castor and Pollux, forming a one being, Dioskuri, even now they watch diligently as the holy mother endures the pains of labor. Her egg will hatch the conditions for a new heaven, one in which all are welcome."

Amaralda stood behind Caiaphas with her arms crossed behind her back and stated in a monotone voice, "Yes, glory be to our church, holding to the pure laws set forth by God."

Caiaphas smiled, adding, "We were cast from Eden never to return by God's holy word and only by taking refuge within the establishment that is the Church of Law may we be exonerated from the sins of Vulgata. The purity of this church depends upon the righteousness of the saints. Amaralda, are you willing to obey me your father even unto death?"

"This body, mind, and soul is yours to command, even to death," Amaralda replies. Caiaphas then pulled out a legendary sword that belonged to the Voltoro family line; still in its ceremonial sheath, the hilt holds the insignia of the Shield of David. Followed by a single command, "In order to protect the purity of the church, we must do whatever is necessary. You are our youngest and most loyal disciple, and although my oath is to celibacy, I regard you as my daughter whom I love dearly. Under the charge of defending our cathedral of hope, you are to put the heretic Zacharias Desteeran to death!" At this point, he pulls the sword from the sheath, tapping her on the left shoulder with it. "I dub you, Amaralda, Celestial Constable of the Church of Law. I hereby absolve you of sin and shoulder your soul to new heights, your spirit now dwells within the fourth echelon of human potential." She says nothing. The two guards bow then stand as Caiaphas returns to his throne. He then concluded, slamming the scepter on the ground, "The world must see this cursed man fall before the chosen of God! Although Damascus may possess superior strength, speed, and technique, Zacharias is a direct descendant of Sir Abraham Desteeran, the first of the false holy knights, demon's blood courses through his body. That is why he was not killed when Sodom and Gommorah was pulled to Hades by the dragon Apollyon. The Devil returned his other agents home, but this one he keeps to wreak havoc on the scattered believers soon to come home at the end of the reformation. One should not regard this lightly for he holds the key to the completion of the Trial of Kings, which shall bring forth the Sword of Sacrilege. As precaution, you are to poison him before his fight. Execute this deed accordingly so that it catches up to him in the match with Damascus. I want the kings of the earth to watch him fall. Both the Desteeran and the Voltoro names shall be forgotten this day, one by venom and one by the blade of the family that stood against our New Way Forward, denying the sacred apocrypha now one with canon. Now go, Amaralda, you above most know of the seriousness of protecting this loving establishment." Amaralda stares putting her right hand to her chest, left down her leg. "Make your father proud," Caiaphas said as his guards crossed their scythes, creating a picture of his face encircled within the blades. Amaralda hid the sword within her cloak and left through one of the windows, able to oversee all of Alexandria.

Malfius had taken Zac to the Courtyard of Heroes where the statues of all those who had won in the Coliseum of Vindication remained. "Zacharias, you have to see this. Carlyle brought this to my attention!" Malfius stood before the statue of a great warrior, holding the same claymore he was and the inscription read: Alcus Desteeran. He turned to Malfius with a life-changing expression "How did you know?" Malfius who was petting Grear answered, "I didn't, it was Carlyle who told me. He said he knew Alcus and that you fought just like him, so it was more of an educated guess, I suppose." Taking a deep breath, Zacharias placed Tala on the ground; she hopped up by the foot of the statue and played around it. "Thank you, Beck, you are a true friend," he stated. Malfius then went to speak, but Zac accidentally interrupted him, "Beck, this may be my last day alive, may I ask you one final favor?"

Malfius patted his friend. "Anything, just ask and I will do it." Desteeran drew Titulus and plunged it into the ground and sat, with the statue behind. "Will you listen to my story?"

"Yes, I would be honored," Malfius replied, sitting and facing the statue as Grear rested beside him. He then began to tell Malfius the story of his secretive past stricken by grief.

THE BACKSTORY OF ZACHARIAS JOHN DESTEERAN

I never met my mother or my father, but instead, I was raised alone by my grandfather Alcus Desteeran in the nation of ruin, Vendalas. My grandfather was the greatest warrior in the nation's western region, which was where we lived in a quiet little village. My grandfather was a widower from before the time I was born and my mother, I was told, died in childbirth, as for my father, he was never spoken of. My mother's name was Dinah Desteeran and she was my grandfather's only child. In the year 2970, my birthday had once again arrived, making me six. My grandfather knew I wanted to be just like him, a warrior. It would be then on my sixth birthday that he would give me my very first sword, which now is my dagger. I'll never forget that night when together, he surprised me along with the entire village giving me that weapon. Grandfather taught me lessons on how to use it all throughout the night; it was the greatest day of my life. In those days, the feelings were real, my love for my grandfather true, and I wished it could be that way forever. Later that night, I fell asleep in the old cabin by the fire, grasping the sword to my heart. My grandfather carried me to my room, and even though I knew it was happening, I held my eyes tightly shut so he'd hold me just a bit longer. He tucked me into my bed and the words he spoke I will never forget; he said that my mother would be proud. I remember the next morning, we trained out by the lake, and eventually, he tossed me in as a joke. He pulled me out of the water, and it was that moment when I began to see Alcus as my father. For many months, I trained with my sword after my chores were complete. But one day, everything would change, for Alcus had to travel to a nearby town, but this time alone. I was upset because I wanted to join my grandfather on our very own adventure, he then promised me we would when I was older. That day, as I was left in the care of our neighbors, I decided to go out on an adventure of my own. I would prove to my grandfather that I too could be a warrior and he would have to take me with him. I journeyed beyond the mighty walls of Vendalas and would come across Death's Trail. It was said that trail was haunted by the souls of the slaughtered refugees from WWI when the drudge knights overcame the defenses. Traveling up the winding trails, I could feel a darkness growing inside of me, and although I was only a child, I knew that something was not right. At the end of Death's Trail, I came to an ancient terrifying black tree known as the Tree of Lament, it rested upon a small mountain. It was said that the very essence of death had made its home in this spot; this tree was completely barren. Something worse grew inside of my mind as I gazed upon the tree. A warrior had to be strong, a warrior had to be brave just like my grandfather, I told myself repeatedly. Mustering my courage, I charged forth, slashing the tree with my blade, pretending it was a monster, but little did I know, this dream was a destined nightmare. Blood showered down the tree as the screaming pains of all those who died on this trail were heard all around me. I had experienced fear to a level I had never yet seen, but that would prove only the beginning as I tried to wipe the red stains off my drenched body. The voice of a young boy was heard by the mountain calling my name for help. Running over, I was met by a single door bearing a strange symbol, an image of a scale with its right side being pulled down by a majestic looking apple. Below the scale, the words "Stipendium Peccati Mors Est" were written; to this day I have not forgotten those words, but I know not what they mean.

I opened the door into a well-lit room that extended out into a mine. To my side, the shadow of a man sat upon the wall and began to speak to me with the voice of a frightened boy my own age. He asked me to help him regain his body for it had been stolen. I was scared at first, and as I backed up, the little boy began to weep and I felt sorry for him. I agreed to help him because a good warrior helps everyone, I thought, and then asked what we needed to do. The shadow explained that he wanted to play a game called The Trial of Kings, but we needed thirty pieces of silver to pay the bridge man his toll. The shadow then promised that if I was to save his body, then he would make me a king among warriors. Knowing I didn't have any silver, I remembered that my grandfather had a bit stashed in a large chest. I would then leave to get it, believing that he would understand that I did this to help the young boy. After he was saved, he'd come back and meet grandfather and he'd proudly accept me as a warrior and never leave me behind again.

Once I returned, the shadow and I headed down the mine deep below the mountain. As we journeyed for over an hour, the shadow was unable to be seen but would lead me with his voice. When I asked his name, the shadow revealed to me that his name had also been imprisoned, but very soon I would learn it. At the end of the mine, there was another sharp drop into a black pit I had to stumble into. It began to get hot like a furnace as we traveled down the pit and a glowing light could be seen not far. Finally, we reached the other side where a long wooden bridge extended to a small island. Red hot lava lay below and a gargantuan charred capstone sat alone on the island that looked to be the top of some pyramid with a great marking of a closed eye. Atop the ceiling, giant roots wrapped all the way into the lava as if drawing strength for the tree above. At first, I was afraid and questioned going forward, but the shadow urged that to become a true warrior, you had to see your fears directly. The shadow then went on to explain he could not cross the bridge but would have to hold on to me only with my permission. I told him it was all right, and as the shadow reached out for me, I could physically and emotionally feel him enter into my being; it felt the opposite of being alive. His voice whispered into my every thought and he said that to cross the bridge, I must throw the silver into the lava. As I threw it in, the faces of people began to form in the lava, screaming for me to run away. The shadow told me that they were the ones who stole his body and begged me to go forward and so, denying every warning, I did. Passing over the bridge, the voices wailed out in pain and agony as the shadow reminded me I would become a king for this. Walking on to the island, the shadow grew silent and no longer spoke as I stood before the giant capstone marked in bizarre writing.

As Zacharias pressed his hand against the blank cold gravestone; the eye opened eerily and stared for several seconds. Then when he tried to pull away a large skeletal hand came forth from the earth and snatched him to the grave. For three days, he remained inside, held to the embrace of a massive skeleton with the monster petting Zac's unconscious head gently as if he was very valuable to him. Zacharias was left asleep for these days trapped inside a horrific nightmare in which the skeleton manipulated on his own accord. It would be revealed that the skeleton's name was Manistof and that he was the father of Zacharias. Manistof first showed him the truth that his mother was raped by a stranger, who let an unclean spirit overtake him. Manistof was the spirit that influenced the man to rape dear sweet Dinah Desteeran and Zacharias would be conceived in that way. Manistof would go on to terrorize him in the fallen celestial realm that he, being the force behind the rape, was his true spiritual father and that Zac was bound to him forever.

As the child was trapped, Alcus and the village searched for him day and night but would not find a single trace. Alcus prayed and wept over his missing grandson for he was the last of his biological family.

On the third day, after nonstop unspeakable nightmares of watching people brutally tortured in hell as was his own soul, Zacharias began to awake inside the grave. He was trapped by the embrace of the skeleton, tightly held inside the ribcage. Being underground, he struggled but could not break free, he hollered and screamed but only swallowed dirt in the silent tomb. Manistof's great jaws slowly fell around him with the soulless gaze of the absent eyes. The voice of Manistof cried as a child, "The Trial of Kings stands complete, and you are the king who opened the gatehouse of the damned unto the rivers of life!" Manistof presses his hand against the child's back searing a scorched handprint as the brand of his kingship. Without hope, Zacharias called on his mother, and at that moment, a miracle of divine proportion occurred. A great light shone penetrating into the cell, and Zacharias was pulled from Manistof's grip. Crashing onto the ground, he saw a white baby dragon encased in celestial golden armor from heaven standing atop the capstone in indescribable light. The glory of this armor brings tears from all whether by dread or reverence, Manistof remained in his grave taken by eternal fear of the Lord. The holy dragon's head is hidden by sacred helm forged in sweeping angelic feather and combined with the armor seven hundred seventy-seven spiked pillars point to the Father above. Every piece of the golden encasement around the white dragon unites perfection that is justice. Around its neck was a clear medallion also generating light that began to speak by clashes of thunder, its name was Law. A soul-stopping scream battled for audible control as Manistof rose eerily from his grave; it was like Satan was pushing him from the earth to get the child. The baby dragon sprawled its merciful wings and lifted its tail that held the shape of the cross. This produced an even greater light from its mouth and these rays of holy truth blasted Manistof into the pit of fire. Standing in everlasting victory, the capstone around this savior was taken by a heavenly peal of thunder revealing the name of Atyrael, the evil eye was obliterated and also cast into the fire. Above, many angels girded for war watched Manistof as he drowned in lava, the holy guardian flew toward the exit, commanding Zacharias to follow. He spoke directly to his heart and soul, but the words were not in language, they were in the fullness of love that humanity could not understand without the mercy or grace of God. He could see the many angels overcome Manistof by the sword of the Spirit that was the word of God. They slashed apart his body, pulled bones out of place, and struck him with his own intestines as so he could see the fullness of sin. The blameless dragon lit the way and guided him out of the mine and then was taken up into the sunlight. Zacharias could feel loneliness return to him as the protector ascended to heaven, but he would never forget this the day he was saved.

As he ran to return home, Manistof began to resurface from the lava, but no longer was he a skeleton. His body was a mixture of demonic flesh with his organs inside out along with patches of bone dislocated in all direction. He held his body in agonizing torture, which was completely inside out. Flesh like wings stained in sin and lava sprouted from his back as he rose above the capstone. Manistof screamed out, still holding his face yet melting, "I may not be able to kill him, but you hold this oath true! I will not rest, I will not stop until you are dead, Zacharias John Desteeran! If I cannot have you by my own means, then I will force you to kill yourself and join me in hell! As I promised, you were given a crown, but the crown of death and any who get close will die because of you!" Manistof then slammed into the capstone, piercing his body, and as his black blood ran down the sides, the floor began to consume it. Sliding down the slippery stone, his bones began to crunch back into place, and soon after, he undertook the prophesied hunt for Desteeran. Although Zacharias was not present for many of these things, Manistof would reveal this to him many times in years to come by use of continual nightmares. Returning home, Zac met his grandfather who was dearly worried, but before he could explain to him, everything fell apart. The sun turned black like sackcloth made of goat's hair. A thunderstorm raged throughout the village as rains hit hard, and on the horizon, the demonic giant's eyes appeared over the wall. Manistof entered into the village and murdered everyone in his path, ripping them to pieces and coating himself with each kill as he tried to get the boy. In the chaos, he was separated from his grandfather as the village ran in horror. He was left alone in the village square as Manistof's naked inside-out body approached magnetized by his black glowing eyes with red focused pupils. No words could describe the fear he felt before Manistof, but even dying would not have saved him.

Alcus ran into the square, knocking Zacharias out of the way, and with his claymore, he called upon the Lord Almighty in which his sword transformed into the Sword of Abraham. Alcus injured the demon who was then pulled inside the earth back to hell. Manistof held one outstretched arm, reaching for the boy as the opening to the abyss let off a boom that went across the world of Vulgata, people all over the world remember it to this day. Zacharias awakened not having seen the battle for he was knocked out momentarily. Alcus was mortally wounded, lying in the rain, soon to die. Staring into his eyes, he wept, knowing he had caused all of this. Alcus told him to reach inside of his pocket for he had gotten him a gift from the city he had to go to. The boy pulled out a Holy Bible, and Alcus put his hand to the Bible, which in turn he held to his grandson. His blood touched the pages, which the rain soaked deeper into the very fiber of its binding. Alcus blessed him in his final words, stating that his Father would never forsake him. Alcus Desteeran died that day, embracing his grandson he loved with all his heart.

After this, Zacharias buried his grandfather and kept his sword, which had turned back into the claymore it was before, Titulus. Taking with him his dagger and his grandfather's blade, he went inside, grabbing one final item, an alabaster box in which he kept the Holy Bible in. He headed east to an abandoned tower from WWI known as Chivalry's Tower and for many years lived in seclusion. Living by hunting and scavenging, his emotions regressed to a point where he was in complete solitude even among his mind. Haunted most nights by terrible nightmares of the rape of his mother, demons, and everything in between his soul was tormented to a point beyond the realm of explanation. Manistof pledging to kill whoever he got close to held him in that tower cursed endlessly to the thoughts of suicide, which would only bring further pain below. In the first year, not a single word was said even unto himself for it took that amount of time just to understand Alcus was never going to return. All that kept him sane were the books and songs he'd find among the ancient ruins of Vendalas. He'd read these books over and over again temporarily parting from the wastelands of reality. In these books, he learned of great adventurers whom everyone so dearly admired and precious romances where a man found a loving wife and no longer had to face life miserably alone. What he learned in these was carried out in a violin he found within that fortress of solitude. Eventually, Zacharias would begin to travel to Darseal as a lone vagabond, hoping for just one person to reach out to, but whoever he got close to did die within weeks of meeting him. Many an attempt did the lonesome boy make, desperately reaching out for fellowship, imploring chance, karma, and even destiny if only to hear a whisper of care. But alone he was not, for the weapon of his forefathers, Titulus, was always beside as was the only book he never read that was there from the beginning.

COURTYARD OF HEROES

Malfius held many tears from the story, having trouble looking at his friend, but held his hand out to him, speaking in absolute care, "I had no idea, I am sorry, my friend."

He then wrapped up his story, "I went to Salem to die, and for many weeks, I sat alone in the ruined playhouse. Just being able to watch people from the distance really was pure, but little did I know Salem would not yield death but life. Fourteen plus years I've watched the world from outside the box, and now, after all that knocking, I've finally been allowed in. And you know what, it all happened because of the faith of a child." He remembered the day Mariana had saved his life as did Joseph and Penelope. He remembered when Joseph had bandaged him, but did not become sad; instead, he sighed with relief, stating, "I've never told anyone that before, to be honest, it feels superb." He began to laugh, and soon, Malfius joined until he spoke again, "Joseph was the first person who ever shared the message of Jesus Christ with me in my aimless wandering." Zacharias then went over to Grear and pulled out an alabaster box and smashed it on the ground; inside was that Holy Bible. Picking it up, he looked to Malfius. "In all the years I've held this book, I couldn't bring myself to open it for I always selfishly blamed God for what had happened. Finally, I can see the truth because of people like you and the Voltel family, because of Jesus." Desteeran could feel a strange sense of renewal overtaking his body as he yelled out, "Beck, not only does Jesus Christ exist, he has always been with me. I was never alone!" He continued to cheer this loudly and Malfius, taken by empathy, watched as a man endured of so much pain came to faith in the one true Lord that is Jesus Christ. Zac kept speaking on it, then added, "I don't know how but Jesus was a part of the white dragon, the Lord is holy. He saved my life that day, Beck, it's not his fault, I walked with the curse of death, he can free me from it. I can feel it just as that white dragon did! Jesus, you were always there and I never believed it, and if you hold the keys of death, then I am free in my true Father!" Zacharias fell to his knees, holding the Holy Bible to his heart as the eternal love of the Lord embraced his soul, confirming that he was in fact not alone. Although he had reached out to God in the forests of Scera, the true salvation was coming in the name of God's only begotten son, Jesus, for by him and him alone are men able to come before the throne of God unto salvation. Malfius stretches his palms to the sky, thanking the Lord for opening his friend unto Him, and a bright light illuminated the garden of heroes. "Look," Malfius yelled out. Titulus that was sticking into the ground had transformed into the most beautiful and powerful blade either had ever seen. "Titulus is," Zac said, followed by Malfius, "The legendary Sword of Abraham."

16

The Trial of Kings

Paralyzed by the Sword of Abraham's glory, Zacharias could not bring himself to touch it. The sword that was in the statue hands of Alcus was gone, and sitting on the now white wooden hilt of the Sword of Abraham was a single white dove. "Grasp your destiny," Malfius declares in righteous tone while bowing and giving a constant praise within. Zacharias kneels before the legendary blade and the dove stares directly at him; images of the white dragon that saved him long ago flash swiftly to him alone. In his soul, Zac speaks to God, "My entire life I have felt alone and without a loving father trapped by the curse of death, claimer of my lineage. I have been lost for so very long, struggling to find a home once more. You are my Father, I now understand that, Jesus my Lord and savior has revealed this unto me by his boundless love shed upon the cross. I've always believed Manistof was my father and I hated you for it, but the fact is, although he was behind an immoral and ungodly act, it was you who brought light out of what most would call a tragedy. Only you can bring life, Father, and now I understand that, thank you." Zacharias could still feel the warmth and excitement of something far greater than adrenaline. This feeling spoke to him not of what we deem as word but the loving word that is truth, it commanded him to rise. Zacharias stood up and the dove rested on his shoulder as he touched his right hand to the wooden hilt of the sword. Memories of all the pain and suffering now flood, but instead of them hindering him, they begin to fade away and better yet draw testimonial strength. He grasps the hilt of wisdom, and at that moment, only for a second, he can see Joseph standing beside his grandfather and mother smiling at him. All at once, he pulls the giant two-handed blade from the ground and holds it to the sun in all its divine majesty. Grear and Tala bow before the Sword of Abraham and the dove then flies off into the sun just as the white dragon Atyrael had. Lowering the sword, Zac then speaks, breathing heavily, "Beck, this is too much. I feel like I'm going to have a heart attack." Malfius smiles, for such a scene is more than most could bear as Zac also smiles in return. In all seriousness, he then states, "Malfius, I have to be baptized before this fight, the dove spoke into my heart and gave me that order. Will you bless me by doing so?"

Malfius then stands back up, replying in all decency, "It would be my honor, Sir Desteeran." They could hear the crowds cheering not far as another coliseum battle commenced. "Zac, I'm going to baptize you inside the Church of Law," Malfius added, not knowing of his reaction. He nodded in approval for he understood why Malfius was ordered to do it; he knew on a spiritual level that they needed to witness this, but what he did not know was this was part of a prophecy foretold from before mankind. Zacharias was no longer seeing things through a temporal worldly outlook, but now, he was beginning to see things in their absolute spiritual truth that testifies to the one true Lord Almighty. Before they left, another question was asked by Desteeran. "Was Atyrael telling me that the Lord is the capstone?"

Malfius explains gently, "Well, to those who believe in the Lord Jesus Christ, he is actually the cornerstone, which means the foundation or placed first whereupon the structure of your life rests. The capstone is referencing the final stone placed. A hard truth many will not realize until it's too late is that Jesus is the capstone if you choose to reject him. And if that is to happen, then being a sinful man for we are all sinners, then one will be tossed into hell forever.

> For it is written, As I live, saith the Lord, every knee shall bow to me, and every tongue shall confess to God.
>
> Romans 14:11 (KJV)

"I understand the words you preach, Malfius."

Beck then scooped up Tala, and Grear followed as they marched to the Church of Law, out of sight from the legions of crowds. Walking up the plaza staircase, a man noticed Zacharias and the sword, which he was trying to hide for it would not fit within the scabbard. "You are the sign, the one we have been waiting for," he yelled out. Malfius urged him to keep moving as the man then left, spreading the good news.

A few silver paladins sat before the Church of Law's doors just as before, and seeing the sword, they bowed not to him, but to the Lord. "Sire, we have long awaited your return," one of them said gallantly, his name was Sir Galahad. Opening the door for them, they entered into the church followed by Grear. There were only a few clergy left inside for the rest had gone on to the coliseum. "Is that the challenger of Damascus?" one of the clergy said to another.

"Yes, it is happening," another said out loud, seeing the sword. The clergy converged on his position with smile and friendship.

"Don't worry, these are friends, these are some of the clergy left standing up for the truth in this place," Malfius whispered to him.

"God has answered our prayers," another yelled out as they gave praise together.

"Come, come," another called out to the silver paladins outside. The paladins at the door followed them in and removed their helmets with the twinkle of childlike faith in their eyes. The silver paladins and the clergy of the church were also divided much like the factions of Northcross and Southcross, and these guys would definitely be north on a compass.

"We wish to have my friend baptized here," Malfius requested politely.

"Yes, yes, that would be positively the best blessing seen here since the days of Abraham," one of the clergy shouted out gleefully.

Zacharias held out his hand, asking in a hopeful voice, "Would it be all right if Malfius baptizes me?"

"Of course," the clergy and the paladins answered together. Then the church doors opened one final time and in walked Joan dressed in her magnificent forest armor. Seeing the sword, she scurried over and hugged Zacharias with all her might for several seconds. As that was happening, one of the clergy asked their names. "Mine is Malfius Simeon Stirling, and this is Zacharias John Desteeran." At the mention of the last name Desteeran, the clergy and the silver paladins felt hope for their nation had been revived. Malfius put his arm around Zacharias and led him to the main altar of the church. Atop this altar, another small marble staircase led to a pool of water. Stepping in first was Malfius, who gave a joking shriek to the coldness of the water. The clergy and paladins numbering less than a dozen sat together in one of the front pews as did Joan. Zacharias removes his shirt, revealing the scorched handprint of death upon his back and the watchers, and Malfius tear at the sight. A delightful nervousness was with him as he stepped into the water overlooking the magnificent church. "This church is beautiful, now that I think about it," Zac said to Beck. Malfius put one arm to his back and the other to his chest, preparing to baptize him and then said in all confidence, "We are the church." Zac then took a deep breath and exhaled as Malfius asked him, "Are you ready?"

"I've never been more ready," he answered, looking to the ceiling but really to God.

Malfius then began to speak in front of everyone, "Zacharias is my newest friend, and he has already taught me more than most. This man loves others unconditionally without asking favor in return. Without hesitation, he is willing to lay down his life for Eurus just as Jesus laid down his life for us, just as Jesus stated there is no greater love than to lay down one's life for one's friends. This man has been through more than most of us could have ever withstood, and today, the answer to that reason is given. Who is Jesus Christ to you?"

Zac turned to everyone sitting and answered, "My entire life, I've denied the word of God and blamed Him for everything bad that ever happened. Today, I can stand here and say that I was unimaginably wrong and I am sorry to a level I could not pay without the love shown from Christ Jesus. The only thing I ever wanted out of life was to be loved by a family I did not have. Jesus Christ is my Lord and God is my Father who will love me no matter what as he is Father to us all. Only He can give life and today after all the misery and sorrow I can see the truth. Through all of that, he forged me into the man He wanted me to become in order to glorify Him properly." Everyone smiled, fighting back individual tears of jubilation they felt as a man lost had now been found. Malfius then spoke, "Upon your profession of faith and in accordance with the Lord's command, I baptize you, Zacharias John Desteeran in the name of the Father, the Son, and the Holy Ghost. Buried in the likeness of His death." As he was saying this, Malfius submerged Zacharias who had the Sword of Abraham with him in the water and raised him up, saying, "And raised in the likeness of His resurrection." Together, everyone gave a standing ovation as Malfius held a triumphant fist to the air, yelling, "Hallelujah!" Malfius then hugged him and then Zacharias stepped out of the water as a cleansed and free man who was a new creation. The mark upon his back is gone death is vanquished for this child of God. The clergy and paladins ran up with towels, drying him off and also hugging their new brother in Christ. He was able to dress himself also as he was handed his Holy Bible whom had been held by Sir Galahad. After they were done, Joan embraced him one more time, crying into his shoulder. Sir Galahad, the silver paladin, then recited:

> For when ye were the servants of sin, ye were free from righteousness. What fruit had ye then in those things whereof ye are now ashamed? for the end of those things is death. But now being made free from sin, and become servants to God, ye have your fruit unto holiness, and the end everlasting life. For the wages of sin is death; but the gift of God is eternal life through Je'-sus Christ our Lord.
>
> Romans 6:20–23 (KJV)

"Zacharias, we will always be with you," Joan added.

Malfius then spoke, "Yep, now you're stuck with us as long as were on this earth and then forever in the next life!" Together, they laughed at this joyous occasion, forgetting about the troubles of the world, praying over him as a family that they now were. A family is something that lasts forever, something that cannot be broken by even death most of all a family is a revelation of who God is. One of the clergy ran to grab both the bread and the wine for the Eucharist (Holy Communion) but noticed all but a single gulp of wine remained. He prepared that and a single piece of bread for Zacharias. Bringing it out to him, Malfius explained the act of this symbolizing the Last Supper (New Testament) before Jesus gave his life. Zacharias took in the bread that is the body of Christ and drank the cup of wine that is his blood, shed for all who call upon his name. He then took a few precious moments in prayer to thank the Lord for all He had done for him also repenting of his sins unto Jesus Christ.

Seven minutes later, the great trumpets of the coliseum are heard throughout the city for the final battle of the week is being called to action. "The time has come," Malfius says to him as he signals Joan to grab something. Malfius handed Zacharias the Sword of Abraham and Zac grasped it tightly. "Aren't you forgetting something?" Malfius asked him, pointing to the hilt of the sword where small notches sit awaiting fulfillment. Joan returned, giving Zacharias the holy knight helmet of Sir Joseph Voltel. "I lied when I said I didn't know Joseph, I'm sorry. I know he is with you now, the spirit of the holy knights did not die with him for they are eternal in the eyes of the Lord," Joan proclaimed.

Taking the helmet, Zacharias closed his eyes, holding it to his chest, thinking, *"Thank you, Joseph."* He then remembers the cloth that fell from the body of Ephestus. Desteeran attached the final piece containing the blood of Jesus Christ to the Sword of Abraham, they are now one. An undeniable feeling to place Joseph's helmet atop his head surfaced and he obeyed. At that the appointed time before their eyes, Sir Abraham Desteeran, firstborn of the holy knights of the Gentiles, stood in front of Sir Zacharias John Desteeran equipped in the celestial armor with his red cape flapping in majestic energy. His spirit-like figure walked into the body of Zacharias and the armor of the holy knights encased him in a single blinding flash. The white celestial plated armor with golden fringe on the edges confirmed that Zacharias was now indeed a holy knight held close to the Lord's embrace. The helmet of Sir Joseph Barnabas Voltel, which held the wings of a golden eagle wrapped around it, began to change. The wings of the eagle sprawled out gloriously and its head raised, glancing unto heaven receiving perfect instruction, it then bowed straight out in front ready for war. On his back sat a ceremonial black cape with the golden symbol present that was the cross in the image of the sword, and as for the Sword of Abraham, it too had transformed. No longer the Sword of Abraham, it had ascended to the Trinitarian Blade, symbolizing The Father in the hilt, The Son in the cloth, and The Holy Ghost in the sacred steel. The blade had increased in size and thickness dramatically and the symmetrical claymore was now equally serrated on both sides with a sharpness not of this world. On either side of the blade, the legendary feather of Atyrael, the white dragon from heaven, was seen shining within the sword itself. All the while, the cloth around the hilt became one with the newly risen holy knight. Slowly, he bowed along with everyone in the room as he held it out horizontally, offering it up to the Lord God Almighty. The glow of the feather then dissipated, but twelve unique symbols of heavenly numerals glimmered in the image of infinite blazing glory. Half the symbols lay on one side, the rest on the other, but as these were burning within the blade, the numbers of 1, 7, 4, and 8 burned far more powerfully one by one in that exact sequence, 1 Samuel is imprinted upon their hearts. The Holy Spirit was now with Zacharias to a complete degree, and he knew God's will would be done in this battle against the giant for the rock was his weapon and that rock was Jesus Christ. Everyone else continually gaped before the awesome majesty of the now risen Exile bearing the foretold holy Trinitarian Sword. The forsaken vagabond once lost had now been found alongside the sword, the day of rebirth had finally arrived, it was indeed magnificent.

After that Grear poked his nose into his back, and as he turned, Grear was seen in a white and black caparison covering his body. Each side of this covering also has the golden symbols of the Sword of the Cross. Zacharias mounts Grear, equips his Bible in an armored slot to the rear of the Belt of Truth and looks to Malfius, saying, "You know, it's funny, most of my life, I've sought death, and now that I face it, I prefer to live." Together, they laughed one final time as Grear began to take him to exit the Church of Law. Joan and Malfius opened the door for him, outside he was overtaken by the scintillating sun, it took a minute for sight to adjust. Standing within the square and within the streets of Alexandria, over fifty thousand people gaze upon him. Joan put her hand over her mouth, and Malfius put his arm around her shoulder. "It has begun just as General Voltel said it would," Malfius says to Joan. Held fast in the raiment of glory before the masses, the holy knight gazes upon the great firmament above.

First the powerful bell atop the Church of Law rings seven times before the pause. Further understanding is gained and the white gauntlet of his hand presses unto his heart. Grear then begins to proudly descend the stairs with his head held high as all seven bells ring continuously. He has now returned to earth a new creation and it is silently realized. The crowd is silent as a single man steps out in front and faces them all. "Praise to Christ Jesus for raising the Seventh Exile to testify to his holy and righteous truth that salvation is not through the mediation or penance of priest unto God before men, but through the free gift given by the love of God for all to hear!" At that time, the crowds of over fifty thousand plus erupted in cheers that shook the very foundation of the Valencian Empire. Reaching the bottom step, Zacharias raises the Trinitarian Blade to the citizens and it turns red hot like magma as he points it to the direction of the Coliseum of Vindication. It was as if the very wrath of God had finally come to the false church that had purposefully denied the complete truth that was the death and resurrection of His only begotten son. It would be right then Zacharias finally knew his destiny that he was the Seventh Exile. He began to march forward as the thunderous audience shouted the name of Desteeran. He moved not only with the hopes of saving Eurus and the forest of Scera, but now another purpose. The hope of a nation was now behind him en masse, the hope of everyone who believed in Jesus was now united in Alexandria. Zacharias, after everything, was now shouldering what all God's children are commanded to by the Lord which is the cross. A cross of hardship, of loving others even when they do not love you in return, a cross of denying yourself for what is righteous and just, a cross that testifies to the life and truth of why Jesus Christ died and was raised in glory to the right hand of God in heaven. The cross is the Trial of Kings, for none know how to lead unless led themselves by the King of kings. As he rode off into the crowds, Joan followed soon to enter into the coliseum beside the Amerius family. Malfius stood atop the stairs, watching his friend go on to fight the battle no one else could.

More and more people began to flood the streets into utter hysteria by the battle ground. Grear could barely push forth as people cheered, all trying to get a single glimpse at the return of a holy knight, the unveiling of an Exile. Finally, he had reached the coliseum where all things would be revealed. A once lost and unknown man led by faith would now rise up against the most powerful church in the land. Over three thousand silver paladins stood at the gates of the massive entrance with the iron gate raised and the red carpet leading to the entrance. The paladin's captains stood in two long rows, extending their swords as a bridge for him to ride under. Dressed in his general's armor, Carlyle sat on his horse with his helmet visor ajar and falchion to his side. Flower petals began to fall, taking all vision around the stadium. People from all walks of life cheered together, reaching in hope that the nation they loved could be restored as to honor Him who gifted this land. Carlyle led Zacharias past the red carpet as the silver paladins began to hail the name of the Seventh Exile. Passing through the iron gate, two other paladins helped Carlyle off his horse and Carlyle brought him into the armory alone.

Standing inside Carlyle bows and rises, then pulling on Zacharias's chest plate as to check the perfection of his pristine armor. "You look good, my boy, I knew there was something special about you," he says.

"This is right, Carlyle, I feel alive," Zac states with opened visor and an unbelievable heart rate pounding profusely. They both believed it was because of the battle to come, but the harsh reality was he had been poisoned. Unknown to him, Amaralda had been on his tail from when they left the courtyard of heroes. Seeing that he was to be baptized, the papal assassin placed a few drops of venom within the wine, leaving only enough for him. Within the Church of Law, the passages are many, and none knew how to utilize them better than the now Celestial Constable Amaralda. "Zacharias, listen to me I've watched Damascus fight for many years. He's going to try to destroy you right out of the gate in order to dishonor you. Damascus fights in three interchangeable manners switching from power to speed to defense. He may even utilize javelins for range if he becomes nervous. The most dangerous weapon against you is his great ball and chain, Votum, destroy that and lure him close with the Trinitarian Sword. That sword will pierce any armor, but more importantly, don't forget to keep level headed, you can win this. His strength, speed and stamina are unparalleled but he has one major weakness."

"What is that?" Zac asked.

"His pride is his weakness, play to that to tune, and he will be cast down as the Tower of Babel," Carlyle exclaimed. An ear-piercing cannon blast was then heard signaling for the contestants to enter the arena and Carlyle began to leave the room.

Stepping out of the room, he said, "You know, Alcus would be proud."

Dashing to the doorway, Zac yells, "Wait, tell me who my grandfather was!" Before he can reach the door, a woman enters. It is Cordelia, the woman known as the Angel's Voice, the woman who held the most protected piece of his heart, never revealed. Cordelia's hair was white at this time, and she stood in front of him silently with an agonized stare. He removed his helmet with an astonished face, melding shy as his words progress, "You sang beautifully the other night."

Cordelia was choked up and began to say something unexpected. "I wish I'd have known the kind of man you were back in Salem. You're a good man and I will never forget what you're doing here today." Cordelia gave him a letter and then began to leave; she tried to escape. Noticing an all too familiar stamp on it, he held up his fingers, signaling for her to wait. "Cordelia, this is from the Voltel family, is it not?" he asked. Cordelia brushed hair out of her eye and answered with her back to him without breaking eye contact. The tone is mournful but the conviction unseen is far more tragic. "On the day I left Salem, Joseph gave me that letter, saying it was for you, and at the time, I didn't understand. Joseph explained to me that he could not share with me the contents of the letter, but that it would make sense to me soon. When I asked when or even where to give this to you, he said I would know. I understand that he has passed on along with his family and I'm sorry for that. I wish there was something more I could say, just one thing I could do to ease your pain, but I cannot. Please win this fight for all of us and most of all for yourself." Cordelia stated dramatically, glaring at the ground unhappy with herself. He smiles to her and speaks as he walks over. "I'm really grateful you said that, but the thing is this fight, this trial is not about me. It's what God wants." Now standing behind her, he rests his hands on her shoulders; she turns around and the gaze enchants union. He states passionately, "The other night when you sang, you made me feel at peace. Like when I was a child and my grandfather held me to his bosom from the troubles of the world." She wanted to look away but could not; instead, the longer the glance connected in the chaos of emotion, the more a lost peace is reborn. Tears streamed down Cordelia's face, but not like a regular human being's; these were tears of a Cruatian, the tears of the very ocean that reflected the mercy of heavenly bodies in the sky above. "Zacharias, I can't, I," but before she could finish speaking, he pulled her close. Cordelia wept bitterly into his neck, he rested his head atop hers with eyes closed, taking in the sweet scent of her hair, wishing she could be his wife. Feeling this much hurt from another, especially from the one he wanted to become one with, he finally understood just how important the need of Christ's love really was. After she was done crying, he began consoling her, but she pushed him away and tried again to escape. "I'm sorry. I don't want to hurt you. I'm not a good woman!" She declares almost gone. "My last name is Desteeran," Zac said to her, recalling the past. Cordelia turns to him ardently as she had now become self-aware of his altruistic nature. After this, she stated, "My hair changes not of my will, it is my affliction." Her hair began to turn blue as she smiled, reviewing him one last time, exhibiting desire; she then left immediately.

He then pulled out the Voltel family crest around his neck and compared it to the insignia on the letter in which they are the same. Opening the letter, it read:

> Dear Zacharias John Desteeran, if you are reading this, then I have passed on into the next world to be with my Father. Please understand that there were so many things I wished to have shared with you, but it was not the right time for you to hear, please forgive me my friend. Know that you meant the world to Penelope, Mariana, and I and we would have given anything to share more time with you, we cherish the days spent together. Sometimes in life, we have to take the hardest path presented and it may not make sense at first, but from an eternal standpoint, everything adds up. I know what I know because God revealed to me many things within my dreams. I understand that my weapons or armor as a holy knight could have aided us in Malastay or missions soon to come, but no one was to know until the appointed time. If you are still wondering exactly what a holy knight is, then this letter hopefully explains, here is my final gift to you. A holy knight is nothing more than a man who follows Christ Jesus, holding faith in the sacrifice and resurrection, and obeying his sound order given in the unification of the Holy Bible and the Holy Ghost. The person is not holy for the flesh is sinful, but being born of the Spirit now that is holy for that is rebirth in Christ. The three persons of God that are all different yet the same are holy for God alone is holy. When one is called a holy knight, what that is saying is that the victory within you is holy for it is Christ's work that has overcome the evil within yourself. Many will come clinging to the vernacular of holiness, but know and discern for all men carry within them a sinful heart only cleansed by the blood of the cross. A holy knight is the good shepherd. Zacharias, you are my brother, know that

my family and I will always be with you, but most of all, your Father is with you. You are both a holy knight and the Seventh Exile, you never were nor will you ever be alone. As your general, I give you this last order. Watch over my family in Antioch and send my love.

Love, First Commandant General of the Holy Knights Joseph Barnabas Voltel

PS: Oh, and just in case you hadn't pieced it together. I was the First Exile known as Alpha and you are the Seventh known as Herald of the Spirit; blessings on the difficult journey ahead, pilgrim, I know you will succeed. God be with you, my brother, we will meet again.

After folding the letter, he grasps the Trinitarian Sword and slashes the head clean off a ceremonial piece of armor with ease. He is not saddened by the fact that Penelope and Mariana have moved on because he knows they are now with Joseph in heaven, but what he does not know is that the family Joseph speaks of is far more extensive in Antioch. Smirking and marching out of the armory, he says, "May the flesh be laid to rest, the Seventh Exile now ascends." With the powerful last words of Joseph, he is now ready to do battle with the master gladiator Fearstein Damascus for he has now come to the final threshold of knowing he is a holy knight and the Seventh Exile, but more importantly, he is a child of God. Passing one final iron gate into the sands of the coliseum, he steps out in front of the kings and nobles of the west. The once cheering audience silences as the commoner walks out in holy knight's armor long since seen. Caiaphas, sitting on a throne by a multitude of clergy and silver paladins, drops his staff in horror; the two giant guards beside him bend down to pick it up, but their shrouded faces do not leave Zacharias, for they hate such men. Royal trumpets break the silence as the iron-gate slams behind, sealing him within the colossal arena. Blood stains the sands from battles recently held along with broken pieces of armor, arrow, and shield. Caiaphas orders he remove his helmet, so they may know that it is him. At the sight of his face, Caiaphas becomes very angry, whispering something in the ear of one of his clergymen. Large amounts of nobles begin to applaud, causing further frustration and tension between the audience divided. Alveria calls out to him from the audience, but he does not notice her for Damascus began to stomp out the opposing gate. Many more of the nobles begin to cheer for Damascus calling for the opposition's demise. Damascus clad in golden thick armor with blue marking drags his great ball and chain to his side, parting the sands like fin in water. On his back rested a two-handed shield twice the size of a man also covered in spikes, and to his sides, two bastard swords desire to pierce the marriage of the Spirit. Inside of his shield were three long silver-tipped javelins jetting out. *"So many weapons,"* Zacharias said to himself only having the one main with his hidden dagger. Damascus saluted Caiaphas as Zacharias drew the legendary blade, pointing it to him. At the sight of the blade, the whispers of the Seventh Exile spread throughout all nobility. Caiaphas held his staff tightly, attempting to remain in positive atmosphere, but in his mind, he was becoming one with malicious intent, his heart was hardening. Snapping his fingers, one of the paladins signaled others, standing high up in the coliseum's main watchtower. Inside of the watchtower, they began to turn a large iron crank lowering a cage. Slightly above, Eurus lay inside as everyone within the coliseum waited for the next move from either faction. Seeing the prison lowered, the tens of thousands outside began to ridicule the church, screaming the name of prophet as others began to cheer for the death of the heretic. Fights began to break out in multiple areas outside as the paladins attempted to quell the violent outbursts soon to take the city. Seeing Eurus naked and beaten to inches of death now presented in humiliation, Zacharias took to his corner as commanded and readied himself for the fight of his life. Damascus, standing over a foot taller than he and easily three times his size, began to laugh for all to hear. "Is this the best Sword of the Cross can sum up after three hundred years of exile!" Damascus yelled out, drawing the majority into a comical riot. King Victor Carthright sits beside dozens of his drudge knights in a stoic nature curiously waiting as to whom he will confront. In his mind, he is surprised, thinking, "So the holy knights make their return here in front of the world. Necromancer Veil, King Coprulus, King Herod, and most of all, General Dante will be most displeased to hear of this revelation. Then again, they could serve to make profound examples in the removal of Vulgata's religions." Carthright smirked to himself but allowed no one else to see it.

Caiaphas declares the battle begun and a massive cannon from the watchtower fires off into a lone field. Over thirty feet apart, both warriors begin to circle around, slowly awaiting for the other to act. "Come on, Zacharias, show them the mettle of a holy knight!" King Drake Amerius screams out. Caiaphas then shouts out to Damascus, pointing his finger with ceremonial ring to the opponent, "By the might of the saints, advance now!" Damascus charges forward with the animosity of the church, ripping the sands of the ground apart with his metallic boots while dragging the gigantic ball and chain behind him. Zacharias can barely breathe at this time for the poison is now taking complete effect. Damascus launches the ball and chain vertically down at Zacharias who in turn dives out of the way. It smashes with such force that a great crater is left in the sand. Immediately, Zac returns to his feet, gasping for air as Damascus begins to bring the deafening weapon with unrivaled precision again and again. Sand and rage collide as unyielding Damascus attacks relentlessly. Alveria shuts her eyes, falling into her father. "I cannot watch this!" Carthright interlocks his fingers and leans forward and Caiaphas grins with delight, thinking, *The sands of judgment shall hold true.* Not a word can be understood as cheers for both opponents fight for control. "Die ye abomination!" Damascus yells to Zacharias as he switches to the new tactic of swinging his ball and chain horizontally over his head. Zac's eyes locked on the hands of Damascus as he readies for his precise moment of attack. Damascus tosses the ball and chain at Zacharias who in turn dodges, slashing the chain in a valiant soar. The steel ball crashes into the wall, releasing stone all over the field. In a single moment, the heels of the holy knight harness the strength of the ground; they are shod with the gospel of peace. Zacharias charges furiously to Damascus with all his might, ready to enter into direct melee combat. Damascus pulls the chain close to him and begins to whip down on the ground, creating a cloud of sand and dust. It begins to partially blind the holy knight as the great chain begins to strike against his armor, echoing throughout the coliseum. Each crack of the chain worsens as the knight attempts to block by sword and vambrace. The armor withstands the attack, but the chain wraps around the arm and Damascus pulls him onto the ground. Damascus's shadow is seen sprinting toward him, but Zacharias counters, cutting the chain and freeing himself. Damascus desperately stops, almost falling into his opponent, who then moves in for the attack. Zacharias lets out the war cry of the lion as he swings the legendary blade, Damascus barely ducks. The blade swings over his head, and in one motion, Damascus turns around with the giant spiked shield upon his back and jumps backward, slamming into Zacharias. The impact of the blow launches him multiple feet back, but Zac does not let go of his blade. Damascus drops his shield to the ground and lying inside are his three javelins. Zacharias, struggling to fall back, sees the first one fling past his head. Out of breath, his body begins to fail as the poisonous task is all but complete. Another javelin is thrown with inhuman accuracy, crashing into the left stout pauldron, stealing the last of his air. He yells out in pain and drops his sword as his back is now up against the iron-gate. Damascus prepares to use his last as the holy knight's body then becomes paralyzed from the tampered communion; he slides down the gate, facing Damascus. The final javelin is hurled with an immense scream from Damascus who throws with such running force, he falls forward onto the ground, the javelin crushes into the breastplate. The impact knocks the Exile's helmet off and cracks his breastplate from the middle, but does not pierce to the skin. Those for him watch in dismay as those for Damascus can feel victory has been obtained. "Damascus, finish the blasphemer," Caiaphas screams. Damascus picks up his two-handed shield and holds it out in front of him. He slowly begins to march toward his enemy, unsure of whether this is a trick or not. "I cannot move my body, I cannot breathe, I cannot do anything, I'm helpless," Zacharias frightfully thinks, unable to budge. Step by agonizing step, Damascus drew closer with each footprint sounding the alarm of defeat. "God, I believe in you, please help me here and now. Don't let what Joseph died for go in vain," Zac screamed out in his mind, desperately trying to move his body. His hands trembled as he attempted to reach out for the sword. Memories of his entire past began to flash throughout and then the shadow of Damascus had found him. The image of Manistof reveals himself on the great shield, glaring at Zacharias for only him to see. Alveria shrieks out his name in distress. Carthright watches Caiaphas intently as Caiaphas grasps the sides of his chair, readying himself to stand triumphant. Damascus held his shield ready to crush the Exile and then yelled for all to hear, "Let all know that I, Fearstein Damascus, am the greatest warrior in all the land! See that it is I who destroyed those of the reformation! Now die bowing before the Church of Law!"

Zacharias then yells back in a divine voice that overtakes the coliseum, "God calls us to bow so that in Christ's name we may stand!" As he bellowed this, he rose, grabbing the sword and gaining a strength he has never known. The Seventh Exile struck Manistof on the shield of Damascus with every fiber of his being. The sword crashed into the shield, destroying it to a full degree, sending the pieces into the crowd with the sound of thunder deafening everyone even outside. Damascus was hit with such energy that it sent him flying across the arena, bouncing in and out of the sand into the other side's iron gate. Zacharias stood in complete unison with the power of the Holy Spirit and pointed his sword at Caiaphas, proclaiming, "You, Caiaphas, who sit upon a throne of your own avarice and vanity shall be judged in full circle for you are a false prophet preying upon the flock! How dare you use the name of God to advance your own wicked desires for your allegiance is with Lucifer! Let all know that no one is above the perfect judgment of the Lord Almighty and that death has been conquered by his son Jesus Christ who fulfilled the Law!" Caiaphas tore his clothes in outrage. Damascus regained his stance with his armor dented heavily and the iron gate behind him also damaged. His armor was jammed into his skin, causing blood to overtake the lower half of his body where it leaked out. Removing his helmet, his face was stained far worse. Damascus spit out a grouping of his teeth into a pile and stumbled in a way, testifying to severe internal damage. Wiping away a fraction of his own blood, he drew the two bastard swords at his sides. His pride is wounded profoundly, and now, his patriarch is openly mocked. Damascus stampedes across the arena calling upon the twin griffons of Castor and Pollux, yelling so loud that even those outside the coliseum tremble. Zacharias in turn charges to Damascus with the Holy Spirit as his guide and all of Northcross pushing for victory. They clash swords in the middle of the arena. Damascus swings wildly like the griffons' talons, screaming obscenities and prideful decrees with each strike. The holy knight deflects and blocks each incoming strike and then cuts one of the swords down, leaving only a sharpened hilt. Damascus drops the broken blade and grasps the Trinitarian Sword with his left hand, but it is so sharp, it cuts off all of his fingers even past the gauntlets. Damascus crushes his skull into Zac's, disorienting him as he takes the other blade and plunges it into the center of the cracked armor. Damascus's sword pierces the armor and Zacharias's sword plunges through the stomach of Damascus and out his lower spine. Blood mixed with saliva gushed forth from Damascus falling on the eagle's head and armor of Desteeran as he yells out, "I am more than a man, I am the Dioskouri, the rule of Valencia is mine!" Damascus removes his blade from the chest plate and goes to strike him down, but Zac pulls his sword up with all his remaining strength. The Trinitarian Sword cuts to the sun, splitting Damascus from stomach to face. The wound is agape, and for that second, Damascus remains alive, realizing the extremity of his finale, as his soul bears witness to the drawing curtain of the final act soon to be unveiled unto mankind. He shifts out of balance then folding open. Pieces of his brain and intestines fall into each other along foul-smelling bodily liquids as his eyes appear as a beast's, his lifeless body then crashes to the ground.

The world around watches in terrified astonishment at the defeat of the legendary hero of Valencia as the revolting excrement and gore run as a broken dam. His pride was the wall, the water lost is his salvation forfeited for the want of personal glory. Not a word is said, the masses are all the same, Zacharias, staring at Caiaphas, kicked the dust off his feet unto the body of Damascus. A lone tear finds its way down the shaken Caiaphas. Carthright alone rises when all remain seated, now staring directly at the holy knight his adversary of the west. Alveria, as most did, held hands to mouth while Zac then looked up to the cage holding Eurus. Eurus's talon reached for Zacharias, but as he did, the Exile collapsed on the ground for the poison had finally destroyed his heart. The sword lay sitting stabbed into the ground in front of his body. The crest of the Voltels had saved his life, absorbing the sword of Damascus. The bonds of that family gave him the ability to finish the battle, but the toxin had finished its clandestine deed. Cordelia stands behind the iron gate, weeping to his fallen body, she is shattered within for denying true love's first and final kiss. Her hair drains splotches of blue dye now shifting white. She is the pen, and every drip of aquamarine is her soul exuding her spiritual connection with him who is now gone. All the words of their ill-fated romance were to be written too late. Cordelia's years of prayer just to be held are not yet realized. One at a time, various nobles in the crowd begin to call for him to get up, but he does not. Alveria continually weeps, also seeing the life she planned for them end; Caiaphas finally rises from his throne. All nobles gaze upon him as he begins to speak after exhaling a vast amount of mortification. In a saddened voice, Caiaphas proclaims, "My Damascus, our dear sweet defender of the church, killed by the tainted sorcery of the white knight's unholy blade!" His tone then advanced to anger, he signaled his paladins and clergy, "Take the wolf in sheep's clothing and burn his body now!" Caiaphas's voice echoed in such pure malevolence that even his own paladins and clergy were scared. Nobles from all over the world break out into a complete riot and begin to fight each other for even those of ruling lineage cannot overcome basic human instinct. The conflict escalates to a point where the entire coliseum is engulfed as Carthright's drudge knights surround him, knocking away anyone who gets close. Caiaphas is surrounded by his own royal guards as hundreds of silver paladins take to the arena ready to take the body of Desteeran and take control of the riot of kings. As they advance, nobles shout out to leave the body of the Seventh Exile. Joan appeared, grabbing the Amerius family, while Amaralda also appeared, secretly gifting Caiaphas the Voltoro blade. One of the lesser nobles gained entry beside Caiaphas's throne, and both of his sacred guards hack him asunder by their scythes in parallel onslaught. "Joan, you have to do something," Alveria cried out to her. Desperately, Alveria attempts to push past the violent mobs. She cannot leave him alone again. Joan, also taken by grief, violently snatches the princess yelling, "It's my job to protect you, we have to go now, Zacharias is dead!"

"No, I won't accept that, I love him, if he is dead, then let me go die with him, I command you!"

Joan slaps Alveria immensely and pulls her away. The Forest Maiden of Devok is mightily angry by the royal Sceran's outlook, she knows Desteeran wouldn't want her to act this way. Alveria is able to look back only one last time and in that moment, a lone prayer is painfully made. In the midst of this pandemonium, Carthright stood behind his drudge knights, holding the sharpest grin, thinking, *All the king's horses and all the king's men could not put the shattered church back together again.* A mighty gust of wind sweeps through the coliseum raising a veil of sand and dust in the battle area. Eurus's cage is heard crashing to the ground like the hammer of fate. The silver paladins halt as the riot stops; every mouth is denied the gift of speech for something unprecedented is happening. Slowly, the same gust of wind begins to remove the cloud, and Tala stands howling before the arena from the watchtower. Standing in front of his body is a single holy knight wearing an even more profound variation of the armor, but this one has the waning moon as his golden insignia; it is Silent Night, the Second Exile. His helmet indicates the status of a great general as does his cape embody the Fear of the Lord. Holding a celestial in appearance weapon—that is, a mace, a sword, and a cross all at the same time along with a combative-looking shield, the holy knight draws a single line in the sand, staring at the silver paladins. The unconscious body of Eurus lay beside Zacharias with his right wing shielding his corpse. As the rest of the dust clears, four other holy knights taken by incandescent light surround the Seventh Exile. But these are more than that, these are the Exiles united, numbering from two to seven, yet the first is there in spirit. In front of the fallen (seventh) Exile with a majestic bow of crystal drawn, the appearance of a female stands, a lone raven, also armored, rests on her shoulder. Behind the bodies, a tremendous man slings Desteeran over his left shoulder, holding a grand double-sided axe in right hand and a towering shield upon his back. To his left, a holy knight holds an unnaturally lengthy lance that had blades running down the sides and a secondary handle as to alternate between sword and lance, this was indeed one of the fabled blade lances. To his right, a remarkably tall holy knight wields a long gigantic steel war hammer that is drawn from the highest peak of Eregia (the Mount of Transfiguration). No one moves, no one speaks as the female Exile fires her bow to the sun. A beam of light reflects off the Trinitarian Sword and overtakes the arena blinding everyone but the Exiles. Above the sword, the image of Jesus Christ is witnessed as every single celestial number one to twelve sparks immensely from the sword, leaving their marks permanently in the ground all thirty degrees apart. As the light begins to dissipate the arrow lands directly on Caiaphas's staff breaking the cardinal's bent cross, leaving only a mouth stuffed with false tongue. But one voice speaks from up high, and His voice is great and almighty speaking of the holy truth that is His name in the sound of the everlasting trumpet that is the word of God. Behind the five who arrived at the call of the King, five hundred holy knights are now seen standing their ground, overtaking the other half of the arena. The Coliseum of Vindication has now become battleground over the newly risen now fallen Exile, the holy knights and the silver paladins each stand their ground with the drudge knights patiently reviewing from a throne of their own. Sir Zacharias John Desteeran had spent a lifetime adrift the seas of extinction, praying for just one person to reach out, and in the end, someone did; the kindness of a stranger saved his life. Any man left alone ponders that hurt, desperately searching for a way to escape, and if abandoned by the world around will most likely to succumb to his hidden pain, his secret war. It is this reason Jesus explains to love the lost for it is by his love that loneliness is vanquished; it is by his love that purpose is cemented to the rock. Most of all, it is by his love that God's nature is revealed unto men for His glory. Although the body has been broken for the world to see, the spirit lives on in the one and only happily ever after for as Zacharias's name declares, "God hath remembered," so does God remember all who call upon His name, for the Lord shall never forsake His children. Here before the kings of the earth, at the sign of the first eagle, after three hundred forty-five years of exile, the holy knights are reborn before the Trinitarian Sword, which was bound to the Herald of the Spirit. The prophesied time of the Exiles had now begun at the accomplishment of the Trial of Kings undertaken so very long ago by the love shown from the Christ whose name is Jesus.